REGARDING FLORIANS

REGARDING FLORIANS
Part Two:
GENESIS

Kelly Jo Pardue

Dedication

I dedicate this book to my Mom and Dad. I hope you have both found peace.

If you or someone you love is having thoughts of suicide, please call the Suicide and Crisis Lifeline at 988. Press "1" for veterans.

Contents

PROLOGUE

He was so nervous. But he was also excited to work with General and Dr. Harlow on their secret project. Daniel Williams had recently come into Dr. Harlow's service as a freelancer for emergency medicine. He wanted to be a doctor, so Daniel was elated when Dr. Harlow singled him out to work on one of his inventions.

However, watching General Harlow use insane powers that *nobody* knew existed was frightening, especially because she was already intimidating without them.

"Are you sure we should be doing this inside?" she asked Troy.

Troy shrugged and said, "No, I'm not sure, but we don't have a choice right now because of the approaching storm."

"Can't we wait?"

"No, Dia, we can't."

"Why?"

Daniel enjoyed watching them interact with each other. These two larger-than-life figures were indeed just like everyone else. They would argue, make fun of each other, laugh at him, and even eat tons of junk food. In the end, they worked well together, and he was honored to see what they could do.

Finally, Troy convinced his wife to stay indoors. Daniel watched as Dia walked into the middle of the training room and looked up at the ceiling. She was wearing her uniform except for the outer jacket and anything else with metal. She had learned the hard way that her belt buckle made for an uncomfortable branding iron. She faced Troy and asked, "Okay, now what?"

Troy stepped to the side. "I want you to absorb the energy from this Wel pod and *gently* cut the steel plate in half without melting it."

"You know I've only been doing this for a few weeks, right? That seems pretty advanced." She turned to Daniel. "It's too advanced, right?"

Daniel was caught off guard by her question and stumbled over his response. "Uh, um, sure?"

"You know, kid, you've been working with us for a while now. You *can* talk. Troy's the only one who bites."

Daniel glanced away, embarrassed but amused.

Troy rolled his eyes and said, "You can laugh too, even when the general is being an asshole. Now, let's go."

Dia turned her attention to the Wel pod, and Daniel watched her place her hand over the tiny glowing orb. He was amazed as she transformed. Her body became bathed in cool green flame, her hair went from brown to a bright blonde, and her fingertips glowed white. But what was always so striking were her bright, iridescent, emerald eyes. She was beautiful and terrifying at the same time.

When General Harlow finished absorbing the energy from the pod, Daniel watched as she pointed her finger over the top of the steel plate, and a small line of green flame began to reach down.

Dia had difficulty controlling the fire, so she pulled back in frustration and tried again. When it happened a second time, she took a step back and stared at the plate.

"Talk to me, Dia," Troy said. "What's wrong?"

"I don't know. It's like something is… interfering. Like another energy source is trying to interact with me, but I can't identify it. I've never felt this before," Dia said, concerned.

Not far away, Daniel heard thunder from the approaching storm.

"Sounds like the storm is here," Troy replied. "It's a good thing we stayed inside."

Daniel noticed Dia starting to act very strangely.

She said, "Troy, something isn't right. Something's reaching out to me, and when I repel it, it comes back stronger."

Daniel could see how distressed she was, which wasn't like the formidable general.

"Okay, we're done for the day," Troy said. "Let's clean up."

Suddenly, a bolt of lightning hit the training room's roof, and the residual energy poured straight into Dia. The power of the blast knocked her back, and she slammed into Daniel. They both fell to the floor, causing her to release all of her power. Dia ended up on top of the young man. As she went to stand, she pushed herself up with one hand on the ground and one on his chest.

She stood, then laughed, extending her hand to help him up. "Sorry, kid, hazards of the job."

Daniel didn't move. His eyes were open, and he was staring at her, but he was completely motionless. Dia leaned down and said, "Daniel."

She knelt beside him when he still didn't move and yelled, "Troy! Come here, now!"

Troy, who was trying to process why the lightning strike and her energy release didn't blow them all to hell, ran over to where Dia and Daniel were and asked, breathless, "What is it?"

Dia, clearly worried, said, "He isn't responding, Troy."

Dr. Troy Harlow was one of the best physicians in the galaxy. He dropped to his knees and started evaluating Daniel's condition. Troy was sure their assistant was just stunned from being knocked down and would recover soon. Daniel was chosen for this project because he was Florian, so his risk factors were extremely low. Troy placed his fingers on Daniel's throat but didn't feel a pulse.

Troy tried to assess the rest of Daniel's vitals, assuming he was in survival stasis, but he had none. By all accounts, Daniel Williams, a *Florian*, was dead.

Troy looked up at his wife and whispered, "Dia, I think he's dead."

"No, that's not possible!" She shook her head frantically. "We have to get him to the hospital!"

Troy wanted to grab her shoulder and make her calm down, but an overwhelming feeling of dread came over him. He breathed, "Dia…"

"No, he can't be dead, Troy. He's one of us!" she exclaimed as a tear ran down her cheek.

"We still have no idea what this power can do."

Dia stood up and began to panic. She kept shaking her head hysterically, and Troy could see she was becoming unstable and needed to release her absorbed energy. He ran and got the battery they used to store her excess power and put it on the ground in front of her. "Try to push it into the battery."

"What do you mean? It all released when I hit the ground. I don't—"

She finally noticed her hand and saw that she was still holding on to some energy. She barely felt it. It wasn't like the usual power that buzzed through her veins. This felt more lucid, like it had its own life—or soul.

Her eyes shot to Daniel William's body, and horror filled her petrified face. She placed her hands on his chest and tried to push the energy into him. Nothing happened. Dia tried several times, but it wouldn't go. Alongside her, Troy used all of his medical knowledge to revive their Florian assistant, but to no avail.

Exhausted, they both sat back, staring at each other, speechless. Dia studied her hands and said softly, "Troy, this energy is different. It's him; this energy is Daniel's life force. And I can't give it back!"

Troy gazed at her, glowing with a faint green flame, her emerald eyes glassy with tears. He didn't know what to do or say; neither had ever anticipated anything like this. He stood up. "Come on. We need to get you discharged and figure out what to do with his body."

"This isn't just any power, Troy. It's *his* power, his life, that I stole! I killed him!"

Troy was known to be sensitive. The resilience he had gained over the years was from Dia, so she was usually stern with him, but not this time. He reluctantly grabbed her hand and pulled her to her feet. "I know, Dia, but we can't sit here and dwell on what just happened, at least not now. You need to pull yourself together and help me hide this before someone finds out."

Her mind switched into the compartmentalized state she saved for battle and handing out dangerous orders to her soldiers and pilots. She helped Troy by doing precisely what he told her.

First, Troy had Dia release her energy into the empty battery. Next, they moved Daniel's body into the adjacent locker room. He called for a transport to come and take them to his office as his assistant had collapsed. Once on his worktable, Troy again tried several times to revive their aide but couldn't. Dia sat down and just stared at the wall. He had never seen her so shaken, and Dia had been through a lot in her lifetime.

"There's nothing I can do for him, my love. We need to get him into cryostasis. It's the best way to preserve his body and keep this incident quiet."

She asked, subdued, "What will we tell his family?"

Troy thought for a minute. "His family lives off-planet. They don't have much contact with him."

"Let's get this done. I want to go home."

***

Once they were finished hiding their tragic mishap, Troy and Dia went home. She immediately got into the shower, and Troy could hear her sobbing as he got undressed. He went into the bathroom and joined her in the shower. She turned into his arms and wept against his chest. Troy could no longer keep his own emotions in, and they cried together for quite some time. She said, "What should we do now?"

"We leave. We can't stay here. It's too dangerous."

Dia stepped back. "No! We can't leave. Can you imagine what the consequences of that would be?"

"Can you imagine the consequences if our enemies found out what you can do? We've been training for you to be the ultimate peacekeeper, yet we just discovered that you could be the ultimate *weapon* against Florians if you fall into the wrong hands. We must leave to keep our planet and species safe," Troy said quietly.

Sadly, Dia knew he was right.

***

A few days later, after securing documentation from a trusted associate for a new life in Deep Space, Troy and Dia strapped into her DREX fighter. She was known for taking her ship on recreational flights, so it wasn't unusual for her and Troy to go on an evening cruise.

As they got ready to leave, Troy asked, "How're we getting out of here?"

Dia finished her preflight check of the ship's operating systems and said, "Summerset Cave."

CHAPTER 1
BOREDOM

"How long has she been doing that?" asked Carl.

Brody glanced at the monitor and said, "Ever since you left."

"Wait, what? I left two days ago!"

Brody turned his attention back to the motherboard he was fixing. "Yup, I know."

Carl shook his head and looked back at the monitor to marvel at the strangeness that was Heather Stone. She was lying in the garden, drawing in the dirt with her finger. Her fingertip was hotter than the surface of the sun, so the sand was turning to glass. She had moved all over, drawing elaborate designs. Brody was right, though; she'd been at it since Carl left to take care of some business for Roger. She hadn't eaten or slept, either. Brody was just glad she periodically stopped to use the bathroom.

Carl said, "I'll go talk to her."

"Good luck! She's being pretty difficult."

"When isn't she these days?" Carl mumbled.

It'd been six months since Brody called them all together to announce that he believed Heather was ready to take on the world as *Flashpoint,* the bonafide superhero. However, Carl and Roger weren't prepared to let her do anything in the real world. Roger hadn't seen enough activity from their mysterious enemy to warrant letting her existence be known. Therefore, Heather had been cooped up at the mansion for almost a year.

He slowly approached her from the rear and heard her say, "Dr. Carl Johnson returns. How was your trip?" She rolled over and gazed at him. "Did you remember my Happy Meal this time? I asked for chicken nuggets."

Carl said, "Yeah, with hot mustard sauce. I forgot."

She rolled back over. "Figures."

Carl walked around her and sat on a bench. He studied the design she was drawing in the sand. It was a triangle with what looked like a wagon wheel in the middle. He said, "You really are an artist."

Heather stopped, and the light in her fingertip faded as she pushed it back into the shell she was wearing. She raised herself onto an elbow and stared at him with her strange, upturned eyes. She had recently cut her hair, which sat just below her shoulders; her silky curls swirled around her face in the breeze. "I'm tired of being an artist, Carl. You told me I'd be doing something months ago. Every time I ask, you shut me down. I'm losing my damn mind!"

Carl was worried about her behavior as of late. It was as if she was acting out like a child not getting their way. An incredibly brilliant, dangerous child who had figured out all of the hiding places for the candy.

"Come on, Heather. Brody said you've been out here for two damn days. What the hell are you doing?"

Heather glared at him for a moment, then got up and started walking toward the house.

He ran after her, asking, "You have nothing to say?"

She just kept walking until they were in the curved room. A large bowl of bananas was on the table, and she stopped and took one out. She looked Carl dead in the eye as she peeled it, took a big bite, and with a mouthful of banana said, "Nope."

She turned and ran toward the stairs.

Carl swore under his breath and went back to Brody's lab.

As Carl walked through the door, Brody said, "I told ya. Difficult."

Their physician's assistant, Penny Singleton, was also in the lab. "Carl, she's a caged animal who knows how to escape this enclosure," Penny said. "It's only a matter of time before she takes off. I can feel it. We need to take her to do something outside of this compound."

Carl shrugged. "Where? What can we do with her that doesn't risk her being discovered? No, she stays here until I say so."

Brody shook his head. "When she hits her limit here, who knows what'll happen."

"Thanks, kids, I'm aware of that. Have a good day."

Carl turned and stormed out of the lab. Although reluctant, he needed to find her and make things right. His relationship with Heather had become awkward, but that didn't mean he wasn't still responsible for her well-being.

***

Heather was lying on her bed, staring out of the ornate skylight in her room. She had closed and covered all other windows and doors to concentrate on the light above. Brody had gotten her an iPod and loaded a large assortment of music for her to experience. She had taken a particular liking to the *Pirates of the Caribbean* movie scores and loved listening to the powerful music and feeling the energy that emanated into her ears through the headphones. It was one of the few things that kept her mind from racing.

However, Heather couldn't help but think back to the night a few months ago that started the change in her behavior. For a time, she and Carl met on the porch to enjoy the peace and quiet and spend time together. Some nights they would talk; sometimes, they would sit and listen to the fountain's bubbling. Some nights they would indulge their growing feelings and cuddle on the bench or share a kiss.

But one night, their usual innocent kisses turned into more than that. Their first kiss that evening lasted longer than usual, the next even longer, until finally they stopped, shocked by how far they were letting themselves go. Surprised by their actions, Carl said, "I'm sorry, uh, I should probably go to bed."

"Yeah, totally—me too."

They awkwardly stood up, and Heather said, "Uh, good night, Carl."

"Yeah, good night, Heather, good night."

They faced each other, waiting for the other to leave. Then, Carl bravely said, "Would you like to come to my room?"

Heather barely let him finish. "Yes, I'd love to."

They fell into each other's arms onto Carl's bed. Heather pulled his shirt over his head, and he untied her robe, putting his arm around her waist. Carl couldn't believe how different she felt. She was so warm; her skin was so smooth. Then, he looked into her eyes in the darkness.

On the porch, with the solar lights casting a pale glow, Heather's eyes were their usual brown, but in the dark of his room, he could see a line of iridescent green surrounding her irises. He couldn't help but wonder where she pulled that energy from. He sat up and stared at her face in shock.

Heather, surprised, said, "What? What did I do? I know I'm new at—"

He stopped her. "It ain't that, love. You're perfect, but I don't think this is a good idea."

Heather rolled off his bed and tied her robe, sad, confused, and scared. She knew what he saw. "I'm sorry."

Carl stood up next to her. "No, no. You don't have to be sorry, Heather. It's—"

She put her warm fingertips on his lips and said, "I understand, Carl. I'm scared of me too."

Heather concentrated on the memory and the music until she heard a knock on her door. She turned off the iPod, waiting for whoever it was to just come in. She had no privacy, even in her cavernous lair of a bedroom.

Carl opened the door. He shoved his hands in his pockets as he walked over to her bed and gazed at her. After a moment, he reached out, pushed a curl off her forehead, and said, "How was your banana?"

"Okay, I guess. Chicken nuggets would've been better."

Heather was surprised when he sat down next to her. This was the closest he had been to her in a long time. He said, "I'm so sorry, love. I can't even begin to imagine what you're going through in this place. You're lightning in a bottle, and I have to keep the cork on so you don't get away."

Heather cleared her throat. "Am I just an asset to you, Carl?"

"To me? No. But you are to our benefactor."

She leaned back against the pillows, crossed her arms, and said, "Our benefactor. The nameless, faceless entity who provides all this glory and keeps me bottled up, ready to do their bidding at a moment's notice."

Nervous, Carl said, "Heather, it's not like—"

An unfamiliar voice interrupted Carl from the door. "Actually, Carl, that's exactly what it is. Hello, Heather. My name is Roger Miller. And I think it's high time you and I met."

CHAPTER 2
EXPLAIN YOURSELF

Veronica considered herself superior to the Coronians she worked for. However, they were still in charge—for now.

In the six months since Dr. Troy Harlow had been rescued by the Rygonians, she had come under a lot of pressure to get him back, to no avail.

The Rygonians and their allies were on the highest alert they'd ever been. Troy Harlow was taken deep into hiding, and there'd been no sign of him, even from her spy in his employ. They were also at a complete loss as to the location of his wife, General Dia Harlow. She hadn't been seen since the day the Coronians captured Troy on Rygone a year ago. Many felt she was gone for good, lost to the vacuum of space. Veronica knew they weren't so lucky. Dia would be found, and she would return.

Veronica stood up from her extravagant desk in the office that overlooked what used to be Troy's lab. She walked to the railing that she and Renee Conner had fallen over as they'd fought like rabid dogs. Veronica hated fighting her own battles, but Conner wouldn't have let her escape without one. She could still feel the hand of that Coronian beast hitting her face.

The truth was Veronica missed Troy. During the battle of the Breger Dunes, she'd become unhealthily obsessed with him. She turned an order to get close and distract him into a full-blown sexual relationship. When he sent her away, choosing his wife over her, she fled to the Coronian home planet of Darsayn. She glanced around the large, open room and saw a Crailion scientist trying aimlessly to make heads or tails of Troy's work. He had been attempting for six months to figure out what Dr. Harlow had accomplished. Much to Veronica's displeasure, it seemed the answer was *nothing*.

Two male Coronian beasts came up the stairs and approached her. One said, "His Excellency wants to see you, Veronica."

"I'll be there soon. I still have some thin—"

The other guard interrupted her. "You'll come now."

She noticed their weapons were drawn and ready to take her by force if necessary. *What the hell is this all about?* she thought.

She nodded and walked toward the stairs, followed by the guards.

The barren desert in which the research facility resided was several tols from the edge of the capital city of Tonwal, so she and her guards took a transport. The city was surprisingly beautiful and modern. Most believed the Coronians were a primitive, uncivilized species, but much of their home world was incredibly stunning.

As they entered the royal palace, Veronica walked toward the Premier's chambers with her head held high, just like she always did. The rabble that usually bowed and pined for her instead stepped aside with disgust.

Two royal guards opened the door and gave her an accusing look as she went in. Veronica walked proudly down the red carpet toward the ornate wooden thrones of Premier Baxelhoff and his Gorman wife, Premieress Lydia.

Veronica stopped at the customary ten feet away and knelt on one knee. "Good morning, Premier. You wanted to speak to me."

The Premier was almost twice as tall and much more refined than all other male Coronian beasts. She wondered how he and his tiny Gorman wife managed to have two children. He stood up, which she didn't expect, and approached her. Veronica stayed kneeling, waiting to see what he would do. He placed a hand on her shoulder and said in his surprisingly clear, quiet voice, "Walk with me, Veronica."

Veronica was afraid, but she had to appease him or risk facing worse consequences. She stood up and fell in line beside him as they walked back up the carpet. He put his big arm around her shoulders as they stepped into the hall. Once out of view and earshot of the others, he turned and slammed her against the wall. He pulled her up until her face was even with his, only inches apart, and growled, "Where are the Harlows? I've given you more than enough time to primp and play queen with *nothing* to show for it! *Where are they?*"

His grip on her was excruciating, and she could hardly breathe. She managed to squeak out, "We cannot locate Dr. Harlow. We think the Rygonians moved him to a different planet."

He growled again and shoved his arm against her throat. "No, they didn't! Troy Harlow was seen on Rygone within the past few weeks. Why do you not have this information? Your so-called spy isn't doing a very good job. Explain yourself, Florian!"

Why hasn't he told me this?!

He dropped her, and Veronica knelt on the floor, trying to catch her breath. The Premier bent down and put a finger under her chin. He gently pulled her face up to look at him. "Ever since you learned about the EIP binding to Dia Harlow, your work has gone off the rails. You were a great partner for many years. You helped us defeat so many of your people and their allies. I've always cared deeply for you, but now all you can think about is that fucking doctor. Pull your head back into the game, Veronica, or you and your spy will suffer painful consequences."

He dropped her chin, stood up, smoothed his fine robes, and walked back into the royal chambers. He left her in the hall to catch her breath and stew in her embarrassment. She sat against the wall, reached into her pocket, and ran her fingers over Troy Harlow's wedding rings. It would only be a matter of time before he returned for them.

CHAPTER 3
I'M SO TIRED

Colonel Renee Conner was now High Colonel Renee Conner. After the successful rescue of Dr. Troy Harlow from the planet Darsayn, she and her crew received promotions and a choice of whatever assignment they wanted.

While she was on Rygone to gather potential recon on Dia's location, she decided to look in on Troy. She sat in the corner of the hospital commissary hall, watching him stare off into nowhere. After they'd made it back to Rygone, there had been two small attempts by the Coronians to attack Baltica City to take him back, but they were quickly thwarted. Commanding General Toni Smith decided to keep Troy on a rotation, traveling to different strong allies. Troy didn't usually say much. He just went where and did what he was told. The brilliant doctor was on autopilot, and Renee was afraid he was heading for a big crash.

It'd been over five minutes since he had moved, so she decided to blow her cover and talk to him. She went and sat across from him, but he didn't notice her. Renee reached out and touched his hand. "Troy, look at me."

He snapped his gaze to her face. His eyes were bloodshot, and he looked like he hadn't slept in a month. He smiled and said, "Hey, Renee, it's nice to see you. How's your search going?"

Renee had learned that saying Dia's name was a mistake. His mental state couldn't handle talking about his wife. "We're still looking, but I think we have a few leads."

"Same as always, then?"

"Yeah, same as always." She was quiet for a moment, then asked, "When was the last time you slept, Troy?"

He laughed. "Are you going to be another person who tells me I look like I'm not sleeping? I wish I wasn't sleeping. I sleep every night, Renee. It's the nightmares that make me look like this."

Concerned, Renee wondered if he should be practicing medicine in this state. She asked, "Troy, what're you doing? For work, I mean?"

Troy swallowed hard. "This probably isn't a good place to talk about that."

"Okay, I'll stop by your apartment this evening." She glanced at the plate of untouched food in front of him. "I'll even bring dinner because it looks like you're starving yourself too."

"I haven't been—"

She cut him off. "I'll be at your apartment at six. Be there," she said sternly.

He didn't say anything. Renee put her hand on his shoulder before she walked away, feeling helpless.

***

That evening, Renee arrived at Troy and Dia's apartment right on time. She rang the bell and was surprised that he opened the door immediately. He motioned her in, and she said, "I got Gorman plantains with no fish."

Troy chuckled. "I'm glad everyone remembers I hate fish."

Renee set the food on the counter and caught Troy off guard with a hug. At first, he was uncomfortable, but being close to another person felt good. He gently hugged her back and realized Renee was crying. He was surprised, as he had never seen her cry. After a few minutes, she pulled back, wiping her face. "I'm so sorry. I don't know what came over me."

"Fear, anger, exhaustion, sadness. I could go on because I feel it too."

Renee nodded. "Let's do something nice and mundane and just eat."

They put together plates of food, and Troy had to admit it smelled better than anything he had eaten in weeks. They quietly sat side by side until he said, "I'm so tired, Renee."

"So am I. I feel like my wheels are spinning as fast as possible, but I'm not getting anywhere."

"I feel like I'm sitting in a corner watching myself try to make something of my existence. My father keeps telling me I have trauma disorder, but it's more than that. Too much has happened, and I can't process any of it anymore." He turned to her and asked, "Do you want to know how many times I've slept in our bed since I've been back?"

She swallowed her bite of plantain. "How many?"

"Once, that first night. When I'm in Baltica, I usually stay in my office or sleep out here. Whenever I close my eyes, I see her or that bitch, Maria. I feel like I'm being tortured. I keep having this one dream over and over. I'm in our room, and I see her by the window. She walks toward me wearing this crazy green bodysuit with black boots. Her eyes are the only part of the EIP active, glowing emerald green. We talk, but she doesn't know me, and I can't understand what she's saying. It's killing me."

Renee stared off into space with a strange look on her face.

"Renee?" Troy asked, puzzled.

"Can you describe the suit?"

"Okay, um, it's form-fitted, a stretchy material, thin with what looks like wires running through it. There are yellow stripes down the sleeves and the sides of her legs."

"And her hair is pulled back in a high ponytail?"

Troy gave her an odd glance. "Yes, how do you know that?"

"Dominic has had that same dream."

***

Ten minutes later, Troy and Renee were waiting for a ground transport outside his door to go to the Strom family apartment. She studied the wall beside the doorway and saw several notes attached with different gifts. She couldn't help but laugh and say, "You have admirers, I see."

He rolled his eyes. "I've even had women break into my house! They were almost arrested as Coronian spies."

"You're quite the catch, Troy Harlow, even when you haven't showered in days. Unfortunately, I'll have to kick these ladies' asses if they think they have a chance."

"I don't think they're all ladies," he said with a quiet laugh.

With how protective Renee had been of Troy since they returned, some might think they were becoming too close. However, after many long years of trying, Dominic had finally broken through Renee's shell, and they had gotten back together. He was now living with her in the officers' quarters because she refused to stay in his parent's apartment. She needed to work on getting him to grow up.

Once the transport arrived, they sped off to the Strom family apartment. Troy was nervous to see the Chancellor, as they were barely on speaking terms. When they pulled up, Dominic opened the door and walked out. "Hey, Troy! It's great to see you, man!"

They had seen each other almost daily, but Dominic loved to tease Troy. It was his way of showing that he cared for his brother-in-law.

Troy was greeted with a hug from Lady Pamela Strom as they walked in. Troy could see the strain of civil unrest and Dia's disappearance were wearing heavily on her. He kissed her cheek. "Hello, Pam. How are you?"

She took a long look at Troy's drawn face, even thinner frame, and sad eyes. "I think I'm better than you are, dear."

Troy sure was enjoying everyone telling him how he always looked like shit.

"Dom, we came because I want you and Troy to talk about the dreams you're having. The dreams about Dia," Renee said.

Dominic tilted his head toward Troy and asked, "Crazy green suit, glowing green eyes, and can't understand you?"

Troy nodded. "Where is she when you see her?"

"She was standing at the end of a long table in a room with huge curved windows. There was a cool garden outside, and every time I have the dream, there's a storm in the distance."

Troy turned to Chancellor Strom. "I know you don't want me on Renee's team because of the liability issue, but I need to be. I want—"

Chancellor Warren Strom, who'd been sitting back for the past year watching the efforts to find Dia fail, said, "Fine, do what you need to. Get her back."

Troy nodded and studied his hands nervously. "Unfortunately, it won't do us any good just to get her back."

"What do you mean?" Warren growled suspiciously.

Troy took a deep breath and faltered when he went to spin the absent ring on his finger. "Dia has no memory of us, of anything in her life before the attack," he said sheepishly.

Renee asked, "How do you know that, Troy?"

"Because I took them from her."

CHAPTER 4
ROGER

Heather sat on her bed and studied the small man who had just walked into her room. He was short, older, with gray hair and large round glasses. He had a meek voice and a pleasant smile. He said, "I'm sorry it's taken me this long to introduce myself. I needed to wait for the perfect moment."

"And this is it?" Heather asked.

He nodded and smiled. "Yes, this is it."

"Hmm... why?"

"Please, come. We're going to go out today. All of us," Roger said, avoiding her inquiry.

Heather glanced at Carl and slid off the bed. They both followed Roger downstairs, and when they were on the landing, he turned to them and said, "Carl, I need to speak with Miss Stone. Can you please gather the rest of the team and meet us in the garage?"

Heather got excited and asked, "We're going in a car? Really?"

"Yes, dear, I think it's time you got out for a bit." He glared at Carl, and Heather watched him walk away apprehensively.

Heather and Roger were quiet for a moment, then she asked, "Why now?"

"Pardon?"

"Why're you introducing yourself to me now? I know I'm here for some nefarious purpose, but it's been a long time."

Roger shifted nervously. He cleared his throat. "Heather, dear, do you truly have no memory of your life before a year ago?"

She shook her head, lifted her hand, and spun the ring on her middle finger. "These rings and a few strange dreams are all I have of my past."

Roger asked, "May I see?" Heather held out her left hand, and Roger examined the rings on her fingers. "Beautiful."

"Brody has no idea what they're made of."

"Do you mind if I ask about the strange dreams?"

She shrugged. "Well, two were in the same bedroom, and one was on a beach, but they all seemed to have the same man in them."

Intrigued, Roger asked, "What did he look like?"

"Tall, thin, with short, dark-brown hair. Very handsome. In the last dream, I noticed he had stunning dark eyes. Oh! And he has a symbol on the back of his neck like I do. His is different, though."

She's dreaming about her husband, he thought.

Roger's observations of Heather over the past several months were curious. When he grew up, his father always liked to watch the news reports from their quadrant of the galaxy. He remembered how his father would groan and get irritated when there was an announcement from "Rygone and their precious Florians." Roger would sit by him as they watched the woman standing next to him report on any conflicts in which Rygone had their dirty hands. Dia Harlow was a stern, seasoned, well-loved military general known throughout the galaxy for her prowess in battle and as an ambassador. Yet, the being beside him could blow up the house with a flick of her finger, then go outside and draw in the sand. Dia had over a million years of life experience; Heather had only had a year to play with a dangerous toy. He had good reason to be nervous.

Before Roger could question her further, Carl and the others walked up, and Brody said, "Road trip? Awesome!"

"Kind of." Roger laughed. "We're going out to dinner. Should we go to Applebee's or Olive Garden?"

Carl said, "Olive Garden."

"Applebee's!" Penny exclaimed.

Brody mumbled, "Ruth's Chris."

Heather furrowed her brow. "What're you all talking about?"

"I think we'll try Olive Garden," Roger decided. "Better food."

"Do they have chicken nuggets?" Heather asked inquisitively.

CHAPTER 5
WHEN YOU'RE HERE, YOU'RE STILL FLORIAN

It was the first time Heather had been beyond the mansion's grounds since she arrived. She'd never interacted with the everyday people of Earth, and she was more nervous than she thought she would be.

They were in Roger's Tesla. He was driving, Carl was in the passenger seat, and Heather sat between Brody and Penny in the back. Brody said to her quietly, "I was expecting you to be a bit more excited. Are you okay?"

Heather nodded. "I'm okay. Remember that I haven't always received the warmest welcome from humans. Except for you guys, I guess."

Penny put her arm around Heather and pulled her into an embrace. The two women had become close. Heather had become hopelessly attached to the physician's assistant, and Penny had actually benefitted from it. Heather loved to run and would drag poor Penny out into the garden and make her do laps or swim with her. Now the two women were best friends, and Penny had lost nearly thirty pounds and was fit and healthy, all thanks to Heather.

Heather glanced past Penny out the window and watched the buildings and people whiz by. "Where are we?" Heather asked.

Carl said, "In town."

"What town, what country are we in?"

"We're in Kno—" Brody began to say.

Roger stopped him. "We're safe, Heather. We're safe."

Heather said sarcastically, "I don't think that's a place, Roger."

They pulled into the parking lot, and everyone started to get out except Heather. Penny almost closed the door before realizing Heather hadn't moved. She peeked her head back in and said, "It's okay, Heather. I'll be with you the whole time."

Heather nodded and slowly slid out of the car. She surveyed the area and was glad to see it was a sunny day, with no storms in sight. Penny linked her arm with Heather's, and they all walked into the restaurant together.

The fantastic aroma of the food hit Heather, and she smiled widely. "I hope today's a cheat day," she said. "This place smells so good."

"Yes, we'll eat pasta, drink Bellinis, and inhale cheesecake."

"Cheesecake," Heather repeated dreamily.

They were shown to their table, and as they walked through the restaurant, Heather observed the people in their everyday settings. A husband and wife out for their anniversary, a family celebrating their child's birthday, a young couple on their first date. It was fascinating.

They sat at a round table, and Heather asked to sit on the far side to observe the room. Everyone thought it was to learn, but Heather was scared and becoming overwhelmed by the amount of energy extending feelers toward her. She sat down, closed her eyes, and took a few deep breaths.

She heard Carl ask quietly, "Are you okay, love?"

She opened her eyes and smiled at him. Carl didn't look much different from the first day they met. His hair was a little less mussed up, and his dark beard wasn't as scruffy, but his green eyes lit up when he smiled, and his gruff voice made her feel at ease. "Yeah, I think so. What's a Bellini?"

The waitress arrived and handed out the menus. Heather was amazed by the choices. Luckily, she had been watching a lot of cooking shows and pretty much knew what everything was. Except for calamari, but she didn't want to know what calamari was.

She asked Carl, "What're you getting?"

"The Tour of Italy."

Heather read the description. "Sounds good. Is it good?"

"It's delicious. It gives you a sampling of the most popular food. And it's big, so that's good for you." Penny laughed.

Brody said, "Is that too big, though?"

"You've watched this woman scarf down an entire rotisserie chicken in ten minutes. Do you really think that's too much?" Carl asked.

Brody nodded. "Yeah, Tour of Italy would be a good choice, Heather."

"Okay. What about dessert?"

"We order that when we're done eating our meal," said Penny.

"You guys should've coached me before we got here," Heather said, frustrated.

The waitress came with the drinks and took their order. Heather stared at her Bellini and thought, *Maybe this wasn't a good idea.*

She took a sip of the sweet, bubbly drink and immediately wanted to chug the whole thing, but she saw Carl staring at her from the corner of her eye. She put her glass down and asked, "Want a sip, Dad?"

"You're a shit. You know that?"

She took a bite out of a breadstick and nodded.

Heather sat back and observed the room. She picked out the specific spots where feelers reached out to her if the need arose to use them. Her initial fear of people knowing who or what she was and wanting to hurt her was unfounded. When their food arrived, everyone ate in a relatively typical fashion.

Heather drained her drink and wanted another, but she knew Carl and Roger wouldn't allow it. She had almost finished her food and didn't realize she was sitting low in her chair, staring at a spot on the wall. Heather's full attention was on the wall when she heard a loud bang from the other side of the restaurant.

There was a commotion from around the room, and she was immediately brought back to the moment. She turned to Carl, panicked. "What happened? Was it me?"

Carl, concerned, said, "What, love? The pop? That was a kid celebrating his birthday with a confetti cannon."

Heather was breathing hard and scanning the room for an exit. Carl looked at Roger and said, "Settle up here. I'm taking her outside for a breath of air."

Roger examined Heather's flushed face. "Okay, we'll be right out."

Carl took Heather by the hand and led her through the restaurant. They got stuck in a bottleneck, and she was caught in a crowd of bodies. The feelers from everywhere were screaming at her, but she calmly ignored them.

Then, Heather felt someone touch the birthmark on her neck and say, right into her ear, "Nice tattoo! So cool. Where'd ya get it?"

Realizing a drunk college student was about to get thrown across Olive Garden by a petite, pissed-off alien, Carl grabbed Heather and pushed her through the crowd. When they finally made it outside, he pulled her along to the car and stopped at the trunk. He turned around, and seeing her ashen face, asked, "Are you all right?"

With her famous stare, she asked, "Is Olive Garden always like that?"

Carl could only laugh.

CHAPTER 6
TROY AND WARREN HAVE A CHAT

Troy and Warren were alone in his and Dia's dining room, staring at each other across the table.

Before now, Warren didn't know the full extent of what happened during Breger Dunes. He just knew that it brought the Coronians to their front door. He wasn't aware of the complexity and strain it put on his daughter's marriage. In all honesty, Warren wasn't concerned about Troy's affair with Maria Granby. Florians were known for their infidelity, including himself and Lady Pam. He was worried about what it did to the outcome of the war. He asked, "Did your affair with that traitor have anything to do with the attack on the rear guard?"

"I can't say for sure, but I don't think so. I don't know the extent of Granby's involvement because she…"

"She what, Troy?"

"She was around me most of the time, and I never saw her do or say anything out of the ordinary." Troy cleared his throat and continued, "But that doesn't mean she wasn't."

"She was distracting the husband of the commanding general. That's what she was doing out of the ordinary. What about the

Pexallun? Where did it come from? Did it do anything permanent to Dia?"

Troy was amazed at how calm the Chancellor was, and it scared him. Dia got her temper and unpredictability from her father, so he knew this conversation could go south at any moment. He answered, "I ran as many tests on Dia as she let me. She's had no adverse reactions, physical or psychological. The Pexallun did not injure her permanently."

"What about the EIP? Have you discovered why it bound to her? Do you think the Pexallun had anything to do with that?"

"Oscar and I wondered about that. I can't necessarily test to see if that might be the case because that would mean subjecting another Florian to Pexallun. I refuse to do that, Chancellor," Troy said defiantly.

Warren nodded and became quiet. The tension in the room was almost more than Troy could take. But he knew this discussion was necessary for Warren to be behind him 100 percent in finding Dia *and* her memories.

Finally, Warren asked, "Where did the EIP come from?"

Troy had always had an answer ready for that question. "A few hundred years ago, when the Coronians first began coming after us, I wanted to help Dia find a way to keep Rygone safe without putting so many of our people at risk. I began working with the energy absorption calibrator we use in the operating room to keep patients' vitals stable when they're in critical condition. It circulates energy from a small battery connected to the patient's temples via leads. I worked to make it larger and bondable to a person rather than keeping someone connected to some power unit. I struggled to get results, so I asked Oscar to help me. It didn't work on anyone or anything beyond what we use it for in medical applications. Until it hit Dia."

Troy sat uncomfortably as Warren studied him enquiringly. "But why her? Why nobody else, Troy? Something doesn't add up. Dia's power can't just come from some upscaled operating room gear. Oscar showed me some videos of your tests with her, yet he says he doesn't know either. Why are you lying to me?"

"I'm not lying to you, Chancellor," Troy said defensively. "I don't understand what happened with Dia, so I can't reproduce her results. Even if I could, I wouldn't. Our enemies somehow know about her powers, and they're stopping at nothing to get their hands on them. Sir, we must find Dia and hide her as far away as possible!"

"Who do you think the spy is?"

This question caught Troy off guard. It'd been so long since he had worked with most of his research team that he couldn't even think of anyone who might have acted suspiciously. He shook his head. "I have no idea, sir. I truly don't."

Warren took out his communicator. "I should've shown this to you sooner."

Warren played the video of Tristen, Troy and Oscar's freelancer, taking the envelope out of Troy's desk. "When did this happen? How did Tristen have access to my office?" Troy asked, exasperated.

"Oscar thinks he was able to forge your ID. The problem is that he disappeared with that envelope immediately afterward. Nobody has seen him since." He leaned closer to Troy and asked, "How well did you know that kid?"

Troy thought back to his interactions with Tristen Black. He was a Hanner-Florian freelancer hired by Oscar to help them both in their labs. Tristen was an average lab tech who stood out more for his prowess with the girls than his work ethic. He had wavy black hair, dark bluish-violet eyes, smooth light skin, and a winning smile that women loved. Troy even saw Dia take notice of Tristen a time or two. As he watched the video of the young man look directly into the camera, then get into his desk and remove the envelope Maria gave him the day of the hospital attack, Troy tried to think of what Tristen's connection to all of this could be. He asked, "Nobody has heard from him since? Is this who you think the spy is?"

"Yes, we believe he's the spy. Everyone else in your and Oscar's employ before and since have been vetted and cleared, but he's gone."

Troy watched the video a few times and tried to figure out why Tristen would go through so much trouble to look into the camera if he were a spy. After a few moments, Warren asked, "Why did you keep the envelope? Such an odd souvenir, Troy."

Troy glared at Warren with disdain. "Yes, it's an odd souvenir, but not for the reason you think. I had that envelope from the day of the hospital attack to when Dia was rescued. It has the coordinates General Smith gave me where they thought she crashed. I took notes from Oscar about what he thought the Pexallun would do to the DREX. So yes, it's strange, and sometimes I wonder why I kept it, but it wasn't because of Maria Granby."

Again, Warren studied Troy closely, just as he had since he was a kid, whenever the Chancellor felt Troy was up to no good. After a moment, his gaze softened, and he said, "Maybe that's why he took the envelope. To either provide or hide something?"

Troy looked back at the screen. It was frozen on an image of Tristen sitting at his desk, glancing up at the camera just as he was about to stand up. Was this kid really a traitor, or was he trying to tell them something? "I don't know, and honestly, at this point, I don't think we need to worry about him. We need to get Dia back, but I first need to get her memories from the Coronians."

Warren laughed. "I'm not sending another team back to Darsayn. That's what they're expecting. We need a way to get this Granby woman away from the Coronians, capture her, and get those rings back."

Troy nodded and said, "She's looking for that too. I think there's only one solution."

"What's that?" Warren asked.

"We need to invite them to dinner."

CHAPTER 7
CARL NEEDS A DRINK

W hen the team arrived back at the mansion from their interesting dinner at Olive Garden, Roger pulled Carl aside and said, "It's high time I showed you something. After the rest of them are asleep tonight, especially Heather, come to my control room."

"Why? What're you going to show me?"

Roger rolled his eyes. "You'll see tonight. Make sure you aren't followed. Understand?"

Carl nodded, confused. Roger turned to everyone and said, "Thank you all for participating in our outing today. I think we learned valuable information about our friend's ability to function outside of our mansion." He glanced at Carl. "I must attend to some business now and hope to see you all soon."

Without further ado, he turned and rushed out of the front door toward the garage.

"I'm so thrilled everyone likes to reference me in the third person. Sometimes I forget I'm just a commodity with a special gift," Heather said quietly.

Penny pulled Heather into a hug and said, "You aren't a commodity. But you can be a drama queen."

"That's for damn sure," Brody mumbled.

Carl huffed. "Knock it off, all of you. Take the rest of the day off. Heather, I need to talk to you."

Penny let her go, kissed Heather on the head, and said to Carl, "Go easy on her. Today was rough."

Carl watched as Penny and Brody walked away. He turned to Heather and said, "Meet me on the porch in fifteen minutes."

"Why there?" she asked inquisitively.

"Quiet and private. I think things are about to change significantly around here, and I want to see how you're doing without prying eyes."

Heather studied his face. "Okay, fifteen minutes."

Carl watched as she ascended the stairs toward her room. He knew Roger was about to make some move, and Heather was beyond prepared as a tool, but she was a liability as a person.

***

Heather walked into her room, and it was almost pitch black. There was significant cloud cover from an approaching storm, so even her skylight was dark.

She turned on a few lamps and wondered why Carl wanted to talk to her alone. They had spoken a hundred times on that porch, but not since the night they almost crossed the line in his room. Heather thought about that moment all the time. Before that, Carl was the only person in the house who didn't make her feel lonely. She longed for his touch and imagined how it would have felt had he not become scared, how things would be now if they had made love that night. Carl stopped them due to his fear of her power. Could she have hurt or even killed him if they went too far?

Heather pushed those thoughts to the back of her mind. She took a pair of sweatpants and a loose shirt out of her dresser and changed. She glanced in the mirror and decided to pull her short, tangled curls into a ponytail. She examined herself and thought, *Unappealing. It's perfect.*

She went onto the porch and sat on a bench close to the middle. Not a minute later, Carl came from the direction of his room and walked up slowly. His handsome face was drawn up into a smirk, and his green eyes danced as he chuckled at her. Heather's heart began to race as he sat down, and she wanted to run. She asked, "What's so funny?"

"I knew you would change into the most comfortable clothes you had. You're the most predictable unpredictable person I've ever met."

Heather turned her gaze to her hands. "Person. Am I a person?"

Carl reached over, took her chin in his hand, and tried to turn her face toward him. She resisted until he said softly, "Look at me, love."

She glanced up at him and asked, "Are you still scared of me, Carl?"

Heather could tell she'd caught him off guard. He cleared his throat and immediately changed the subject. "Heather, do you feel comfortable about what happened today?"

"No. The breadsticks were dry."

Carl stifled a laugh. "That's not what I meant. I mean the whole thing. Driving there, seeing other people, eating out, but mostly, the asshole who touched you."

Heather had almost forgotten about the man who touched her birthmark. "That part pissed me off. People shouldn't touch others without permission."

He nodded, but he wasn't really paying attention. His concerns consumed him. Taking a breath, he said, "Love, I think things are about to change drastically for all of us, especially you. You'll be thrown back into the world in a manner that I'm not yet certain of, but it'll be scary. You'll need to use your abilities, but I'm unsure how or for what. I'm..."

"You're what?"

"I'm scared shitless, love. I'm terrified of what'll happen and that I won't be able to protect you," he said.

Heather could easily see he was flustered and embarrassed, but there was something else she couldn't quite place. She said, "I'll be okay, Carl. You won't need to protect me."

He smiled and caressed her cheek. "I'm sure you won't need it, but I want to anyway."

Heather took a deep breath and asked again, "Carl, are you still scared of me?"

He stared at her, uncertain, for a long time. Just as he opened his mouth to answer, she stood up and took his hand. "Follow me."

Carl let her lead him to his room. She turned and closed the door, pulling the curtains. The only other light was a lamp by his bed. Heather turned it off, and the room went completely dark. She could see, but Carl was still standing where she'd left him. Heather could actually hear his heart pounding. She walked back over to him, took his hand, and carefully examined his confused face. She asked, "What do you see, Carl?"

He turned toward her and tried to look at her face. "Nothing."

Heather put her hand on the back of his neck and pulled his face to hers, locking lips and kissing him deeply. Carl lifted her off her feet and stumbled to the bed. They both feverishly took off each other's clothes, and as she laid back, she whispered, "I don't remember how it feels."

He kissed her lips deeply, and Heather pulled him into a tight embrace.

And of course, like clockwork, Carl's phone rang.

He reached over toward the nightstand as Heather kissed his neck and ran her fingers down his spine. The caller ID was Roger. He'd forgotten he had a meeting with him. *Damn it!*

He turned his attention back to the beautiful woman giving him all of her trust and love. "Love, I need to go do something."

Heather kissed his lips again and said, "No, it can wait, please."

Carl kissed her hard and fell back into the ecstasy of the moment. He whispered, "Are you sure you want to do this?"

Heather breathed, "I've been ready for this for a long time."

Just as Carl was going to satisfy both of their desires, his phone rang again. Heather grabbed it before he could and threw it across the room. "Please, Roger can wait."

But the ringing began yet again. And again, and again.

Heather laid back against the pillow with a huff. "You should get that."

Carl turned on the lamp and got out of bed to search for the phone. She hadn't seen a man naked—at least, not in person—since landing on Earth. Carl was younger than he let on; his body reflected that, as he was very fit and lightly muscular. He found the phone and sat on the edge of the bed, pulling the blanket around his waist. He answered the persistent Roger. "What is it?"

Heather slid over and sat behind him. She ran her fingertips down his spine and smiled when he shivered. She rested her forehead against his back and slid her arms around his waist as he continued his heated discussion with their so-called benefactor. Finally, he said, "I'll be there shortly."

Carl put his phone down, and they sat quietly for a long moment, savoring the feel of their bodies being close. Heather traced her fingers along his sides. Carl whispered, "God, that feels good."

Heather sighed. "Why do you have to go talk to him tonight? It's late."

"I was supposed to go earlier."

Heather sighed again, frustrated. "Can I at least stay in here until you get back?"

Carl turned around and gave her a long kiss. "You better."

***

Fifteen minutes later, Dr. Carl Johnson, physicist, walked into Roger's control room. He said, "This better be good, mate."

Roger studied Carl. "Please don't tell me you finally broke down!"

Carl narrowed his eyes and said, "If I did, I wouldn't tell you."

"Well, it's written all over your face. I have something to show you that'll completely change whatever feelings you have for Heather Stone."

"What the fuck are you talking about?" Carl growled.

Roger motioned to the bank of monitors on the wall and brought up a series of photos. "I was able to get these images from my home planet. I'm sure you'll find them interesting."

The image that caught Carl's attention was in the middle. Roger enlarged it, and all of the air escaped Carl's lungs as his throat seized up. It was slightly blurry, but the woman was perfectly distinct. She wore a black uniform with military insignia on the collar and shoulders. Her long hair was pulled into an elaborate braid with a silver ribbon woven into it. She had large, up-turned brown eyes with black liner and dark mascara. She was pointing to the side, and he could see other people in the picture running in that direction. Her face was stern, commanding, yet still beautiful. He could only imagine what she said to make them jump to action.

Carl choked. "It can't be."

"Isn't it one of our jobs to find out who she is, even if we keep her for ourselves?"

Carl nodded, even though he didn't want to. Was that really the same woman lying in his bed, waiting for him to return? "I need a drink. Now."

CHAPTER 8
LEARNING CURVE

"Do you know who she is?"

"Yes. Sit down."

Carl sat down hard, gripping the bottle of whiskey Roger'd given him. He'd taken three long pulls and was almost ready to hear about the woman on the monitor.

Roger cleared his throat and said, "This is Commanding General Dia Harlow of the Florian Army on the planet Rygone. Her species is Florian, who are said to be direct descendants of the Beginners. Neither are known here on Earth, even though they should be."

Carl took another long pull of the whiskey.

"Go easy on that, or you won't remember any of this."

Maybe I don't want to, Carl thought.

Roger zoomed in on another picture. This time, though dressed the same, Heather—*Dia*—was standing next to a man. He was tall, much taller than her, and very slender. He had dark brown hair and eyes and an unnaturally handsome face. The picture was clear enough for Carl to see his left hand, and plain as day, he wore the same two rings Heather did. In whatever society these two were from, they were connected somehow.

He said, "Her husband or whatever, I suppose?"

"Yes. His name is Dr. Troy Harlow. He's the most brilliant doctor in their quadrant. Hell, in the galaxy, even."

Of course. Why wouldn't he be?

Roger sat down in a chair across from Carl. "Look, you've been working for me for a long time and are the only person who succeeded in bringing us a viable tool to—"

Carl interrupted him with slurred words, "She is *not* a tool."

"You're right. She's not a tool. She's the most dangerous, volatile, and useful weapon the galaxy has ever known, and she's ours."

Carl was getting pissed. Earlier that day, Heather had said people only thought of her as a commodity. She was right.

Carl studied the face of the woman in the picture. Everything about her appearance proved she was Heather, but the way she presented herself said she wasn't the same person. Carl felt sorry for that beautiful and terrifying face. *What happened to you, love?*

"Do you want to know something even more amazing?" Roger said with a hint of excitement. "Florians are immortal. They cannot be killed and heal almost immediately in the very rare instance they're injured. Case in point is the warehouse incident. General Harlow is over one *million* years old."

The fact that Roger said her age was lost on Carl, but what name he used was not. "Here, on Earth, until she remembers that she's the woman in that damn picture, she's Heather Stone. Are we clear?"

Roger noted the growing anger in Carl and said, "Of course."

"Why is everyone all up in arms about her? Don't all these Florians have powers like this?"

"Nobody has ever seen anything like Heather. The consensus from my people and our allies is Troy Harlow was working on a weapon that bound with her, maybe by accident. The Coronians will either want to use her or destroy her," Roger explained.

Carl thought about the woman upstairs, probably still lying in his bed. Her sweet voice and love for coffee, bunnies, and Happy Meals. There were people out there who wanted to destroy or exploit her. It was all he could take for now. He stood up with the bottle in his hand and said, "Well, they aren't going to get to use her, destroy her, or do shit with her until we find out why she's here," he pointed at the first picture, "and make her back into *that*!"

He started to stumble toward the door, but he turned back to Roger and growled, "How long have you known?"

Roger cleared his throat. "I've known since the moment you brought her here. When I was a boy on my home planet, my father would watch the news from our quadrant, which we share with Rygone, and that woman was always doing something incredible. She was either a commanding general reporting on military operations, teaching the Florian Army Air Corps pilots how to fly DREX fighters and destroyers, or working as an ambassador alongside her father, brokering peace and trade amongst the known galaxy. The point is, she's a priceless individual to the galaxy, even more than anyone on this planet knows. She has a powerful family who loves her very much, and I know they'll want her back. Carl, she's ready for whatever comes next."

Carl fought back tears and approached Roger. "Agreed."

He reared back and punched the smaller man in the mouth. Roger hit the ground, holding his lip, and Carl continued, "You knew who she was, knew that she was married, and you didn't do more than warn me not to get close. She's in my bed right now waiting for me. And now I have to send her away. I love her, asshole. Go to hell."

***

Heather had put her clothes back on but refused to leave Carl's room. She was convinced that whatever Roger had to tell Carl would derail anything they were about to share earlier, but she still wanted to see him when he came back.

She had wrapped herself in a soft blanket that smelled like his soap and was in the midst of dozing off when the door opened. She sat up straight and watched as Carl walked in. He was holding half a bottle of whiskey and seemed to be stumbling. He came to her side of the bed, turned on the lamp, sat down, and stared at her.

Heather had never seen such emotion on his face. He was sad, angry, and confused. He reached out, took her left hand, and gently turned the ring on her index finger. "I've taken all of this for granted. This project. The way we're so proud of making you into what you are. We've lost sight of something," he said softly.

Heather asked, "Lost sight of what?"

"*Who* you are, love," he said, staring into her strange eyes. "Where you come from, and who out there is missing you. Roger may want you to stay here for his selfish reasons, but I'll do my best to find all of that out."

Heather's eyes spilled over with tears, and she squeaked, "What if I don't want that?"

He pushed a curl behind her ear and said, "I'm afraid of what we've done to you, love."

Heather moved next to Carl, and she put her arms around him. "You haven't done anything. You saved me from the people who would've made me into something worse!"

"Maybe. Hopefully. But I still want what's best for you." Carl reluctantly pulled away from her embrace.

Heather knew she shouldn't, but she asked, "Can I at least lay here with you? I'm so lonely, Carl."

His eyes were deep with what seemed like a new knowledge she couldn't fathom, and she knew he wouldn't share it with her. She could only hope he would agree. He smiled weakly and said, "Yes, love, that would be nice." He stood up, unsteady, and continued, "I'm going to take a shower first. Drinking whiskey and learning new things is a dirty business."

"Okay. I'll be here," she whispered.

Carl gazed at her wondrous face, leaned down, and kissed her, hoping it wasn't for the last time.

CHAPTER 9
VERONICA'S HISTORY

Veronica stared at the screen on her desk with frustration. Since her confrontation with the Premier, she had been on edge about not being able to find Troy, Dia, *or* her informant. The little bastard had disappeared, and she feared he had turned tables on her. However, the Rygonians would know precisely where she was and what she was doing if he had. *Where are you, ya little jerk?*

She had managed to covertly access the Coronian's top-secret database revolving around their known planetary systems in the quadrant and Deep Space. She searched for planets that could sustain intelligent life, specificially ones they might know about but Rygone didn't. The Rygonians were incredibly intelligent but stayed in contact with only the species communicating with them and their allies. Rygone had no interest in dominating the galaxy, even though they easily could. They only knew a fraction about their quadrant and Deep Space, which she always found odd.

However, the Coronians had delusions of grandeur. They wanted to take over the entire galaxy and make it in their image. At first, their efforts were futile, but they were able to turn spies from all over the galaxy to their cause. Soon, societies crumbled under their endeavors in even the most formidable civilizations.

So far, the most robust resistance was from Rygone and its allies, which weren't as many as they used to be, thanks to Darsayn and Baxelhoff's relentless pursuit of power. Rygone was much more of a tyrant than they made themselves out to be, thanks to the Florians. Her species was arrogant, selfish, and controlling—especially the "old blood" families, namely the Stroms. Warren Strom was great at making the citizens of Rygone, both Florian and refugee alike, believe that he and his core group of supporters were making a positive difference in their way of life. He was regarded as the greatest Florian to ever live because he could bring all the people who called their planet home together and live in harmony. Yet, when the "lesser" groups, such as refugees and Community Florians, wanted to participate in the government's running, they had to follow the election laws put in place long ago by Strom. He welcomed the diverse elections of officials as long as all politicians, ambassadors, community chiefs, and military leaders operated per his regulations.

His influence led to a resistance that wanted to take control of their communities, especially those in the towns and cities outside of the three Baltica cities. Many people left those cities, hoping to find a better life in the outlying areas of Rygone as simple farmers or community leaders taking care of the smaller populations. Sadly, as local governments were formed, and the federal system was tested, Strom and his aptly trained accomplices would come in and take control of the insurrection, as they called it. Several communities were left in ruins because of riots and resistance against Strom's judgment. There was even a terrorist faction that attacked all three Baltica cities, disrupting the entire government, financial districts, and even the entertainment industry for months. It was rumored that many high-profile Florians, even Strom himself, were taken prisoner. The insurrection was brought to its knees by an unlikely Florian hero named Perry Contreau, an artist, of all people. But that was before Veronica's time, and she learned about most of Rygone's history in primary school. Perry

Contreau was still a prominent member of Rygonian society, but he had left his war hero mantle behind. Veronica and the residents of Rygone only knew him for his music, entrepreneurship, philanthropy, and championship for the gay and lesbian community.

It wasn't only the parliament that stood against the resistance. Many citizens of the remote communities also reveled in the federal rules. They loved the Stroms and old, traditional leaders. The terrorists were reminded that Rygone was mostly refugees from all over the galaxy. Those who escaped tyranny and genocide at the hands of their rulers. Many civilizations had come and gone in the timeframe that Rygone had been established for the Florians. The rules of existence the Beginners set forth for their rejected children were much different than other intelligent life they created intentionally. They interfered little with the Florians, contributing to their success. At least for now.

The Beginners. Were they truly real?

The more time passed, the more younger generations of Florians perceived the Beginners' existence as garbage. Lies their parents fed them to explain their differences to the others around them. Veronica remembered her mother telling her, "We Florians are so special, Maria. No other race in the universe's history is as important and extraordinary as ours. Our ancestors are the great Beginners themselves, and we're descendants of power and grace, brought here to start our own life and flourish."

Yet, when Veronica asked where they went and why they left their children on a strange planet, her mother had no solid answer. Nobody did. Not even the third generation and beyond. The first generation had disappeared from Rygone, and nobody could give a good explanation as to why, not even *their* children. Many believed they left to search for their incredible parents, but none had returned to tell the tale.

Veronica cried foul. The Beginners were a lie, just like the old families who claimed to control their lives. But no more. She planned to use the Coronians as pawns to take Rygone by force. It was time for the community to rule the planet.

Veronica had been working with the Coronians on a varying basis for almost two hundred years now. Her plans for a takeover were a work in progress and took time. She wanted to do it right and ensure that those she was planning to overthrow couldn't return and take her prize easily.

That was why she needed Dia Harlow.

Veronica had waited so long for something that could defeat not only her people but, in turn, take on the Coronians once she had control of Rygone. She needed to get Dia Harlow captured and under control. It was paramount for her plan to work. All she had to do now was find the bitch.

Dia was known to challenge her father and superiors, occasionally playing in the community's favor. Like so many young girls and women, Veronica had wanted to be like Dia for thousands of years. A strong woman who rose through her government's ranks to take the top spot in the Florian Army, but Veronica figured it was a ruse. A ploy put together by Warren Strom to make it look like she was resistant to his rule, when in actuality she was also his puppet. Veronica had lost all respect for her hero.

The Coronians had decided to make their big move on Rygone, starting with the Waleetrs, who had begun to rebel again Strom's rule. They took up the plight secretly, providing them with equipment and training. The Premier came to Veronica with their plans and outlined what they wanted her to do with Troy Harlow. They wanted to eliminate anyone who could interfere in their plans for getting their hands on the brilliant doctor, namely Dia Harlow. With her gone, grabbing a bewildered Troy would be much easier. They discovered the Pexallun and located a remote source unknown to the Florians. They took the gamble that it would kill the commanding general in a crash in the swamp. Veronica, or Maria, was tasked with distracting Troy from treating or investigating any suspicious injuries so they could test the poison on the community. Their plan couldn't have worked better. They knew she went further with her feelings for the doctor than expected, but he was putty in her hands. The perfect, faithful, and diligent doctor was seduced by a beautiful face and caring touch for the first time.

Unfortunately, Dia Harlow survived her horrific crash and the physical and psychological injuries it inflicted. It took time, but Dia returned more robust than ever, and their plans were pushed back to square one.

Until they found out she was the one who finally bonded with the EIP. The mighty general would be the perfect candidate to wield such a weapon, and they needed to grab her as soon as possible. Veronica had planted a spy in Troy's lab many years before, and he kept them informed on every move the Harlows made, all through training and experimenting, until something happened, and they spooked and tried to flee. The day the unknown incident occurred, their spy said the Harlows were in shambles and not acting like themselves. He followed them as much as he could but didn't figure out what they were doing until the day before their departure. He informed Veronica that Troy and Dia would flee Rygone with no intention to return, so they scrambled an assault on the planet. The spy even knew what direction Dia planned to take to get to the other side of Rygone so they could leave the atmosphere undetected. Unfortunately for the Harlows, the Coronians were there. Unfortunately for the Coronians, Troy had a contingency plan, and Dia was lost to the vacuum of space. She was still yet to be found.

Which left Veronica to figure out what to do on her own. Her informant hadn't contacted her in a few months, and now the Coronians were somehow getting the information she would feed them before he could get it to her. She had to assume he was captured and in prison. Whatever the case, he would pay dearly if she ever got her hands on him again.

Veronica continued scanning the planetary systems until she came across one she didn't recognize. She zoomed in and investigated further. There was one star and what looked like eight planets with varying moons. The system's information showed only one planet suitable for intelligent life. She was shocked to see that the Coronians had already visited it. They were scoping out different systems without her even knowing! *Baxelhoff still doesn't fully trust me, that bastard*, she fumed. What else could he be hiding from her?

She opened the files with pictures, language programs, and historical records. They had documented everything about this planet for at least two hundred years, and Rygone had no idea it existed, even with it being surprisingly close. *Florians. A bunch of blind idiots we are.*

The planet was fascinating but strange. There was advanced life support, energy production, farming, and community development, even more than Rygone had outside the Baltica cities. A concerning part of their existence was how divided they were, even more than Rygone, and willing to use their advanced intelligence to fight each other rather than move their society forward. They had only left their planet a few times and stayed close. They didn't even have spaceships capable of going to the next planet in their system, let alone across the galaxy. What did the Coronians want with such a primitive place?

"Earth," she whispered. "What's so special about you?"

CHAPTER 10
WHAT THE F@#$?

After Carl got out of the shower, he left the bathroom expecting Heather to be gone, but much to his pleasant surprise and terrible dread, she was still there. She was lying on top of the covers, curled under a soft blanket. He tentatively walked to his side of the bed and watched her for a moment. All he could see was her head; most of her face was covered in curls. He smiled and gently slid under the comforter, putting a layer between them on purpose. He turned off his lamp. The moon shone from above and bathed the room in cool light. Carl could see the blanket move up and down with each breath as he listened to her snore softly.

He was reluctant to close his eyes, afraid she would disappear, but the remaining effects of the whiskey and exhaustion took over, and he drifted off to sleep.

What seemed like only a few minutes passed, and Carl felt the gentle brush of fingertips on his cheek. He sighed and smiled in his light slumber. After another moment, he felt the same touch, only longer. His brain finally registered what was happening right as he became aware of a weight on his stomach, and his eyes flew open.

Carl knew he'd turned all the lights off, but his lamp was now on for some reason. He was frozen in shock to see a familiar face staring back at him.

She was beautiful with large brown, smoky eyes. Her skin was smooth as light-peach porcelain, and her lips were painted dark red. Her hair was pulled back into an elaborate braid that had a stunning silver ribbon woven into it. She wore a black uniform that was trimmed with gold. Her collar had a logo of what looked like a roaring cat with two swords crossed beneath it, and she had three gold stars on each shoulder. On her left breast were several ribbons and what looked like flight wings, and a nametag was on the right. He couldn't read the alien writing but assumed it said Harlow.

She smiled pleasantly. "Hello, Carl."

His eyes went wide, and he tried to move back, but she put her hand on his chest, holding him down. "No, no. This is your dream; you have to stay here for it."

Carl glanced to the side and saw that Heather was still lying there fast asleep. He turned back to the woman sitting on him, who was staring at Heather too. "You're..."

She glanced at him with a smirk. "I'm... who, Carl?" she asked.

He asked, "Dia?"

She nodded. "Very good." She motioned with her head toward Heather and continued, "So is she. At least, deep in her head, she is."

Carl studied her face and tried to figure out the differences. She was the same person, but the personalities were significantly different. "Why are you here?"

"I can't tell you that right now, but I can tell you that you're the only person who can protect Heather. Protect her until I can return, Carl. She's extraordinary, yet very fragile and dangerous... but you know that already."

Carl shifted his gaze between Heather and Dia. "I can't understand how you're so different from each other."

"We aren't different, Carl. We're the same person. What you see in her right now is a lack of life experience. I'm 1,248,152 years old. She has one year of knowledge of a foreign planet.

Who you call Heather doesn't remember the joy, the horror, the thrill, and the sadness that goes along with being immortal. I've won wars, lost battles, and watched dear loved ones be born, live, and die without me aging a day. She manipulates energy dangerously and plays with animals in the garden. I need her to remember me soon so our combined experience and power can save both of our worlds, Carl."

He could feel the pain of her words. He asked, "What do I need to do, Dia?"

She leaned in and whispered in his ear, "Take her to Las Vegas."

Eyes snapping open, Carl sat straight up and took several deep breaths. He had never had that vivid of a dream in his entire life. His eyes darted to Heather as she began to stir.

She purred, "What is it?"

He shook his head. "Nothing, love. Go back to sleep. It'll be morning soon."

She curled back into the blanket and immediately started snoring again.

Carl lay down and ran through the dream in his head before he could forget it. How had he manifested Dia in his mind? Was that really what she was like? Why Vegas?

Surprisingly, he started to fall back to sleep. Just as he slipped into slumber, he thought, *I need to book us rooms at the Venetian. I've always wanted to stay there.*

CHAPTER 11
CARL WANTS TO TAKE US WHERE?

When Heather woke up that morning, Carl was lying next to her, sleeping soundly. With the previous evening's events weighing heavily on her mind, she decided to leave before he woke up.

The kitchen was cool and quiet when she walked in and made coffee. She wondered what Roger could have possibly said to Carl to make him so emotional last night. Heather still longed for Carl but had to come to terms with the possibility that maybe it was better for them, for all of them, that they remain platonic. Whatever that meant.

Finding a pomegranate, Heather sat down at the kitchen counter and tore part of the maddening fruit open, spilling tiny seeds across the counter. She grunted in frustration just as Brody walked in. As he made his way to the coffee maker, he watched her struggle and asked, "What the hell are you doing to that poor piece of fruit?"

She stopped what she was doing and asked, "Have you ever eaten a pomegranate?"

"Nope, too much of a pain in the ass for such a small reward."

"Well, then shut up." She grumbled, "I'm determined to try."

"That's understandable coming from you," he said with a smile.

Penny was next to arrive in the kitchen. She came from outside and was sweaty from running.

"Why didn't you come get me?" Heather asked. "I would've loved to take a run."

Penny took a big drink of water and wiped her mouth. "I did."

Embarrassed, Heather realized she hadn't been in her room that morning. She was sure that would eventually become a topic of conversation for her and Carl. She cleared her throat and said, "Oh, right."

Brody was about to inquire about what they meant when Carl came breezing into the kitchen and went straight for the coffee maker, pouring a cup. He chugged half the scalding liquid and said frantically, "Brody, grab a cup of coffee and a piece of toast. I need you to work on something with me in the lab." He raised his voice for all of them to hear. "All of you, get a bag packed. Tomorrow morning, we're taking a trip."

"Where to, Carl?" Roger's voice came from right behind Heather, startling her and Penny. "What are you talking about?"

Carl painfully chugged the rest of the cup, poured more, and said, "We're going to Vegas."

Hmmm, scary, Heather pondered, concerned. *Lots of power on the Strip, from what I've read. I'd like to try playing poker for money, though.*

Carl said, "Come on, we need to get this together." He turned to Roger and asked, "With your infinite supply of money and resources, can you manage travel? We must get there fast and can't take her on a commercial plane. She would never make it through without identification."

"Identification isn't a problem." Brody proudly explained, "I've already created a foolproof identity with passports, social security number, and driver's license. Her problem would be the danger of possibly interfering with the aircraft itself. Are you certain we can't drive?"

Carl shook his head. "We need to get there as soon as possible." He looked over at Heather, who was eating the few seeds she managed to extract from the mangled pomegranate, and asked, "Do you think you can handle flying on a plane, love?"

"It isn't something we've ever discussed, but I don't think there's anything to worry about. I know how to control this power." *For the most part.*

"Good enough. Brody, let's go. Penny, I also need you to book the biggest suite at the Venetian. I want us all to stay in the same room. Or adjoining rooms if we need to."

"How long?" Penny asked.

"Three days," Carl said, breathless.

As Carl started walking toward the lab with the tech, Roger tried to stop him. "Can we talk first?"

Carl didn't even look at him as he said, "No, just make what I said happen."

Penny and Heather looked at each other awkwardly. "Come on, Heather, let's go upstairs and see what clothes we can scrape up to head out to the most glamorous and tacky place on Earth."

"Sounds good." The two women hurried up the stairs.

***

Once in the lab, Carl said, "Okay, I need you to pack her suit and a few shells. But most importantly, I need you to make something special very quickly."

Brody clapped his hands and rubbed them together. "Okay, boss, whatcha got for me?"

"I need two cocktail dresses made with a shell built into the lining. And they can't look any different from an ordinary dress. They also need to make it past any security screeners without detection."

Brody laughed and said, "And you want this by tomorrow? *Morning*, no less?" When Carl only stared at him, the brilliant technologist laughed louder. "That's a good one, man! I thought you were serious! Do we still get to go to Vegas?"

Carl took Brody by the shoulders and glared desperately at him. "Brody, you're a fucking genius. I know you can make this happen. We need to get there tomorrow."

"What has you so flustered, Carl?" Brody asked with a furrowed brow. "What's in Vegas that has you in such a rush? Who did you talk to?"

"A trusted source told me we need to get Heather there as soon as possible. I believe them wholeheartedly."

"Who was it?"

"You wouldn't believe me if I told you."

Brody rolled his eyes and said, "Everyone always says that! I'm a pretty open-minded guy, Carl."

Carl considered him. "You're right. You probably would believe me and then turn around and tell everyone, even if I don't want them to know."

Brody nodded in begrudging agreement and said, "Okay, I'll do it. But I want extra cash for blackjack."

"If you do it, I'll make sure Roger gives you an extra five grand. How about that?"

Brody clapped his hands again. "Hell yeah, boss man. Lemme get started!"

Carl turned to leave, but Brody stopped him. "Hey, Carl, what colors?"

"Huh?" Carl asked.

"What colors do you want the dresses? You wanted two, and I need to know what colors so I can make her as hot and incredible as possible!"

Carl thought for a moment. Heather needed to be beautiful but classy. "One black, one red. Keep them simple but appealing. Don't make her look like a whore."

"Don't get me wrong, I like scantily clad women, but Heather isn't that type of girl," Brody said, slightly offended. "She'll be respectable and sexy at the same time."

"Good." Carl hoped he and Brody had the same idea of sexiness.

***

Penny and Heather went through each other's closets and dressers. Penny put together enough outfits and accessories for two women to live it up in Las Vegas for a few days.

Penny sat on Heather's bed and gushed, "I'm so excited. I've only been to Vegas once, and it was so much fun! And there are so many hot guys there! I looked up the convention schedule, and it's totally booked. Almost every hotel will be full!"

That was exciting for Penny but terrifying for Heather. After Olive Garden, Carl wanted to throw her into one of the highest populated and energized places in the United States. What did he know?

She was quiet, making Penny look up at her. She patted the bed and said, "Come over here, Heather."

Heather sat next to one of only three friends she had in the world. "I'm so scared, Penny." She asked, "What if something goes wrong and I hurt or even kill someone?"

"I can't sit here and say, 'Oh, it'll be fine; that will never happen' because I don't know what'll happen, sweetie," Penny acknowledged. "What I do know is that you're so much more capable and confident in your abilities than you were when we first found you. I'm quite sure you'll be able to control yourself perfectly."

Heather feigned a smile. She thought, *I wish I had that much confidence in myself.*

***

They all spent the rest of the day getting ready to go. Not even Carl knew that Roger had a private jet. Roger did, in fact, have an infinite supply of money and resources on Earth. His home planet of Zole was very rich in minerals scarce on Earth, like titanium and gold. Every so often, a transport would secretly deliver these precious metals, and Roger would slowly invest them into the different monetary systems worldwide. One of Earth's benefits of not being a single government like Zole or Rygone was exploiting other economies for the most significant yield of funds. His quality of life on Earth was better than he ever had back on his home planet. He would be very disappointed if they ever decided to call him back from this assignment.

After packing, Penny and Carl went into the lab to help Brody. Like Carl expected, Brody put together the two dresses that Heather would use as shells. Unfortunately, due to the limited amount of available fabric, there wasn't much room for wire to store power. He was confident that Heather could manage because of the immense electrical energy flowing through the Las Vegas Strip. A constant amount of fuel would surround her, but she could get overwhelmed. Everything was all one big unknown. He could only hope Heather was ready for whatever Carl had in store for her.

Once finished with the first dress, Carl called Heather into the lab and said, "I want to do a test run to see how you handle this before we commit to being finished."

He handed her the black cocktail dress, and she went into the lab bathroom and changed. When she came out, they were all impressed by Brody's work. He did an excellent job making the dress simple yet elegant and respectably appealing.

"Damn, man, you should be a clothing designer," Carl said.

"I thought about it. But I prefer science to fashion."

The dress was form-fitted, and the length fell above Heather's knees. A small slit up her left thigh was more for function than style, but it helped the look. It had wide shoulder straps and came down in the front to a V. Brody knew she never wore a bra, so he took that liberty and brought the V down to the middle of her breasts, and the fabric hugged their firm shape.

She stood before them, shifting on her feet, and asked, "How do I look?"

"Spectacular!" Penny said, beaming.

Brody said smugly, "Like a work of my art."

Carl just cleared his throat. "We should get out to the field and get this test done. There's still a lot to do today."

"Not yet. I have another piece of gear that will be perfect for this trip," Brody said.

He pulled out a small jewelry box and handed it to Heather. She opened it, revealing a beautiful pair of diamond earrings and a matching diamond necklace. She ran her fingers over the delicate chain and whispered, "These are beautiful, Brody."

He grinned. "And very useful." He took the necklace out and walked behind her. She lifted her hair as he put the chain on, purposely brushing his hand against the birthmark on her neck. Next, he showed her how to put on the magnetized earrings.

She looked in the mirror and admired the jewels. "Now what?"

He put a small device in his ear and said, "Hello."

She was startled by his voice in her ear and jumped. "Wow! How'd you do that?"

"Very carefully. Now, the earrings are what you hear us through, and the necklace is the speaker we use to listen to you. You need to keep these on when we're there, no matter what."

Heather smiled at herself in the full-length mirror. Between the dress and jewels, she almost didn't recognize herself. Until she looked at her slippers; they were more her speed.

They walked into the curved room, and Heather continued alone into the garden and made her way down the path to her Field of Fucks—Carl's name for the empty field that she regularly destroyed with her powers.

When she got to the end of the path, she turned to one of the solar panels Brody had installed. Heather held her hand over the panel, absorbed the energy, and pushed as much into the dress as possible. She couldn't store as much as she wanted, but it was better than nothing. She gazed back down the field and held her arms out. She drew the stored energy and released it all at once, carving a crack in the earth twenty feet long and about three feet deep. With so much energy storage capability and the fact that infinite amounts of available power would surround her, she was confident she could do whatever Carl needed, whatever that may be.

She walked back into the house and asked Brody, "Will that work?"

He glanced at Carl. "So?"

"That's perfect. Thank you all," Carl said.

With that, he turned and rushed away toward the front door. Heather watched longingly as he disappeared.

Brody asked, "So. Heather, you and—"

She cut him off. "No. Nothing happened." Then it was her turn to walk away.

The tech reached into his pocket and took out a dollar bill. He handed it to the physician's assistant and said, "One day, it'll be me who wins this bet."

"Highly unlikely," Penny said as she snapped the bill.

***

The team did their own thing for the rest of the day. Heather made homemade pizza and chocolate chip cookies for dinner and dessert. The closer it got to bedtime, the more excited and terrified she became.

After dinner, she and Carl were cleaning up, and he asked, "You left early this morning. Were you okay?"

She nodded, not knowing what to say.

Carl leaned up against the counter. "I want you to know something, Heather. Please look at me."

She put down the dish she was drying and turned her eyes to his. He was worn from whatever was stressing him out. "If you ever feel lonely, you can always come to visit me like last night. No pressure, no expectations. Just company."

She liked the idea but would probably never do that again. She enjoyed sleeping in Carl's bed just as friends, but she was afraid it might turn into more than that one day. Heather couldn't entirely remember what love felt like, but she was beginning to believe she was experiencing it with Carl. After he told her he would stop at nothing to help her find out where she came from, the prospect of leaving and losing him became more real. Yet, she also felt incredibly alone because she didn't fit in with the people of this world. She smiled. "Okay, thank you."

He asked, "Are you nervous?"

She shook her head. "Nope, I'm completely terrified."

Carl smiled warmly and put his arm around her shoulders, pulling her into a loose embrace. His touch made her feel wonderful and scared at the same time. *Why do I have these feelings for him?* He must have felt the tension in her body because he let go awkwardly. *I think this is the beginning of us drifting apart,* she thought.

Once they finished cleaning, Carl said, "We should hit the hay. We'll be up very early tomorrow to leave for the airport."

"Hit the hay?" she repeated curiously.

Carl laughed. "It means to go to bed."

"Hit the hay. I like that."

They walked up the stairs and discussed different ways to say "going to bed."

By the time they parted ways, Heather still liked "hit the hay" best.

CHAPTER 12
WE'RE DOING THIS ALL WRONG

Troy was lying in bed, staring at the ceiling, overthinking everything he was trying to do. He had tried to reach out to the Coronians on Darsayn, but Rygone received no response. They weren't a species that usually bartered for peace or resolution, but he had hoped they still might find him a desirable target, yet all of their efforts fell on deaf ears.

Troy was beginning to think he was failing at convincing Chancellor Strom that he was up to the task of getting his rings and Dia back when Warren came to see him that evening. When Troy answered the door, the Chancellor of Rygone came into his living room, looking terrible but bearing a gift of Capole liqueur, Troy's favorite.

The two men sat silently across from each other in the living room, sipping the sweet cordial that Troy had mixed with glacier water. Warren finally said, "There's something we're missing. The Coronians know something we don't and couldn't care less if we try to negotiate, even for you."

"We're going about this all wrong, and I can't figure out why," Troy agreed.

Warren took a sip of the super-sweet drink and tried to hide the grimace that crossed his face.

He said, "I think the only use the traitor is to us is to get your rings back. After that, I'm sure she's worthless. They used her to get to you, and now you're no longer valuable. Well, at least it seems that way."

Troy considered his words. He sipped the Capole, and a very distant memory flashed into his mind. He smiled and asked, "Do you want to know why I like this garbage liqueur?"

Warren looked at the dark green liquid in his glass. "Yeah, kinda."

"During one of your and my parents' famous Herrow Day parties when Dia and I were about eleven or twelve, we were bored out of our minds. We were pretty much the only Florian children on the planet, and all we had was each other."

"Back then, you both hated being forced to spend time together."

"Usually, yes, but one year we were jealous that all of the adults, including Dominic, were getting wasted." Troy continued with a grin, "So, we snuck into your and Pam's kitchen, and she found the last remaining bottle of booze in the pantry—Capole."

Warren chuckled. "Oh, yeah. You both took it into Pam's and my shower and drank half the damn bottle. When we found you, you were passed out, and Dia was puking. Fun times those were."

"It was a fun time, kind of. Dia and I rarely connected when we were kids, but there were a few memorable moments. Some were better than others." He glanced up at his father-in-law, knowing Warren knew he was referring to the year he and Dia lost their innocence to each other at another one of their parents' famous parties.

Warren drained his glass and stood up. "I'm going to go talk to Oscar. Hasn't he been working on something to trace the energy profile the EIP emits?"

"Yes, but he either doesn't have it calibrated right, or the range of the DREX scanners aren't as powerful as we thought. He can adjust the frequency from here, but it's taking time."

"Okay, I'll see if there's anything else that can be done from my side." The Chancellor walked toward the door, then turned back to Troy. "Troy, I know this is hardest on you; you're receiving the most flack from the rest of us. But you're the brains that can figure it out, right?"

Troy didn't hear the voice of the Chancellor but that of a father longing to find his daughter. He stood up and walked toward Warren. "No, I'm not the *only* brain that can solve this. The Coronian problem goes way beyond the EIP, my transgressions, or Dia's missing memories. Even beyond the effects on our people since Breger Dunes. We all must come together and prepare for an all-out war, which will likely be on our soil again."

"I fear that as well. Hopefully, we can find Dia before that comes to pass."

The Chancellor of Rygone sighed, turned, and walked out the door. Troy was left alone again in the eerily quiet apartment.

He had been forcing himself to sleep in their bed, hoping he would get used to not having Dia there. Throughout their marriage, there were hundreds of times that they spent months, even years, apart, but this loneliness was different. Then, he always knew where she was or at least why she was gone. Now he didn't know if she would ever lay beside him again.

He took a deep breath and turned onto his side, toward the window. All three moons were in the sky tonight. It almost looked like daytime on the plains outside of the city. He concentrated on the outline of the mountains until sleep finally found him.

Troy felt someone get into bed behind him and move close. He was frozen with fear until she said, "Hello, Troy."

He slowly rolled over and met her gaze. "Dia? Do you know me? You understand me?"

Beneath the blanket, he could tell she wasn't wearing any clothes. She had a sultry look in her eye and a slightly devilish smile. She traced her finger around the edge of his jaw and leaned in, kissing his neck. She said breathlessly into his chest, "Yes, I can understand you. And I need you to understand me."

Even though every ounce of his being wanted to embrace her as tight as possible, he couldn't move. "Understand what, my love?"

"You're right about the energy frequency. Oscar is looking for the wrong signature. The EIP is different now; it's stronger and more consistent. Instead of an undulating wavelength, look for a steady, extremely high-power emission."

She ran her fingers down his chest, sending goosebumps all over his body. She moved even closer to him and whispered against his neck, "Also, widen the search pattern from just our known quadrant to the entire galaxy. I know it'll weaken the signal, but you must do this."

Troy was trying to concentrate on her words, but the feeling of her being so close was driving him insane. He wanted to hold her, kiss her, love her, but he couldn't seem to move. *What the hell is going on?*

Finally, she moved up the pillow and was face to face with him. She took his cheeks in her hands and kissed him gently. Dia pressed her forehead against his. "Know this, my dearest Troy. I'll always love you the most."

Troy's eyes flew open, ending the wonderful but vexing dream.

I need to write down the energy shit she just said. And the whole galaxy thing. But what the hell did she mean by loving me the most?

CHAPTER 13
OUT OF THE FRYING PAN AND INTO VEGAS, BABY!

The next morning, they woke up super early and loaded the van. The team, especially Heather, was nervous and uncommonly quiet, even Penny.

Roger's plane was stored at a small airport on the city's edge, so when they arrived, nothing kept them from loading their gear, getting in, and taking off. The plane was a Bombardier Global 7500 private jet that could accommodate at least twenty passengers. There were two pilots and one flight attendant.

Penny guided Heather to two very plush and comfortable seats across from each other. Heather didn't say a word as she tentatively watched the rest of them get settled. She barely heard the flight attendant ask her a question, and it snapped her out of her head. "Huh?" she said.

The attractive and pleasant woman smiled and asked again, "Would you like a drink, ma'am? Or a small snack before departure?"

Heather just gave the woman her famous, strange stare. Penny laughed. "She'll have coffee, and I'll have hot tea."

"Very good," said the flight attendant as she walked away to ask the rest of the team if they wanted refreshments.

"Sorry, I froze for a moment," Heather said.

"It's okay." Penny said warmly, "You'll catch on fast."

Heather leaned back in her seat and gazed out the window. The sun was just starting to appear, casting a warm, orange glow across the tarmac. A loud whir and a gentle bump of the plane made her nervous. She scanned the cabin to see how everyone else reacted. No one seemed concerned, so she relaxed. Then the plane started to move backward as they slowly pushed out of the hangar. The flight attendant gave Heather her coffee and said, "Please buckle your seatbelt. We're ready for departure."

Heather placed her coffee in a cup holder next to her seat and buckled her seatbelt. She noticed that Penny was already getting ready to take a nap. Heather turned her attention back to the window and watched as the buildings passed by. The plane turned and slowed to almost a stop, and she sat with bated breath, wondering what would happen next. They suddenly started moving forward again, and there was a roar of the engines. The sleek aircraft began speeding down the runway faster than any car. After a few moments, Heather felt a strange sensation as the plane left the ground. At first, they felt like they were floating, but then the weight of gravity hit her, and she was pushed back into her seat.

Heather had a split-second flicker of what she could only imagine was a memory of her past life. She somehow knew the sensation of flying. It was a component of who she was before. She smiled wide and closed her eyes, taking in all of the feelings her body was experiencing. *This is who I am. Flight defines me somehow.*

The flight to Las Vegas took about two hours, and the team mostly slept. At first, Heather concentrated on the sounds and sights of the aircraft and tried to place how it brought back a faint glimpse of who she used to be. Near the end of the flight, Roger came over to Heather and sat next to her. He asked quietly, "How're you doing, my dear?"

"All right, I guess. Somehow, flying is making me feel a connection to my past. Like it has something to do with who I am, but I can't quite place what that is specifically."

Roger nodded, and she could tell he wanted to say something but stayed quiet. He patted her hand and said, "I hope we'll find out someday, Heather. I really do."

On cue, the pilot came over the speakers and announced they were on approach to Las Vegas and would be landing soon. He said it was eighty-four degrees under partly cloudy skies.

Heather met Roger's gaze and asked, "Do you know why Carl is bringing us here?"

"I don't." He added sincerely, "Carl hasn't told me anything, but he's a smart and trustworthy man. I've never had cause to question his judgment. I'm sure the reason we're here is a legitimate one."

"Are you nervous about not knowing, though?" she asked, concerned.

"Yes, dear, I am. I think we all should be. Erring on the side of caution should always be your first instinct, Heather."

"Good advice. Thank you, Roger," she said with a smile.

Before returning to his seat, he said, "I want you to know that we all legitimately care about your well-being, my dear. Even an incredible person with unimaginable powers needs someone to protect them."

"Person."

Roger nodded. "Yes, Heather. A person."

He went back to his seat and put on his seatbelt. Heather couldn't believe Roger had made her feel more at ease. She still didn't trust him, but he seemed sincere this time. As her gaze lazily traveled around the cabin, she noticed Carl staring at her. Her eyes fixed on him, and he smiled. She smiled back but wondered how long he had been watching. He turned and looked out the window. She closed her eyes, concentrating on the sensations of the plane.

It wasn't long before they were on the ground, exiting the aircraft. When Heather stepped out, she couldn't believe how much warmer and drier the air was. A large black SUV was waiting for them in the hangar, and they quickly loaded their gear. Carl was nervous and wanted to be as close to Heather as possible, so he had

Brody drive. Soon enough, they were heading away from the airport toward Las Vegas Boulevard. Heather could feel the immense energy around them. It came from everywhere, not just from the direction they were traveling.

It took about half an hour to get to the Strip, and Heather couldn't believe what she saw. The enormous hotels, signs, and crowds were exciting yet overwhelming. She leaned over Carl and stared out the window. He asked, "Do you like what you see, love?"

"Yes and no. This place might be a little too dangerous for me."

Penny laughed. "Most people say that about Vegas."

Brody pulled up to the Venetian Resort's front entrance. The moment the hot air and immense power hit her, Heather nearly collapsed from the confusion of thousands of feelers practically attacking her. She started to panic and turned to the team. They all reached for her with concern. Roger said, "We need to leave. Coming here was a bad idea. It's way too much, way too soon."

Carl studied Heather closely, who was now leaning against the SUV with a nervous, overwhelmed look on her face. He said, "You're right. Call the airport and have them get the plane ready."

Heather yelled, "No! We aren't leaving, not yet. I just wasn't prepared for how much energy would hit me all at once. I'm already compensating for the change and feel better. We need to do the task we set out to do."

Brody asked, "Are you sure? You still look like you're going to puke."

"I feel like I'm going to puke, but that isn't enough to cancel our trip, is it?" Heather asked, determined.

"Good point. Let's check in."

While unloading the SUV, Heather took a long moment to survey her surroundings. There were people everywhere dressed in all different kinds of clothes. Two handsome, young valets came to the SUV and asked if they could take the luggage to their suite. One winked at Heather, making her blush. *Do they always do that?* she thought.

Brody and Roger walked out in front of Carl and Penny, keeping Heather between them. Heather thought she would be irritated with their overprotectiveness, but now she was glad for it. As they approached the check-in desk, Carl said, "Wait here. I'll get checked in, and we'll all go up together."

Carl walked off, and Heather noticed that Roger was scanning the lobby hard, as if he saw something he didn't want to. She asked, "Are you okay, Roger?"

He stopped for a moment and smiled at her. "Of course, dear. Just getting a lay of the land."

Heather caught Brody's eye, and she could tell he also thought Roger was acting odd.

Carl came back up to them with a handful of plastic keycards. "Okay, we have two adjoining queen suites. The ladies are in one, and we'll be in the other. Let's go up."

Heather noticed the valets from outside had been patiently waiting close by with their gear on carts. The team, except Brody, got into one elevator, and he and the valets waited for the next. He didn't want to let any of Heather's dresses, shells, or monitoring equipment out of his sight. As Heather stepped into the elevator, the valet who winked at her before smiled and nodded at her. She didn't know what it meant. *Is he just being nice? Is he flirting? Does he want to show me how to play the slot machines?*

Penny noticed the perplexed look on Heather's face and asked, "What's up, buttercup?"

"That valet is weird," Heather said. "He winked and smiled at me."

Roger told her, "You'll get that a lot here. You both will. Be careful."

"But why? What did he want?"

Carl grumbled, "A bigger tip."

The elevator stopped on the thirty-third floor, and they walked down the ornate hallway to their rooms. Heather and Penny entered their queen suite with two huge beds, a separate living room, and a beautiful marble bathroom. "Oh, yeah, this is a perfect place to stay a few days in Sin City," Penny said with a slightly sinister smile on her lips.

"Sin City?" Heather asked.

"Yup, that's just another name for this opulent place. Once we're out and about, you'll see why."

The same valet came into their room to deliver their luggage. He unloaded the gear and special case with her shell dresses. Penny handed him a twenty-dollar bill and said, "Thank you."

He took it, glanced at Heather, then bowed. "I hope to see you ladies again." He ducked out the door and was gone.

"He is a little odd, isn't he?" Penny observed.

She turned to Heather just as she cracked open a mini bottle of Grey Goose vodka and chugged it. Heather's eyes widened, quickly realizing her horrible error, and she spat out what was left in her mouth into the ice bucket. "That's not water!" she sputtered.

Penny burst into heavy laughter, and Carl came into their room through the adjoining door. Heather was still choking on vodka, and Penny couldn't talk over her amusement. "What the hell are you two doing?" he asked, puzzled.

Heather held up the small bottle and said with a harsh voice, "This isn't a cute little bottle of water."

Carl couldn't help himself and laughed at the poor woman. Soon, the whole team had a good chuckle at the naive Florian's expense, even Roger.

When the moment ran its course, Carl gathered them all together and said, "I think we need to do a bit of a test this afternoon. I know it's hot, but Heather, please put on an outfit that can fit a shell beneath it. I want to see how you feel walking around with it on. We'll get lunch too." Then he, Roger, and Brody returned to the men's suite to get ready.

Heather walked to where the valet had left her suitcases. As she went to grab hers, she noticed a note attached to the handle. She pulled it off slowly, examining the envelope for anything suspicious.

Penny came up from behind and glanced over her shoulder. She asked, "What's that?"

"A note attached to the handle of my suitcase. Should I read it or give it to Carl?"

"Read it, then maybe give it to Carl."

Heather slowly opened the envelope and pulled out a small piece of paper. It said:

We are glad you have finally arrived.
Be careful of your friend.

Penny and Heather exchanged a confused look. "Come on. I want Carl to see this," Heather said.

She knocked on the adjoining door, and Brody opened it. "Sup, Flashpoint."

That name always made Heather feel strange. "Can we come in? Is Carl in there?"

Brody stepped out of the way, allowing the two women to walk in. Their room was the same, only with the addition of a pullout couch. Roger drew the short straw.

Carl asked, "What is it, love?"

"This was on the handle of my suitcase." She handed him the note. "I didn't notice it until just now. That valet must have left it."

"'We are glad you have finally arrived. Be careful of your friend,'" Carl read out loud.

Brody mused, "You know when you're reading a book or watching a movie, and something like this happens, and it's vital but vague as shit and pisses you off because of the lack of information? That's how this feels. I wonder which friend."

Heather shrugged and said, "Probably you."

Brody shook his head. "Nah, my bet's on Penny. She's too nice. Very suspicious."

"Maybe we should go down to the sportsbook and place a bet on it." Roger chuckled.

"Wait, did you make a joke, Roger?" Brody asked, feigning suspicion. "It has to be you, then."

"Okay, all, let's be serious," said Carl. He glanced at Heather. "Did the valet say anything else to you earlier?"

Heather thought back to their interaction as he delivered their belongings. "Well, when he left, he said he hoped to see us ladies later. That's just another thing I thought anyone would say here."

Penny said, "That's usually a correct assumption, but this is getting creepy." She furrowed her brow and glanced at Carl. "I think you need to tell us why we're here, Dr. Johnson."

He cleared his throat and awkwardly explained, "I received a confidential lead from the ISC that there could be a credible threat to Las Vegas. They wanted us to come and investigate, possibly putting Heather and her powers to the test."

Heather felt an immediate surge of anger come from Roger, directed toward Carl. She could only imagine what that was about. Her own suspicions and anger boiled forth, and she growled, "I'm glad you told us this *after* we were already here, Carl."

"Would you've come so willingly if I'd told you before?"

"Yes," she said with certainty. "Because you said I could always trust you, remember?"

The room became uncomfortably quiet. Heather and Carl stared at each other, waiting to see what the other would do, but neither said another word.

Finally, Roger broke the tension. "If we're going to do this so-called test, we need to get ready. I'm starving."

CHAPTER 14
NEW ASSIGNMENT

Veronica was escorted into the Premier's chambers by two guards. He looked up from whatever he was working on and said with feigned kindness, "Ah, Veronica, please have a seat."

Male Coronians were large, clumsy, boar-like, voracious beasts. They were seven to eight feet tall with brown, bumpy skin, thick lips and brows, and muddy yellow eyes. Their voices were more of a growl, and it was hard for them to speak, even in their language. But not the Premier. He was very tall, taller than most, but he had a more elegant Florian-like body, and his eyes were green. His skin was still brown but much smoother. He had a passive, kind voice, but you couldn't let that fool you. He was one of the most brutal leaders their species had ever known, though he wasn't cruel to his own people. Premier Baxelhoff was revered as one of the most remarkable Coronian leaders ever to live, and he had been alive for a long time. His longevity was due in part to his mother being a Hanner-Florian. Baxelhoff had become Premier over three hundred years ago and set his sights on the systems he wanted to dominate. His mother was always insistent on him not attacking Rygone, as the Florian Army would be their most formidable opponent. Still, he wanted to destroy the Rygonians, especially Dominic Strom and the Asset, for what they did to his mother. Someday soon, he was determined to get the chance. In the meantime, he had been slowly taking over minor planets and systems around the galaxy, making the citizens believe they were being cared for by the Coronians, then exploiting their homeworlds for whatever resources he could collect. Ever since coming to power, Baxelhoff had made every Coronian prosperous. His planet was abundant and thriving due to the thievery inflicted on the rest of the galaxy.

Veronica walked smugly to the chair across from Baxelhoff and sat down. "You wanted to see me, Premier."

"We received an interesting hail from someone today," he mused quietly. "I thought you might like to know about it."

"Oh? Who?" she asked.

"Troy Harlow himself sent a message from Rygone, requesting a peace summit with you and me."

Veronica swallowed back her excitement and fear and asked, "Interesting. When will it be?"

"We aren't even going to answer. Fuck Troy Harlow; he's worthless." Baxelhoff leaned forward and continued, "Or is he? Is there something I need to know, Miss Granby? Is there something you're keeping from me?"

Veronica could feel the rings in her pocket. "I have nothing to hide anymore, Premier. I'm an open book."

"No, you aren't." He sat back, resting his elbows on the arms of his chair and putting his fingers together like a steeple. "You've found a way to access classified areas of our computer logs, haven't you?"

She knew Baxelhoff used to love her. They even had a romantic affair; however, he stopped that after Breger Dunes. She had still been able to exploit those feelings from time to time when he would get angry with her, but those days were over now. She cleared her throat, answering defiantly, "Yes, I have. I've been looking in the expanded database for other locations around the quadrant that Dia Harlow could be hiding in."

He stared at her for a moment; his large, clear green eyes searched her face to find a lie. When he was satisfied she was telling the truth, he said, "Earth. What's your interest in it?"

"I'd never heard of it before. It's relatively close to Rygone, and they seemed to pass it by, almost like they don't know it's there. If Dia Harlow could use the EIP to move through space, maybe she's there."

Veronica was nervous about the topic. She was telling the truth, but Baxelhoff had a way of making anyone question their actions, even if honorable. She shifted in her seat under the weight of his gaze until he said softly, "Rygone is too arrogant to think about everyone and everything around them. That's why we were fortunate enough to have you join us. Right, Miss Granby?"

She nodded. "Yes, sir."

Baxelhoff took a deep breath and closed his eyes. He sighed and gently rubbed his temples. Veronica knew he suffered from blinding headaches, and she could tell by his behavior one was coming on. Caring for him during these painful episodes used to be a ploy to weasel her way into his cold heart, but not anymore. "Can I get you anything for your headache, Your Excellency?" she asked.

He opened his eyes and smiled at her warmly. "You've been here longer than any of my men, much longer than my wife. You probably know more about me than I know myself."

Probably. "I highly doubt that, sir."

He leaned forward again, pointed behind her, and said, "Veronica, I'd like you to meet Major Jafol Baryly. He has a team of female Coronians on Earth doing recon as we speak. When Dia disappeared last year, there was an incident that could've possibly been the EIP. Since then, they haven't found anything, but it's still our best lead. Since Troy Harlow was a waste of time and resources, we need to double our efforts."

"What would you like me to do, sir?"

Major Baryly said in his guttural growl, "I can't show my pretty face around the humans on Earth, and you know General Harlow better than my team already there. You're going to find her."

Veronica felt fear blooming in her gut. "I mean, that sounds like—"

The Premier cut her off. "And you're going to deliver her to us. Or I'll deliver you personally to Chancellor Strom and let him freeze you in the Ice Lake, right before I steal his pretty cannon on Nexxus and blow up his pathetic fucking planet. Are we clear?"

"As a bell."

"Good. Now get the hell out of my face," he said with his sickeningly sweet, kind voice.

CHAPTER 15
COULD IT BE?

Renee Conner didn't like the heat. She wasn't born in any of the Baltica cities, so she was a Community Florian. Her family was from a small town in the Raltain Mountains called Sailpro. It was never hot there, but geothermal features weren't far away, keeping the air moist and warmer during *icewane*. Those geothermal features were what made her town and family prosper. Her father was born in Baltica City but left at a young age to make a life for himself elsewhere. He knew that many citizens from all over the planet loved soaking in the warm pools and mud pots of the Raltains, but they were hard to find and get to. He invested what money and resources he had to start tours and set up camps. He eventually received permission from the government to build a hotel. It was now the oldest and most popular resort on Rygone. People from all over the galaxy came to rest and play in the healing water. When Renee told her father she wanted to go to the Academy instead of taking up the family business, she thought he would be angry. She was surprised when he beamed with pride. As Renee's career progressed, he supported her in every way. Dia would sometimes be jealous of Renee and her father's relationship.

The Chancellor and his commanding general had always been assholes to each other.

She walked across the landing platform on the fortieth floor of Baltica City toward one of Oscar Strom's many workshops. It was high *albesun*, or summer, on Rygone, and she was miserable, especially with the sun bearing down on the Karon steel and concrete beneath her feet. *Some days, I wonder why I didn't stay in Sailpro.*

She reached Oscar's workshop, and the cool air felt fantastic. She went into the small kitchen and took a bottle of glacier water out of the cooler. She could grab a much less expensive container of regular water, but glacier water was always cold, crisp, and healthful.

As he was working, Renee sat down on Oscar's desk and took a long pull on the bottle. "Remind me to buy you another bottle of this later, Os."

He barely noticed she was there, as he was working feverishly on his datapad. He mumbled, "Yeah, okay."

She playfully sucker punched him on the shoulder and said, "Hello, paging Dr. Strom!" He then laughed, stood up, and exclaimed, "Come with me!

Renee followed him out into the Research and Development priority hangar. Several large projects were being developed, some for civilians but most for the army and air corps.

She saw something exciting that made her heart skip a beat. "Os, I thought the Chancellor scrapped this project?"

"He did—until Troy got home. I guess he felt we needed a much more capable first-strike weapon. Beyond the EIP."

Renee walked toward the most beautiful DREX she had ever seen, but it wasn't a fighter or destroyer. Oscar had been trying to approve this particular craft with different Chancellors for several thousand years. He was always told they weren't necessary or too expensive, even by his father—especially his father. But times had changed. Chancellor Strom came directly to Oscar three days after Troy was rescued and recommissioned the DREX Gunship Program.

She ran her hand down the smooth Karon-steel finish. She glanced back, excited. "Well, Os, let's see it!"

Oscar slid a finger across his communicator, and the huge gunship purred to life. Renee squealed like a little girl getting a new puppy. "It's so quiet! What does it run on?"

"It still has a Wel Reactor, but the fuel pod is much smaller and lasts hundreds of years. I'm already working on retrofitting all military and government aircraft to this new fuel system. It takes little to no energy to run all of the ship's systems. The Jump, the operating and weapon systems, even the Requiem Fusion Cannon. Although, it has its own Wel pod for operational purposes."

Renee looked at him with shock. "You got a Requiem Fusion Cannon on a ship this small? Won't it fall apart?"

"Shut up and get in. See for yourself," he said enthusiastically.

The bridge ramp opened, and Renee walked into the belly of the beast. The gunner was about four times as large as the biggest DREX fighter. It only needed four crew members: the pilot, co-pilot, weapons tech, and captain. The captain would have to be utterly proficient in every system, so she knew it would take time to get these ships on the front lines, but she would do everything possible to get them out there.

Oscar said, "Both crew members of a DREX fighter can live in their ship without resupply for, what? Seven or eight months, right? And it's uncomfortable as hell. No shower, and your bed is a small cot pulled out of the wall. Taking a shit is the worst, I know."

Renee snickered. "You just called your own creation uncomfortable. Have you lived in one for that long?"

"Well, this craft is a luxury resort compared to that!"

They started walking around the ship's interior. Impressed, Renee took note of all the features. Full quarters for sixteen people. A complete galley with a food replicator loaded and programmed to make thousands of different meals from systems all over the galaxy. Two full bathrooms with showers. A medical bay complete with state-of-the-art equipment developed by Troy. There was even a recreation room with entertainment and exercise gear.

Oscar said, "As is, this ship could sustain a crew of sixteen for five years without ever having to be resupplied."

Renee, beaming, said, "How long do you think it'll be before she can be tested?"

"Today. I need you to test it."

"I would love to, but—" Renee started to protest, but Oscar interrupted her.

Sterner than she had ever seen him, he said, "Renee, we're on the verge of a war to end all wars, and the major aggressor wants to destroy us first. This ship is equipped to stop them from doing that. The time for waiting years to introduce new technology is over. I need you to get a crew, test the systems, and let me know if this ship is mission capable."

"When's the mission?"

"The minute you tell me it's ready. I think I know how to track the EIP."

Renee smiled. "Let me make some calls."

CHAPTER 16
FEAR OF THE UNKNOWN AND LUNCH

Heather remembered how hot it was to fly through the star on her way through space before landing on Earth. It was almost as miserable as Las Vegas. The shell she was wearing was only a tank top and shorts, but with that and her outer clothes, she was sweaty and irritable. Wherever the mansion was located could get hot, but moisture was in the air due to frequent storms. This place was hot and dry as a bone.

The team walked together down Las Vegas Boulevard, or the Strip. Heather was amazed by the elaborate resorts, attractions, and people trying to hand her pamphlets for strip clubs. The most incredible part was the amount of power reaching out to her from such a small area. She had quickly acclimated to her surroundings and had absorbed enough energy in the shell but kept none in herself. Another interesting thing she couldn't shake was a strange feeler far away that reached out to her. She decided to ignore it and followed the lead of her human companions.

Carl was the closest to her and the most protective. After walking in silence for a long time, he asked her, "How are you doing, love?"

"Fine. The initial shock when we first arrived is completely gone. I've adapted to control everything reaching out to me completely, and…"

"And what?"

She smiled slyly and whispered, "I'm enjoying the feeling quite a lot."

He placed his hand on the small of her back, making her shiver. She had to admit that she enjoyed it, heightened by the feeling of the immense power surrounding her. Vegas was growing on the Florian general.

They stopped at a restaurant close to the hotel called The Yardbird and were seated immediately. Once inside, Heather felt the immense power subside as there were now walls and windows blocking many of the feelers. She looked around the elegant restaurant and said to Penny, "This is nicer than Olive Garden."

Penny giggled. "Yes, it is."

Heather poured over the menu and noticed that there weren't many dishes she recognized. Luckily, the children's menu had chicken fingers, and she was satisfied to order her favorite food.

Much to Brody and Heather's dismay, Carl advised that they not order alcohol so they could stay on their guard, especially after the note found on Heather's suitcase. Heather decided to try lemonade and enjoyed the sweet and tart drink.

While waiting for their food, Heather tuned out her team and studied her surroundings. She needed to grasp how to react to different feelers, especially in a place like this. Heather located every one of them in the large, open room of the restaurant. She determined the strongest and most pure as fast as she could. She assumed that if she had to use her powers in a real-world setting, she would have to ascertain what to pull instinctively. She was a bit irritated with Carl for not taking her out into the world sooner to hone her skills. Putting her into a situation like this with no experience was dangerous to her and everyone around them.

Roger gently laid his hand on Heather's arm, making her jump. He asked, "Are you okay? What are you doing?"

"Studying."

Brody said, "So basically, you're trying to figure out how to blow up the joint?"

She flipped him off.

"You have completely corrupted her. Both of you," Penny said accusingly.

Carl said, "Well, I'm not the one who introduced her to *Pornhub*."

Roger blinked at them all in disbelief. "Pornhub? Really?"

Heather just shrugged. "It's fascinating."

Of course, none of them knew just how inappropriate, obnoxious, and personally- destructive Dia Harlow was in real life, not even Roger. Pornhub and foul language were nothing.

Once their food arrived, they ate and enjoyed small talk. Heather listened to everyone share their past visits to Vegas. They mostly seemed to revolve around gambling, drinking, and debauchery. Carl even told them how he married his second wife in a drive-thru wedding chapel about two miles from where they were. Heather took a bite of chicken finger slathered in ranch dressing and asked, "How long were you married?"

He chuckled and said, "Too long."

"I'm sorry. I shouldn't have asked that."

He smiled warmly at her and placed his hand on hers. "It's okay, love."

Brody stopped the awkward exchange by asking, "So what's on tap for tonight?"

"Observation," Carl answered. "It's time for you to be on your own, Heather."

"What do you mean 'on my own'?" she asked, concerned.

"Well, you have your dresses and can play a mean hand of poker, as good as some of the professionals. I want to see how people will react to you."

"Why can't I have someone with me?" The fear in her voice was palpable.

Penny glared at Carl and said, "We'll be close, very close."

Roger said, "Yes, we will, but I agree with Carl. We need to assess your ability to handle yourself alone accurately." His eyes flicked to Carl. "Especially if we're here based on a credible threat."

The waiter returned, and Roger paid the tab. Heather felt the rush of feelers come at her as they stepped outside. She instantly ignored the weak and picked out the robust and pure power without thinking about it. Yet, a feeling of dread was growing in her. Once in the hotel, as they approached the bank of elevators, she asked Carl, "Can I speak to you alone for a minute?"

"Of course." He looked at the others and said, "We'll be right up."

Carl spotted a private alcove across the casino and led Heather there. Once she was sure they were out of view of any other person, she turned to Carl with pure anger and fear on her face.

He was scared for a moment but could see no sign of absorbed power coming off her. However, he knew she was wearing a shell, so could he still be in danger? She came close to him, almost touching. "Why are you doing this to me? I thought you were my biggest protector, my ally. You know I'm not ready for this, but you don't seem to care. I deserve to know what this so-called credible threat is!"

He said, trying to control the fear in his voice, "Yes, you do. But you gotta trust me, love."

She stepped back, tears welling in her eyes, and choked out, "I've already mastered how to control the energy here. I can handle the immense pressure that might come with whatever we're here to do, but there's something I cannot get over." A tear ran down her smooth cheek, and she continued, "Innocent people will be hurt or killed. I can feel it."

"All we can do is hope it doesn't come to that, Heather," he said.

"You don't know what the threat is, do you?"

He sighed and shook his head. "Not specifically, but we'll know when it presents itself. Again, you have to trust me."

She crossed her arms and just stared at him. Something came over Carl, be it stupidity, sadness, or longing, that made him step forward and pull her into his arms. She didn't resist, but she didn't return the embrace either. After a moment, he kissed her on the forehead, and she released the tension in her arms and slipped them loosely around his waist. She slowly looked up at his face, and their eyes met. He kissed her, but she didn't respond, so he boldly kissed her again. This time she pressed her lips into his; they were completely captivated by each other by the third. Heather tightened her arms around him and immersed herself in his carnal energy, but only momentarily. She tensed and pushed away from his embrace in embarrassment and horror. She whispered harshly, "What're we doing?!"

Carl could only gaze at her in disbelief and sadness. Heather smoothed her skirt, met his stare, and breathed, "This, too, is unfair. For both of us."

She turned and walked quickly toward the elevators and got on the first one that opened. Carl pressed his head hard against the wall and took a moment to gather his composure. As he turned to walk out of the alcove, he looked up. There was a surveillance camera pointed right at him. He glared at it in pissed-off shock and growled, "Fucking awesome."

***

The camera operator in the security room, surrounded by his coworkers, said, "Damn it, I lost this one."

They all exchanged bets as the losers thought the hot couple would've kept going. One of his friends said, "You can't win them all, dude. Those two were too strait-laced. Not two drunks out of the casino for a quicky."

"She was gorgeous, though, man."

His coworker nodded. "So was he."

CHAPTER 17
ON HER OWN TWO FEET

When Heather returned to her and Penny's room, she was relieved to hear her friend singing in the shower. If Penny saw Heather in distress and crying after talking to Carl alone, she would never hear the end of it. Heather went to the minibar, found a whiskey bottle, and drank it all at once. She looked in the mirror and saw the anguish on her face. Since Penny was in the bathroom, she opened a bottle of water and splashed some onto her cheeks. She decided to lie down for a few minutes. She lay on her side, gazing out of the huge windows that overlooked the Strip, and realized the sun was setting. She ignored all the feelers making their way through the glass and quieted her mind. She soon drifted off to sleep.

Heather dreamt vividly about what happened in the alcove. How he felt, how his lips tasted, how tightly he held her. Her sleeping mind let go of her inhibitions and analyzed every exciting and dangerous detail. Her mind moved past when she stopped them just as Heather felt a gentle hand on her shoulder and heard, "Heather, wake up, honey. We need to get you ready."

Heather opened her weary eyes and trained them on Penny's face. She asked, "Do we have to?"

Penny pushed a wild curl off Heather's sweaty forehead and asked, "You okay, honey?"

Heather's head was spinning from the whiskey and what happened with Carl. "I can't do this, Penny. I don't want to be here anymore."

Penny climbed onto the bed behind Heather and pulled her tiny body close. Heather always considered Carl her chief guardian, but Brody and Penny also had significant roles. As the tech expert, Brody always ensured that what he created for her and had her do was safe. At first, Brody considered Heather a project, a way to become famous. But as time passed, she became part of his family, like a dangerous, naive little sister with superpowers. Penny was Heather's nurturer. Even Carl couldn't make Heather feel more comfortable and less anxious like Penny could. They were indeed like sisters; even though she never really talked about it, Penny would do anything for her precious alien.

The two women lay close for a few minutes before Brody burst into the room via the connecting door. "Are you ready to—wow, this is interesting. I'd say something inappropriate, but I'll be nice."

Penny shot Brody a blazingly angry look, and he realized Heather wasn't doing well. "When you're ready to put on the dress, let me know. I want to make a few last-minute adjustments," he said respectfully.

Heather rolled on her side. "Okay, I'll take a shower and let you know soon."

Brody turned to leave but paused and asked, "Heather, do you know where Carl went? He didn't come back to the room after lunch."

"I don't," she said, very concerned. "We spoke in the lobby for about fifteen minutes, and then I came upstairs alone. I don't know where he went after that."

"I'll send Roger to go look for him. In the meantime, we need to get cracking. It's Saturday in one of the finest casinos on the Strip. Whatever Carl is up to, we need to get down there soon."

Heather rolled off the bed, shuffled into the bathroom, and closed the door.

Brody whispered to Penny, "Did she say anything to you about what she and Carl talked about?"

"No, but she seems pretty shaken." Penny pointed to the empty Jack Daniels mini bottle and said, "I assume something considerable happened."

Brody picked up the bottle and spun it in his fingers. "She doesn't always handle her alcohol well. This'll be an interesting night. I'll see you soon."

***

Roger gladly went down into the lobby, searching for their wayward leader. Luckily, he found him quickly, sitting in a tavern. Carl was at the bar with an untouched glass of bourbon in front of him. He stared blankly at the wall when Roger approached and growled, "What're you doing, Carl? We're all depending on you, and you're hiding from us in a bar far, far away."

Carl kept studying the wall and wanted to blurt out that he stupidly brought them all there because Dia Harlow told him in a fever dream that they needed to be in Las Vegas. Even more exciting, he and Heather Stone nearly went at it in the lobby for the whole world to see. In fact, the entire world might actually see, depending on how perverted the assholes behind that security camera were.

He sighed and said, "I'm sorry, Roger. My loosely laid plan is unraveling due to my misgivings."

"What happened after lunch between the two of you?"

Carl glanced sidelong at Roger, reached into his pocket, and threw too much money for his drink onto the bar. He said to the bartender, "Keep the change," then to Roger, "I didn't drink any of this if you want it."

Carl got off his stool and walked toward the elevators. No matter his doubts about why they were here, he needed to get his head in the game and pull it together. Dia had to be onto something.

Roger watched him walk away, then looked back at the drink. The bartender stared at him, waiting to see if he would drink it or if it would go to waste. Roger grabbed the glass and downed the entire thing in one swallow. He grimaced as he set the glass down and walked away. The bartender laughed, then gasped as he picked up the two-hundred-dollar tip for a twenty-dollar bourbon.

***

When Carl made it back to their room, Brody looked at him in shock and said, "Jesus Christ, boss! What the hell were you doing? You look like shit! If we're going to hang around the casino supporting Heather, you need to get it together."

Carl stared at the brilliant tech wizard with uncertainty. Brody waited to be yelled at for insubordination, but Carl calmly went into the bathroom and closed the door. Brody couldn't be sure, but he swore he heard quiet sobbing.

Next, Roger came into the room with glazed-over eyes and a bewildered look on his face. He asked with slurred speech, "Is Carl hereish?"

Brody scoffed and said, "Yeah. I'm not going to ask what happened to you."

"Vegas," he said and collapsed onto his pull-out bed.

What in the actual hell is going on?! Brody thought, both confused and alarmed. *Penny and I are supposed to be the subordinates, but these so-called leaders are falling apart at the seams!*

***

Brody waited impatiently for his male counterparts to get it together and his female companions to finish primping Heather, which didn't take as long as he expected.

Penny poked her head into their room and said, "Okay, she's ready for the dress. How will we do this, as she's only wearing panties?"

Brody hadn't thought about that. "Go ahead and have her put it on first. I'll be in there in a few minutes."

Penny gave a quick nod and went back into the room. Brody studied the room around him. He could hear Roger in the shower. In front of the closet mirror, Carl was expertly tying his tie. Brody was thankful to see that he had put himself back together. Carl was wearing a gray suit with a white shirt and black tie. He had trimmed his beard and fixed his hair instead of leaving it a mangled mess. *Much better.*

Penny poked her head back into the room and said, "Okay, ready."

Brody picked up a few instruments and went into the ladies' room. He was taken aback when he saw Heather, as Penny had made her into a work of art more than he could have ever managed. Her hair was in an ornate updo, accented with silver pins that matched the jewelry he gave her. Her makeup was stylish, with her liner drawn out in black to make her already upturned eyes stand out. Penny had expertly created a color palette for her eyeshadow in purple and an iridescent cream. She wore light blush and a subtle red gloss on her lips. The black dress hugged her curves just as he wanted. Penny had her in black heels with a wide heel to help her walk easier.

Brody cleared his throat and approached her. He would usually have a quip or off-color comment, but he could only manage, "You look incredible, Heather."

She blushed. "Thank you. I wouldn't know how to pull this off without you or Penny."

Again, he thought, *the lower ones on the totem pole are pulling this shitshow together.*

He handed her a thin copper wire and said, "I need you to slide this into the seam on the slit of your dress. It'll help you stabilize the stored power on the bottom edge." He took out a small skin-colored patch and said, "I know you won't like it, but we need you to wear this over your birthmark. We're in Vegas, and tattoos are crazy, but yours is distinct to people we may not want to be looking for you."

He walked around her, and Heather closed her eyes as she felt the cool patch cover what identified her past life. Brody and Penny watched as the material bonded with her skin and matched the color perfectly.

"You need to take off your rings as well. Don't even try to argue with me."

Heather opened her mouth to protest, but Brody gave her a look of pleading authority and said, "Again, they're not made of anything found on Earth. They could be a beacon to you being different."

She gently slid them off her fingers and handled them to Penny. The physician's assistant said, "I'll put them in your suitcase, safe and sound."

"What else?" Heather asked stoically.

He stood back and glanced at her up and down. He gave her an approving side smile. "Nothing, you're ready. At least in terms of appearance."

Just then, Roger and Carl walked in. Roger said, "Are we about ready? That casino will be insane very soon, and it'll be hard to find an open poker table."

Carl and Heather didn't hear him. They were staring at each other in awe and disillusion. Heather snapped out of it first, and steel determination flashed across her face. She said, "I'm ready. Let's stop dicking around and get this damn operation started."

She grabbed the black clutch off the bed with her fake IDs, casino cards loaded with fifty thousand dollars of Roger's cash, and lip gloss. The rest finally came to their senses as she was already out the door.

CHAPTER 18
BACK IN CHARGE

I t took Veronica a few days to research everything she needed to know about Earth. Major Baryly turned out to be a decent partner and let her know all the places on the planet where his teams were stationed. He told her that if Dia Harlow was on Earth, he expected to find her in one of three places.

One: Bruce Nuclear Generating Station, Ontario, Canada. The human-made power station produced nuclear energy for roughly six million people. However, there didn't seem to be anything outstanding in the area, so it was a contingency.

Two: Las Vegas, Nevada, United States of America. This city was smaller than many but had a vast and extravagant entertainment industry that used a considerable amount of electrical energy from several different sources. There could be five hundred thousand people concentrated in a tiny area at any time. This location was highly visible. Anyone looking for her would probably start there first.

Three: Yellowstone National Park, Wyoming, United States of America. It was a long shot, as the area was remote, but the geothermal energy from the lava dome under the ground was more than the top two regions combined. It had an undulating population as it was a "tourist attraction," and most people there were just visitors.

Baryly had teams in all of these locations embedded into the surrounding communities. He had four workers at the nuclear plant, several cocktail servers at the raunchy casinos and hotels in Las Vegas, and park rangers who were able to travel all over the park in Yellowstone.

A year ago, his division detected an unusual energy emittance, similar to what they were tracking on Rygone when the Harlows tested the EIP. They sent a team to the planet and found primitive footage of the event that occurred a week after a significant meteor strike. His team reviewed the footage and determined with 72 percent certainty that the source was indeed Dia Harlow. Unfortunately, she was picked up by authorities on the night of the incident and completely disappeared. There hadn't been any other EIP signatures detected since.

Veronica asked, "What makes you think she's still on Earth? Maybe she found a way off."

"Earth has a considerable level of intelligent life with technology created by the humans, but they have barely been able to leave their atmosphere," Baryly explained. "They've visited their moon a few times and sent crewed shuttles and rockets into low orbit, but nothing more than that. It's doubtful that she left. We assume the government of the country she landed in, the United States, has her somewhere secure. Maybe even exploiting her power themselves."

"What now?"

"We aren't going to find her without more knowledge. You're the only Florian we can trust to help us locate her. Do you think there's a way you may be able to do more than we have?"

Veronica thought, *No.*

She shrugged and said, "Maybe. Where do you think we should go first?"

"I think we should try Las Vegas first. The other two places are more docile and spread out. If she's working there, I hope it'll be easier to find her."

Veronica quickly read through the information. "Good; English is the language for all three locations. I learned English as they speak it in most countries worldwide, but I found over sixty-five *hundred* languages when I researched the planet. I thought Rygone had a lot of diversity, but this planet takes the cake. It seems that's one of the problems they face in their society. Too many different voices are trying to control one thing. They're more of a fighting species than all of us."

She leaned back and crossed her arms. Veronica liked Baryly and looked forward to working with him. She asked, "So, who's going on this trip?"

"You'll be the point. I'll be the leader in the air with ten of my soldiers for background support if things don't go as planned."

"When do we leave?"

"Tomorrow. My team is already getting packed. We have a new ship outfitted with an old Jump Drive from a downed Rygonian cruiser. It isn't as fast or as accurate as newer versions, but at least we were able to get it to work."

Veronica was impressed. Oscar Strom made it his life's work to ensure that his propriety systems, like the Jump Drive, were never reverse-engineered by Rygone's enemies. Strike a win for the Coronians.

***

Later that day, Veronica was in her quarters, ready to take this huge step toward *her* goal, not the Coronian one. She was just pissed that the intel didn't come from her source. She had been trying to locate him since the Premier assaulted her in the hallway. Had he turned on her?

No. There was no way he turned on her. She groomed him for years before embedding him into the Rygonian inner circle. He was a nobody in a place of high importance. All he had to do was do his job, pay attention, and report to her. He had done incredibly well up until now. *When I find you, kid, I will make you pay painfully.*

Veronica took a deep breath. *It's finally time.*

CHAPTER 19
NERVES OF STEEL

Renee lay in bed, restlessly staring at the ceiling. Her mind was methodically going over everything she needed to finish for her team and the gunner to be ready for an immediate departure. The craft, with all of their gear, needed to be prepared to leave immediately if Oscar detected a signal with the new calibrations Troy gave him for the EIP. Troy wasn't at liberty to tell them how he knew the changes needed to be made, but the moment Oscar did so, his readings were immediately more promising.

She took a deep breath and closed her eyes, picturing all the lists and procedures she had put together for their journey. Renee was excited and scared at the same time. She knew they were on the precipice of finding Dia and figuring out the next step to fight the Coronians, but there were still too many unknowns.

Regarding the four people going on this journey, she had no problem choosing her team. She was captain of the ship and commander of the mission. Dominic was the weapons expert on both the gunner and, if needed, on the ground. Captain James Ramsay would be the pilot, and Troy would be the co-pilot. Dia had always insisted on teaching him to fly and fight, just as he taught her to treat patients and even to do simple surgeries.

Earlier that day, she had shown her team their incredible new ride, and even Troy was impressed. He was very excited about the ease of the flight controls and the med-bay. Dominic was enamored with every weapons system the ship possessed, from the Requiem Fusion Cannon to the most advanced thermal pistols. There was even an electric whip that could quickly subdue an enemy without serious injury. He later told Renee that he wanted one for the bedroom.

Captain James Ramsay was the quiet one of the crew. He was short and stocky with curly brown hair and blue eyes. James was one of Dia's best students and used to be a loud-mouthed, cocky asshole, just like her. But after the recent wars, he became subdued and quiet, though that didn't mean he became weak. James was one of the best pilots and secret operatives in the Florian Army and Air Corps. He had been taught by the flight trainers, Dominic's teams, and even Oscar and Troy's people in certain areas, making him an indispensable resource. Renee never let him out of her sight because she didn't want another unit to steal him from her.

She gathered them in the passenger bay and asked, "So? Will this work, Troy?"

"Yes," he said calmly.

Dominic asked, "You aren't very excited, Troy. Why?"

"I'm not excited by our circumstances at all. But as ships go, this'll be our best bet to find Dia and move forward. What do we do now, Colonel Conner?"

"On this trip, I'm just Renee. We're all friends here on a special mission for someone we love. Even James."

The subdued captain just smiled.

"Anyway, all we can do is keep close, monitor Oscar's transmissions, and be ready to leave at a moment's notice. Oscar said that once the location is locked into the Jump Drive, we can be in the outer atmosphere of wherever we're going in two minutes with only one Jump."

"Wow, impressive," James said quietly.

"Very," Renee agreed. "Now, go home, all of you. Stay close to your communicators. I have a feeling we're going to be leaving soon."

***

Renee ran those words over in her mind and hoped she was right. She hated being on the edge of something so huge but unable to move forward. Every person on her team was a mover, not a waiter. The delay was going to be excruciating for them all, especially Troy. But they all had nerves of steel, and there wasn't a complaint or misgiving from any of them. They were ready.

She turned on her side and watched Dominic as he slept. He was lying on his back with his face toward her. She was always curious about why petite little Dia snored all the time, but big, bulky Dominic was a silent sleeper. She rested her head against his shoulder and gently took his hand in hers. He sighed and shifted a little bit before his breathing was rhythmic again. She whispered, "Let's go find your sister and kick some Coronian ass."

Dominic opened his eyes and gave her a lazy smile. "Yes, ma'am."

CHAPTER 20
POKER AND SUGAR DADDIES

After her grand exit from the hotel room, the team caught up with Heather. Brody gave a rundown of where they would station themselves around the casino. He had a live camera view of the poker tables and pinpointed a quiet table with only three other players on the edge of the floor.

"Okay, Heather, do you remember what we discussed about entering the game?" Brody asked.

She nodded confidently. "I sit down, wait until the next hand to play. Then they'll swipe my card for the amount I want and give me chips."

"Perfect. Once you have your chips, start bets small and don't look too smart out of the gate. Fold or lose a few hands before starting to play to your ability, and we'll go from there."

"Okay. What am I supposed to look for in people?" she asked. Her confidence shifted to nervousness.

Carl said, "Anyone paying extra attention to you, either friendly or angry. You'll have a lot of admirers no matter what because of your appearance. Be careful." His tone had a touch of concern. "If you feel threatened by anyone or anything, say 'mousetrap.'"

Confused, she asked, "Why 'mousetrap'?"

"It's a safeword. We'll all come to your aid if you say it," Penny said.

"Okay. That makes sense," Heather said with a nod.

Brody made a few adjustments on his tablet and opened a small case with four earpieces. He said proudly, "Here's my next Avenger-level invention. These are earpieces for all of us with Bluetooth sensitivity, enough to pick up our voices. We can hear and talk to each other and Heather."

Heather asked, pouting, "Why didn't I get that?"

"Because we want you to look elegant, not like a spy," Carl said.

Brody put his tablet down and gently placed a hand on Heather's shoulder. "You and I have been working up to this for a year. Do you think we're ready, Flashpoint?"

"I think so." She flashed the team a confident smile. "Let's play some cards and find out."

***

The team split up and went down to the main floor in different ways. Heather rode the elevator alone and went straight into the casino. She navigated the confusing layout like a pro, quickly making it to the designated table. At first, Heather was nervous about being on her own. The environment was chaotic and the immense amount of different feelers screaming at her was overwhelming, but she quickly adjusted to her surroundings and relaxed.

Roger and Penny went down together and played as a sugar daddy and his baby. Penny looked nearly twenty years younger than Roger, so they fit in perfectly.

Brody dressed like a young man there for the sportsbook. He went straight there, as it had a direct view of the table Heather was going to play.

Carl sat down at a small bar in the middle of the card floor that was also a perfect vantage point to observe Heather and those around her.

From their respective locations, the team watched as the Florian general approached the table confidently. There was an empty chair on the end, close to the dealer. She sat down, watching the current game intensely. There were now four other players at the table, and they were all sizing Heather up. The dealer asked her chip amount, and she took twenty thousand out in chips, as Brody had instructed. The current hand was finishing, so Heather prepared herself to be dealt in. A tall, blonde cocktail waitress with a deep voice asked, "Can I get you a drink, ma'am?"

Heather smiled and said politely, "Yes, please. I would like a small amount of iced tea in a rocks glass."

The waitress gave her a strange look. "Not bourbon or whiskey?"

"Oh no, I'm not drinking tonight. However, I want to look like I am."

The waitress and the man sitting closest to her laughed, and she moved off to get Heather her drink. The older man leaned over to her and said, "Nice touch."

"Thank you," Heather said with a self-assured smile.

Heather was dealt the next few hands. She lost one, folded twice, and won a small pot. In the meantime, she had been able to assess the area around her for feelers. The energy in that room was pure and potent from all sources. She could feel the people, lights, emotions, and even the water fountains on the edge of the floor. She knew that even without a shell, she would have a constant supply of power from this room if it came down to it.

Brody said quietly, "Okay, Flashpoint, you aren't on many people's radars right now, so let's turn up the heat. Start winning more."

Heather began to play like Carl had taught her. The boring late nights in the curved room when the four of them would play poker was about to pay off, literally.

Soon, the gorgeous woman in the black dress playing high-stakes poker began making some card sharks look like amateurs. She quickly proved that she was a brilliant, cool player who wasn't intimidated by anyone or anything around her.

After about an hour of winning, a crowd gathered around Heather, and the team lost visual contact. Roger and Penny moved to a small café directly behind her table. Brody found a different spot in the sportsbook with a partial view, but Carl struggled to find a way to see her. So, he did the next best thing. He joined the game.

Heather glanced at him when he sat down but gave no indication that they knew each other. Penny said, "Good job, Flashpoint."

Carl was also dealt in at twenty thousand dollars, and the game continued. Heather won a few more hands, and Carl watched the crowd become more and more intrigued by her. It made him nervous, but she was handling herself beautifully.

Until the Texas oil tycoon showed up.

The chair next to Heather was empty, and a large, unkempt older man in a Western-style suit and cowboy hat sat down next to her. Heather smiled at him pleasantly, and he put his hand down on hers and said, "Darlin', aren't you just one of the prettiest things in the universe. Can I play wit' ya?"

She cleared her throat nervously and said, "Well, we're all playing together, right? Deal in."

He pushed up against her and laughed drunkenly. "That ain't the playin' I was talkin' about!"

His entourage laughed, but many other patrons, including Carl, came to Heather's defense. He said, "Oh shut up, I was just teasin' the poor thing." He pressed his arm against her again. "But damn..."

Heather turned, grabbed his wrist, and held it like a vise. "Sir, I would really appreciate it if you would stop touching me. We're here to play poker. Now let's play."

"Fine, bitch." He pulled away from her and staggered up drunkenly. "I could've been your best ever."

Heather swallowed back the laughter she wanted to blurt out. "Perhaps, but we'll never know. Will we?"

Carl could tell the man thought about taking it further, but Carl, three other men who had been politely watching her play, and the blonde cocktail waitress stood in his way. He turned and staggered off with his followers.

The cocktail waitress asked Heather, "Another iced tea, dear?"

Heather adjusted her dress and gave Carl a brief, nervous glance. "I'll have that whiskey now. A double, please."

"Comin' up, gorgeous!"

Heather played for another hour, and soon, the whole casino knew about the petite woman in the black dress who won over a hundred thousand dollars on high-stakes poker. Men wanted to buy her drinks, women wanted her to join their bridal parties, and almost everyone wanted her to accompany them to their rooms. Attention was also paid to the man in the stylish gray suit at the same table. He was losing all of his money to her. Three women were hanging on Carl, waiting for him to cash out and pamper them for the rest of the night.

Brody was a perfect coach. Penny and Roger were great at reading the room for dangers, even from the tycoon. But Carl was torn. He sat close to her most of the night, having to pretend they were strangers, and she was perfect at it. She won most of Roger's money from him without even trying. She was sweet, dazzling, intelligent, and lovely all at once.

Heather was exhausted and having a hard time keeping up with the act. They'd been there for hours, wearing them all down. The test of whether she could handle the Vegas nightlife had been a success. So far, they weren't aware of any danger.

Carl intentionally lost a hand that he could've won and said, "Oh, it looks like I'm finished for the evening. Time to move on." He cashed in his remaining chips and stood up, with the three women following him as he walked away.

Brody said quietly in her ear, "Make that your last hand, Flashpoint. It's time to wrap this night up."

Heather dealt into the hand by going all in. Her chances of winning were low, but she wasn't playing with her own money. It was between her and a tall, attractive brunette woman in a white sundress. Heather and the woman played respectfully, and she won. She cashed out with a round of applause, and the tall woman came around and extended her hand. Heather shook it graciously and smiled.

The brunette said, "It's not often someone walks in here and can play like you. Impressive."

"Thank you. Your skills are remarkable as well."

"Are you here tomorrow? I'll be playing a tournament if you want to join. You sure as hell won enough tonight to buy in."

Heather didn't know how she was supposed to answer and hoped Brody or Carl were listening. Luckily, she heard Carl's calm voice say, "You can't make the tournament, but maybe you'll see her on the floor in the evening."

Heather repeated Carl's words, and the woman smiled. "I hope to see you…"

"Heather."

"I'm Julie. Have a nice evening, Heather."

As Heather walked away, Brody told her, "Go to the south elevator bank by the French bakery. We need to keep you and Carl apart for a bit."

Heather quickly walked across the casino, reached the elevator bank, and hit the up button. While she was at the table, she was confident and capable, but now she felt alone and scared. Something didn't feel quite right.

When she got onto the elevator, three other people followed her: a couple who were drunk and laughing, not paying attention to their surroundings, and a man whose face she had seen before. She searched her memory and realized he was one of the tycoon's entourage. Feelers of anger reached out to her from him, but Heather couldn't react as they were in an enclosed space with two innocent people.

He moved closer to Heather and whispered, "My boss would like to see you tonight, little lady. Hit the thirty button."

Brody heard what the man said. "Take it easy, Heather. We're coming for you."

Brody and Carl ran toward the elevator banks and got on the first one going up. They hit the button for the thirtieth floor, but the hall was empty when they arrived. All four tried to listen to her. Hearing nothing, Carl yelled, "Heather! Say something! Say mousetrap!"

Suddenly, an elevator door opened, and a man scrambled out, holding his bloody nose, and ran down the hall. Carl and Brody trained their eyes toward the open elevator door and saw Heather rubbing her elbow. She said, "I had to drop the couple off on twenty-three before getting him to his floor."

"Holy shit!" Brody exclaimed. "I don't know if this is a good thing or not, but well done, my dear."

The two men got onto the elevator with her and were quiet as it took them to their floor. When they got to their rooms, the team met in the ladies' living room for a quick debrief.

Roger said, "For Vegas, this night went well. We knew you would be noticed, but we definitely underestimated how much."

"Sorry," Heather said sheepishly.

"I think it was more the Texas guy's fault," Penny said. "Hopefully, he won't be around tomorrow."

Carl agreed. "Yeah, hopefully. I'm sure his crony is nursing a nice headache right now. How much power did you pull for that move?"

"None. He lunged at me, and I used his drunk body momentum to knock him off his feet and bash his nose with my elbow. Basic self-defense. I read it in a book."

Carl put his arm around her and kissed her on the top of her head. "I think you'll be okay, kid. We underestimated the hell out of you."

Heather beamed. "Yeah, ya did."

They all said their goodnights, and the men retreated to their room. Even Penny, usually the most energetic, was exhausted; the two women went to bed without another word.

But Heather lay awake, thinking about Carl across the table from her all night. She had felt the energy of the tension in his body from him wanting to protect her, especially when the tycoon began harassing her. *What are we to each other, Carl Johnson?* she thought as exhaustion took hold, and she drifted off to sleep.

***

The blonde cocktail waitress walked into a room on the fourteenth floor. Sitting on the couch was the tall brunette from the poker game. She looked up and said in Coronian, "Ah! Allra! Wonderful work tonight!"

The blonde sat down and looked at the other two women sitting in the room. One was a tall redhead with green eyes, and the other was blonde with hazel eyes. All were attractive women who many on Earth compared to the mythical Amazons or Scandinavian Vikings. Either way, even as Coronians, they fit in with the humans, and now, they had found their target.

The waitress said, "I could smell her from across the casino. Blech, Florian stench."

"After all this time, she finally shows up. I'm glad we stayed," the redhead said.

The four women leaned forward, took glasses of a black, tar-looking liquid, and said, "Potar!"

They all slammed the liquid back. "What now?" asked Allra, wiping her mouth with the back of her hand.

"I've already informed fleet command," replied the brunette. "Major Baryly and his team will come in, and that Florian bitch the Premier loves so much will capture her."

"We've done the work, and that cunt will get the credit."

"Perhaps, but who cares. Our people will have the first weapon that can kill Florians! And it's one of their own!"

The women cheered and pounded their fists on the table.

It had been a good night.

CHAPTER 21
THE SPY

I t had been a long time coming, but he was finally on his way to achieving his goal. He had left Rygone about six months ago, after purposely leaking the footage of him taking the envelope out of Dr. Harlow's desk. But now he was back, sitting in a small bar in Baltica South, sipping *hashel*. He wore a sandy-blond wig, and his color-changing contact lenses were set on brown.

He had to make sure the Rygonians saw him making a connection to his benefactor on Darsayn without actually telling someone. Oscar Strom knew him and his benefactor well, so he hoped they would make the connection and run with it. So far, he had not heard of the Rygonians going after Maria Granby, or as she now calls herself, Veronica.

After years of her grooming him as a spy and traitor to Rygone, he had been ready and eager to join the Coronian resistance and to help bring down the "old blood," as she would say. However, when he started working for Dr. Harlow and Dr. Strom, he realized the Rygonian establishment as a whole that Maria painted for him wasn't as terrible as she made it out to be. Indeed, issues needed to be addressed, but they were minimal compared to how helpful the Rygonians were to the galaxy around them.

He paid particular attention to General Dia Harlow, as Maria despised her the most. From her perspective, he understood why. Dia won the war for Troy and recovered from the injuries Maria had inflicted on her in the swamp. Dia was still the beloved Florian everyone on Rygone adored. He liked Dia, for the most part. She was a fantastic leader and one of the most well-respected people he had ever met. Whenever she came into Troy's or Oscar's lab, the whole place changed based on her mood. If she was happy, everyone smiled and made jokes. If she was mad, they stayed quiet and out of her way. If she was sad, they were miserable alongside her without knowing why. Even he fell into that pattern. At first, he hated that he enjoyed his surroundings and so-called enemies. But after a few years, he began having a change of heart and stopped feeding Maria accurate information. He gave her enough to get them by with the Coronians but tried not to hurt Rygone too much.

Yet, when he noted the Harlows' odd behavior after a particular EIP test, he fatefully contacted Maria. She insisted that he watch them as closely as possible, and when he happened across their documents to flee to Deep Space, he reluctantly let her know. To his dismay, Maria acted on his info immediately and dispatched the two Coronian destroyers that attempted to subdue both Harlows before their escape. When he discovered the extent of the carnage from the attack on Rygone's citizens, he was beyond horrified.

Once Troy was captured, and Maria had the doctor all to herself on Darsayn, he tried everything he could to keep the enemy of Rygone from learning anything about Dia's location or the source of the EIP. When he left Rygone, he stayed in touch with Maria occasionally but didn't have any information to give. He knew he had worn out his welcome and would be immediately executed if the Coronians found him. So now he was back on Rygone... where he would be immediately executed if they found him. Well, at least they would try.

The day before, he had snuck into the Research and Development hanger and saw the DREX gunner being readied for a mission. When he saw who the crew was, he knew they were close to finding the elusive lost general. He had to make himself known or sneak onto the ship. He decided on a very bold, very foolish move.

***

Troy was in his home office, closing patient notes from that day when someone rang the doorbell. It was pretty late, so he checked the camera on his datapad and saw a kid with sandy-blond hair standing there. Troy hesitated for a moment, then said through the communicator at the door, "Can I help you?"

The kid cleared his throat. "Uh, hi, Dr. Harlow? I was wondering if you could look—"

"Office hours are tomorrow."

The kid lifted an envelope to the camera.

Troy scrambled through the apartment, opened the door, grabbed the kid by the shirt, and slammed him against the kitchen counter. He angrily growled, "Who the fuck are you?"

Tristen Black painfully reached up and pulled the wig off. "It's Tristen. I used to work for you."

Troy leaned into the kid and hissed, "Why did you take that?"

Tristen was having a hard time breathing. "Please, Dr. Harlow," he whimpered, "let me explain myself."

Troy stood back but kept a hold of his shirt. "You have one minute until I show you what my wife calls 'the dreaded kneecap.'"

"Um, I took this from your desk after you were captured. I know you've seen the video of my doing so. I had to show you somehow that I was the spy for Maria Granby."

Troy felt his throat tighten. "So you're the traitor." He kicked Tristen hard in the shin, knocking him to the floor. He picked up his communicator and went to call security when Tristen painfully stood up and lunged at the much taller man, catching Troy off guard. He fell back into the dining room table but recovered quickly.

A familiar burning deep in Troy's gut began to simmer. He turned toward the disgusting spy, not realizing how his appearance had changed until he read the terror on Tristen's unusually handsome face.

Tristen put his hands out in front of him and said, "Dr. Harlow, please let me explain. I must go with you on your mission with High Colonel Conner."

Troy stalked toward him, staring with his angry dark eyes but not saying anything.

"You need to listen to me very carefully. I need to go on that mission with you."

"Why? So, you can tell your precious Maria more about us? Is she your lover? Is that how she made you into a spy?"

Tristen cleared his throat and said, "No, she's my mother."

He slowly turned around and lifted his hair off his neck.

Troy's head hit the ground so hard that he didn't just get knocked unconscious but went into survival stasis.

Tristen knelt beside his father. "Well, fuck."

CHAPTER 22
FAMILY MATTERS

After Troy went down, Tristen poured a glass of glacier water over his father's head to wake him from the deep stasis he had fallen into. It worked like a charm, though Troy got up sputtering and very unhappy.

Tristen said, "You should sit down, Doctor."

Troy, soaking wet, stumbled to the couch as Tristen sat in an armchair. Troy glared at the young man in the chair across from him, and Tristen cast his eyes to the floor, avoiding his father's intense gaze. Troy wasn't taking his revelation well.

After a moment, Troy said very quietly, "I knew it."

"Knew what?"

"That she was pregnant. That Maria had you and hid you from me. How I know, I couldn't tell you. I've just always felt you were out there somewhere. And the fact that you were right under my nose for years? And you're a *spy*, *her* spy?"

Tristen looked down at his hands, ashamed.

"How many of our people have been captured or killed because of the information you fed her? Do you know what they do to Florians on Darsayn?"

"I'm sure it can't be good," he mumbled.

"My personal favorite was being submerged in a cesspool of wastewater from the sewers for a few days. They would pull me out right before I could slip into stasis and leave me in my cell to rot without food, water, or help. It would take two or three days to expel the water and toxins from my system. It was so painful and humiliating. But that wasn't the worst part of it. Do you want to know what the worst part was?"

"No."

"She would *watch*!" Troy exclaimed in anger.

"You should call security, Father," Tristen whimpered. "I'll face the consequences of my actions."

"Don't call me that. It wasn't supposed to be this way. Maria shouldn't be your mother." He looked away toward the balcony door and continued, "I failed her again."

Tristen was confused. "What do you mean?"

Tears filled Troy's eyes as he said, "Dia has wanted a child since the day we got married almost eight hundred thousand years ago. She would've happily dropped her entire military career to stay home and raise a child. I always convinced her otherwise, that we should wait. She didn't complain much. Every once in a while, she would tell me stories of her family back on Kalow 9 and how much she loved raising her children with King Ben." Troy turned his gaze back to his newly revealed son. "Now, here you are. I don't care if this hurts you, but Dia deserved to have you, not Maria."

The young man swallowed hard and boldly said, "You're probably right, but be that as it may, I still love my mother."

Troy only scoffed and glared at Tristen, but instead of a rebuttal, he stood up unsteadily and asked, "Well, do you want a drink? I sure as hell need one."

Tristen was a little shocked by his offer. "Uh, yeah. I'll take something."

Troy was shaking. The shock of the news and hitting his head was catching up to him, so he hoped the alcohol would help calm his frayed nerves. Troy poured them a glass of *Merela*, an expensive whiskey Dia drank. He raised a toast.

"Here's to the fucked-up universe. I hope the Beginners are happy."

Tristen sipped his drink as Troy slammed back the smooth, amber liquor and poured himself another. After finishing that one, he asked, "Why do you want to go on our mission?"

"The Coronians are looking for Dia just as hard as you are. I can help you keep an eye out for them."

"Yeah, um, no," Troy said, his speech slightly slurred.

"Please, I want to help bring her back too. They want to exterminate us. So much of this is my fault. I want to make up for at least some of my mistakes," Tristen pleaded.

"Make up for your mistakes, huh? The mistakes that have cost thousands of Rygonians their lives, you mean. I don't trust you. Is your name really Tristen?"

He nodded.

Troy said, "Come with me." Tristen reluctantly followed Troy into his office, where he pulled a small trundle bed out from under Dia's desk. "You're staying here tonight. I'd suggest you piss now because I'm tying your ass to this bed. I haven't decided what to do with you yet."

Tristen knew Troy was serious, so he went into the bathroom and took care of his business. He returned to the office and sat on the bed. Troy took Tristen's hand and secured his arm with a metal clasp to the post. "You better be here in the morning, or I'll have Dominic Strom turning Rygone upside down looking for you. Do you understand?"

"Yes, sir," Tristen said, much like a little boy being scolded by his father.

Troy stumbled out of the office and turned off the light. Tristen was left alone to process everything that had happened. He'd never imagined that would be how he revealed himself to his father.

***

Troy drank half of the Merela and threw himself onto his bed, hoping to pass out and have Dia appear in a dream and tell him what he needed to do. No such luck.

He dreamt about a place filled with people, lights, and dazzling displays. Then a disheveled man threw up on his shoes.

***

The following day, Tristen woke up to the smell of lavender tea and breakfast. The metal clasp was gone, so he hesitantly walked out to find Troy making *betal* eggs and sweet bread.

When Troy saw Tristen, he poured him a cup of tea. The younger Harlow sat at the dining room table and looked around the apartment for the first time. He knew Troy and Dia were some of the highest-paid public servants on Rygone. Many people with half their salaries lived in opulent apartments in North or South, but Troy and his wife lived well below their means. Tristen asked, "Can't you get a bigger apartment, even here in Baltica City?"

Troy shrugged. "We can, but we choose not to. Despite a few technical interruptions, we've lived here our entire marriage, and we aren't even home half the time. Plus, the view is one of the best in the city. And we were waiting…"

Troy trailed off and turned away. Tristen knew he was going to talk about having children, so he dropped the subject. Troy walked over with two plates and set one in front of him. "Dia makes better sweet bread."

Tristen couldn't remember the last time he had a home-cooked meal and said, "This looks wonderful, thank you."

Troy sat down across from his son. They ate in silence until Troy asked, "You know what I find interesting?"

"No, what?"

"Florians don't look like their parents. You look nothing like your mother, which makes sense."

Tristen knew what Troy was going to say. "We look almost exactly alike. Some of the other techs would tease me in the lab."

"Dia even mentioned it once."

The more they were together, the more Tristen felt guilty about even mentioning Dia's name. "I'm very sorry about General Harlow," Tristen said stoically. "I always enjoyed it when she came in to see you. You couldn't not notice her."

"Especially when she was mad."

"Or very happy."

Troy sighed. "Hopefully, we'll find her."

"I hope you do too."

"You're going with us. I know the Chancellor kept the video of you taking the envelope out of my office very quiet, so I have to assume Dominic Strom hasn't seen it. You have to cover your birthmark so well it hurts. If he finds out you're my son, he *will* find a way to kill us both."

Tristen believed him.

CHAPTER 23
DAYTIME ACTIVITIES

Heather and her team had breakfast together in the guys' room. She was quiet for the most part, thinking about the night before and what she could've done differently. She was glad that nothing happened that required her to use her abilities. *Will it be that way for the next two days?*

With a mouthful of bacon, Brody asked Carl, "Is there anything specific we're doing during the day today?"

"Relaxing, for the most part. We're taking a gondola ride and seeing a magic show," Carl said.

"Yeah, no," Brody said, "I'm playing blackjack."

Penny shook her head. "I think I'm going to hang out by the pool. It's too hot for anything else."

"I have a friend in town who wants to meet for lunch. Anyone is welcome to join us," Roger said, overly kind.

With wonderment in her voice, Heather asked, "What's a magic show?"

Glaring at Roger skeptically, Carl said, "Fine. I'll join you for lunch, Roger. Heather, maybe you should spend the day at the pool with Penny. I want us all to meet back here at four. Tonight will be another test."

Penny asked, "Poker again?"

"Maybe a little, but I think we need to move you around a bit more, Heather. From bars to different gaming tables."

"Alone?"

"After the tycoon incident, I think one of us should be her date," Brody stated.

Everyone volunteered, even Penny.

Heather was flattered. "Brody, aren't you the most experienced with the casino stuff?"

He nodded.

"I guess we're dating now."

"Well, let's head out," Carl said as he stood, giving Heather a slight longing glance. "Everyone still needs to wear their communication devices. Ladies, don't get in the pool above the waist."

***

Once everyone else got up from the table and began going their separate ways, Carl pulled Roger aside and asked, "Who's this friend?"

"A former colleague. He may be of assistance."

"I'm not comfortable with this," Carl whispered suspiciously. "You should've told me you were meeting someone you may give information to about our endeavor."

"You should've told us what we're doing here. Yesterday was almost a disaster, and we still aren't sure why we're here."

Carl cleared his throat, scanned the room to see if anyone was listening, and continued, "You'll think I'm crazy, but here it goes. Dia Harlow came to me in a dream and said we needed to come to Vegas."

Roger stifled a laugh but was still intrigued. "Interesting. How do you know it was Dia?"

"She was in her fancy general uniform and looked like a fucking Viking shieldmaiden. Plus, she didn't act like Heather, at least not completely. It felt real, and I believed her enough to drag you all here. Maybe it was a mistake. We'll see in a few days."

Roger studied Carl's face closely before saying, "That's the most uncharacteristic thing you've ever said, but I'm curious to see if something plays out. My colleague can still help us."

Carl shrugged and walked away. *We'll see*, he thought.

***

Both women got ready to head out to the pool. Penny called the concierge and booked a cabana for the entire day. One with all the food, drink, and valets they could desire. Heather put on her bathing suit and cringed in the mirror. It was a bikini, which she felt safe in at the mansion, but in public, she was nervous. She also had no suit or shell, so she was all on her own if something happened. *Maybe I should go with Carl and Roger*, she thought nervously.

But Penny was ready to show off her new body to the world, and she wanted Heather for moral support. Both women left the room and headed toward the massive fifth-floor pool complex. Heather was wearing a cover-up, but a few people noticed them as they made their way to the elevator. Penny was excited, but Heather was uncomfortable.

When they arrived, Heather was mortified to find that not only were there *several* pools but bars and restaurants too. Luckily, once they made it to their lavish cabana, the commotion of the Venetian fell away, and they were in sumptuous comfort. Heather was amazed; it looked almost as lovely as their room. There were oversized lounge chairs, a small mini bar, overhead fans that eased the oppressive heat, and even a television! She felt better having a retreat to escape to if need be.

As they settled in, a waiter came into the cabana and asked, "Can I get you lovely ladies a drink or a snack? We have a wonderful charcuterie board, exotic fruit plate, or perhaps a selection of pastries from Bouchon?"

Heather glanced at Penny as she had no idea what they were. Penny said, "We'll start with the fruit, please!"

Heather took another good look at the waiter and realized he was the other valet from the day before. As he walked out, he winked at her. She said, "Penny, that was the other valet from yesterday. He winked at me too. Do you think they're working together?"

"Possibly. Did you guys hear that?"

Brody said, "I was ignoring you."

"What's the point of these things if you ignore us?" Carl asked angrily.

"Sorry," Brody groaned. "The sportsbook is hot today."

Carl said, "Yes, I heard you, Penny. Let us know if you need anything."

"Mousetrap?" Heather asked.

"Yes, love."

Penny slipped her earpiece out and whispered to Heather, "He sure calls you 'love' a lot. Does that bother you?"

"Sometimes. It depends on my mood." *I wonder if they all heard that.*

The waiter returned with their fruit. Penny gave him a generous tip, and he bowed to Heather as he breezed away.

Heather scrutinized the plate for another note. Penny said, "We'll keep an eye out for anything strange."

Heather nodded as she nibbled on a piece of starfruit. When she determined she liked it, she shoved the rest of it into her mouth. She could see Penny watching in amazement. She turned to her friend, and with a mouthful of the juicy fruit she mumbled, "What?"

Penny laughed. "One day, you're gonna choke."

Heather swallowed hard, coughing as the bite was too big. "Doubt it."

***

Carl and Roger were still in their room after Brody walked them through how to adjust their earpieces so they could hear, but their conversations could be muted. He explained to Heather through her earrings that the jewelry was incapable of this; therefore, she stayed quiet.

Carl left their room and strolled through the casino to find something to do before lunch. His mind was on who Roger's friend might be when someone bumped into his shoulder intentionally.

Carl stepped to the side and said, "Whoa, buddy, are you okay?"

It was the oil tycoon. "Was that little thing tasty?"

Carl burned with anger and got into the bigger but older man's face. "Do you have any decency? She didn't want you, so you have to make her out to be a whore?"

"So, she was tasty!"

Carl shoved him aside. "Go to hell."

Usually, Brody would've come to Carl's aid, but since he taught them how to tune each other out on the communicators, they were practically useless. Carl was on his own when the tycoon's band of thugs came to their leader's aid.

Carl realized he had been set up and prepared to be laid out when the valet who winked at Heather the day before came to his assistance. He said in a commanding voice, "Sir, I do hope you will leave this patron be. I watched your interaction, and if you refuse to calm down, I will be forced to call security and have you expelled from this hotel."

The tycoon growled at the valet and wanted to turn on him, but the pit boss noticed the commotion and stood close with his radio in hand. The disheveled man straightened his suit coat, the same one from last night, and sneered, "I hope she was worth it."

You have no idea how much more she's worth than anyone in this world, Carl thought.

As the four men stumbled away, Carl turned to the valet. "Thank you. Can I ask you something?"

The overly polite man said, "Of course, Dr. Johnson."

Carl was shocked that he knew his name, but hotels like these studied their guests, so he chalked it up to that. "The lady yesterday who came in with me. She had a note on her luggage that said she needed to watch out for her friend. Did you leave it there?"

"No, sir, I did not," said the man, smiling. "But I know who did. Unfortunately, he's no longer at the hotel. Just know that your friend has been anticipated here for a long time. Which is both exciting and dangerous. She is needed here; however, what will happen is perilous and could result in much devastation." He bowed and rushed away.

The only thing Carl could do was stare into space with his mouth open. He turned his communicator on and asked, "Brody, where are you?"

Brody said, "Yo, in the sportsbook, talking to Lacey."

Carl rolled his eyes. "I'm on my way. We may need to make some changes."

***

Heather and Penny sat in their cabana, sipping mimosas and eating exotic fruit. Between the heat and alcohol, Heather was drifting off. Penny kept poking her with a large green and blue feather, but finally, Heather crashed and fell into a dream.

A man came into the cabana. He was very tall and had long unruly black hair and bright gray eyes. He was wearing a strange black uniform that almost seemed familiar.

He said, "Hey, sis."

Sis?

"Huh?" she muttered.

He said in broken English, "I know you don't remember me yet, but we're trying so hard to find you. There's something you aren't gonna like when we do. Ask Troy."

He handed her a warm towel, then disappeared.

She snapped awake, turned to Penny, and asked, "How long was I asleep?"

Penny was chewing on a piece of mango. "I dunno, maybe two minutes."

"I had another vivid dream."

"You and your damn dreams. Was the hot guy in it?"

Heather shook her head. "No, he was really tall and had long unruly hair. He looked kind of like the Hound from *Game of Thrones* without the burned face. He called me sis."

"Whoa," Penny said, intrigued. "Did he say anything else? Did he speak English or the weird language?"

"English, but he had a hard time with it. He said they were looking very hard for me, but when they found me, there was something I wasn't going to like and to ask Troy."

"Troy is the hot guy, right?"

Heather shrugged and said, "I think so."

"As I said, you and your damn dreams."

Heather sat back and thought about the man. *Do I really have a brother?*

***

Carl found Brody with a cute, expensive-looking redhead in the sportsbook bar. As he approached, she asked, "Hello, sir, how're you today?"

"Tense, can I borrow your friend, please?"

She stepped away. "Sure thing, but maybe you can join us when you're done."

Carl glanced at Brody and said disapprovingly, "You know she's a prostitute, right?"

"I haven't gotten laid since before you locked us in that damn mansion, so I'm willing to go for a guaranteed thing. Especially because it's not my money paying for it."

Carl couldn't disagree; he had come close himself, but the world said otherwise. "Okay, I get it. But you have to get a different room, and be careful about what you say in the throes of passion."

"She has a room, and Jesus, what the hell is your problem?"

"I could've used your help earlier. The oil crew almost jumped me. Luckily, Heather's odd valet stepped in. He's fucking off and said things I didn't quite understand. We may need to adjust Heather's gear. Or put her in a situation where she can get to her suit in a moment's notice."

"The suit might be an issue if you want her down here mingling. She can't wear a superhero-looking weapon in public without actually using said superhero weapon. But we could forego the red dress and have her wear something that can cover an actual shell."

Carl liked that idea. "Yeah, that'll work. Heather?"

No answer.

"Heather!"

Penny said, "She's asleep."

"Wake her up," Carl demanded. "Did you hear our conversation?"

"Yup, Heather and I will hit the Promenade!" Penny exclaimed.

Roger sighed. "Great."

***

Penny woke Heather up and said, "Come on, little one, we need to do some shopping!"

Heather was enjoying the relaxing comfort of the cabana and whined, "Do we have to?"

Three voices yelled, "Yes!"

I hate this jewelry, the Florian general thought.

The ladies gave their friendly waiter the full hefty tip he would have gotten if they had stayed for the rest of the day. He bowed to Heather again and said, "It is such a pleasure."

They returned to their room, changed into more appropriate clothes for shopping, and went to the Promenade.

Heather was in awe. She had never been shopping before. The shops were filled with many beautiful things, from clothes to purses to jewelry. The moat with the gondola ride was in the middle of the expansive room, and she was so amazed. *I wish Carl and I could've gone on this. Maybe tomorrow*, she thought.

Penny took Heather into Saks Fifth Avenue, and they were set upon by two eager salesmen. One gasped and said, "Oh my, gorgeous ladies, Vegas is in for it! What's the occasion?"

Penny said, "We're looking for sexy but coverage, preferably pants or chinos. Short sleeves instead of sleeveless or tank tops. Other than that, surprise us!"

Heather was wearing the long shell shorts and sleeved top, hoping to get something that would cover them both but be attractive. The salesmen delivered. She wound up with a flowy white blouse that went well with the black shell. Her salesman was very interested in the material, but Heather did her best to keep him from touching it. The last thing they needed was someone unknowingly damaging the fabric. She wore a pair of loose black chinos that came to just below her knee for her pants and a pair of black wedge heels.

When they were perfectly dressed, Penny and Heather admired each other in the mirror. Penny was wearing a light sundress with exposed shoulders and tan sandals. Heather smiled at her beautiful friend and whispered, "We are so hot."

Brody groaned. "Shut up, please."

Roger came to the ladies' defense. "Be nice; they are."

They paid for their items, and Penny gave both salesmen a considerable tip. Heather could tell Penny loved spending Roger's money.

Heather looked around, wanting to experience more of the intriguing Promenade. "Now what?"

"Wanna see if we can go on the gondola?"

Heather smiled. Penny was probably a better date than Carl anyway. "Sure!"

***

Roger stood in the bathroom, nude, and looked at himself in the full-length mirror. He sighed, slipped the earpiece out, and set it on the counter. He was sure something would happen tonight since his contact was already at this hotel. *Darsayn is up to something, finally.*

He closed his eyes and felt his body begin to change. It had been quite some time since he was in his actual form, and he'd almost forgotten how he looked.

When he opened his eyes, the image in the mirror would drive any human mad with fear.

Roger was now twelve feet tall; his skin was pitch black and had intricate tattoo-like designs all over his body that were etched down to the muscle in silver, gold, and red. His eyes were now twice as large and bright red with long, black irises. His hair was long and silvery-white, and his hands bore three-inch razor-sharp claws. Roger now looked as sinister as a devil to the people of the Earth. Yet, he was still as meek and quiet as his human form. Would anyone on this planet ever trust him when he looked like this?

He heard the door to the room open, and Carl called, "Roger, you in here? It's almost lunchtime."

Roger changed back into his human form, put in his earpiece, and said, "One minute, I'm getting changed."

He quickly got dressed and left the bathroom. Carl was sitting on his bed. "Now what?" he asked.

"Lunch is in the Wynn," the Dailing said. "It's right next door, so we can walk."

They both made their way downstairs, and as they crossed the lobby, Carl saw the tycoon again. He said for the whole team to hear, "The tycoon and his crew are still here. I feel they might be an issue before the day is done. Keep an eye out."

Penny giggled. "Okay, boss."

Heather was giggling as well. "Okay, Carl. Have a nice lunch, don't do anything I wouldn't do."

"You mean nothing or blowing up a field?" he asked.

"Both." Loud laughter.

Brody breathlessly whispered, "Yeah."

"Thank you for keeping it so we can't hear you, Brody. Jesus," Carl said, slightly jealous.

Well, at least they're having more fun than I am. I hope Penny is taking care of her. He sighed, exasperated. *How am I supposed to be her only protector if I'm not with her? I planned today all wrong.*

Roger and Carl arrived at the Wynn and went to the Wing Lei restaurant to meet Roger's contact. As they were shown to the table, a familiar face stood up. Carl exclaimed, "You're the valet who left the note."

The man nodded politely. "At the hotel, at least, but that's not who I truly am, just as Roger here is not a millionaire alien finder."

Carl squinted his eyes and asked, "What friend did you mean Heather Stone needs to watch out for?"

The valet smiled. "Sit, and I will go over what I know for you."

Roger motioned for Carl to sit. He reluctantly did and scanned the room. *I wonder how many others like Roger are in this place.*

The valet had already ordered rice wine and vegan spring rolls. Carl wasn't thrilled about them being vegan, but he didn't want to offend their guest. He took a small bite and was surprised at how good they were. "Which friend? I'm taking great care to ensure she's safe, yet here I sit with someone I don't know," Carl said.

The valet nodded at Roger, and his benefactor said, "He meant you, Carl. She needs to be careful of you."

Carl realized that he didn't hear anything in the earpiece anymore and took it out. Something was interfering with the Bluetooth signal. Carl was about to go into a rage when the valet put up his hand as a peace offering and said, "Dr. Johnson, please. I wasn't expecting you to be here for lunch today, but I'm glad you are. Your dear friend is distracted by you. What you and Dia Harlow fear is about to happen must be a priority."

Carl breathed, "How do you know about that? Who are you?"

"Roger contacted me after you told him about your dream. My name is Goli. I'm a part of the mission that set out from Zole to find individuals like Heather Stone. We were so grateful when you found her; now that we know her true identity, it is a blessing and a curse. Everyone in the galaxy will want to get their hands on her. I cannot say how many different planets have agents here in Las Vegas. A world-changing event for humanity is about to go down, and Heather Stone or Dia Harlow or Flashpoint, as you call her, is center stage. If she is distracted by you, all may be lost."

Carl stood up, very flustered. "Piss off. Roger, I'm leaving."

"Carl, don't overreact," Roger said quietly. "I've been warning you. I realize you and Heather are close, but it isn't just her husband. It's who she is beyond Earth. She isn't a pretty woman with a special gift anymore. You know that and need to accept it."

Before Carl could say anything, Goli said, "Please, watch something for me. This video was taken before she was bonded with the EIP."

After Carl sat back down, Goli handed him a phone with a strange video. It showed who he knew as Heather but depicted as Dia, standing on the platform of what looked like a rooftop landing pad. She was staring straight up at something he couldn't see at first. Then a large craft that looked like something out of *Star Wars* landed near her, almost within touching distance. The video skipped to a view of her sitting in the pilot's seat next to another woman. She looked like a Japanese anime princess or something but had a steely sneer, a lot like Dia. The two women spoke what he figured was their native language, but the authority in Dia's voice was striking. The video then skipped to the aircraft flying along a cliff face looking over a lake. They flew incredibly fast, performing intricate moves while seeming to joke and pick on each other. In the next shot, they were maneuvering through a cave. The only light was from the craft, and he almost got sick from how the video moved around. The women we no longer joking but working together to make their way through the cave system, flying faster than they did over the cliffs. A video feed in the corner showed her face as she focused on her flying. She was virtually nothing like Heather, and he now understood what Roger and this new asshole meant. Heather wasn't Dia. Whatever happened to her when she landed on Earth, her former self was gone. And with him as a distraction, she may do more harm than good with her dangerous abilities.

Carl returned the phone and said, "She could probably get a job with United. And that's what it's called, huh? The EIP?"

His joke fell on deaf ears. "Carl, if you want to protect her, keep your distance," Roger said.

Carl took a sip of the rice wine. "Don't you think that could be counterintuitive at this point? If I keep my distance, she may take it badly and become even more distracted. She's still trying to figure out what she's feeling right now. Unfortunately, you didn't tell me about her damn husband. I'm blaming this on you, by the way."

"It doesn't matter now. You need to stay away to protect her, Carl," Roger said, exasperated.

Carl downed the rest of his wine and grabbed a spring roll. "Again, I'm leaving. Me coming to lunch was a mistake."

Carl stood up and left without looking back. His mind tried to wrap itself around the video they showed him. Did it even matter? So, Dia was a great spacecraft pilot. She was determined and confident, even cocky. He remembered the night they escaped Mallory's facility. Heather improvised immediately and was able to handle the situation perfectly. Something changed in her at that moment. Maybe her instinct as a fighter like Dia came to the surface. He was worried about her, but no more than he was before discovering Roger hid her identity from him. *How long have his friends been here on Earth?*

As he walked into the Venetian lobby, he saw Brody stepping into the casino with his red-headed friend. Carl stopped him and said, "Sorry, the party is over. We're starting this night early."

The girl pouted but walked away. Brody asked, "Is everything okay, boss?"

"I don't know, but we need to get together and put a plan in place. Heather is our number one priority from this moment forward. Also, someone at lunch jammed my earpiece. I need you to look at it."

"Who the hell did that?"

"Roger."

CHAPTER 24
CONTACT AND MOVE

"So, how the fuck are we going to do this? Hold her down and wait until the pretty bitch shows up and steals our prize?"

"Perhaps," Major Baryly said. "Veronica needs visual confirmation before we grab her. We can't screw this up, or the Premier will throw us all into the Pestual Grinding Pit."

He heard the woman on the line growl. "How far are you?"

Much to the blonde cocktail waitress's irritation, Veronica answered, "We're on the dark side of their moon. The stolen Jump Drive is powerful enough to put us into the desert outside of the city. Let me know when and where she is in the casino, and I'll grab her. Then you can call in the battlecruiser. We can get our prize and eliminate half a city in an hour." Veronica ran her fingers over the rings in her pocket. She wished Troy were there to see this.

"You know she'll attack when you grab her, right?"

"Yes, we're prepared for that. I watched the videos from the first contact, and at one point, it looked as if Dia was hit with a mechanical ram that put her down, forcing her to release her energy. I need you to find one of these rams in the hotel police's riot gear and have it in a secure but accessible place in the casino."

The waitress growled again and said, "Fine."

"Fine, what?"

"Fine, Captain."

Veronica smiled. "Much better." She turned to Baryly and asked, "When am I going in?"

It would take roughly an hour to Jump to the desert outside the city and drive in a primitive vehicle to the hotel where Dia Harlow was located. He said, "The sun in the human's city will start to set in about one Earth hour. We'll Jump to our desert location then. That way, we aren't likely to be spotted. We'll drive to the hotel and wait in the parking structure until called."

Veronica almost wanted to skip with excitement. Her plans were finally starting to come together.

Baryly asked, "How are we going to keep her on the ship without destroying us all?"

Veronica opened a small case with several vials of clear liquid and a small face mask with a cylinder on the bottom. She said, "The moment we take her out with the ram, we need to gas her with this. It's Polley, the strongest sedative that works on Florians. I've personally seen how it affects Dia Harlow, and she goes down hard. Hopefully, nothing has changed because of the EIP. This is enough for about ten days. More than adequate to get her back to Darsayn."

He nodded. Veronica could see his apprehension but didn't care. *This will work; it has to work!* she thought.

***

The cocktail waitress made her way onto the casino floor with a tray of cosmos for a party of women celebrating one of them getting divorced. Allra had been on Earth, working at this casino, for a few months now. She was intrigued and disgusted by the humans' mating habits. They "married" each other, whether man and woman, man and man, woman and woman, or whatever, claiming to love and cherish until "death do us part." Then they often turned around and got "divorced" or separated without dying. She knew there were similar rituals on other planets like Rygone and Kalow 9, but Darsayn and her kind were more intelligent about the other sex. If they wanted it, they found who they wanted and mated with them. Any children were celebrated as a gift of the god Hallbole, and each community raised the young as a whole unit. This practice kept the new generations from forming their own ideals, and the Coronian way of life would remain constant and pure.

She smiled and placed the drinks in front of each woman. One of them ran her hand up the back of Allra's thigh to the bottom of her buttocks. The woman cooed, "Very nice. You should come to room 3817 later."

Allra could snap the disgusting human's neck with one slap but knew she had to refrain. She pushed the woman's hand away and said, "Thank you, but I'm sorry. I'm not permitted to fraternize with the guests."

The woman scoffed. "I bet if I were a man, you would do it. Go away."

Allra had thick skin; nothing these humans ever said to her was surprising. She smiled kindly and walked back toward the bar with her empty tray. *Pathetic garbage. I can't wait until you are Batol shit.*

As she turned the corner toward the center of the casino, she was surprised to see Dia Harlow and the other woman in their group walking toward the elevator. They were talking like children, gushing over the material garbage they had paid too much money for in the shops.

Last night at the poker tables, General Harlow, who they called Heather Stone, seemed off her game. Allra knew who the commanding general was before taking this assignment, and the woman at the table wasn't her at first. Once she gained her confidence, Allra saw the Florian that most of her kind feared. Some Coronians even considered her a god of old when she survived the Breger Dunes swamp. But Allra knew better; Dia Harlow was just another Florian—irritating beings who needed to be removed from the Coronian path to galactic domination, especially Dia.

She muttered in Coronian, "Tonight, you'll be ours, dear general. I can't wait to see your face when we disembowel your precious humans right in front of you."

Someone touched the small of her back and said in her ear, "Why don'cha get me and the boys some beers, darlin'? I can make it worth yer while."

Allra glanced over her shoulder to find the oil tycoon standing too close. He was swaying and reeked of beer and Mexican food. She smiled politely and said, "Sure thing, sir."

She turned and looked him straight in the face, hoping he would lean into her, which he did. Allra palmed a small device that she pressed into his inner thigh. He took it as an advance, but it wasn't.

He stumbled toward her a little more, and the smile drained from his face. His eyes filled with dread; he opened his mouth and tried to speak, but his throat seized up. Allra screamed and yelled, "Somebody help! I think he's choking!"

The pit boss and several other casino employees came to her and the man's aid, but it would be to no avail. Allra had pierced his skin with the tiniest amount of Coronian cyanide, giving him an instant, untraceable stroke.

When they assured her they would take care of him, Allra turned away.

This is my gift to you, General. That disgusting human will not interfere with our work.

***

The sun had set enough to Baryly's satisfaction, so they Jumped down to the desert outside the city of Las Vegas. Even from there, almost sixty human miles away, they could see the lights of the Strip.

I hope this works. That place is pretty, Veronica thought.

Baryly still felt exposed even with the reflection mirrors turned out on the skin of the ship. One of the tools the Rygonians had not shared with their allies was a foolproof cloaking drive. One of the issues many in the galaxy had with the Rygonians was that they would refuse to share particular technology. They were happy to sell their partners state-of-the-art DREX fighters, but they didn't have Jump or cloak drives. Most systems loved Rygone because of the Florians, but they were also despised by many for their selfishness. These sentiments played to the Coronians' advantage for hundreds of years.

The red-headed Coronian woman, Jella, was at the landing site with two Earth vehicles. Veronica laughed and said, "They have wheels on their vehicles for more than just farming?"

Jella pretended to smile. "Right? Such a primitive species."

Baryly said, "That bank of lights is where General Harlow is?"

"Yes, she's in a hotel called the Venetian. She's planning to mingle in the casino tonight, playing games." Jella took out her phone and turned it toward them. "This is her appearance now."

Veronica was eager to see her, and the differences didn't disappoint. Dia's hair was much shorter than she usually wore it by choice. Her makeup wasn't much different but not as sinister as usual. She looked like a doll more than the commanding general Veronica remembered. Veronica committed the white blouse and short black pants to memory, but what caught her attention was Dia's lack of rings. *Did she take them off or lose them?*

Jella showed them three other pictures of Brody, Carl, and Penny. "These are the three humans she's with. They are extremely protective of her, and I think she might have a personal relationship with this one." She pointed at Carl's picture. "A surveillance camera caught the two of them in the lobby, nearly fornicating. She ran away, upset, and he was left confused. Their relationship seems complicated and might work to our advantage."

Veronica couldn't help but laugh out loud. The Coronians looked at her curiously, and she managed to say, "I'm so sorry! I've caught so much hell for Troy Harlow, and now his wife is screwing a human! This is hilarious!"

Baryly asked, "Does she know who she is down here?"

Veronica shrugged. "I dunno, but I doubt it. Either way, it's still funny. Go on, please."

"And this is the Dailing." Jella continued, "As you can see, he's going for as low of a profile as possible. He goes by Roger here, but this is Loi himself."

She showed them a picture, and Baryly gasped at the human form of such a great Dailing warrior. He'd fought Loi in several battles for the control of Zole. Loi was a great warrior and spy, which had to be why he was on Earth.

"We're going to grab her tonight. The humans she's with don't have her up to the task of fighting. She isn't outfitted for a battle. She's in pretty dresses and eats chicken. It'll be easy to finish this," Jella said with confidence.

Veronica took another look at the picture of Dia in a flowing shirt over what looked like underclothes. She didn't look like the military leader they knew, but that didn't mean she wasn't capable like Dia. "Don't underestimate her or the humans. They're probably coming into this not knowing anything about her past before landing here. From what it looks like, just from these pictures, she doesn't know who she is. Therefore, this is home to her. She's going to protect it and these people."

Jella waved her hand dismissively. "Ah! It doesn't matter. We'll have her before she even has a chance." She nodded her head at Veronica and said, "Florian, you're with me. We need to get there quickly."

Veronica had to hide it from her companions, but she was beaming with excitement. Not only were they going to grab the greatest weapon in the galaxy—maybe even the universe—but that weapon might be having an affair with a human! Did she remember Troy? Did she think she would never get home, so she gave up and went to this new man? It didn't matter. It was absolutely poetic to her. She reached into her pocket, ran her fingers over Troy's rings, and wondered what had happened to Dia's.

She smiled and said, "Lead on, Jella."

CHAPTER 25
THE BEGINNING

E very member of the team had reservations about that
evening.

Roger knew his colleagues were ready to grab Heather
and get her away from Earth, even with their limited ability to do
so.

Penny was aware it was going to be more complicated than last
night. She didn't like that Carl wanted Heather to move around
more.

Brody was nervous about how intense of a test this was on his
tech. If something went down tonight and Heather had to rely on
something he created, but it didn't work, he would let her down.

And to Carl? This was the beginning of the end of everything
he knew.

Heather felt something deep inside. She knew, without a doubt,
that this wasn't just the end of one thing but the beginning of
another.

***

Penny and Heather combed over their appearances thoroughly. Penny made sure the skin patch covering Heather's birthmark was flawless. They tested the earpieces and jewelry, and everything was functional. Heather even tried the shell she now wore instead of the red dress. She was relieved that it held much more power.

Heather wore her hair down this time, and her curls fell unimpeded to her shoulders. Her makeup was nearly the same, but the shadow was green and yellow on purpose. The white blouse flowed whenever she walked, breaking up the shape of the shell she wore underneath. Heather was unfamiliar with the wedge heels but was catching on fast.

Carl instructed everyone to pay attention to what the other team members wore. Brody was in a fitted black suit with a white shirt, unbuttoned at the top. Roger wore slacks, a white shirt, gray vest, and a black bowtie. Carl had on a dark gray suit, maroon shirt, and a black tie. All men wore a white handkerchief in their suit or vest pocket. They looked like a bunch of players ready to tackle Vegas.

As they were getting ready to head down, Heather reached into the side pocket of her suitcase where Penny had put her rings. Her chinos had a hidden pocket on the inner waistband, and she slipped them in. *No matter what happens, I don't want to lose these.*

Heather and Brody went down together. In the elevator, Heather watched him fuss with his jacket and said, "You look very handsome tonight, Brody. Thank you for everything."

He gave her a sad smile and pushed a curl behind her ear. "Thank you. You too, kid. Tonight will be just like last night, I promise."

She smiled and nodded, but she knew he didn't believe her.

When they stepped off the elevator, Brody said, making sure the team heard him, "Flashpoint and I are in the casino. We'll be in the blackjack area."

Roger said, "Got it."

"Okay," Penny confirmed.

Carl took a deep breath. "Be careful."

Carl's voice felt like a knife piercing her heart. Something was wrong, and the further they went into the casino, the more dread she felt. Heather said nervously, "Something isn't right. We need to leave now."

Brody turned to Heather. She was flushed; she had absorbed a small amount of energy, and was faintly glowing green. He grabbed her, pushed her toward a column out of the way, and said, "What is it? You're glowing!"

Heather realized she had been pulling in the feelers around her and the shell was already full. She placed her hand on a light fixture close to them, and it blazed brightly for a moment as she pushed the excess power into it. She breathed, "I'm sorry, I'm sorry. Something's wrong. We need to leave. Now!"

Brody whispered harshly, "She's right. We need to go. Even I can sense that something doesn't feel right. We need out of this hotel now."

"No! Vegas, out of Vegas. *Now!*" Heather was almost screaming.

She scanned the casino past Brody's shoulder, looking for the source of the dread she was feeling.

Just as she felt they were in the clear, her eyes caught something. *Haven't I seen that face before?*

***

Veronica sneered as Dia Harlow fixed on her. *She's uncertain about what's going on. Not like the general at all.*

Veronica started walking toward Dia and the human with her. A young man with sandy-blond hair and dark blue eyes. Considerably attractive; too bad his head was about to be smashed on the floor.

Unfortunately, Dia spooked and shoved the kid as hard as possible to get him out of harm's way. Veronica scoffed as the general exposed herself to the entire casino floor. People started to panic and ran away from the woman bathed in green flame with emerald eyes and fiery blonde hair. Dia touched a table with one of her bright fingertips, and it instantly burst into green flame. She asked cooly, "Who are you?"

"I'm one of you, Dia. We're Florian and don't belong on this primitive planet. You need to come home with me."

Heather glanced at Veronica's left hand and saw that she wore the same rings she carried in her pocket. She smiled at the strange woman and started to walk toward her.

"It's been so long."

Veronica stepped back just as Dia shot a strand of rope-like flame from her hand, wrapping it around her left wrist. Veronica's face filled with horror as Dia whipped her arm back, jerking the traitorous Florian toward her. Just as she reached the smaller general, Dia grabbed her throat and said, "I am nothing like you."

Heather stripped the rings from Veronica's hand and threw her across the casino. She landed near the sportsbook and was knocked unconscious.

When she came to, the casino was in utter chaos. People were trampling each other from all directions, and the fire alarms were blaring. Veronica felt someone grab her, and as she turned to fight, she saw that it was Allra, one of Jella's team members. Allra growled, "What were you thinking, Florian?! Now she's gone!"

Veronica pulled her arm away from the much larger Coronian woman and said, "No! She's going to head toward the street. I got her to expose herself here. That way, the humans are already panicked. Her fight will be with the ship, distracting her from us."

Allra had to nod in agreement and said, "Where now?"

"The ram."

*****

Carl was in the lobby and could see what was happening in the casino on a bank of security feeds behind the front desk. *Who the hell is that woman?*

Penny had found him, but Roger and Brody were still missing. Carl yelled through the earpiece, "Report in!"

"Here, with you!" Penny cried.

"Under a roulette wheel in the casino," Brody growled. "I'm not moving. Heather just went off the fucking rails."

Carl asked sternly, "Roger? Heather?"

Roger said nothing as he had destroyed his earpiece and was running to meet with his colleagues.

With an authority none of them had ever heard before, Heather said, "Brody, I just saved your ungrateful ass. All of you need to get out of the city and to safety. Everything changes tonight, and I don't want any of you here."

The three remaining teammates heard the crunch of the diamond necklace under her heel.

Heather was theirs no more.

***

Heather calmly stood in the middle of the Venetian hotel's front drive, wondering what her next move should be. *Should I try to go back upstairs and get the suit? Or stay here since I'm close to the action already?* She considered her options closely. *I'll stay here. Who was that woman? Why did she have these rings? Didn't the man from my dream have these rings too?*

She decided the shell was good enough but ditched the heels and went barefoot. As she walked toward the street, several police officers ran at her, shouting for her to stop. *Well, at least I understand them this time.*

She stopped and said calmly, "I have no quarrel with you, but I believe there might be others here that do. I'd like to help you defeat them."

They ignored her. Several officers drew their weapons, yelled at her to get down, and put her hands behind her head. She rolled her eyes, disregarding their order. Then, she heard a familiar voice behind her.

Carl yelled, "She isn't going to hurt anyone! You need to let her do her thing! Please!"

An intelligent cop yelled, "Who the fuck are you?"

"My name is Dr. Carl John—"

Heather had spun around before he could finish, whipping a green rush of flame and air around herself, and demanded, "Leave now, Carl! All of you!"

By the time the flash of air diminished, Heather was already at the end of the driveway, running west down Las Vegas Boulevard.

Heather didn't know how she did it, but she surrounded herself with a bubble of invisible energy. People could still see her but couldn't get close. If she walked toward them, the power automatically pushed them out of the way. She pulled the strongest feelers from the powerful hotels, lights, and vehicles around her. She was almost as powerful as she had been after flying through the star. Heather started to feel an immense amount of euphoria and satisfaction from the force running through her veins. She could feel every milliwatt of energy flowing through her body, and she had never felt this excited. She began to forget why she was there.

***

"She's already made it to the damn street! Let's go!" Allra growled.

The crowd on the Venetian driveway was in chaos, and the police were trying to regain control. Everyone wanted to follow the green flame lady, but she was in the middle of the street in some sort of daze.

"We're inbound. Where's the asset?" Baryly asked.

Veronica yelled breathlessly, "She got away! She's on the street but moving slowly to the west. Look for the signal when to attack."

"What signal?"

"A ball of green flame."

Veronica, Allra, and Jella ran out of the casino toward the street and were immediately confronted by what they could only describe as hell on Earth.

Roger and the two valets were in their proper forms. All three were over twelve feet tall. One of the valet's skin designs were bright blue and undulated as he walked. The other's design was pure gold. With his gold, silver, and red designs, Roger stepped toward Veronica and said in Rygonian, "Leave now, and you will not be attacked. I'm sure Rygone misses you."

Veronica laughed hard. "Rygone can die for all I care. I'm with them." She gestured at the Coronians.

Both Coronian women made ready to fight, and Allra said to Veronica, "Catch her with the ram, Florian, or I'll find a way to shove it up *your* ass!"

The two women went at the three Dailing warriors from Zole as Veronica slipped by, lugging the heavy ram with her.

***

Carl recognized Roger's voice as one of the Dailing warriors. He was sitting on the curb, watching the world descend into chaos around him. But that didn't matter because he had lost her. Heather was gone.

Suddenly, a hand slammed down on his shoulder and pulled him to his feet. "She's right, boss. We need to get the hell out of here. There are reports on the news that there might even be an alien ship nearby. Heather *has* indeed gone off the rails, and who knows who she's fighting for."

Carl looked at Penny, who stood next to Brody. Her cheeks had streaks of black liner from crying, and her arms were crossed. He stared at them sternly and said, "What did we expect this situation to look like when it happened? Haven't we been working toward this for a goddamned year?"

Brody looked around and gasped, "This? No. What're you saying, Carl?"

Penny whispered, "We need to help her."

Brody exclaimed, "*How?*"

"The suit. She needs it to control the power better, right? I think the power is controlling *her* right now."

Brody nodded. "Okay, let's get the suit. How do we get it to her?"

Penny looked at the alien battle about to take place in the driveway and said, "Maybe Roger can help."

***

Aren't I supposed to be fighting someone or something? Heather thought.

Heather was still walking down the street with the invisible energy field surrounding her. Some people were in awe, some were trying to attack her, and others were cheering. She didn't even know who her enemy or ally was. She just kept smiling and walking.

Behind her, she heard a commotion, so she turned. *Ah, you again.*

"Hello. Do you want to play again? Nice toy," Heather said as she threw a ball of flame toward Veronica. But the Florian traitor was expecting it and jumped out of the way. The flame ball hit a parked car, and it blew up, spewing flaming debris all around them. People were screaming, but Heather just said, "Pretty."

She continued her walk when Veronica came at the Florian general with the ram, only to be repelled by the energy field. Heather laughed. "That was cool!"

The blonde woman looked at her quizzically, then said, "Do you even remember him? Do you remember Troy?"

Heather stopped, studying Veronica inquisitively. She asked, "Who is he?"

Veronica smirked. "Well, he's your—"

Out of nowhere, a barrage of nonlethal bean bags slammed into Veronica, sending her to the ground and making her drop the ram. Heather pointed at her and laughed, then continued walking.

The police around them were also trying to shoot Heather, but the bean bags bounced off the energy field, making it stronger with their kinetic energy.

Suddenly, Heather felt a massive surge of two different types of power surround her. One was insanely powerful, while the other she had never felt before. She finally snapped back into the present and scanned her surroundings. She couldn't find the more prominent source, but the unknown came from above, fast. Heather looked up and nearly choked. *What the hell is that?*

***

Luckily, the team made it back to the rooms via the elevator before the staff put the hotel on lockdown, per the police's orders. They'd have to worry about that after they got the suit. Penny opened the door, ran straight to Heather's special case, and pulled out the suit and boots. Before she turned to leave, she opened Heather's suitcase and went to reach into the pocket with the rings, but it was already open.

Carl exclaimed, "Come on, we gotta go!"

The team ran to the elevators, which were now shut down for guests. Carl whined uncharacteristically, "Thirty-three flights of stairs?! It might be down, but that's a lot of wasted time!"

Brody cooly took his phone out of his pocket and scrolled through a few apps. Penny and Carl watched on curiously as he made a call. Brody said in his most mature voice, "This is Officer Charles Peyton of the Metro Police on the thirty-third floor. Badge number 1894. I need the elevators unlocked to the lobby."

Carl and Penny glanced at each other in shock. As the elevator started to rise up to their floor, Brody hung up.

Penny beamed. "Wow! That was awesome, Brody!"

"Don't get excited yet. They may have only sent someone to arrest me for impersonating an officer. Like, perhaps the real Officer Peyton."

Carl said, "Still, good work."

When the elevator arrived, it was empty. The ride was less than a minute, but their anxiety made it feel like an eternity. When the team got off, they had to make their way through the chaotic casino to get to the lobby and front entrance. The lobby was filled with police, firefighters, and people trying to make their statements about the aliens taking over the world. *I wonder what Roger is doing*, Carl thought.

Like an earthquake, a colossal crash and rumbling hit the front of the building, filling the lobby with dust and debris. The lights went out, and emergency sirens began blaring, followed by red security lights illuminating the whole area. Everyone, including some of the first responders, panicked, and the main level of the Venetian descended into even deeper disarray. Carl realized the commotion was part of the roof of the front drive collapsing. *Was that Heather or Roger's doing?*

Roger and his colleagues had dispatched the two Coronian female warriors, but at a cost. There was much damage left in their wake. Many humans were injured, and a few had been killed. Now, the entrance into the Venetian was blocked.

Carl turned to his faithful companions, who were backed up against a chocolate shop close to the front desk, and said, "We need to get out the back, preferably before the rest of these people."

"How do we get to Roger?" Penny asked.

"I think we might be on our own now," Brody said grimly.

***

Veronica took a deep breath and shook off the pain in her chest. *What the heck did they hit me with?* she thought.

Several police officers in riot gear had surrounded Veronica with their weapons drawn. They were all yelling in English. Her limited exposure to the language made them hard to understand. She couldn't be killed, but she also didn't have powers like Dia. She wasn't sure what these human weapons were capable of.

She was already sitting on the ground. After a moment, she determined that they wanted her to lay on her belly.

She complied, and they set upon her like rabid dogs. One officer put a knee on the small of her back, zip-tied her hands, and lifted her to her feet. Several were staring at her with shock painted across their faces. One finally asked, "Are you one of them?"

"One of who? One of the beings here to destroy your planet? Yes."

Just as the pathetic cops began trying to drag her away, Veronica saw a silhouette fly over the top of the buildings.

She smirked and said, "It's about to get very ugly, humans."

***

Goli, the valet who smiled at Heather first, was severely injured, forcing Roger—Loi—to leave him at the Venetian. Loi said in their native language, "Stay. I'll come for you when I find Dia Harlow and get her ready to go. I promise."

Goli took Roger's hand. "I'll fight till the end, Loi, my liege."

Loi kissed him on top of his head and turned to run off with Korti, the other valet.

The two giant aliens made their way around the debris on the hotel's drive to the street, looking for the green glow that would signal Dia's location. Korti saw green flames to the west where the car had been destroyed and pointed, "There, my liege!"

As they ran toward the flame, they encountered many horrified humans who ran away instead of approaching them. They came upon a scene of several police officers trying to arrest a tall blonde woman. The police officers were startled by their presence and trained their guns on the Dailings, blocking their way. The blonde woman laughed and said, "Ah, the Dailings. These two might help you, humans."

Loi ignored the Florian woman, knowing she was there with the Coronians and up to no good. He knew they needed to get past the bewildered police officers, but he wasn't willing to intentionally hurt any humans. To his surprise, the Florian woman unwittingly created a diversion that allowed them to move on. She kicked one of the distracted officers in the back of the legs, sending him to the ground, howling in pain. Loi and Korti pushed past and left the Florian to fend them off as the others turned their attention to her. Knowing the tenacity of her species, he was sure she would be just fine.

Loi and Korti started heading toward the green glow, but it had vanished. Loi asked, perplexed, "Where did she go?"

***

Like Loi and Korti, Carl and the team had followed the green flame from the car wreckage. However, they were lucky and found a golf cart near the hotel's service entrance. They were racing down the sidewalk of the Strip, trying not to get knocked over by the bewildered Vegas crowd. Carl saw the police trying to arrest a tall blonde woman. Brody exclaimed, "Whoa! That's the chick Heather tossed in the casino. She had the same rings as Heather's. Heather stole them from her."

Carl wasn't interested in Brody's story and continued to race in the direction of the green flame.

But there was no green illuminating the way. There was only a strange feeling of dread from above.

CHAPTER 26
WHEN THE LIGHTS GO DOWN IN THE CITY

Carl stopped the golf cart and jumped on a tall flower planter. He was frustratedly scanning the people-filled streets when, from behind, he heard a quiet voice say, "I thought I told you guys to leave."

The team spun around, and Carl jumped down to see Heather standing before them, but they could tell she wasn't herself. "Something's here. I don't know what to do."

Carl grabbed her and said, "That's why we're here, love. Penny?"

Penny shoved the suit and boots into Heather's arms. "You need to put this on. Strip down to your shell and get it on now."

They could tell she was shaken to her core when she didn't move.

"It's going to be fucking awkward if we have to strip and dress you, damn it!" Brody yelled.

Heather huffed with determination and took off the blouse and chinos, carefully taking the four rings out of the hidden pocket. Penny helped her get into the suit and the boots. It wasn't long before she was herself again. The rest of the team was in awe as she pulled energy from every available feeler.

As she began to say, "I'm ready," the team was blown back by an enormous shock wave caused by a massive explosion close by.

When Carl regained his composure, Heather was gone.

***

It was Circus Circus first.

Long-time established, trashy-as-hell Circus Circus.

The ion cannon from the Coronian battlecruiser fired directly into the center of the north tower. The building was instantly cut in half, collapsing down on itself.

Next, the battlecruiser turned and shot the top off The Strat.

Thousands of human lives were lost within minutes.

Earth knew without a doubt that there was intelligent life in the universe.

Unfortunately, it was clearly hostile.

***

Carl could see the flames and chaos from where they were.

Penny hugged Brody and asked, "Did we fail?"

Brody nodded. "I think so."

Carl felt tears well in his eyes. *Where did you go, love?*

***

Loi and Korti were next to the Flamingo Hilton as the first blast hit Circus Circus. Loi gasped and scanned the area above the crowd. He said, "Where did our weapon go?"

***

Veronica had managed to escape from the police when the first blast took down Circus Circus. She broke the zip-tie on her wrists and took out her communicator. "Why are you attacking now, Baryly?! I don't have her yet!" she screamed in anger.

Baryly's voice stung. "And you never will. You are worthless, Veronica. The Premier wished you poorly, and we'll capture the EIP ourselves."

***

For the record, the Coronians were incorrect about the Strip's power.

There was another source of energy close enough to throw off their assessment.

A much more potent source.

***

The power grid all over the entire state of Nevada shut down. The city of Las Vegas plunged into darkness.

It was followed by power plants from Flagstaff to Phoenix, Arizona.

Then half of Los Angeles went dark.

Suddenly, a gigantic, bright green sphere of intense flame appeared at the Las Vegas Strip's west end.

***

A rattled reporter with a cell phone was trying to record herself during the chaos, but all that could be seen and heard was darkness, screaming, explosions, and an occasional round of gunfire.

She stopped by a planter box on the Encore hotel's north side, pretty close to Circus Circus. She ran a live Facebook feed and said, "This is Kayley Hammer. I'm in Las Vegas during this unprecedented"—she swept her phone around to show some devastation—"event. Hotels and buses—"

Kayley screamed, but her shriek was abruptly cut off. The last thing her viewers saw was a large, beast-like creature crushing her head with his bare hands.

It was the perfect press for Baryly. He only had a few men, and they could navigate through the chaos that the humans were practically creating themselves, pick and choose a few hands-on deaths that would go out live on their news sources, and the planet would know who his people were. *Idiots*, he thought.

One of his men yelled from the gun deck, "Major, look!"

Baryly watched the feed from the front of the ship and saw the intense green glow only a few earth miles away. He laughed and exclaimed, "There she is! Let's get her!"

His fire control officer asked, "Do you want me to fire, Major?"

"No! She'll absorb it! We need to stun her into submission. Drop a building on her!"

***

The team was carefully making their way toward the street when the power went out. Brody saw Heather's display first. He started laughing hysterically. "How the hell didn't we know?"

Penny, scared to death, screamed, "What are you talking about?!"

Brody pointed to the west, out of the city. "Whoever sent us somehow knew we would be fighting aliens on the Strip. And what better source of energy to fight them with than the *Hoover*! *Fucking*! *Dam*!"

Carl watched as the blaze began moving onto the street. Bewildered, he said, "Oh my God. She knew they would come here all along. But how?"

"We can ask philosophical questions later, Carl. We need to move!" Penny yelled.

Carl was torn. Should they get closer or move away from Heather? He knew whatever happened between her and that alien ship would be messy.

He said to his team, "Okay, guys, we'll sit back and watch this one. We need to stay away because us living through this is the help she needs."

***

Veronica was perplexed by the betrayal of the Coronians but knew she needed to get away to regroup. In the dark, she could see the cruiser turn and slowly drift toward the green flame. She scanned her surroundings and saw an intact parking garage by Treasure Island. She slipped into the structure amidst people running in pandemonium.

Many were trying to help the wounded and dying. Police and firefighters were arriving to help, even though the threat was still above them. *Humans are as misguided as Florians*, she thought.

Another big explosion suddenly went off in the middle of the Strip.

She didn't care; she had to find a way to flee the area. Veronica was needed there no longer.

***

Baryly watched as the glow moved slowly toward his ship. The brightness was so intense that he couldn't see if Dia Harlow was even there, but he knew she had to be. There was nothing else in any galaxy that could manipulate power like that. And he needed to get it out of her.

He turned the ion cannon toward the Mandalay Bay resort. He sliced the top five floors off perfectly, sending them toward Harlow. He expected the debris to land on and crush her, hopefully releasing her energy, but he was wrong. Very wrong.

Everything seemed to slow as he watched the rubble stop in midair over the flame. There was a deafening *crack*, and the debris seemed to dissipate. Not fall, not break up, but *dissipate* and disappear.

That's not possible!

***

There was no more time to play games. She knew they were going to keep throwing everything they could at her. Flashpoint took a deep breath and closed her emerald eyes. She thought hard about what every cell, molecule, and element of her body needed to do. She needed to achieve something she had never tried before.

Flashpoint opened her eyes and threw her arms out toward the approaching spaceship. She released two wide arcs of flame that attached themselves to the front of the craft, instantly stopping it in midair.

***

Baryly panicked and yelled, "Full reverse throttle! Don't let her pull us in!"

***

Carl breathed, "Holy shit, she grabbed them."

***

Loi and Korti watched on in utter awe. "This will go down in the history of our galaxy," Korti cried. "Maybe even the universe! She is such a thing of beauty."

***

Flashpoint began walking backyards, using the Coronians panicked engine thrust to their disadvantage. The longer they struggled, the more of their ship's power she stole. Finally, the only thing keeping them in the air was her.

She closed her eyes again and took a deep breath.

One.

Two.

Three.

Flashpoint turned and threw her arms toward the sky as hard as possible, sending the ship with them. She hurled heat hotter than lightning with it, instantly incinerating the entire battlecruiser.

All that remained was residual dust that fell to the ground like fine snow.

CHAPTER 27
IN AN INSTANT

C arl watched as Heather released most of her power to destroy the ship, and once it was gone, everything at their end of the boulevard went eerily silent and dark. The team knew that Heather became incredibly weak when she wore her suit after releasing just a fraction of what she had just done. Hoping she could hear him, Brody yelled, "Heather, don't let anything go yet! We need to find you a snack!"

But Heather didn't hear him.

"She can't hold what's left for long," Carl said. "This shit isn't a perfect science yet."

He started to run toward Heather as she turned toward the Hoover Dam, which was forty miles away. She raised her arms and gently released the remaining power from the suit, the shell, and her body. Less than a minute later, the electricity across the southwest United States began to return.

Carl yelled, "Heather!"

She turned toward his voice, but the exhaustion hit her hard. Heather's head started to swim, and her legs couldn't hold her weight. She faintly heard Brody's voice scream, "Carl! Get down!"

Heather fell to her knees and heard two distant gunshots. She collapsed forward right as someone crashed to the ground in front of her.

It happened in an instant.

Heather lifted her head and realized it was Carl. He was lying on his side, looking at her. His eyes were wide, and she watched a tear slowly trail over the bridge of his nose. His eyes fixed on her beautiful face, and he whispered, "I'm sorry, love. I failed to protect you."

Carl coughed twice, and blood splattered all over Heather's face.

Two bullets from Major Jason Mallory's sidearm had pierced Dr. Carl Johnson's heart.

He exsanguinated in less than a minute.

Heather would never forget the life draining from his eyes.

Just as the grief and exhaustion sent her unconscious, Heather felt a strange rush of wind.

And the last thing she heard was Penny screaming.

CHAPTER 28
REACTIONS

While the battlecruiser was still in existence, Major Baryly had been able to hack into all news and private feeds from the surrounding area. He was able to send real-time footage to Premier Baxelhoff back on Darsayn.

The Premier, his wife, daughters, and close associates watched the humans' destruction in their private chambers. The mood in the room was joyous and happy as they observed their comrades destroy the hotel with one blast, killing thousands. A feed from one of the human reports showed the power going out around the entire surrounding area. Not long after, several news feeds began showing the ball of glowing green flame at the end of the road.

Baxelhoff watched in joyful suspense as Baryly turned and slowly started moving toward Dia Harlow in her full glory. He wondered how this would play out just as Baryly shot the top of a building toward the Florian weapon. But to the Coronian leader's shock, she stopped the attack and instantly destroyed the debris. She then turned her sights on the cruiser and grabbed it with two robust arcs of flame. Within minutes, she had drained the power from one of the most advanced battlecruisers ever developed and threw it into oblivion.

Baxelhoff wouldn't have known what happened to his ship if one of the remote news feeds hadn't run for a few more seconds. All that remained of Major Baryly was dust in the wind.

Baxelhoff immediately called his generals to find out exactly who was on the ship and get another cruiser out there as soon as possible. Unfortunately, Baryly's was their only Jump-enabled craft. It would take a little preparation, but they could travel to Earth with one of their fastest destroyers in ten Earth days.

After dismissing his generals, Baxelhoff stood at the window, staring out at his beautiful city, Tonwal. His wife, Lydia, came up behind him and placed an arm around his waist. She was nearly half his height and only came up to the bottom edge of his shoulder, but that didn't deter her from being close. Lydia wasn't afraid of her husband, unlike so many others. He never gave her a reason to be. Baxelhoff hadn't been looking for a woman to be in his life when he met her. He was bitter about the unrequited love he had for Veronica. He wanted their relationship to be a starting point for a Florian-Coronian union, but Veronica was vain and selfish. Lydia came from a humble planet and species and never looked at him for who or what he was. She started as a cook in the palace kitchen, and Baxelhoff loved her salted fish. One day, he asked one of the other servants to bring her up to talk to him.

Usually, they trembled at his feet when he asked to see a servant, even for a good reason. Baxelhoff used to enjoy that, but he had grown sad and lonely by then. Lydia came into his chamber, walked straight up to the ten-foot mark, and bowed, as confident as ever. Her boldness struck him profoundly, and he often called on her in order to talk and spend time with someone who didn't care who he was. Baxelhoff could have forced her into marriage, but he simply asked if she wanted to be the Premieress. She accepted without hesitation, and their union was among the strongest in Coronian history. He truly loved his wife, and she him.

She asked meekly, "What is your next course of action, dear husband?"

He kissed her on the head. "We need to get a much larger force back to Earth and concentrate only on finding Dia Harlow. And perhaps Veronica."

Lydia looked down and pushed the edge of her dress with her tiny foot. Baxelhoff knew how much his wife despised Veronica, but she stayed dutifully quiet. He embraced her and said, "I don't want to ever see her again, but she may still be of use."

Lydia mumbled into his chest, "Use for what? Destroying General Harlow?"

"No, my dear, harnessing her."

***

Loi and Korti quickly changed back into human form after the Coronian ship disintegrated. Roger knew they couldn't get back into the Venetian to find clothes, but there was so much unrest surrounding the entire area that they were able to slip unnoticed into a large curio shop and find shorts and shirts. They looked like any other Vegas tourists in a crisis.

Roger said to Korti, whose name was also Peter, "We need to get down there. I need to find my team. I hope they made it to her."

"What will she do now?"

"Using this power takes a lot out of her. She gets very depleted and needs to recharge. Brody and Penny were still working with her gear to combat that issue, but it wasn't going well."

The two men were jogging down the middle of the street when several Army Humvees sped past them. "Oh no. Come on!" Roger exclaimed.

They ran as fast as they could to where the ship had gone down, but the closer they got, the more people gathered, trying to get close to Heather.

Roger saw the Army vehicles had parked, and several armed soldiers were surrounding the area where he assumed she was. Roger was pushing through the crowd when a familiar face came out of one of the Humvees. His sidearm was drawn, and Roger faintly heard Brody yelling something at Carl. Roger watched Mallory bring his weapon up and fire two rounds.

People started screaming and running away, letting Roger see Heather and Carl lying on the ground, face to face. A growing pool of blood was coming from his friend's chest, and Heather looked too exhausted to react.

Roger started to run toward them when a strange sensation sped through him, and a cyclonic breeze swirled around the area.

In the confusion, there was more random gunfire, creating chaos among the humans. Roger tried to race toward Heather, but Mallory's men were already loading her into one of the vehicles.

The cyclonic breeze moved west, and Roger heard Penny scream.

And like nothing had happened, everything went quiet.

Roger ran to where Carl lay with futile hopes that he might still be breathing, but he wasn't. Roger's heart ached for his loyal friend and colleague. *Where are Brody and Penny?* he wondered.

"Things are insane, my liege. What do we do now?" Peter asked, concerned.

Roger glanced at Carl's body, then around the surrounding area for Penny and Brody. He said, "We need to find Penny, Brody, and Goli, and get back to the airport. We need to go to the mansion."

Unfortunately, they could not locate the physician's assistant or tech expert.

***

Earth was descending into madness.

News agencies ran as much footage as they could find of the incident: the giant spaceship destroying hotels; tall, black aliens that could break concrete pillars apart with their hands; beast-looking creatures who had crushed people like they were bugs.

Most of the footage revolved around the woman bathed in green flame who stole the Hoover Dam's power to save the city and its citizens.

There were several pictures of Heather in Vegas compared to grainy images of her from Kentucky last year. There was an interview on CNN with Maeve Marco, who was the first to have prolonged contact with Heather Stone.

The favorite moment that every outlet showed, from Facebook to CNN to local news channels, was several different angles of Heather throwing the enormous ship into the air and incinerating it completely.

People cheered for her. People jeered at her. Even vigils were held for the Coronians, and Heather was called a murderer. A college-age girl with blonde braids was interviewed in Los Angeles and said, "I'm sure if she asked first, they would have stopped destroying those hotels. She just assumed they wanted to hurt humans and murdered them all!"

Doctors, scientists, politicians, and military leaders showed up to tell the people of Earth that they would work tirelessly to address the new threat from above. They would find out who she was and ensure she had no ill intentions for their planet. The aggressors would be repelled, and a scene like Las Vegas would never happen again.

Over the next several days, video surveillance from all over the Venetian began to pour in, pulled from facial recognition software. They showed her at the pool with Penny, shopping, playing poker, and blending in well with humans. Luckily, the alcove video of her and Carl didn't get released.

But there were questions.

If she had been there a year, where had she been hiding?

She disappeared from Las Vegas; where was she now?

Who was the man that was shot by what looked like the Army?

Most of all, now what?

CHAPTER 29
STARTING OVER

If she were human, Heather would be suffocating to death. But since she was Florian, she was suffocating to torture. All she knew was she was in some sort of container that was blocking any kind of energy. It didn't matter. Even if she wanted to pull in a feeler, she was too weak.

She needed water so badly. The toll of the final release was more than she had ever felt. The power she took from the dam was almost as pure as the star. It was so exhilarating, but she had known it would have consequences the moment it hit her veins.

When they worked in the field, sometimes she and Brody found ways to release energy to help her move farther or faster. Her favorite was pushing power down toward the ground and 'riding' the wave either up or jumping forward. That helped her get from the middle of Vegas to the dam and back to Vegas in less than five minutes.

The suffocating sensation came back as she thought about Brody and Penny. She hoped they escaped the turmoil and Mallory. Who knew what he would have done to them.

But Carl. *Is he really dead?*

When he hit the ground by her, she thought he was getting down to help get her to safety. She knew he was in trouble when he didn't move and just stared at her.

I'm sorry, love. I failed to protect you.

She could feel the dry blood splatter on her face still. The thought was more than she could take. She screamed herself into stasis.

***

Mallory's new compound was quite different from the run-down facility in Kentucky. They were now in the heart of the Cheyenne Mountain Complex in Colorado Springs, Colorado. Formerly the home of NORAD, now it was the top Space Force Command. The perfect place to take an alien.

The lab they had set up for Heather was an old hangar bay with several large, Lexan-walled rooms. The closer you got to the center room, the less power generation and thicker the Lexan. Finally, the center room was a completely clear compartment with a simple bed.

Heather was lying on the bed, unconscious.

The staff could see her from anywhere in the enclosure. Either through the glass or on a monitor. There were several cameras behind energy reflective shields, watching her from every angle.

Mallory was two rooms in, Dr. Helen Grace at his side. His arms were crossed over his chest, and he mumbled, "Come on, bitch, wake up."

"Jason, stop. She had a rough night."

Mallory glared at Helen, but she didn't return his gaze. Helen Grace was very conflicted by the events of yesterday. Especially him killing Dr. Johnson unprovoked.

"Come on, Helen, you know he was in the way and needed to be eliminated," Mallory said earnestly. "I found an easy solution and took it."

She scowled at him. "I know he was in the way; I don't even care that you killed him, but you did it *right* in front of her! She has been with him and that team for a whole year. She isn't going to take it well."

"Well, it won't matter if she doesn't fucking wake up," he retorted.

Helen picked up her tablet and clicked on a music file. The center room began to fill with quiet classical music, and just like she expected, Heather began to stir.

The entire compound stopped what they were doing and watched the small woman roll onto her side and look around. Mallory smiled and said, "They're all waiting for her to destroy us."

"If she could, I bet she would," Helen said. "I'm going in. Wish me luck."

Mallory nodded as she walked through the door, taking her to the first block of rooms, right up against Heather's glass enclosure. As Helen opened her mouth to talk, Heather said in a very raspy voice, "I know you're there, Helen."

Hearing Heather address her sent chills up Helen's spine. She cleared her throat. "Hello, Heather. How are you, dear?"

"Uh, let's see. I saved your civilization from a different, more sinister alien race. You're starving and dehydrating me on purpose because you know I can bring this whole goddamn mountain down on top of us if I get my hands on a simple battery. And your piece of shit boyfriend killed one of the most incredible men in the world right in front of me. Thanks for washing his blood off my face when you stole my suit. How's the weather, bitch?"

Heather covered her head with the thin blanket they gave her and tried to hide the sobs racking her body, but all could see her pain. The rant she gave was all the strength she had left, and she slipped back into survival stasis.

"Damn it," Mallory whispered.

Helen walked back into the second-level room with him. "We need to get some food and water into her, or we may as well just leave her like this."

"How?"

Helen turned back to the lump of a white blanket with barely detectable vital signs and said, "We strap her down, gently put a tube down her nose, hope it won't wake her up, and slowly introduce IV fluid until she starts to come back around."

He sighed heavily. "I don't like it, but do it. Pay close attention to anything entering that room. Also, you cannot add any light."

The light already illuminating Heather's cell was from an exergonic reaction, like a glow stick. It still produced free energy but with very little output and was behind the Lexan. They had no choice but to try something.

Helen chose a brave team to help her insert the nasogastric tube. When the four people entered Heather's cell, Helen could feel their tension as she gently removed Heather's blanket.

The Florian general was completely nude and very pale. Helen could see that her breathing was labored and felt a tinge of sadness. She remembered when they first took custody of Heather back at the other facility. She wasn't in much better condition than right now. Helen shook off the nostalgic feeling and ordered, "Lay her out straight."

Two nurses reluctantly put their arms under Heather's body and laid her flat on her back. They were relieved when she didn't move or make a sound. The fluids needed to be gravity-fed, so Helen brought in a foam wedge and said, "Raise her head and torso so we can put this under her body."

Again, Heather was lifted and didn't move.

"Now starts the tricky part. We need to strap her down."

All three of the other team members gently circled straps around Heather's ankles and wrists and across her legs, waist, and chest. Helen felt terrible that this was happening while Heather was naked and vulnerable. When they finished, she laid the blanket back over her.

Once the straps went on, without even a twitch from Heather, Helen said, "Now we need to insert the tube."

The medical doctor who'd joined them quickly set to the task. He tilted her head back as far as possible and was startled when her eyelids slid open. He backed away and breathed, "She's waking up."

Helen examined Heather's face. "No, her eyelids aren't functioning. When she's in stasis, her body only uses the systems she needs for survival. Her eyelids aren't necessary to keep her alive."

One of the nurses whispered, "Creepy."

"Come on, we need to get this done," Helen said impatiently.

The doctor reluctantly took the lubed rubber tube and gently pushed it into Heather's nose. She never reacted despite the pressure needed to get it to her stomach. He murmured, "If I didn't feel her breathing, I'd say she was dead."

Heather twitched and gargled slightly.

The doctor jumped but quickly finished inserting the tube. He taped it in place, picked up the fluid bag, and turned to Helen. "Now what?"

"Hang the bag, but don't start the flow yet. The three of you leave, and I'll start it as I run out and bolt the door."

Heather yelled, "Boo!" and started laughing.

All four people panicked and ran out of the room. Luckily, Helen managed to start the fluid but faster than anticipated. They made it out of the door, and Helen slammed it shut behind them. The doctor and two nurses didn't stop until they were at the furthest level, but Helen stayed in the second, observing their prisoner.

Helen looked on curiously as Heather continued to laugh but didn't struggle against her restraints. As a matter of fact, she seemed to relax.

Heather sighed and said, "I was awake the whole time, you know. If I had moved, y'all wouldn't have finished, and I would still be wishing for death." She yelled, "Hey, doc! You did an excellent job with the tube. Sorry I scared you!"

Heather's humor faded, and Helen watched her face darken. The Florian general turned her haunting eyes to the glass and seemed to be looking directly at them.

Mallory asked Helen, "Do you think she can take the energy from a living being yet?"

"I know Johnson and Patterson were going to test that, but they never did it for us. Why do you ask?"

"Because that's literally a look that can kill."

CHAPTER 30
ALL THE SHITTY TIMING IN THE WORLD

When Heather destroyed the car on the Strip, Rygone could finally detect the EIP's location on Earth. The team, including Tristen Black, was on board the gunner in record time, and Renee was able to load the coordinates into the guidance system immediately. Unfortunately, the lack of appropriate testing resulted in a simple miscalculation. The Jump Drive was boosted for the physical size of the gunner, but not the displacement. The displacement was still based on the largest DREX fighter. So, when they Jumped, the location setting was off. Renee and Oscar knew this happened with all DREX, but they were in such a hurry that a straightforward error was the difference between rescuing Dia and losing her again.

Their calculations would've had them landing inside Earth's atmosphere within ten Earth miles of the EIP's detected location. But because of the displacement, they ended up on the wrong side of Earth's moon. Not even close to being in the atmosphere. Renee and James realized immediately what had happened, and she kept her head. They had to recalculate not only based on the location zone but the difference in the displacement.

It took four Earth minutes to make the adjustment. They Jumped to the exact location of the original detection. Renee had them cloaked, and they arrived close to the ground amidst absolute pandemonium.

The entire team saw Dia. Dominic and Troy confirmed that the suit she was wearing was what they saw in their dreams.

She was lying on the ground next to an injured human. Another group of humans was running toward her, and as they went to grab the unconscious Dia, Dominic yelled, "Captain, do I have permission to fire?"

Renee froze; her head was spinning.

"Captain!"

Renee yelled, "Cloaked fire, the vehicles only!"

Dominic set a target lock on seven military vehicles, and Troy yelled, "No! Do not shoot!"

Renee turned to him with fire in her eyes and growled, "You are not the—"

Troy pointed to the display. "Look! Attacking them for Dia makes us no better than the Coronians. And it could interfere with finding her later. She can't go anywhere far!"

Renee sneered. "Retract order to fire, Colonel." She turned to Troy and said, "You better be right, Doctor."

"Captain, two humans are looking after the dead man close to the general," James said.

"Grab them," Renee ordered. "Maybe they'll know something."

Unbeknownst to the panicked citizens on the ground, another alien warship flew directly over and sometimes through them. The only evidence was a swirling wind that was easily explained away.

James expertly pulled the huge craft alongside the two bewildered humans, who seemed to have no idea where the sudden blast of wind was coming from. They were within Dominic's reach through the open bay door. The hysteria outside would cover the fact that two people instantly disappeared from the street, right next to Dr. Carl Johnson's dead body.

Troy grabbed the girl and Dominic the boy. They injected them with a sedative, instantly rendering the two humans unconscious.

They carried their victims into the holding cell and laid them on the floor. Renee moved the ship out of the city to an area not far away to regroup.

Dominic and Tristen stayed by the cell while the rest of the team gathered on the bridge. They all watched the two humans begin to stir. The girl sat up, scanning her surroundings in shock. When her eyes fell on Dominic, her face filled with dread, and she screamed at the top of her lungs. Her shriek woke the boy, and he snapped up quickly. He embraced the girl, and they moved to the corner of the cell. He held her as she sobbed.

Dominic activated his coms and said to the bridge, "I'll watch them for a little while and try to figure out what the hell we're going to do next."

Renee sat with her arms crossed and grunted. "Dr. Harlow, a word."

Troy followed Renee to a small office close to the bridge. She grabbed his collar and snarled, "You are *not* a military officer, Doctor. I don't care what mission we are on or what orders we are carrying out. You will *never* undermine my authority again. Are we clear?"

"Renee, I didn't—" Troy started to say.

"Right, Troy, you didn't *think*!" She sighed and continued, "I know you mean well, but sit back and observe. You're the co-pilot, not the commander. I need your head in the game for when we find her, not how we find her."

"You're right. I'm sorry. However, I'm still glad you held fire."

Renee let go of his collar and said, "Help me get the displacement bullshit fixed so the next time we Jump, we land in the right spot."

"Yes, Captain."

***

Dominic stared at the humans, enjoying intimidating them. The boy's eyes were fixed on him. His gaze was full of fear but curiosity as well. *Little man wants to know who we are.*

With a meek voice, Tristen asked Dominic, "Do you need me to do anything?"

Dominic looked him up and down with curiosity. "Why did Troy bring you again?"

"I worked with him exclusively on the EIP. He thought I might be able to help find it."

Dominic didn't buy it, but extra help finding Dia wasn't a bad thing. He turned back to the humans. "Get them some water."

Tristen went off to the galley, and Dominic began assessing their captives. The girl was still sobbing, but she said something to the boy. It was the first time he had heard either of them speak, and of course, he didn't understand their language.

James was running the English language through their translation software, hoping to have it deciphered within the hour. Both of their languages could then be loaded onto translation disks. Each person would carry a disk; when they spoke to each other, they would automatically translate the opposite language. It would be cumbersome at first, but they'd be able to communicate.

Tristen returned with two cups of water and put them on the tray inside the cell door.

Dominic said, "Let's see what they do."

CHAPTER 31
ARE WE SAFE OR SCREWED?

B rody swore he had to be in a nightmare. He was pressed into the corner of what looked like a holding cell. Two of the walls were clear, and he could see into an incomprehensible open space.

Penny was pushed up to him as tight as possible, and even if she wanted him to, he would refuse to let her go. She was all he had left in this world, and he would protect her to his dying breath. She kept her face pressed into his shoulder, quietly sobbing. She whispered, "Is he still staring at us?"

"Yes, and the other one keeps stopping to stare as well."

The tall man grunted at Brody, and he immediately looked away.

Penny started to say, "What are—"

Brody shushed her as the tall—not tall, *gigantic*… man? How the fuck would he know?—came walking toward the glass door. He was well over seven feet tall with long, unruly, dark hair and a scruffy beard. His eyes were an insane light gray and scary as hell. He was wearing what looked like a uniform, a black jacket with red trim, and it had what Brody assumed was a name tag written in some sort of script that resembled a mix between Chinese and Arabic. Brody could tell there was an emblem on his collar, but his hair hid it. They both looked exactly like humans, so maybe they were from a different country with a super-advanced alien spaceship.

The smaller one came over again. He looked less menacing, except for the same weird brown eyes as Heather. What was with aliens having scary eyes? He was maybe five-ten, had black wavy hair, and wore a black jacket with no markings and tight slacks with tall black boots.

He carried two cups, opened a small door, and set them on the tray. He closed the door, and both aliens stared at Brody and Penny, obviously waiting for them to take the drinks.

Brody was frozen. *Do I get it, drink it, and wait to die? Do I not get it, offend them, and they shoot me? Both have some kind of gun. Do I get it, drink it, realize it's water, and feel better?*

Brody took the chance of not being fried with some sort of blaster and said to Penny, "Sit up a little, sweetie. They offered us something to drink, and I don't want to offend that big guy."

She grabbed his arm. "No! Please don't."

"Just a second, Penny," Brody said as he kissed her forehead.

He slowly stood and walked to the tray. He stared the tall man in the eyes and picked up a cup. He examined the contents, brought it to his nose, and quickly sniffed. It sure seemed like water. He looked back at the super scary tall man, whose gaze had not changed, and took a sip. He then nodded at the two aliens, grabbed the other cup, and took it back to Penny. He was now waiting to die a horrible death from some alien poison.

Brody sat back on the floor and gave Penny her cup. "It's just water. We shouldn't provoke them."

Penny was parched and took a sip. "This is excellent water," she said, surprised.

Dominic turned to Tristen. "Stay here and keep an eye on them. I need to find out what we're going to do."

Tristen nodded, sat in a chair outside the cell, and watched the two humans, who looked almost exactly like Florians, sip glacier water. He figured if he was going to get them water, it should be the best. Hopefully, they didn't swell up and die from it.

***

Troy watched the two humans on a monitor on the bridge. *Do you know Dia? Do you know where she is? Can you help us find her?* he thought desperately.

Dominic clamped his hand down hard on Troy's shoulder and said, "They seem pretty harmless. Hopefully, they aren't worthless."

Troy nodded. "Yeah."

"So, what's with the kid? Diego, right?"

Troy cleared his throat and said, "Yes, Diego. He worked in Oscar and I's lab on the EIP for years. I guess every little bit helps."

"Uh huh. It does," Dominic said, slightly suspiciously.

Troy hid his growing concern about Dominic finding out who Tristen really was. He might not seem like it, but Dominic was highly intelligent and would figure them out sooner or later. But he wasn't about to let his son out of his sight, and he damn sure wasn't going to stay on Rygone while the team went after Dia. Maybe the extra help would be good.

James said over the ship coms, "Everyone, please come to the bridge. The translation disks are ready."

***

Brody heard the alien voice overhead, and the little man walked away. Penny asked, "What's happening?"

"Not sure. I hope it's good."

"Me too," She placed her head on his shoulder and whispered, "Carl…"

He rested his face on her head and choked back tears. "I know, sweetie. But you know what?"

"Hmm?"

"These people didn't kill him. Our own did."

***

Renee passed out the disks to the team and took two extra. She said, "Dominic, please move them to the galley. I want to talk to them in a less intimidating space. It's not like they can hurt us." She glanced at Tristen and said, "Well, maybe you."

Everyone other than Troy thought Tristen was Hanner-Florian.

She continued, "Troy, James, hang back. I don't want them to see everyone just yet. I'll wait at the table."

They all went their separate ways as Renee sat down at the head of the galley table. Troy and James went to the bridge to watch the meeting on the monitor, and Dominic and Tristen returned to the cell.

Brody watched as the same two men opened the door. The tall man waved for them to come with him, and Penny froze. Brody took her hand and said, "It's okay. I think we're okay."

She gazed at him with concern, and he saw all her trust being put into his hands at that moment. *God, please don't let me let her down.*

They got up, Penny holding onto Brody's arm, and slowly walked to the door. Dominic held it open and walked out in front with the smaller man behind them. Brody was amazed at the ship. Nothing on Earth could even begin to compare with this technology. He wanted to tear it apart and play with every piece.

They walked into what looked like a galley or a kitchen. At the head of the table was the most beautiful and intimidating woman he had ever laid eyes on. She looked like she'd stepped straight out of a Japanese manga. She had straight black hair pulled into an elaborate bun, and her cat-like eyes were even bigger than Heather's. She wore smokey black eye makeup and dark purple lip color. Her smooth skin was almost pure white and flawless. Her uniform was the same as the tall man's, but the trim was white, and there was some sort of rank on her shoulders. The insignia on her collar looked like a mountain lion with swords crossed beneath it.

She gestured with her hand for them to sit. They both sat down, and she placed small yellow circles on the table in front of them. She gazed at them for a moment, then said something in her native language. The yellow disk in front of her flashed blue and a pleasant female voice said, "Hello."

Penny gasped, and Brody jumped. He hesitantly said, "Hello."

His disk flashed red, and presumably said whatever hello was back to them.

The anime queen said, "My name is High Colonel Renee Conner. I'm the captain of this DREX gunner from the planet Rygone, here on a mission to rescue the commanding general of our army, General Dia Harlow."

She gestured toward the tall man and said, "This is High Colonel Dominic Strom of the Rygone Security Force and Diego Keller, our technology specialist."

Brody gazed at the three of them, knowing there had to be more. He cleared his throat. "Uh, my name is Brody Patterson. I'm also a tech expert, and this is Penny Singleton. I'm, um, sorry, but we don't know a General Dia Harlow."

Renee blinked slowly and let them stew for a moment. "The woman who destroyed that battlecruiser *is* General Harlow. You went to the spot she was taken from; do you know that woman?"

Brody swallowed hard, and Penny squeezed his hand. He choked, "Yeah, we know her. She's a member of our team."

"Where is she?"

While fighting back tears, Penny said, "If we knew, we would tell you, I swear. We weren't with the psychopath who kidnaped her and killed Carl!"

"Who is Carl?" Dominic asked. It was strange to hear the male voice from the translator.

"The dead man on the ground. He was our leader and was murdered trying to help Heather," Brody said mournfully.

"Who is Heather?" Renee asked.

"I guess to you, she's General Harlow," Brody explained, "but to us, she's Heather Stone, or when she's working, Flashpoint."

Dominic turned away, ruffling his hair in frustration. Penny gasped. "She has that same mark on her neck!"

Dominic ran his hand over his birthmark. He said, "All of our kind have them."

When Renee showed hers, Penny didn't expect to recognize it, but she couldn't think of from where. "Why is yours different?"

"We inherit them from our fathers," Dominic explained. "Dia is my sister."

Brody asked Tristen, "What does yours look like?"

Tristen showed his blank neck and said, "I don't have a mark. Only full Florians do."

Penny utterly forgot her fear and was about to ask about their species's history when a new voice asked, "Who took her?"

Penny and Brody watched the newcomer walk into the room. They didn't need an introduction to know exactly who he was. Penny asked, "Are you Troy?"

He gasped and asked, "How do you know that?" It was odd how the translators couldn't express their feelings.

"Well, Heather would occasionally have vivid dreams. And most of them were about someone who she described looking just like you."

Troy stared at the girl. She was pretty, with smooth, dark skin and light brown eyes. He asked quietly, "What did she dream exactly?"

"The one I remember most was of you at the beach, sitting on a bench, and she tried to ask who you were, but you said, 'It's too early' and left. Strange, but it was just a dream. The girl has weird dreams."

Troy inquired, "What did the beach look like?"

"She said the water was crystal clear, and the sand was white as snow, I think."

Renee looked at Troy, and he whispered, "Kalow 9."

"Did she ever say anything else about where she came from?" Renee asked.

Brody shook his head. "All she had were a few dreams. Oh, and her rings."

Troy visibly tensed. "What rings?"

"Two stone rings with gold and silver threads through them. They were beautiful, but who knows what happened to them— *oh my God!*" Everyone startled as Brody stood up and exclaimed, "That's what started the attack in the Venetian! It had to do with her rings!"

"Brody, what the hell are you talking about?" Penny asked, confused. "Her rings were in the room."

The Florians listened intently as the humans worked through the story.

Brody said, "When we were in the casino together, she saw this drop-dead gorgeous blonde chick. The one on the Strip getting arrested, remember?" Brody pointed at Troy. "She talked about you! And the blonde somehow had Heather's rings! So, I kid you not, Heather lashed out a rope of flame, grabbed her by the arm, and yanked the bitch toward her. She pulled the rings off that chick's hand, said, 'I'm not like you,' and *threw her across the casino into the sportsbook*! It was crazy!" He cleared his throat and sat back down. "Sorry, I got a little bit excited."

Dominic asked eagerly, "Did Dia recognize her? The blonde chicken?"

Brody ignored the chicken mistranslation. "No, I don't think so. But who knows, Heather had just shoved me under a roulette table for safety."

Troy and Tristen's eyes met from across the room. *Veronica*, Troy thought.

Penny said, "Come to think of it, when I returned to the room for the suit, I went to get her rings out of the suitcase, but they weren't there. Maybe she had them on her."

"Did she ever wear them?" Troy asked.

"All the time; Brody had to practically pry them off for this mission," Penny said.

Renee stood up. "We need to start a search for her. We need your help," she said.

"Of course. She means a lot to us too," Brody said. "I know where we can get the best start. How do you put coordinates into this thing?"

CHAPTER 32
SHE ISN'T GOING TO COOPERATE

"This bag is empty. Who's brave enough to come take this tube out of my nose? I promise I won't hurt you. Unless it's Mallory."

Helen said, "Heather, threatening us won't improve your situation."

Heather shook her head. "I just want someone to take the tube out. I'm sure I can figure it out myself, though."

She pulled on the wrist restraint hard and broke the braided wire. She carefully grabbed the tube, pulled it out, and threw it on the floor. She settled back on the wedge and said, "Much better."

"How did she do that?" Mallory asked, shocked.

"I can hear you, cocksucker! Whoever put that buckle on didn't tighten it very well, probably because they were scared shitless. I just pulled on it. No extra power, just physics."

Just the word physics brought Carl back into her thoughts. He rarely worked in his chosen science at the mansion, but when Brody needed help, Carl was always there to assist brilliantly. She couldn't get different memories of his face out of her mind. When they first met and he'd been so irritated with her. When he angrily realized how much she had learned from the tablet. His concern when he watched her recover in the warehouse. When he laughed, watching her enjoy French fries for the first time. His warm smile when she marveled at the fish in the fountain at the mansion. The feel of his arms around her and the roughness of his beard on her face. The sensual press of his body when they were in the alcove. The look of confusion and pain as the life drained from his eyes in the middle of the street.

He didn't deserve to die like that, and no matter what had to happen, Mallory would pay.

She pulled the blanket over her head and began to cry quietly. Since arriving on Earth, she had been cared for in the highest and lowest ways. The humiliation of being back on display for the world to see was almost more than she could take. She reached out for feelers but couldn't find anything. Mallory had learned a lot after Kentucky, and her cell was well insulated. If she were going to make a break for it, she would have to wait until the door opened.

"I have to pee."

"You'll have to hold it, Heather," Helen said.

Heather pulled the blanket off her head and yelled angrily, "Hold it for what? For one of you assholes to get over your fear and help me? Holy shit! Or is that another thing you want to put on display for the world? The alien lady having to piss on the floor for all to see?"

Helen turned to Mallory. "She has a point. If you ever want to get through to her, you'll need to start small."

He crossed his arms again and said as he walked out of the room, "Let her piss herself."

Helen gasped and turned back to Heather, who was laughing again. "I heard him. I wasn't expecting anything different. Be the go-between, Helen. Get me a bucket."

Helen was genuinely starting to feel like a go-between. She walked through the door, taking her back into the first level. She asked quietly, "Do you really have to go to the bathroom, Heather?"

Heather didn't have a snide comment or sarcastic remark. "Did you know he was going to kill Carl?"

"I suspected he would take out anyone in his way, including Carl and his team. I admit I didn't think it would happen as it did."

"I loved him, Helen."

Helen sighed. "I figured as much."

"So, Helen, I want you to think about something. When I escape, not *if* I escape, but *when*, how would it make you feel if I snapped Mallory's neck in front of you and let you watch him die? I know you love him; it was all over your face in Kentucky, and I didn't even know what the hell I was back then."

"That's not who you are, Heather. You know that."

"That's not who I *was*. I have no ill will toward anyone else in this facility, not even you, but I will kill Mallory if I can. He changed the game."

"Nothing I say will bring Carl back—" Helen said desperately.

"Then don't say anything. Get me the bucket."

CHAPTER 33
MANSION SWEET MANSION

Brody worked with James to get the coordinates for the mansion loaded into the gunner. He asked, "How long will the flight take? I bet this baby is fast!"

James gazed at Brody with confused wonder and asked, "This isn't a baby. Is it?"

"Never mind, it's an English figure of speech. I need to stop using those."

Veronica was now permanently the hot chicken.

James said, "The gunner is fast as you say, but we're going to Jump."

"Jump?" Brody asked inquisitively.

James slid his fingers down the flight controls. The ship jerked gently, and Brody nearly passed out when he saw they were in the field at the garden's edge. He choked out, "You literally dematerialized and rematerialized that quickly? How?"

James smiled warmly at his new human friend. "It isn't what you said. We moved through space. Just faster than any other being has ever gone—that we know of."

Brody laughed slightly. "Holy shit, you guys are cool as fuck!"

"Cold as wh—"

Brody shook his head. "Never mind." He returned to the galley and said, "We're here."

"No way, that's not funny, Brody," Penny scolded.

He pointed to a monitor that showed the gunner sitting at the edge of the field, looking over the garden toward the curved room. All she could say was, "Wow."

Troy asked, "Where are we?"

"We're home. Come on," Penny said.

The two humans and their new friends walked out of the ship. This was the first time the Florians set foot on Earth, so they were curious about their surroundings. It was nighttime, and a storm was approaching. Brody gazed down the field and stopped. He said quietly to Penny, "She would be out here right now."

"Why?" Dominic asked.

Brody pointed toward the storm and explained, "She learned how powerful she really was by working with thunderstorms. It was beautiful and frightening."

"She worked with storms? What do you mean?" Troy asked with a hint of tension in his voice.

"She could absorb and manipulate the energy, not just the lightning, but the thundercloud, wind, even the rain. That's why Brody nicknamed her Flashpoint," Penny said. "I'm sure all of this sounds strange to you. But we also don't have a Jumping spaceship."

Renee laughed. "True." She turned toward the house and said, "So you live here? With how many others?"

"I'm not sure if Roger even lived here since we never saw him, so with Heather and Carl gone, I suppose it's just the two of us," Brody said sadly.

Dominic looked at him strangely and asked, "You two people in this large of a dwelling? Even four of you are incredible."

"Yeah, Roger kept us in the lap of luxury."

Just then, a flash of lightning streaked across the sky above them, and thunder quickly followed. Penny said, "Let's get inside. It'll be much more comfortable, and we can tell each other what we know about her."

Renee turned to the gunner and powered down the ship with her communicator. It went silent and disappeared.

Brody was still beside himself about the ship. "That's so amazing. I can't even imagine creating technology like that."

"Our brother Oscar designed and built these ships. He's pretty much built all of our army and air corps technology and equipment. He's a brilliant man."

"I can imagine. I'd like to meet him someday."

Dominic smiled. "If all goes well with finding Dia, you just might."

Penny authenticated her identity on the door scanner, and they went into the curved room. The lights came on automatically, and Dominic exclaimed, "Wait, I know this place." He slowly scanned the room. "This is where I dreamt about her. Where she was in that crazy green suit."

Troy nodded. "Makes sense."

Penny programmed the lights on the wall between the curved room and the kitchen, and the whole bottom floor of the mansion came to life. The Florians weren't strangers to opulence. Some very wealthy and influential Rygonains lived well in Baltica North and South, but only four people living in such luxury was criminal where they were from. Of course, it could be criminal on Earth as well.

Penny said, "Uh, well, are you guys hungry or thirsty? We can make some food because Brody and I haven't eaten in, like, I don't know how long."

The Florians were initially skeptical, but appreciated their attempt at hospitality. "That sounds nice. Thank you," Renee said.

"Here, we should all sit in the curved room. Other than the garden and the porch, this was Heather's favorite place," Brody said.

What each side was calling her was making them all feel awkward. As it was, neither one was willing to let her go. Luckily, Penny was the best bet to help the situation resolve itself.

Brody and the Florians sat at the table, and Dominic started looking around, amazed at the room's architecture. He said, "You're impressed by our ship, but this dwelling is incredible."

"Roger, our benefactor, is very wealthy. This is his house, and he provides all of our funding for research and development."

Troy, who was comparing the dwelling's extravagance to places he used to live on Rygone, asked, "Where is this benefactor?"

"He was in Vegas with us, and we got separated." Brody said sadly, "I'm not sure if he made it out. I hope so."

Penny came in with a tray of glasses and a pitcher of iced tea. She said, "Here's my favorite drink. I hope you like it. Brody, can you help me in the kitchen for a moment?"

Brody got up and followed her into the kitchen. She said, "Help me get the sandwiches out there. Some have meat, and some are vegan because who knows what they eat."

"Heather eats meat like it's going out of style. I'm sure it'll be okay, Penny."

She shrugged. "I don't want to offend them, Brody. They're wearing guns and have a ship that could destroy this house without a second thought. Also, we should call Heather Dia."

"Why?"

"It'll make them feel like we care about their feelings too. Because we do care, right?"

"Of course!" He sighed. "I'll try to remember."

"Good, now get the sandwiches. I'll get the plates and the cookies."

"The ones Dia made?"

"Good job, Brody, and yes."

The humans took the food into the curved room to find their guests doing different things. Dominic was up, admiring the room. Tristen and Troy were dismantling the drying flower arrangement in the middle of the table, looking for anything medicinal. Renee had her head on the table, trying to go to sleep. James was sitting quietly, sipping his iced tea.

Penny nervously set down the tray of food and passed out plates. She said, "Uh, these are sandwiches with vegetables, and some have turkey. I'm not sure what you're all comfortable eating."

They all studied the sandwiches curiously. Dominic was the first to pick one up. He took a huge bite, chewed a few times, looked at Penny, and mumbled, *"Boda."*

She assumed that meant something good as the others each took a sandwich and began eating. Penny was starving, so she took one as well. "Oh," she said, "and these are cookies. Dia made them the other day."

Troy glanced down at the baked goods, secretly shocked. He took a cookie and asked, "Did she make these a lot?"

Penny nodded and swallowed her bite of a turkey sandwich. "She loves to bake. These cookies are her favorite to make."

Troy gave the cookie a longing glance. "She loved to bake at home, too. She used to make a malson fruit cake that was delicious." He took a small bite and smiled. "Not bad."

Dominic slammed his hand on Troy's shoulder and said, "Did you think it wouldn't be, brother-in-law?"

Brody thought, *Brother-in-law?*

"So, do you mind if I ask how you each know Dia?" Penny asked.

Renee said, "She's my best friend. We've worked together since my time in the Academy."

"I only met her a few times, but she was never unnoticed," Tristen said.

"Big brother," Dominic said, "but you know that."

James said, "Her favorite student." Renee laughed.

"I'm her husband." Troy said. "A terrible event caused Dia and I to become separated, and she landed here. I was taken captive by the aliens that attacked Las Vegas. They're known as the Coronians. The blonde woman you spoke of is a traitor to our people and stole my rings while I was her prisoner. I hope Dia has them all, as they are the key to getting her memory back."

Brody and Penny stared at the tall, thin man with dark hair and brown eyes.

Well, the dreams make sense now, Brody thought.

Dominic clapped his hands and said, "Well, that pretty much tells you why we're here! Plus, you know how powerful she is. The Coronians sending one battlecruiser here is just a test. I'm sure they know what she did to that ship by now; there'll be more. But Earth is not the only planet in their sights."

Troy said, so quietly the translator even missed a few of his words, "Dia is a weapon. She wasn't supposed to be, but the Coronians have been our enemies for hundreds of years and are slowly meeting the challenge of taking Rygone by force. I developed the EIP to be bound to someone else, *anyone* else, but it never worked. Dia was in the wrong place at the wrong time, yet she can wield it like none other. Our world needs her, as does yours. As do many others."

"She's amazing," Brody said. "Her work with our technology has made her even more incredible." He cleared his throat and continued, "And dangerous. We were still working on several issues."

A large flash of lightning and crash of thunder startled them all. It was very late, and they were all tired. Penny said, "I believe this is a crucial conversation to continue after some sleep. The storms will be hitting one after another tonight, so we would be remiss not to have you stay in the house. There's plenty of room for everyone."

Renee stood up and began to say, "Thank you, but we—"

Another lightning bolt hit right next to the gunner, and an alarm went off on Renee's communicator. She said, "This storm is strong. It's interfering with our cloaking program. I'm nervous about that."

"This house is what we call a black site. Our technology all over the planet and satellites above cannot penetrate the interference surrounding the property. This area looks like a grove of trees on a map," Brody said.

Dominic said to Renee, "The gunner is fine. I think we should stay here. These storms seem very powerful, not like the ones on Rygone."

Renee glanced out of the window and watched more lightning illuminate the garden. She nodded. "Okay, we'll stay here."

Penny beamed. "Great! We can go upstairs and show you to your rooms."

Tristen covered his translator and said to James, "She's very kind and eager to please."

James nodded. "Yes, and lovely."

The Florians followed the humans upstairs, and Brody showed Dominic the rooms in his and Carl's hall, pointing out the available bedrooms.

Dominic turned to Renee and said, "Finally, some privacy!"

Renee laughed, followed him into a room, and closed the door. Brody scoffed in surprise and said, "Uh, okay." He turned to Tristen, James, and Troy and said, "Take your pick." He side-eyed Renee and Dominic's door. "There's another hall with rooms down there as well."

Tristen asked, "Why so many rooms for so few people?"

"This house was meant for more people to live here, but to keep Heath—Dia safe, it was only us," Penny said.

The three Florians awkwardly walked toward the rooms in the hall. Penny asked Troy, "Uh, Troy. Can I show you something?"

He studied her warily for a moment and said, "Yes."

She was surprised by how different he was from Heather. Quiet and reserved, very refined. He walked beside her with his hands behind his back. As they got farther away from the rest of the group, she began to feel intimidated. Not that he would hurt her, but that he was so perfect. He was uncommonly handsome. His proportions were perfect, and his voice, presence, and demeanor were utterly unnatural. The others, including Heather, were definitely more advanced and sophisticated than humans, but Troy seemed superior to his own kind.

They came to the end of the hall and stopped in front of the double doors that led into Heather's room. She had etched her birthmark into the door, and Penny watched as Troy just stared at the symbol. She said, "This is her room. I didn't know if you wanted to look around or stay in here or, you know, whatever." She was becoming more nervous around him.

She continued, "If you don't want to, there are many other empty rooms." She pointed at her door and said, "Uh, that's my room, if you need me."

He turned his gaze to her, and Penny could swear she saw his eyes darken. He said very softly, "Thank you."

She smiled nervously and said, "Good night."
Penny hurried away, leaving Troy in the hall alone.

***

Troy sighed and slowly opened the door just as lightning flashed, casting bright light throughout the room from the skylight above. It scared him, but he went in anyway. He gazed around the vast space in awe. *This one room is twice the size of our apartment.*

He found a switch on the wall and turned on the lights. The room was filled with a warm glow that showed how well the humans cared for his wife. He walked around, looking at the art, and opened a dresser drawer. Inside, he found her nightshirts and shorts made of delicate fabric. He went into the bathroom and grinned at the towels thrown in the corner on the floor. *Old habits die hard, even when she doesn't know who she is.*

There was a brush and lip gloss on the counter by the sink. Troy picked up the makeup and spun it in his fingers as he walked back into the room. He slowly went to the bed and took a deep breath. *Do I want to stay here?*

He ran his hand over the smooth comforter, turned around, and sat down. Across the room, there was a glass door behind a curtain. *I wonder what's through that door.*

He turned his eyes to the skylight as another flash of light filled the space. The rain was pounding on the glass, and he couldn't believe how beautiful it all was. He looked down and gazed at her pillows for a long while. He reluctantly reached out, placed his hand on the cushion, and felt a lump growing in his throat. He sighed, laid his head down, and closed his eyes. He could smell her shampoo on the fabric, and even though it wasn't the kata orchid brand she loved back home, it confirmed that she was close but still not with him. Troy became consumed by his sadness and guilt and cried himself to sleep.

CHAPTER 34
BREAKFAST AND SURGERY

A few hours later, Penny got up to start making breakfast and saw the door to Heather's room was cracked open, and the light was on. She peeked in and saw Troy lying on his wife's bed. At that moment, she was hit by the uneasiness that could result from him learning how close Heather and Carl had become. Heather didn't remember Troy, and Penny felt she would've never become close to Carl if she had, as incredibly decent as she seemed. But she was so lonely, and he had become so enamored by her that it was a natural progression. Penny knew Heather and Carl never slept together but did come close on a few occasions. Sadly, Carl's death could make this a more straightforward truth to tolerate. She felt slightly ashamed about her reaction to him being beyond perfect. He was curled up in the fetal position, cuddling his wife's pillow, probably feeling the utter pain of her loss. She realized that, whatever he was, he had feelings just like the rest of humanity.

She gently closed the door, made her way downstairs, and looked through the kitchen for what she thought aliens would eat. She tried to think about what Heather liked. She never complained about any food and was a garbage disposal. Penny decided on pancakes, eggs, bacon, orange juice, and of course, coffee.

She heard footsteps behind her and thought it might be Brody but nearly dropped the eggs when she saw it was Roger.

She ran around the island and embraced him. She exclaimed, "Roger! I'm so glad you made it." She realized he wasn't alone and was shocked to see that he was with the hotel's valets. "What happened to you?"

Penny could see that Roger wasn't himself. "We barely made it out of there, but luckily, the plane was still at the airport, so we came here for now. How did you get here, Penny? I heard you scream, but you and Brody were gone when I made it to Carl. We searched as long as we could for you."

A voice from behind said in Rygonian, which Roger understood without the need for of a translator disk, "We brought them here."

Roger spun around and saw Renee and Dominic standing behind him. He immediately recognized Dominic Strom, a Florian almost as powerful as his sister. He said back in Rygonian, "Oh my, how did you know where we were?!"

Dominic asked with suspicion, "How do you know our language? Who are you?"

Roger swallowed hard, but before he could say anything, Troy came into the room and began examining Peter and Frank, both of whom were injured. He asked, "Are you the Dailings from the attack in Las Vegas?"

Peter didn't know Rygonian, so Roger answered, "Yes. We all are, Dr. Harlow."

By then, the rest of the Florians and Brody had joined them in the kitchen. Troy said to Roger, "I can treat their injuries in our ship's med bay." He turned to Tristan and continued, "Come with me and help."

Trying to hide his excitement, Brody asked, "May I come too?"

Troy studied the human. "I suppose, but don't touch anything," Troy said sternly.

Brody nodded sheepishly.

Troy, Tristen, Brody, Peter, and Frank walked through the curved room and into the garden. Brody watched as Troy took out his communicator and deactivated the cloaking program. The ship reappeared and once more purred to life. He was in awe.

***

Back in the kitchen, the remaining Florians were carefully scrutinizing Roger. Renee asked, "How long have you been on Earth?"

Exhausted, Roger sat at the kitchen island, resting his head in his hands. Penny set a cup of coffee in front of him and asked the rest of them, "Would you like some? Dia loves coffee."

Renee sat down as well and nodded. "Thank you."

Dominic remained standing, but James went over to Penny and quietly asked, "May I help?"

Penny was surprised but welcomed the assistance. "Sure!"

The two set to cooking, allowing Renee and Dominic to interrogate Roger.

Renee asked again, "How long have you been here? And *why* are you here?"

"Over ten years," Roger said as he sipped his coffee. "Zole is in just as much trouble as Earth and Rygone from the Coronians. We have vast resources that would help fuel their quest to control the galaxy. Our species has been searching for intelligent life to help defend us from them. Carl Johnson was my contact here on Earth, and he located Heather, or Dia, when she landed a year ago. We've been working with her to refine her powers ever since."

Dominic bristled. "You're exploiting her as well?"

Roger took another sip of his coffee. "Anyone who comes across her incredible abilities wants to exploit her. We do, the humans do, and so do the Coronians. Even Rygone; that's why she exists, right?"

Renee took a deep breath and growled, "We all have much to talk about today. But food first."

***

Back on the ship, Troy was assessing the two Dailings. Peter's injuries were straightforward, and with a few shots of different medicines and an instant healing splint on his ankle, he was good as new. But Frank had several internal injuries that Troy couldn't heal with ultrasonic cauterization.

"You need surgery, but it won't take long. I'll also need you to change into your true form."

Troy laid Frank back, and the Dailing turned into his natural form. He expected Brody to react, but the technologist had seen Frank like that in Vegas.

Troy said, "Everyone close your eyes." He glanced at Brody. "Be sure to keep them closed, please." Troy slid his finger down the primary medical equipment control panel, and a bright blue light scanned the room from top to bottom, then back up again.

"Okay, you can open your eyes."

Brody asked, "What happened?"

"The Dinal Laser sterilized the room. It's harmless to us but is programmed to kill over one million harmful pathogens," Tristen said.

The human gasped quietly, making Troy smirk slightly.

Next, Troy taped a small electrode patch to the top of Frank's hand, and immediately his vitals were observed on the monitor next to Troy's head. The patch took a blood sample and gave an analysis for infection. He then administered strong anesthesia, and Frank instantly fell into a deep sleep. He cleaned the area with a handheld Dinal Laser, then took a small instrument, like a pen, and carefully cut into the skin. A Dailing's skin was very tough, so it took a few passes with the laser pen to open his abdomen. Troy took another instrument that looked like a tiny spatula and placed it in the incision, and a view of what he was doing came up on two large monitors on either side of the table.

Troy located the two sources of internal bleeding and cauterized them quickly. Within minutes of the wounds being closed, another medicine was introduced, and Frank's body began creating new blood to replace what he had lost. The procedure took about twenty minutes, and Frank went from close to death to nearly completely healed.

As Troy finished his work, he turned to Tristen and said, "I need you to stay here with him. I want him to wake up naturally so his body continues to heal without issue. If you need me, I'll be on the bridge."

He quickly walked out of the room with his long, silent strides and disappeared.

Brody watched him go and turned back to Frank, then glanced at Tristen, who was staring blankly at the monitors. Brody asked, "So, obviously, he's a doctor."

Tristen chuckled and said, "He's *the* doctor. Dr. Harlow is the head of the Health and Science Division on Rygone. He's a brilliant physician and inventor. He developed almost every piece of equipment in this room."

Brody slowly scanned the room, admiring the incomprehensible gear. "Wow, very impressive." Quieter, he said, "I have to ask, is he always this quiet and subdued? It's almost creepy. No, it *is* creepy."

"Not always, but he's a very calculating person. And we're experiencing some unusual circumstances. He's very concerned about General Harlow."

"General Harlow. It's hard to imagine her as a general. She sits in the garden, plays with small animals, and draws designs in the sand. She loves to bake cookies and eat. She really loves to eat," Brody said.

"But when you're working on the EIP, does she have that same mentality?" The Florian asked inquisitively.

Brody thought about that, seeing as he was the one who worked with her the most. "Well, not really. She takes it very seriously unless I piss her off, then we argue for about an hour. I usually realize I'm wrong, and we fix it."

Tristen smiled. "I didn't know her well; I work for Dr. Harlow, but sometimes she would come in to visit or give him a hard time. They're both known for constantly getting on each other's nerves."

Brody glanced behind him and saw Troy sitting in Renee's captain's chair, staring into the abyss. It was difficult to imagine him giving Heather a hard time. But then again, he had only just met him, and their present situation was out of the ordinary, as Tristen had said.

Frank began to stir, and Tristen checked his vitals, satisfied that they were normal. He administered a small amount of fluid with vitamins and immune boosters, and Frank sat all the way up. Brody watched how the small amount of liquid made a massive being recover so quickly. He asked, "What's in that medicine you just gave him?"

"Uh, I know it's glacier water, *flotr*, and a few other herbs. Dr. Harlow could tell you exactly what it is."

On cue, Troy walked into the med bay and asked, "What was it you wanted to know?"

Brody said, "One of the major issues Dia has with the EIP, as I think you called it, is recovering after using it, especially when she uses the suit. If that small amount of fluid can almost immediately recover someone as robust as Frank, maybe it can help her recover immediately as well."

Troy furrowed his brow and asked, "What's the suit for anyway?"

"It's a regulatory device. Instead of always absorbing energy, releasing it, and absorbing more, the suit stores it for her. She can also accomplish what she wants to do faster and with much less power. Unfortunately, she collapses when she stops and has released all of her energy. Just like the other night."

Troy stared at the skinny, sandy-haired human in disbelief. "How did you get that to work? We tried everything."

"Thin neoprene fabric and copper wire. I can show you in my lab. I was working on a new one before shit hit the fan."

The word for shit in Rygonian didn't quite match with its English meaning. "What is shit? Why does it hit fans?" Troy asked, confused.

Brody cringed, trying not to laugh. "It's another figure of speech. I'll learn one day not to use them."

***

They all left the ship and headed back toward the house. All told, Troy performed major surgery, and both patients were completely healed in less than an hour.

Troy heard thunder in the distance as they made their way through the garden. He glanced at the menacing, dark clouds and said, "You have a lot of storms here. Isn't that dangerous?"

Brody shrugged. "It can be. But the rain is very beneficial to this area. We have a lot of farms and ranches that depend on it."

"I see. We have storms much like this, but they are very few. Our water mostly comes from lakes and glaciers in the mountains," Troy said.

"Wow! We have glaciers, but many of them are melting due to climate change."

"Climate change?"

"Yeah, between the natural progression of the planet's cooling and heating cycle and the carelessness of humans using our resources irresponsibly, the temperature of our planet is rising and melting glaciers—hell, it's creating all sorts of problems." He coughed and said, "So, can you solve that for us?"

"We don't have that problem," Tristen said.

"Figures."

They made it into the curved room just as the rain started, and Troy stopped and watched the water bounce off the glass. *She can absorb all of this. What else has she learned?* he wondered.

Penny and James were setting out breakfast as they walked in. She stared at Frank and Peter. "Wow! You look amazing! Now, let's eat."

Everyone sat at the long table, and the Florians carefully decided what they wanted to eat. Troy asked, "What would Dia eat?"

"All of it. She loved bacon the best. And bananas. Did she eat a lot at home? I mean, like *a lot*?" Brody asked.

Troy took a small bite of bacon and decided that Dia was correct; it was delicious. "It depended on her mood, but the EIP took a lot out of her, as you said earlier. She needed to replace calories to replenish her body's energy reserves."

Penny said, "Makes sense. The longer she worked, the more she would eat. She once ate an entire chicken in ten minutes."

Dominic glanced up from the sixth pancake he was eating and said, horrified, "I thought the blonde was a hot chicken?"

"Uh, not really. Chickens are birds that we eat," Penny said, trying not to laugh.

Renee gave Penny a dark look and said, "You eat birds?!"

Poor Penny was so scared that she offended them before Renee broke and laughed. "We eat birds too."

Renee's joke went a long way to breaking the tension and helping the Florians and humans bridge the gap in their existences. And of course, Dia was the common denominator.

As the group cleaned up from breakfast before going to the lab to try and find a way to locate Dia, the very quiet James spoke up and asked, "Oh, by the way, what does purple mountain majesties mean?"

CHAPTER 35
AMERICA THE BEAUTIFUL

Penny stared directly at James, making him nervous. She said, "That sounds so familiar. Where did you hear it?"

"I had a dream about a woman at the foot of my bed who said, 'I'm Helen. purple mountain majesties.' And then she disappeared."

Penny and Brody both gasped and exclaimed, "Helen!"

"Who is Helen?" Renee asked.

Penny swallowed back a lump that quickly developed in her throat. "She was our fourth team member, but she stayed with Major Jason Mallory when we broke Dia out of the first facility. Mallory is who kidnapped her and... killed Carl."

Troy said, "I'm sorry about your friend."

Dominic sighed in contemplation. "But what do the other words mean?"

Brody pulled his laptop out. "I know I've heard that before." He Googled the words and said, "Oh! It's from 'America the Beautiful'!"

"Oh yeah!" Penny cried. "I remember having to sing that song every day for weeks in elementary school. I wonder what Helen was trying to tell you, James."

He shrugged his shoulders.

Brody researched the song's history and said, "Katharine Lee Bates wrote the poem inspired by the beauty from the top of Pikes Peak."

Penny said, "Pikes Peak. Colorado? Colorado Springs, right?"

Brody kept reading. "Yeah. But why would she want us to go to Pikes Peak?"

Penny sat back, thinking for a moment. "It can't only be because of Pikes Peak. Colorado Springs is surrounded by some of the country's largest and most important military installations. Including—"

"Holy shit! Mallory took her to NORAD!" Brody exclaimed.

Roger said, "Of course, where else would you want to hide a dangerous alien with her abilities? Inside a solid granite mountain that's now a Space Force installation."

"That doesn't sound like a very easy place to stroll in and perform a daring rescue. Even for us," Dominic said.

"It isn't. Cheyenne Mountain is one of the most secure military facilities in the world," Brody said, perplexed. "You can't get in there. Period."

"Brody, you have some of the most advanced identification-creating software. Can't you just make something?" Roger asked.

"Yeah, they're going to be expecting any other life forms that would want to get their hands on Heather. And Penny and I will be on their radar because we worked with Dia, Helen, *and* Mallory. I heard a rumor that high-security government installations are testing DNA authentications. None of us would make it past that even if we had foolproof identification."

Dominic said, "Let's light them up with the Requiem Fusion Cannon."

Renee shook her head. "The threat of collateral damage is too heavy. We didn't come here to kill humans, but we will kill Coronians."

"What do you mean?" asked James.

"They're well aware of what happened to their ship the other night. You know Premier Baxelhoff has to be sending more battlecruisers as we speak. We just have to be ready when they get here, attack them, and show your planet that we mean you no harm. Then sue for Dia's release."

"Sounds great," Roger stated. "But I don't believe they'll let her go so easily. Even though we all know she made a great debut in Las Vegas, Mallory will deny her existence or that she's their captive."

Penny whispered, "Captive. I hate thinking that's what she's been the whole time."

"She was captive here?" Troy asked with a hint of concern.

Roger said, "Yes, this location is untraceable. She was kept here for her own safety. And ours."

Troy bristled with anger. "That's unfortunate, yet understandable as well. We're aware of how powerful and unstable she can be." *More than aware*, he thought.

Both the humans and his team were surprised by his disclosure. On Rygone, he and Daniel Williams were the closest to her when she tested her abilities, and now Daniel Williams was dead.

Dominic sighed and said, "Well, what're the specifics of this mountain you think she's under? Maybe there's another way we can use the gunner to get to her without hurting anything."

"Everyone, please come with me," Brody said with an uncharacteristic air of authority.

The Florians, Dailings, and Penny followed Brody into his lab. He directed them to stand around a large table. He turned on the lights, and the table lit up with maps and several physics equations, one of which Carl had been working on. Brody used a tablet to clear the screens and brought up a large aerial view of the Colorado Springs mountains.

He pointed at Cheyenne Mountain and said, "We're only assuming now, but this has to be the best place to take Heather—uh, Dia—after the events in Vegas. Las Vegas is only an hour's flight away, so I'm sure they had a plane already set to leave with her after the event. I want to know how Mallory knew to be there."

Tristen asked, "Who exactly is this Mallory you keep speaking of?"

"Before Heather landed on Earth, Dr. Johnson occasionally worked with Major Mallory because he had access to facilities around the country," Penny said. "If an event like Heath—Dia's arrival occurred, Carl could gain access to much-needed resources. Brody and I also worked with Carl on different projects, and we all just so happened to be together when she landed. Her arrival was a mess."

"How?" asked Renee.

Roger said quietly, "Bring up the footage. Let them know everything that's happened since she arrived here."

Brody opened several video files, the first being news footage of a streak of fire across the sky and an explosion where she landed. "Carl couldn't figure out at first how something with such a small mass as Dia could create such an impact, but she told us that not long before she hit the Earth, she flew through our *sun* and absorbed a tremendous amount of energy," Brody explained. "It took her all the way here and blew a hole half a mile deep into the Blue Ridge Mountain cave system. They're still trying to stabilize the area around the crater to keep it from collapsing."

Troy smiled inwardly. *She can do damage, that's for sure.*

Brody showed them videos from her captivity in Mallory's facility. The coffee escape, and the hangar collapse. There was footage of Heather in the hole with Carl and Penny when the beam was lifted, and she contorted herself back whole. Dominic laughed and said, "Ha! That reminds me of when she tried to jump across the fortieth-floor deck! She hit that sculpture hard."

"She said she slipped," Troy said.

"Yeah, that's what she told you, Troy." Renee snickered.

"So wait, all of you are this... durable?" Penny asked.

Troy chuckled. "I'm not sure how that translates, but we can't die. It takes a lot even to hurt us, but we heal very quickly."

"There have been a few times when Heather has knocked herself out pretty bad, and then she slips into a suspended state. What about that?"

"We call it survival stasis. It means our body or sensory systems are suffering from a level of pain, negative stimulus, or potential damage strong enough to shut down, sometimes even mentally. Our regulatory systems only support what's needed to stay alive, and they stay that way until the danger has passed or the pain is alleviated."

"Unfortunately, it differs for each Florian. Some will slip into stasis after stubbing a toe. Some will crash a DREX into a cave wall and be trapped for days, awake the whole time," Renee added.

"Yeah, it sucks to be you sometimes, Renee," Dominic said.

"What's a DREX?"

James answered, "That's what we call our ships. Most of them are fighters, some are destroyers and cruisers, and now we have the gunner."

Brody restarted the videos, showing their escape and a grainy shot of her interaction with Mallory in the gymnasium with the contractor. He paused the video and pointed. "He's Major Mallory. They never had a good relationship. Heather, I mean, Dia knew that his intentions for her were more nefarious than what we had in store. She put a lot of trust in us during the escape."

"She came with you willingly?" Troy asked.

Penny nodded. "Very willingly. Sometimes I felt we took advantage of her trust, but we never intended to hurt her. It's one of the reasons we never left the mansion until…"

"Until… what?"

"Let's finish the footage; we'll get to that eventually," Brody said.

Brody hacked the Venetian hotel security CCTV and found the recordings of when they checked in and left for lunch. Then a video Brody and Penny had not seen came up. It was Heather leaving a nook in the lobby, clearly very upset. Less than a minute later, Carl came out, looking confused.

Dominic asked, "Who's that? She didn't look thrilled to see him."

Penny cringed.

Brody coughed and said, "That's Carl Johnson, our team leader. The man shot on Las Vegas Boulevard."

"Did they not get along either?" Renee asked.

"That trip was only the second time she'd been out of this house since coming here. She and Carl didn't see eye to eye on many things. They must have cut away from the team, so we were spared their argument," Roger said.

Everyone accepted the explanation except Troy. He began having doubts about how Carl and Dia interacted with each other. *It doesn't matter, Troy; the man is dead. Have some respect.*

Penny turned to Roger and asked, "You were there last. Was his…"

"We didn't leave him behind. We can talk about that later."

Next, the video feed from the casino came up with the interaction between Dia and Veronica. It was just as Brody had said; she shot out the rope of green flame, grabbed Veronica's wrist, and pulled her in. It looked natural, like she didn't even have to think about manipulating the flame. Dominic asked, "Is that normal? Her ability to manipulate the energy so finely and without a second thought?"

"Oh, yes. Heather could do everything from absorb an entire thunderstorm, take apart a piece of equipment one screw at a time, or eat her dinner with a makeshift flame fork. Most of the time, it was amazing. Sometimes it was scary," Brody said.

Troy asked him, "What about living beings? Did she ever work with those?" *Please say no.*

"We tried with a mouse one time. She pulled a tiny amount of energy from one of the mouse's legs and couldn't put it back. The mouse died. She had a complete breakdown and didn't talk to any of us for a few days."

Troy nodded solemnly. *Good*, he thought.

The last video showed her throwing the Coronian ship, then collapsing as Carl ran toward her. They all saw Mallory shooting Carl in the back and him hitting the ground next to Heather, who was trying to respond but visibly growing weaker by the moment. The military swept in and grabbed her, leaving his body in the middle of the road. Next, they saw Penny and

Brody run toward Carl before a whirlwind blew over, and they were gone. Not long after, the Dailings arrived on the scene. They spoke for a few moments, then one of them picked up Carl's body, and they ran off.

Penny turned to Roger and began to ask, "What did—"

"Again, we can discuss that later. It's not as important as finding Heather."

Troy watched her nod with sadness in her eyes. They lost a significant team member and were still working to find Dia. He was beginning to develop great respect for these humans.

Brody continued, "Now, back to the Cheyenne Mountain Complex. Since it's now a Space Force installation, it's the perfect place to take an alien like Heather." Brody stopped and put up his finger, "Okay, I have to say something. Her name is hard to change in my mind. I know she's been Dia to all of you forever, but she's always been Heather to us. I hope that doesn't anger you."

The Florians stared at Brody, taking in his heartfelt words. Renee said, "We don't really care. Just stick with Heather. The translator gets confused enough as it is."

"Cool. Anyway, Cheyenne Mountain is a *huge* bunker buried deep inside the mountain. Getting in there may be harder than even blasting away at the front door with your ship, which I would hate to do. We need to find a way to break in."

Roger said, "I'll surrender."

"No, my liege, you must not do this," Frank begged.

"She's there mostly because of me. We all thought she was up to this task, which she was, but circumstances put her where she is. If Space Force has an alien under their mountain, they'll love getting another."

Renee studied Roger and said, "What if we can't get you out with her?"

"I'm willing to make that sacrifice. Heather's existence is much more important than mine."

The room went quiet for a moment, then Dominic said, "Awesome, let's get going. The longer we wait, the more time they'll have to hide her elsewhere."

Renee straightened up and asked, "Let me see the terrain around this mountain. I want to land the ship as close to the front as possible." She asked Brody seriously, "You talked about the DNA issue. How will we get in with that problem?"

Brody closely studied the front entrance to the complex and saw that there was no way to sneak in. "You said your ship is completely invisible when cloaked, right? That someone could walk right through it and not know."

She nodded.

"Well, that ramp is wide and long enough for you to land. If you wait until they open the doors for Roger, you can do what we don't want to do."

"Fire at them."

He nodded.

Renee looked back at the map and scanned her eyes over the entire area surrounding Cheyenne Mountain. She sighed. "I would hate to do that on a whim. What if she isn't there, and we kill innocent people? That's something we don't want to do."

Dominic yelled, "*To a fault!*"

Renee sneered at him and said, "But we need to find her. It's only a matter of time before the Coronians send more ships here, and there's only so much we can do to help."

Brody studied Renee thoughtfully. "Can I ask you something?"

"Sure."

"Why're you so willing to help us? Roger told us that Rygone didn't even know Earth existed before all of this."

Renee squared her shoulders and crossed her arms. "The Coronians have been known to us for thousands of years. About three hundred years ago, they began harassing other systems in our quadrant. They seemed dumb and incapable at first, but they started getting smarter and crueler as time passed. At first, they left us alone and attacked at random, but many victims were allies of Rygone, so they knew we would come to their aid. Over time, they would infiltrate their enemies' leaders and use spies to get damaging information to bring whole civilizations to their knees. They started to mess with us occasionally, but they were easy to deal with at first. Troy is also an inventor and began working on the EIP that Dia is bound with. The Coronians kept an eye on his progress and made their move about fifty years ago. They started an arduous war and led a surprise attack, nearly destroying our civilization. After that, Troy worked much harder on his invention but couldn't get it to work until an accident bound it to Dia. After other circumstances occurred, she found her way to you. I believe you intended to exploit her abilities, which anyone would. But seeing the way she interacted with you and your friends in those videos made me believe you can be trusted. So, you asked why we're so willing to help? If my commanding general and best friend is willing to trust you, so are we. Even if she doesn't know who she is. Yet."

Brody thought about Heather baby-talking the fish in the fountains and drawing in the sand. But she would also argue with him fiercely, like a commander. Heather was even more incredible than he'd realized. He stared at Renee with wide eyes. "Wow, that's amazing. I hope we don't let you down."

"Now what?" she asked.

Brody returned to the maps and said, "We can land outside the front door. Be there as a contingency plan. Roger, there are parks and public facilities close to the first level of security gates. It'll be easy for you to get there. How're you going to present yourself?"

"I'm just going to walk up to the gate, like myself. Hopefully, they won't shoot me."

"They probably will," Dominic said. "That's why I'm going to go with you. I'm sure your government knows every aspect of my sister. A Florian just like the one in their captivity and a twelve-foot Dailing? That'll be fun to watch."

Penny asked, "But what if you can't get out?"

"Oh, we'll get out. And if Dia is there, she will too. I can't believe I didn't think of this earlier."

"If we want to make this peaceful, you can't be armed," Renee said.

"That's where the big fancy ship outside the door comes in, right?" Dominic asked his beloved.

"Right."

Troy asked, "And the rest of us?"

Dominic said, "If they don't just hand her over, which they won't, I might need backup. Stay on the ship until you see all hell break loose, then figure something out."

"It's better than nothing, I guess," James said.

Quietly, Renee instructed, "Get ready to go. We only have a few more days before the Coronians arrive, and we need her out before then."

CHAPTER 36
LOST

Her place in the equation of the impending galactic war had all but been erased. The only thing Veronica could do now was try to get back to safety. She looked just like any other destitute person who survived the attack that night, but now she needed to find a way to regroup.

I need to get a message to Tristen.

Even though she was pretty sure her son had turned double agent and was now working with his own kind, she believed he would still help her. She could prove she was no longer helping the Coronians. *For now, at least.*

Did he reveal himself to Troy? Is he working with his father?

Veronica always dreamt of the day she could bring Troy to her world, and the three could live together as a family. But he never saw her as more than just a—what did he call it?—a means to an end. She fell deeply in love with him, and he never showed any for her.

Since Florian women could choose when and if they *laval*, she made sure she never did because she didn't want to have his child—at that time, at least. Veronica had been mortified when she found out she was pregnant, so she fled to Darsayn. Tristen was raised with a small faction of Coronian loyalists from other systems, including Rygone. He was taught about the ways of Rygone, the Kalow system, and many others. How their ideas and shortsightedness led to the suffering of their people. But even Veronica knew those systems' leaders didn't always bring on the misery. Baxelhoff destroyed many planets and societies to exploit the resources he needed to keep taking more control of the galaxy.

Veronica had a small pocket inside her blouse that held money, IDs, and, hopefully, her saving grace. She and Tristen carried analog communicators that could send a rudimentary signal to the other, showing only a location, so they could reach each other in emergencies. Even when Tristen wasn't working to his full potential, it had never failed before. She took it out and powered on the small device, about the size of a lipstick tube, and a small light illuminated on the top. All she could do now was wait.

***

Tristen was on the bridge of the gunner with James when he felt a buzzing in his jacket's inside pocket.

No! It can't be!

Attempting to hide his alarm, he said, "I'll be right back."

James nodded and kept working on the flight computer to ensure the displacement issue was fixed.

He went into the galley and took the device out of his pocket. It listed the location as Earth and gave the coordinates. He verified the area and knew exactly where it was. Las Vegas, Nevada.

At least she wasn't on the ship. Would she have survived?

The only way to respond was to ping the other way, sending her his location, and he refused to do that. He swore to himself and sought out Troy.

His father was working on his datapad in the med bay when Tristen walked in. He asked quietly, "Troy, can we talk in private?"

Troy continued to work without looking at his son. "What is it?"

"We need to talk in private."

Troy paused, then gently placed his datapad on the table. "Let's go into the garden. Fewer ears."

The two men walked out of the ship into the warm afternoon breeze. The weather had cleared up, and the sky was blue. Troy admired the deep shade and said, "Not much different from Rygone. Earth is a beautiful planet."

Tristen nodded but said nothing.

They sat down on a bench by Dia's glass sand drawings. "So, what does she want?"

"All this gives me is a location, not a message. Usually, I would then activate mine and send her my location. Then we would get back to each other within a day on regular channels."

"Where is she?"

"Still in Las Vegas. I'm glad…"

"Glad for what?"

"That she wasn't on the ship."

Troy just nodded. He looked down at the drawings, marveled at Dia's creations, then realized something. He pointed and said, "Look at her designs. What do you see?"

Tristen studied the intricate glass designs. "Whoa, that's the Harlow birthmark!"

Troy pointed at a triangle with a wagon wheel in the center and said, "There's Conner."

In fact, there were over twenty different family birthmarks drawn into the sand. "She didn't completely forget who she is," Tristen stated.

Troy smiled slightly, feeling the guilt of his actions tug at his heart. He shook it off and asked, "Why didn't you tell me you had that communicator?"

Tristen swallowed hard and said, "I had hoped she wouldn't use it. I'm sorry, but I couldn't completely abandon her. Whatever her faults, whatever she's done to you and our people, she's still my mother."

Troy looked his son hard in the face. "Your mother is a traitor. If she's caught, she'll be taken to Rygone and tried as such. If you ask this crew and me to rescue her, she'll be in a tribunal before the Chancellor himself the first chance I get. Do you understand?"

Tristen knew Troy wasn't lying. He went out on a very flimsy limb and said, "She'll implicate me as well. I'll go on trial too. And you'll be tried as an accomplice for not turning me in. Right?"

Tristen immediately regretted what he said when his father smiled at him with an alarming grin. It took him back to the night when he revealed himself and the uncharacteristically sinister presence that scared the shit out of him.

Troy spoke softly, with a deeper tone, "Is that what you want? For us all to go down together? One big happy family frozen to the edge of pain and torture in the Ice Lake? I kept you with me so that wouldn't happen. If you want all of that, I'll have Renee take us home *right fucking now!*"

Tristen backtracked, stumbling over his words. "No, no. I don't want that at all. I just—I don't know. Maybe she can be of use. Maybe she can help us stop the Coronians."

"You know her much better than I do. Tell me how you expect that to play out. Will she cooperate, use us to get to Baxelhoff, and then turn around and betray us? That's what I'm envisioning."

Tristen knew that was a very real possibility. He said, "For the past year, I haven't been giving her good information because I'd changed my opinion about what she was trying to do to Rygone. Plus, she had me working for you for so long. Standing next to my father, the man she vilified so much, made me realize that you were nothing like she said. I was torn between her love and the right course of action. She may indeed want to get back in Baxelhoff's good graces, but she might not."

Troy sat up and stretched his back and long legs. He stared thoughtfully at the birthmarks in the sand before him, knowing they were put there by the woman he loved and dearly missed. He said quietly, "Don't respond to her here. I don't want to compromise the human's black site. When we land in Colorado Springs, we'll decide only *after* we have Dia. Veronica might be your mother, but my wife is more important than any of us." He stood up. "Now, let's finish. I'm ready to get this over with."

Tristen nodded. "Agreed."

CHAPTER 37
IT'S PRETTY HERE

It was too late in the day after all of their preparations to leave for Colorado Springs. They decided to rest for the night at the mansion and make the Jump in the morning. The public facilities next to the Cheyenne Mountain Complex opened at 7:00 a.m. They planned to drop Roger and Dominic off in a grove of trees secluded enough that nobody would be suspicious of the direction they came from when they approached the gate.

For dinner, Penny made lasagna with James's help again. They hashed out precisely what the plan would be. Dominic said, "Roger and I will approach from the north and walk straight up to the gate. Both in all our glory."

As Dominic was seven and a half feet tall, he looked the least like a human of all the Florians. And since he was Dia's brother, they had the same birthmark. Brody said, "You might want to rock a man bun and low collar. They aren't going to want you to lift your hair."

"What kind of rock is a man bun?" Renee asked.

Penny laughed and said, "Brody just wants Dominic to pull his hair up."

"If they take you in, what do we do then?" James asked.

"Tristen and I figured that out," Brody said, taking out a thin wire. "What's this called again?"

"Hoiltle wire," Troy said. "It's a living thing, yet a very sensitive and conductive metal. We were able to attach a fine camera that we can run into your hair, Dominic. It sounds weird, but it won't give off enough of a signature to be detected by their scanner. Hopefully."

Dominic took the fine wire from Brody gently. "Wow, that's insane! I'll have to remember not to run my hand through my hair."

Renee said, "Once you're inside, look around as much as possible, Dom. Give us a view of the facility if you can. I'm sure she'll be in the second blast vault, according to the schematic we found. We just have to hope they take you that way. If you make it there, and she's nowhere to be seen, we'll knock on the front door with the gunner."

"Knock on the front door, huh?" Troy asked.

"Yes, Doctor, unless you have a better plan," Renee said with an edge to her voice.

Troy shook his head.

Renee sat back and studied her team's faces, including the humans and Dailings. "If we had more time to plan, none of this would be an issue. This facility is more secure than the Vault under Baltica North. If we're serious about getting Dia out of there before the Coronians return, not only here but to Rygone as well, I may have to make the tough decision to fire. Our shot will do mostly structural damage to the outer door, but there's a limited chance of collateral damage. As the mission captain, I've determined that this act will be much more beneficial now than what will happen if Dia isn't rescued."

Troy thought about how these decisions affected Dia. The dilemma of possibly sacrificing twenty to save the one. He studied Renee's stern face and knew her well enough that she wasn't making this decision lightly. Renee was trained to lead by Dia. His wife saw something in her that she didn't in the hundreds of thousands of other officers who came under her command. He thought about the first time he met Renee. A fresh flight officer, right out of the Academy. She saluted him, a civilian, on the flight deck, and he had to correct her. She had come so far since that day. He said, "Renee, we believe in you."

They all agreed. She threw Troy a grateful glance and said, "Okay, let's get some rest. We need to be up and ready to Jump at 6:30 a.m."

Everyone went off to bed soon after cleaning up from dinner. Renee wanted to check a few of the ship's systems before enjoying some privacy with Dominic in their exceptionally soft bed. When she stepped on the bridge, she saw that all systems were in hibernation mode except the med bay. There was a faint glow coming from the room, barely enough to see by. She went down, peeked around the corner, and saw Troy sitting back in one of the medical chairs with his eyes closed. He said, "Hello, Colonel Conner."

She walked in, sat on the edge of the chair next to his legs, and asked, "Is your head or heart sick, Dr. Harlow?" He opened his dark eyes, and she could see the pain he was trying to hide. She put a hand on his knee. "We're going to get her back, Troy, I promise."

"I know we are. Nobody else in the universe could do that but you and Dominic."

"Troy, there's a lot of uncertainty coming up. Trust in your love for each other."

"From what I've deduced from Penny and Brody, Dia and Carl were very close. I have no reason to fault her, yet I'm sitting here in the dark, jealous of a dead man. I can't even bring myself to stay in her room like last night." He sighed. "Renee, what the hell happened to me?"

"Honestly, I think the long centuries of the galaxy holding you and Dia to an unattainable standard caught up with you. Her too. I may as well tell you. A few days before the EIP accident, we had lunch. That weekend, she was planning to tell you she was retiring."

Troy sat up and said, "Really? Why?"

"Ever since Breger Dunes, we've all been off our game, including her. Especially her. She recovered and went back to work because everyone was pressuring her. 'General Harlow, she can survive anything.' Well, she wasn't surviving. A few days before you fled, she told me about nightmares she was having of people who died by her orders. She didn't want to be a soldier anymore."

"She wanted to be a mother."

Renee sighed and said, "Yes, that's what she wants. She'll wait for you forever, Troy. She *has* been waiting for you."

"I know. And she deserves better."

Renee grabbed the back of Troy's knee and pinched the skin hard, causing him to cry out in pain. "I better never hear you say something like that again. You aren't perfect, but neither is Dia. That's why you deserve each other." She let go of his leg and continued, "Now, stop brooding in the dark, and go to sleep. We get her back tomorrow."

Troy rubbed his leg and pouted. "You know, only you, Dominic, and Warren give me such a hard time."

"We're assholes to her too." She stood up and kissed him on the cheek, "Good night, Doctor."

Renee breezed out of the room, and Troy was again alone on the ship. The only sound was the gentle hum of the Wel Reactor. *I wonder if Dia could disable the fuel pod. Probably.*

Troy forced himself to relax and soon drifted off to sleep, dreaming of Rygone and the troubles it faced.

***

The following day, the whole team gathered at the ship, ready to go. The excitement and fear they felt were buzzing through the air, but they were prepared for the task at hand.

Roger and Dominic were going over how they would approach the gate. Brody stayed up most of the night, finishing the new suit he had been making. He perfected the recovery drink storage system and had it so that if Heather needed to replenish calories, all she had to do was drink from a hidden straw that led into a pouch on the small of her back. He filled the bag with the solution the Florians used to revive Frank, hoping it would work just as well or even better.

Finally, Renee prepped each team member on their part of the operation down to which seat they would be in on the gunner. Even though they were Jumping, which virtually never negatively affected any species, she insisted they stay strapped into their seats to prevent any potential injuries.

It was 6:30 on the nose when Renee strapped into her captain's chair on the bridge and said to Troy, "Power and auxiliary systems check."

"Auxiliary systems are ready and online. Wel is functioning at 63 percent capacity."

She said to James, "Flight and Jump controls."

"Flight and Jump systems are functioning normally and ready for departure."

To Dominic, "Weapons and cloaking systems."

"Cloaking is engaged, and all weapons except the Requiem Fusion Cannon are armed and ready."

Renee was quiet for a moment, checking her coordinates and landing site for accurate calculations. She took a deep breath. *We're coming, General.*

"Captain Ramsay, Jump."

Everyone felt the same gentle shift of the ship, and they arrived in the park alongside the most secure mountain in the world. Renee said, "Okay, we don't have much time before the gate opens. Dominic and Roger, you need to get ready."

Dominic watched as Roger changed into his true form. He said, "Whoa, I've never been close to a Dailing in true form. You guys get a bad rap for your appearance, don't you?"

"Yes, by almost everyone."

Renee opened the bay door, and the two aliens walked out into the world, ready to make their presence known. Luckily, the park was empty, so there would be no civilian interference. Roger looked up, glanced down the expansive range of tall mountains, and said, "It's pretty here."

Dominic said, "It sure is, but if we don't get going, the Coronians will change that."

Renee said to James, "Move us to the offensive position. Get us as close to the door as possible."

"Yes, Colonel."

The ship jerked again, and they were sitting outside of the Cheyenne Mountain Complex entrance tunnel. The front of the ship lined up with the outer tunnel perfectly. *If we have to fire, this tunnel may collapse*, Renee thought, concerned.

"Captain Ramsay, can you move us closer? If we fire from this location, we'll collapse the tunnel, and the escape plan will be a moot point. We have to penetrate that door without blocking their escape."

Troy said, "It could potentially cause more casualties, Colonel."

Renee sighed and said, "Yes, Doctor, I'm aware, but that blocked door could become even more of a potential confrontation. We have to take the chance."

Troy nodded, knowing she was right.

They all watched the monitors showing Dominic and Roger approaching the gate. Everyone became tense when the first guards spotted them. They were all counting on the guards to immediately point weapons at them. Renee had Dominic keep his translator, hoping it wouldn't be confiscated. Knowing what the humans were telling him to do would go a long way to keep him safe and moving in the right direction.

***

One of the terrified guards, trying to stay calm, yelled, "Stop! Stop where you are, or we will shoot!"

Dominic and Roger obeyed their commands and said nothing. More guards came running to the gate and trained all their weapons on the pair. Dominic wasn't afraid of being killed, and though he didn't know how resilient Roger was to physical attacks, the Dailing remained relaxed.

"Get on your knees! Hands behind your head! Now!"

Toward the back of the growing mob, Dominic heard one of the soldiers say, "Inform Major Mallory. Tell him there are more of them at the gate."

Major Mallory.

The leader was being mobbed by his men, wondering what they should do with the terrifying beings surrendering at their gate. Most figured Dominic was some sort of human until, in the chaos, a weapon fired and hit him in the chest. He muttered, "Damn."

In an attempt to quell hysteria, Roger said, "We mean you no harm."

Unfortunately, the fact that Roger spoke English in a quiet, calm voice was almost more than the soldiers could take. Suddenly, a man came through the crowd and stood before them, unfazed by their appearance. He was tall and thin with close-cropped gray hair. He narrowed his eyes at Dominic and said, "I knew there had to be more of you."

Dominic said quietly in Rygonian, which wasn't picked up by his translator disk, "You have my sister, and I'll stop at nothing to get her back. You have no idea whom you're dealing with."

Mallory nodded, trying to hide his growing concern. "I don't know what you said, but it doesn't matter. You'll go in but never come out. Since you're the distraction, where's your actual rescue party? They'll suffer the same fate."

"We're alone," Roger said calmly.

Mallory turned his attention to the Dailing. "We saw footage of you in Las Vegas," he said smugly. "You and your comrades were impressive warriors. I look forward to seeing what we can get you to do."

Without warning, Dominic and Roger were hit with large bolts of electricity and fell to the ground. Roger was unconscious, and Dominic groaned, trying to stand back up. Mallory said, "Hmm. I wonder if this one's like her. Hit him again."

Dominic was hit again with a higher voltage, sending him into stasis. The shock also took out the Hoiltle camera and his translation disk.

***

Renee gasped and sat up. Their team had been captured, and they were blind.

The time had come. *Do I fire now or wait?*

CHAPTER 38
THE FIRST RULE OF IMPROVISATION

Troy watched Renee's reaction to what just happened, wondering if she thought they were in serious trouble. He could tell she was concerned but not in panic mode.

James asked, "Orders, Colonel?"

"For the moment, keep our plan on target. This is a fluid situation, and the colonel is well able to handle himself."

Tristen said, concerned, "But Colonel Strom is in stasis."

"Trust me, he won't be for long," Troy said.

Dominic Strom healed and recovered the fastest of any Florian Troy had ever treated for any ailment. He was the largest Florian to ever live, and Troy and his father frequently used him for experiments. If he was willing, of course.

After they had landed, James scanned the area for any CCTV feeds and hacked into several outside the gate. They watched the feeds from those cameras as Dominic and Roger were taken through the front door, right past the gunner. It was hard to sit still and watch their teammates being taken away, but Renee trusted her instincts about Dominic. *Please be okay*, she thought desperately.

Once they were brought inside, the team lost contact with them. They waited with bated breath, watching to see if changes in the activity outside of the facility indicated an emergency within. Renee sat back and glanced at Troy, who was staring at the monitor showing the barrel's view of the forward cannons. They were only a few dozen feet from the entrance blast door, and they marveled at the people who walked through the ship on their way to work, oblivious to what was sitting there.

Brody whispered, "Can they hear us?"

James shook his head. "The ship's structural integrity remains the same, and the cloaking program hides all sound emitted from the entire craft, even the reactor."

Brody still couldn't wrap his head around such advanced technology. The laws of physics were either not the same or were understood much differently on Rygone. Maybe both. But something that intrigued him was Troy said he couldn't create a way to regulate Heather's power like Brody did with the suit. Perhaps they all had something to offer each other.

Renee sighed and said, "Watch all monitors. If there's no sign of them in six hours, we fire."

***

Dominic slowly came out of stasis and tried to survey his surroundings. He could tell he was in a glass-like box with glowing lights. They had removed his uniform jacket and strapped him to a chair, but the restraints were more substantial than anticipated. As his mind became sharper, he heard a voice say in English, "Hello."

He just looked blankly at the glass, which he couldn't see through, and was silent.

"You have the same mark on your neck as Heather Stone. Are you related?"

You're damn right we're related. She's my baby sister, and I plan to rip your head off for hurting her, motherfucker.

Dominic remained silent.

"The strong, silent type, I see. Look for yourself."

The glass wall to his right slowly cleared, and he could see into the box next to him. Dia was lying on a table. She was sleeping, but he could tell she was weak. She was wearing a thin shirt and pants with only socks. Her beautiful curly hair was matted and sweaty. Her breathing was labored, and she had her arm draped over her face, blocking the strange light. He wanted nothing more than to scream for her to wake up. To tell her that he, Troy, and Renee were there to save her, but he remained silent.

"We don't want to hurt her or you. We just need cooperation. If the beings who attacked Las Vegas return, we may need your help in defeating them."

Again, Dominic remained silent and still.

***

Roger was in a box on the other side of Heather's. He was talking, telling the humans their intentions and that Dominic didn't speak much of the language yet.

The interrogator asked, "Why are you on Earth?"

"I've been here for many years, watching the skies for the beings who attacked you the other night. They're called the Coronians, and you can rest assured they have more ships on the way."

"So, the destruction of the first ship is prompting an invasion."

"You existing and having resources they want is prompting an invasion. Las Vegas was a test, and Heather Stone was your savior. But yes, they'll be back, and that was always their intention." He glanced at his friend lying on the table in the next room on the edge of torment and continued, "Yet you torture your only chance at survival."

"She's extremely dangerous; it's necessary to keep her subdued."

"Subdued? You have her at the edge of death, but her kind cannot die. Think of it this way: how would you like to be starving and dehydrated, feeling all of the pain and physical effects, but never die? Never have that anguish alleviated? That's what you're doing to her. Miss Stone isn't just a random being who can manipulate power to her will and protect you. She's a brilliant and reasonable person. The longer you keep her caged up and tortured, the less likely you'll survive an attack by the Coronians. Hell, she might help them."

Roger wasn't lying to the humans. Everything he said was true, and he knew if they didn't change their treatment of her, she would make them pay when she got the chance.

It angered him that they were too cowardly to show themselves. He was in the room alone, tied to a chair. The good part about that was if he wanted to escape, all he needed to do was change back to his human body, and the restraints would fall away. The problem was getting out of the room, finding Dominic, and discovering a way into Heather's cell.

He observed the Florian, his friend, helplessly. He didn't think she could be so sickly. *Maybe it's a good thing Carl isn't with us anymore. He would lose his mind if he saw her like this. Of course, I'm sure Troy would as well. I wonder what they're doing out there.*

Suddenly, he saw Heather stir a bit. She turned on her side with her back away from him and raised up on her elbow. He wished he could see her face because he would've seen her curiosity at hearing a strange voice screaming through the glass.

***

The interrogator hadn't said anything to Dominic for quite some time. He stared helplessly through the glass at his sister. Her lovely face was sunken in from lack of fluids, and her skin was pale and splotchy. As he started to look away, her eyes opened. She stared blankly at the glass, but Dominic felt she maybe knew he was there. *Does she know I'm here? She doesn't even remember me, though!*

Troy had given him a very small vile of the glacier water solution before he and Roger left the ship and told him to hide it in his boot. Dominic could still feel the thin, plastic tube and knew he needed to get through that glass to reach her. Lucky for him, that bastard Major Mallory was a cocky son of a bitch and made a critical error.

***

Renee looked at the six-hour countdown on her console and saw that five hours, twenty-nine minutes, and thirty-six seconds had passed. *A half hour left. Come on, Dominic.*

***

Roger watched Heather sit up and stare at the opposite window. *She knows something's happening. Please be Dominic, and please be positive.*

***

Major Mallory walked into Dominic's cell and stood before the much larger man. He sneered and said, "You're a bit different from your friend there. I don't think you have the same powers, but you're one hell of a specimen. Do you understand me?"

Dominic nodded slightly, and Mallory continued, "What are you? Both of you?"

Dominic cleared his throat and mumbled something. Mallory stupidly leaned in and asked, "What?"

Almost in Mallory's ear, Dominic said, "We're better than you," in perfect English.

Dominic yanked his leg from the restraint, and before Mallory could react, the large Florian kicked the smaller human in the chest, slamming him against the glass of Heather's cell, which caught her attention. Dominic saw she was staring at the window. He had seen the camera in the upper corner with the power-reflecting shield earlier and, with all his might, still strapped to the chair, he kicked the Lexan, causing the shield to shift.

Heather immediately sensed the feeler reach out to her, and she absorbed the power, returning to life in mere moments. She stood in front of the glass, and Dominic yelled, "Heather, break the glass! Break it, and we—"

A barrage of soldiers descended on Dominic and tried to subdue him. He saw his precious little sister punch the six-inch-thick Lexan, shattering it like a thin sheet of ice. Much to Dominic and

Heather's displeasure, Mallory escaped the room, yelling, "Hold her down, *but do not fire!*"

Heather glanced around at the six soldiers and Dominic. He said in Rygonian, almost in tears, "Dia, it's me, Dom. Do you recognize me?"

She didn't answer but stared at the rest of the soldiers, who were scared out of their minds, and said, "As I have been saying, I have no quarrel with any of you, just Mallory. Leave."

Heather pulled in more power from sources around her, and her appearance changed. Rightfully so, the responding soldiers fled from the room to the second level, knowing not to fire. Heather bent down next to Dominic. She quickly broke away the rest of his restraints. "Stand up."

Dominic stood and said, "I know you don't remember me now, but you will. We need to go."

Heather just blinked at him, confused. *She doesn't remember our language,* he thought despairingly.

Since his translator was fried, he had to rely on the few English words he remembered. He turned and showed her his birthmark. She gasped when she saw it, reached out, and ran her fingers over his neck. He said, "Here with Roger. Must go!"

"Roger?! He made it out of Vegas? Did—"

He stopped her and exclaimed, "Talk later. Go!"

They went into the second level of rooms but she stopped and said, "No, I can't leave yet. I have unfinished business here."

Dominic sighed, frustrated, and said, "Di—Heather, no time. Must get out."

"They have something of mine that I can't leave behind."

He glanced at her left hand. *The rings; they're gone.* "Where?"

"I don't know. I've been in this glass box for what seems like days."

Dominic saw that even though she had power, she was still sickly. He reached into his boot and gave her the vial. "Drink, please."

She studied the vile warily at first, then drank the fluid. After a few moments, Dominic watched the color and vitality return to her face as her energy level grew.

They both ran out of the room together and expected to find armed resistance, but there was just one woman. Helen.

"Did the coward send you to be his mouthpiece again?"

She shook her head. She glanced at Dominic and said, "I'm Helen."

Dominic sensed tension from his sister, so he stayed close. Heather said, "We're leaving, Helen. You can make sure it's peaceful. I understand another one of my friends, Roger, is here. The three of us walk out the front door, and no shots are fired. I don't want anybody hurt."

Helen rushed up to Heather and said, "I can't help you with that, but I can with this." She took Heather's hand, put a small pouch in her palm, and closed her fingers over it. She stared the Florian general in the eye and said, "Go. Good luck to you all, and please do more for us than he ever could."

Helen turned and slammed her hands down on a large panel with two buttons. The alarm sounded, and at first, Heather was angry, but then she realized the blast doors were *opening*.

"Thank you," Dominic said.

They ran unimpeded to the end of the glass structure and evaluated their surroundings. The cavernous room was mostly empty except for the Lexan structure. Heather eyed the blast doors and said, "We need to get to them before they close, but where is Roger?"

A bank of monitors on the wall showed the CCTV feeds of all the glass rooms. Heather spotted Roger, in his alien form, as he changed to being human. She pointed. "There!"

The hallway leading to Roger's cell was locked, but Heather pulled the door open with ease. This display of power scared those inside enough to run from the two Florians, making it easy for them to get to Roger's cell. She said through the door, "Stand back, Roger."

He moved to the other side of the chair as the door flew from its hinges. He reveled in seeing her and said, "Oh, Heather, I'm so glad you're okay."

She said, "I'm relying on you two for whatever happens next."

The three sprinted from the glass enclosure to unexpected chaos.

***

When Helen opened the blast doors without authorization, it prompted a lockdown of the entire compound. All soldiers were to report to their assigned station to help locate the reason for the breach, which took them to the area of the front blast door. Heather, Dominic, and Roger were quickly surrounded by dozens of troops with weapons drawn.

Heather didn't want Roger or her new companion to get hurt, so they stopped and stood down. Of course, surrounded by his men, Mallory came up to her and said, "Dissipate your energy, Miss Stone."

"Fuck off."

Mallory bristled with anger. "Do it now. I know you don't want anyone here to get hurt."

Suddenly, Heather reached out, planted her hand against Mallory's chest, and said in a growl, "Except you. You know, Jason, we did work on drawing the energy from a living thing."

Dominic said, "Heather, please don't."

"Please don't do this," Roger breathed.

She ignored them. "I killed a mouse. It was horrifying, and I didn't recover from it for days. However, I won't have that problem with you. Open the door."

Mallory stared into her emerald green eyes and knew she wasn't bluffing. He tried to step away, but she was holding him in place.

***

When the blast doors started to open, Renee and her crew prepared to exit the ship and get their team out, but before they could leave, the doors closed again.

James said, "Now what, Colonel?"

"Our plan remains the same."

***

Helen came rushing through the crowd to the scene playing out at the Cheyenne Mountain Complex's outside door. "Heather, please! Don't do this. I know he killed Carl, but killing Mallory in this way will only leave a stain on you that you don't deserve."

Heather didn't look at her and said, "What makes you think I care?"

Mallory said, "Because that's who you are, remember? No collateral damage."

"You aren't collateral damage. You're a necessary elimination."

***

Back on the ship, Renee looked at the clock with steely determination. "Almost time. Be on your guard for my signal."

***

Dominic stepped forward and placed his hand on his sister's shoulder, squeezing it slightly. "Step aside, Heather. He isn't worth your time. But he is worth mine."

He then pushed Heather in the back just enough to make her release Mallory.

***

Major Jason Mallory would insist that he had thought through all potential scenarios of an attempted escape by their asset. Maybe she would do it herself, have help, or even be rescued by the enemy. One of the situations he thought of prompted him to have several high-powered weapons available inside the complex to deal with outside assistance.

As Heather released Mallory, he made a quick hand signal, and a loud burst of heavy gunfire erupted into the crowd. Several rounds hit Heather. They knocked her to the ground, and she looked around and saw that the tall man had been shot too. She crawled to him, and he sat up, no worse for wear. Heather scanned further and saw Roger, a loyal friend who saw her as a commodity and a savior. His face and chest were covered in blood; she hurried over to him, and he choked, "They're going to fire the Requiem Fusion Cannon! Go!"

***

Renee calmly said, "Five, four, three, two, one. Firing Fusion Cannon at 28 percent capacity."

She slid her finger up the Requiem Fusion Cannon's control panel, the gunner's Wel Reactor revved, and the ship jerked hard. Penny squeezed her eyes shut as she heard the impact and explosion.

Cheyenne Mountain probably hadn't shaken so violently since the complex was built in the 1960s. Renee's shot was perfect for maximum effectiveness and minimum damage.

The entrance door was completely gone, but much of the interior was left intact. She couldn't tell from inside the ship, but she was hopeful that there were few casualties.

Renee said, "Gear up. James, Troy, and I will go and find the team. The rest of you stay with the ship. We're cloaked again, but they obviously know we're here. Be careful."

Brody said, "But she won't recognize you. I should go with you; it should make it easier to convince her to come with us."

Troy argued, "We might not be able to protect you. You need to stay here."

***

Rubble was falling from the ceiling above, and dozens of people were running around, many injured. Heather sat next to Roger, not really knowing what had happened. Dominic, having completely recovered from being shot, grabbed her arm, and pulled her up. He watched as she drew in power from all over the room and began to glow brighter than he had ever seen. She slowly walked toward the hole that used to be the blast door, and he realized, *She thinks the ship is the enemy*!

***

Renee, Troy, and James armed themselves, opened the bay door, and stepped into the chaos. Many soldiers reeling from the blast immediately took the Florians as another threat as they appeared out of thin air. Two shot at them, and one hit Troy in the shoulder. He jerked, but more in irritation, and said in English. "I know you don't believe us, but we're only here for Heather Stone. Let us get her and leave."

Three more soldiers shot him, only pissing him off more.

Several voices started to scream to hold fire out of fear of the newcomers possibly being able to absorb energy as well. The three were able to continue easily toward the door.

Renee said in Rygonian, "Look."

All personnel cleared the tunnel as a bright green flame walked out of the hole that used to be the blast door. Troy was almost overcome with joy to see Dia until he realized she had her hand aimed at the still-cloaked ship.

CHAPTER 39
REUNITE

D ia Harlow was having a bad year.

Her memories were erased. She was propelled through space and crashed on a strange planet. She had her ups and downs with humans and made the mistake of falling in love with one. He was murdered in cold blood right in front of her, and she was taken captive by the man who did it. Now she was staring down an alien ship that nobody else could see.

She saw three more of the extraterrestrials dressed like the tall man who was now beside her. The four of them were yelling in broken English for her to stop, saying they were her family and loved her.

The chaos had come to a halt. Time seemed to stand still as the green flame left Heather's hand and flew directly toward the cloaked gunner.

Right as the flame made it to the tip of the forward cannon, Heather closed her hand, stopping the forward motion. She said very calmly, "Now that I have your attention. Why should I believe you?"

The bay door opened, and Brody came running toward her. Heather immediately retracted the flame and yelled, "Brody!"

One of the tense soldiers pointed his weapon and said to Brody, "Stop right there, or I will shoot!"

Brody stopped and immediately put his hands up, but a shot from elsewhere rang out.

Time slowed again as a single ball of green flame flew toward the young technologist. Just as it got to him, it hit the bullet aimed at his head and disintegrated.

Heather turned around, expecting to see Mallory, but it wasn't him. It was Helen.

She still had her gun aimed at Brody and said, "That was impressive, my dear. I bet I almost killed the person who taught you that."

"Drop the weapon, Helen," Heather said cooly.

"You know, I liked you when you first arrived, but I knew how dangerous you were. How your power would be irresistible to humans and others alike, and our world would never be the same. At first, Carl thought that too. He just wanted to pawn you off to Roger for a quick buck."

"You say that like it would be surprising to me, Helen. I knew it all along."

Helen stepped toward Heather, and the dozens of soldiers and Renee's team tensed. Heather put her hand up to signal not to react. Helen said, "You do that like it's instinct. Like you know how to command others, yet you sat in that mansion and learned how to play with absolute danger—and make-believe with the good doctor and his crew."

She stepped closer to Helen. "Why give me the rings?"

"Because I hope they make your life an even bigger living hell." She glanced past Heather at Troy with an extra focus to her gaze. He was standing like a statue, watching the confrontation, unbeknownst to the dangers that lay ahead.

Just then, several fighter jets flew over the mountain, and a command came over a speaker system that they would fire upon the alien invaders at the Cheyenne Mountain Complex.

Heather glared at the older-looking woman and said, "We're leaving. If they fire on this facility, it will only kill their own people."

She turned quickly and said to Dominic, "Don't make me regret this."

She ran with her brother and the rest of the team and boarded the gunner. Heather glanced around, astonished by the incredible ship, and stumbled into Troy. "Sorry."

Renee stood on the bridge and said, "Get ready for departure; decloak and make for the black site."

"Decloak?" James asked.

"Yes, they need to see us leaving so they don't destroy their own people thinking we're hiding in front of them. Once we fly a certain distance away, we can Jump."

"What if they engage us?"

"Jump before they can."

Heather sat down in a seat next to Penny, who was beside herself with happiness for Heather and grief for Roger. Heather knew the others were definitely like her. *Do they have this cursed power as well?*

She turned to Penny and whispered, "Was I right in trusting these people?"

"Yes. But I'll let them tell you why when we get home."

Heather could feel the sadness in Penny's eyes. She took Penny's hand and leaned her head back in the soft seat, wanting to rest before they reached the mansion.

"We've arrived," James said.

Renee said, "We need to keep an eye on the surrounding airspace for all craft, including drones. Who knows if they found a way to track us. We'll rotate having at least one person on duty in the gunner monitoring the area. James, you'll take the first watch."

Heather was bewildered and said, "Wait, where are we?"

Renee pointed at the monitor on the front deck, showing the path to the curved room.

"Wow," Heather breathed.

Everyone except James left the ship and began walking down the path toward the mansion. The differences between Heather and Dia were laid out perfectly before them.

She walked in the middle of the path, her Earth family on one side and Rygonian on the other. Penny was next to her, holding onto her arm, needing support from Heather. On the opposite side was Renee, a strong and proud soulmate and best friend but not soft.

Brody was quiet, eyes downcast, thinking about Roger and Carl, knowing they would soon lose Heather too.

Dominic was behind Renee, ready to defend his sister at any moment. Willing to die for her. Tristen was silent but still immensely relieved she was safe.

And then there was Troy. Ever since she had bumped into him on the ship, having no idea who he was, Troy was struggling. He knew she carried the heavy burden of her life in a small pouch in her waistband. Should he bring her memories back? Over a million years of sadness and pain? But also over a million years of happiness and love. He had his hands behind his back, eyes lowered to the ground as they entered the curved room.

Everyone was kind of milling about, not knowing what to do. Heather said, "I'd like to catch up with everyone, but it's been a long few days. I need to shower and refresh first."

Troy stopped her and said, "When you're settled in, can you please let me know? You and I need to talk."

She stared at him for a moment, not recognizing anything about him. "Well, I'll be down to speak with everyone soon."

He shook his head and said, "*We* need to talk, just you and I."

She looked around at the rest of the team, and Brody nodded. She said, "Okay, give me some time."

"Of course."

Perplexed, Heather went up the stairs to her room. As she went to get clean clothes from her dresser, she noticed her pillows were out of place. *I wonder who was in here. Probably Penny.*

Heather took off the thin garments Helen had convinced her former captors to let her have. *Why did she turn on me in the end? Why did she shoot at Brody?*

She pulled the small pouch containing her rings from the twisted waistband on the pants. She dropped them into her hand and examined the stone rings with gold and silver spun throughout. She set them on the bathroom counter and studied herself in the mirror. She was much better after whatever the vial contained, but she was still weak and tired. Her hair was a matted mess, and her skin felt like it was covered in wax. She stepped into the hot water and let it run over her body for several minutes. She thought about the day's events and felt there was more to come. She kept thinking about the tall man.

Who is he? Do I know him? Why is his voice familiar?

Release all of the power inside you.

Heather's eyes shot open when she realized his voice was the same. She finished her shower quickly and was about to get dressed when there was a knock at her door.

She threw on her robe, wondering if she should answer, but they all knew where she was. She said quietly, "Come in."

The door opened, and thankfully, it was Penny. She hurried over to Heather and gave her a huge hug. Penny was flustered and said, "I had to have a moment with you before everything changes."

Heather gave her a confused look and asked, "What do you mean?"

"Well, I don't know what's going to happen with all of us. Especially after you talk to Troy."

"Troy is the tall thin one?"

"Yes, he's Troy."

"Is there something you need to tell me, Penny? Has he done some—"

Penny shook her head and said, "No, not at all. He's a very nice man, from what I know."

"Then what?"

"He's—"

There was another knock on the door, and Troy peeked his head in and said, "Oh, I'm sorry."

He turned to leave, and Penny said, "No, I was just leaving!" She breezed out of the room past Troy, leaving him with his wife.

She cleared her throat and said, "Come in. You wanted to talk to me."

He walked in slowly. Troy had an autobiographical memory, therefore had picked up more English than any other team member so far. He decided it would go a long way to keep Heather at ease before restoring her memories as Dia. "I didn't want to seem pushy, but certain circumstances require you and me to speak first."

Heather began drying her hair with a towel. When she was done, she tossed it toward the bathroom door. He turned away, trying not to laugh. She asked, "Why was that funny?"

He stifled his laughter and said, "It'll be easier to understand after we talk."

She sat on the bed, close to the pillows, and gestured for him to sit. "Have a seat and tell me why it's so imperative that we talk, Troy."

He nervously folded his elegant hands in his lap and asked, "Do you still have the two rings?"

"Yes, I do. Why?" She didn't tell him about having four.

"This may be hard to understand at first, but those are your wedding rings."

Which means the other two could be his. Are he and I married?

She sat for a moment, thinking, stood up, and went back into the bathroom. Troy watched as she returned and sat closer to him, nearly driving him mad. She opened her hand and said, "So, are these yours as well?"

He studied the four small stone rings for a moment, then reached out and asked, "May I?"

She gave a slight nod, and he took them all from her hand. He put the two large rings on his left hand's index and middle fingers, then gently slid the other two onto her fingers. She watched his face and his deliberate but emotional movements. He looked at her with tears in his eyes. "Now, this might be hard to imagine, but the memories of who you were before landing on Earth are contained in these rings. I can give all of that back to you right now if you want."

Heather studied his handsome face; he had the most beautiful dark eyes. They were full of beauty and soul but also pain and sadness. Before she realized what she was doing, she reached out and touched his cheek, causing him to shiver. She pulled her hand back and said, "I'm sorry. I sh—"

He stopped her and lifted her hand back up to his face. "You have no idea how long I've waited to feel your touch."

Tears filled her eyes, and she began sobbing. Troy didn't know how to react, and she choked out, "I didn't know. I didn't know you were out there."

He leaned forward and said, "I know, Dia. It's going to be okay."

"Dia... that's my actual name?"

"Yes, your name is Dia Harlow."

She still had tears rolling down her cheeks. She looked back at Troy and his gorgeous dark eyes and said, "I'm ready to remember."

Troy took a deep breath and grasped her left hand, aligning their fingers so all the rings touched. "Are you sure?"

She nodded, and he closed their fingers together. Heather's head began to swim faster and faster until everything went white.

A few moments later, she heard Troy's voice calling to her. "Dia... Dia, can you hear me?"

She opened her eyes, stared at the skylight for a moment, and then glanced around the room. Troy was sitting on the edge of the bed, watching her intently. She was surprised his color-changing lenses weren't set to brown.

She stared at him for nearly a minute, then sat up. Her head hurt from a lifetime of memories being dropped on her all at once. Finally, he asked, "Are you okay, my love?"

Her eyes widened.

My love.

"I'm sorry, love."

The thought of Veronica in the Venetian and the memory of Maria Granby flashed through her mind simultaneously.

She said, "I need a moment."

"Of course. Whatever you need."

Dia stood up, and Troy watched her walk out onto the porch. He desperately wanted to follow her but knew this was a delicate moment, and she needed space. However, only a few minutes later, he heard her call his name.

He stood up, walked out onto the enclosed porch, and was amazed by its beauty. The plants, fountains, and art were beautiful. He slowly approached a corner and saw her standing in front of a large fountain with small, brightly colored fish. She was quiet as she fed the little fish. As the food flakes hit the water, they would all rush to the spot, gorge themselves, and wait for more to be dropped in. "They were starving. Poor things haven't been fed in days."

Dia was never one to care much for pets or animals. She didn't hate them. She just never had the time to invest in their well-being. Seeing her take care of those little fish made it clear that she didn't lose the newest part of her, Heather's part.

She said, "I didn't know about you, Troy. I had no memory of anything and was incredibly lonely here. I didn't fit in, and the only solace I had was the attention I received from this team. Carl most of all."

Troy tried to interrupt her, but she stopped him and said, "Please let me finish before you say anything."

He remained quiet and listened to her sad and painful explanation of the confusing and complicated relationship between her and Carl.

"He was kind but rough around the edges. Yet he always ensured I was cared for, even in the beginning when we didn't see eye to eye. After coming to this place, I felt even more alone—such a big house to get lost in. There was nobody like me who understood my crippling solitude. But he and I slowly grew close. It helped me accept my new life." She looked Troy directly in the eyes and continued, "Although the opportunity presented itself, we never slept together. Not that it wasn't a desire, but something always came up, especially fear."

Troy nodded. He understood that very well. Then, he reluctantly asked, "Did you love him?"

She choked back tears and said, "In a strange way, yes. Part of me still does, mostly because he was there for me for more than just a romantic connection. No matter the purposes I was brought to this facility, Carl always protected me." She took his hand. "I'm so sorry, Troy. I wouldn't have let that happen if I knew you were out there, even if we never found each other."

"I know," he said quietly. "I understand the circumstances of your situation. I know you had no idea what your life was like, and you needed to feel a connection to something or someone. I would be remiss to fault you for that, but I also can't help but be sad and jealous, and I never even met Carl. I also understand the fear you both felt. You were lonely long before arriving here."

Troy had never wanted Dia to be bound with the EIP because of fear of the unknown. After it happened, he became nervous about being close to her. Affection was redefined between them, and they were only intimate in ways that didn't require physical contact. He'd even told her how he felt, and she'd said she understood, but he had known it was breaking her heart.

She asked, changing the subject, "What happened to you after we ejected?"

"I crash-landed right into the middle of the Coronian attack. They took me prisoner, and I was held on Darsayn by Baxelhoff and Maria Granby."

"Of course. Because why wouldn't this whole situation be dangerous to the galaxy and personally hurtful to us both, right?" She shook her head. "I'm sorry, go on."

"She tried for months to get me to duplicate the results of what happened to you, but of course, I couldn't. She and her hoarde tortured me constantly, physically and mentally. But I promise you; I never touched her. She even offered to improve my situation if I slept with her, but I refused, I swear."

Dia heard the desperation in his voice. "Like you, I understand the circumstances were out of your control." She studied his face and knew he was telling the truth. He had come clean about his affair with Maria many years ago, and Dia had made her peace with it and forgave him.

They both fell quiet for a few moments. Troy became intrigued by a curious grin that crossed Dia's lips. She asked, "Are you still scared of me, Troy?"

Surprised by the question, he breathed, "No."

"Prove it."

CHAPTER 40
IT'S BEEN A WHILE

It was probably good that Penny joined James on the ship rather than go to her room a couple of doors down. Troy and Dia didn't hold back on reacquainting themselves and didn't care who might hear.

The dynamic changed when Dia told Troy to prove he was no longer scared of her. He grabbed her hand and pulled her toward him, kissing her lips hard. She responded just as enthusiastically by pushing him against the wall, unzipping and removing his outer jacket. Troy lifted her by the waist, and she wrapped her legs around him as he carried her back into the room, tossing her gently onto the bed. She smiled wickedly and said, "You can do better than that."

Dia watched excitedly as he continued taking his clothes off. He grabbed her by the ankle, pulled her to him, and said, "What's with the robe?"

She laughed and quickly tore her robe off as he fell onto the bed, wrapping her in his arms. Within a moment, they were consumed by each other. Nothing else in the galaxy mattered except how they made each other feel. Troy buried his face in Dia's neck and reveled in hearing her cries of passion. She dug her fingertips into his back and responded to his every move. It wasn't long before Troy could no longer hold back and bit down on her shoulder as he climaxed. She squealed and laughed. "Ow!"

He kissed up her neck to her lips and said, "You make it sound like that was the worst we've ever done."

"Well, that was relatively mild, I admit, but it's been a while. Speaking of it being a wh—"

"Stop! Not fair."

"It's okay, Troy, we can st—"

He put his hand over her mouth and laughed. "We're both a little off our game." She licked his hand playfully, and he pulled it away. He said teasingly, "Difficult woman."

"You like me difficult; I keep your perfect mind and soul in turmoil for a reason."

Troy rolled onto his back, and Dia moved to rest her head on his shoulder. She draped her leg over his, and they both lay quiet for a while. Finally, he said, "Yes, I need and love your difficult turmoil. We all do."

She traced her fingers in circles on his chest and said, "Part of being Heather was not knowing there were so many people out there with an unrealistic expectation of what they want us to achieve. Our lives together seem like they have always been spent trying to solve everyone else's problems, even if we have no idea what to do."

"Renee told me that you wanted to retire."

Dia was quiet for a moment, wishing her best friend had kept that to herself. "I do. I think this Coronian war will be my last. And then it'll be your lot in life to get this damn thing out of me. I don't want it."

Troy pulled her close and whispered, "I'm so sorry, Dia. I've said it a million times, but you weren't supposed to be the one it bonded to."

"You know, I've had this ability for over a year, and it's a part of me now. But I don't think it's just a source of energy to be manipulated by the user. I think it has a mind of its own as well."

"What do you mean?"

"When we first started working with it back on Rygone, it was hard to control, not just because I didn't know what I was doing, but sometimes it would fight me and change what I was doing to manipulate something until I did what *it* wanted. Does that make sense?"

Yes, it does, he thought.

"I think so. How is it now?" he asked.

"I don't have to work to make it do what I want. I barely have to think of where I want the power to go or which feeler I want to pull, and it does what I ask. It's like I work in tandem with it now. Sometimes it's scary."

Troy ran his hand through her thick curls and looked up at the skylight just as a bright flash of lightning lit up the sky. "Brody and Penny said you have a special relationship with thunderstorms."

"It didn't start that way, did it? But yes, for some reason, thunderstorms are greatly attracted to the EIP." She sat up on an elbow and asked, "Did you check on Daniel's body, just to make sure he really died?"

He nodded. "I didn't want to hide anything anymore, so I showed his body to your father, Dom, Renee, Oscar, and my father. Dad even did an autopsy; it turns out Florian skin doesn't stay impenetrable after death."

Dia swore and said, "And I'm going back. This whole thing started because we were fleeing from what this weapon can do, and we'll be right back where we started."

"No, not right back where we started. Being here, training without knowing what it could do back home, gave you the advantage of learning much more control. Yes, it's a calculated risk, but the Coronians are a much bigger problem than we first imagined."

She nodded and kissed his chest.

"There's something else we need to talk about—"

She slid on top of him and pressed her body against his. He moaned quietly, and she said, "Can it wait? We aren't going to have much time for ourselves soon."

She pushed against him harder, and he gasped. He gazed into her eyes and nodded. Dia sat up and slowly started making love to him. Troy watched her move and took in the sight of her body when the lightning lit up the room. At first, the storm being close made Troy nervous. But soon, he was consumed by the euphoric sensations of the moment. As she came close, she leaned forward and kissed him deeply. He sat up with her, and she pressed her forehead to his and said, breathlessly, "Never lose me again, Troy Harlow. Please."

He wrapped his arms around her tight and rolled them over, quickly hitting his peak. "I won't. I will never leave you behind, my love."

They both lay together, panting, as the storm moved away outside. Just before Dia drifted to sleep, she heard him say, "Nobody will ever take you from me either."

CHAPTER 41
THEY'LL BE HERE SOON

The following day, Penny decided to go downstairs to get something for breakfast ready. She was surprised to find the kitchen light was on, and she smelled coffee, Heather's favorite brew.

As Penny went down the hall, she saw someone sitting at the island, sipping coffee and reading a tablet. Her hair was pulled back into an elaborate braid. She wore her makeup much like Renee, only her eyes were drawn more cat-like. She wore a black uniform like the others, but hers was trimmed with gold. There was a lone gold star on each shoulder, and she had the Florian Army insignia on her collar. She said, "Good morning, Penny."

Penny swallowed hard and said, "Good morning... Dia?"

Brigadier General Dia Harlow turned to Penny Singleton, PA, and said, "Yes, Penny, this is who I was before coming here. And this is who I am going forward, but I'll take my experience as Heather and time with you, Brody, Carl, and even Roger with me."

Penny burst into tears, and Dia walked over and hugged her dear friend. "Just because we're at this point doesn't mean I don't still need you. To help us fight the enemy—and as a friend."

Penny said through her sobs, "I know. It's just hard to see how much you changed overnight. I fear you'll lose Heather."

"I'll *never* lose what being Heather Stone taught me. Good and bad."

Penny stepped back and looked her up and down. "I thought Renee looked like a badass, but wow! Is it fun being a general?"

"No, it's not fun at all. But I'm good at it."

A voice came from the hall. "Don't let her fool you. She's *the* general. She just hates to admit it." Dominic ran up and embraced his little sister and said, "Sis! Good to have you back!"

"Holy shit, you're hot!" Brody exclaimed, walking into the kitchen. "I mean, you were hot before, but now you're general hot. That's hotter."

"You're so weird, Brody, you know that?" Dia said.

"Yes, but you love me for it, remember?"

The rest of the team slowly made it into the kitchen and were excited to see that Dia had returned. But everyone was also happy to notice that Heather wasn't all gone as well.

Penny opened the fridge and asked, "Where did the rest of the pork loin from last night go?"

Dia said, "I hadn't eaten in days. Don't judge me."

The last one to come into the kitchen was Troy. When he woke up, he was alone in that vast room. He came down to find his wife reminiscing and joking with their team. He stood back and watched. He loved seeing her there, knowing that she was back as Dia. Back to being the woman he loved and who loved him. But there was a darkness over her that Heather didn't have, the weight of distant, damaging memories. *I hope I've made the right decision. Now I have to tell them about Veronica.*

The team reminisced and told stories about Rygone and Earth. It was fun to learn and enjoy each other's company as they all knew their work would be complicated and serious from now on.

After breakfast, Troy said to Dia, "I need to tell you something."

"Let's go to the garden," she said.

The morning was bright, and the air was warm and sweet. Troy said, "This reminds me a lot of the meadows in the foothills of the Raltains. We haven't been there in a long time."

"Maybe we'll go once this is all over."

He linked his hands behind his back. "Maybe."

"You want to talk to me about her, don't you? I know she's on Earth. She had your rings."

Troy stopped, cleared his throat, and said, "Yes, she—she's still here and in distress. I think we should help her."

Dia glared at the side of his face. He wouldn't look at her.

He continued, "As of yesterday, she was still in Las Vegas. I think we should rescue her. If the Coronians abandoned her, she might be useful to us."

Dia sighed. "How do you know this?"

Troy cast his eyes to the designs in the sand and said quietly, "Maria is Tristen's mother. She pinged a communicator he has, and it gave us her location."

Dia's throat tightened, and her mind began to race. She said, "Why is he with you? Why did you bring him? Did you know he was her son?"

Troy finally glanced at his wife's face. She was trying to hide the panic in her mind as she processed what the truth could be.

She breathed, "Is he…"

Troy knew that hiding the truth wasn't going to help anything. He nodded. "Yes, Dia, Tristen is my son. But I promise I had no idea until right before we came!"

Dia sat down hard on one of the benches and stared into the garden. "Sit down."

Troy joined her, wondering what she was going to say.

"Troy, um, I've always had a bad feeling about this. Something always nagged me that she was pregnant when she disappeared right after the war." She turned to him and continued, "You and I need to address this situation, but not now."

"Are you sure? I mean—"

"No, not now. The safety of our kind and our allies is much more important, and you're right, she might be the key to achieving that."

Troy didn't know what to think, but he did agree. This revelation could ruin their marriage, but they had to set the issue aside and concentrate on saving their galaxy for now.

He sighed and said, "Well, let's go talk to him, then."

***

Troy and Dia went to Tristen and had him ping his mother's communicator. It almost immediately came back with her exact location. Dia and Troy also went to Renee and informed her about Tristen being Veronica's son, but left the part about Troy out for now. As they all went out to the gunner together, Dia said excitedly, "I can't wait to fly this bad boy."

Renee said, "You don't even know how yet!"

Dia shot her a glance. "When has that stopped me before?"

When they got onto the ship, Renee went to the bridge, but Dia took the pilot's chair. She looked over at Troy and laughed. "Remember the last time we were together in a DREX? Fun times, right?" She clapped and rubbed her hands together. "Let's go somewhere special for a quick test flight."

Dia locked in several different coordinates for flight and Jump commands.

"Flight and Jump controls," Renee said after taking her place in the captain's seat.

Dia said, "Flight and Jump are functioning and ready for departure."

"Power and auxiliary systems check."

Troy said, "Auxiliary systems are ready and online. Wel is functioning at 59 percent capacity."

"Put the reactor to 80 percent, Doctor," Dia ordered.

Troy wanted to protest but knew better.

Renee studied the location coordinates and said, "That isn't Las Vegas, General."

"Nope, Vegas is our second stop. Strap in tight."

Troy thought, *Ohhh, shit.*

***

Dia engaged the Jump, and the gunner appeared, cloaked, directly over the North Rim of the Grand Canyon. She whispered, "Let's see how he handles, shall we?"

Dia dove straight down into the narrow canyon and eased the ship level before hitting the Colorado River. She maneuvered the much larger DREX gunner between canyon walls and up and down gorges. Troy was always nervous when flying with her, but Dia was the greatest pilot in the Florian Army Air Corps. Renee was smiling and cheering. Tristen watched the monitors intently, impressed by her ability to move the ship through such tight and dangerous places. Finally, she buzzed the South Rim tourist center on their way out to fly to Vegas. The thousands of humans marveling at the canyon's beauty felt a sudden blast of wind as the gunner took off toward the desert outside the city.

Renee clapped and said, "So? What do you think, General?"

Dia thought for a moment and said, "He handles like a garbage barge compared to a fighter, but still very impressive. Now I want to play with the Requiem Fusion Cannon."

CHAPTER 42
RENEE IS TAKING BETS

The coordinates Tristen received for Veronica's location led to a restaurant in Henderson, a suburb of Las Vegas.

Dia put the gunner down in an empty lot across the street. Tristen had removed the wig and changed his eye color back to their purplish blue. He also borrowed clothes from Brody. He asked, "Who's going with me?"

Troy said nothing, Dia laughed, and Renee said with a sinister grin, "I am."

Tristen had hoped it would have been his father, but he figured Renee would go because the world knew Dia's face too well. Unfortunately, Renee would also be the most likely to return Veronica to Rygone for a possible trial and Ice Lake sentence.

He nodded reluctantly, and they got ready to go. Dia gave each of them one of Brody's earpieces and said, "We'll be able to hear you both if any issues arise. Use as much English as you can. These people aren't going to be happy hearing an unknown language after what happened here."

They put in the listening devices and tested that they worked. Once ready, they both stepped out of the ship. Renee wore one of

Dia's sundresses and said, "This is so strange. You really wore this?"

"Hush and get to work," Dia said.

Tristen was scared to death. Renee said, "Relax, kid. It's your mom. Why're you so nervous?"

Because Dia can kill Florians and knows I'm Troy and Veronica's son. We should all be nervous.

"I just am. She hasn't been to Rygone in a long time. This could be interesting."

Renee and Tristen made it across the street as Dia and Troy watched them from the ship. "You go in first. I'll wait out here for a few moments, then join you," Renee said.

"Uh, why?"

"Just do as you're told," said Troy over the earpiece.

Tristen took a deep breath and walked through the door. He immediately spotted Veronica sitting at a booth facing him, and she got up, nearly running to see her son. When she reached him, Veronica embraced Tristen so tight he grunted. She said, "Oh, sorry, darling. Come sit. I'm so happy to see you."

You won't be for long.

Tristen purposely sat on the side of the booth facing the door. Veronica didn't even notice the change. She said, "I'm so glad you're here, baby; we need to find a way off this planet immediately."

Veronica didn't notice Renee walk up. The high colonel said, "You have one. How's the face?"

The tall, blonde Florian shot a terrified look at Renee and started to panic. Renee pushed Veronica hard against the window and sat down next to her. "We have a ship, your son is part of our team now, and you have no choice but to comply."

"Your—your team?" Veronica asked warily.

"Yes, our team. I'm sure you can only imagine who's a part of it. Now, get up calmly and leave without causing a scene. My ship is across the street, and we'll be on our way back to Rygone soon, where we'll decide what to do with you."

Veronica, full of dread, started to cry and said, "But I'll be—"

Tristen breathed desperately, "Mother, we need to go now."

***

On the ship, Dia and Troy listened carefully to the conversation. Dia asked, "Will she implicate him?"

"Probably."

Dia glanced at her husband, but he kept his eyes on the monitor, not wanting to address the topic with her. She didn't care. "What will you do?"

He sighed and side-eyed her. "I'll let her. Just because Tristen said he had a change of heart and tried to stop sending accurate information to Darsayn doesn't mean he hadn't been for many years. What do you think I should do?"

"I think you should've turned him in back home. Bringing him here for protection because he's your son makes you an accomplice, Troy."

Troy knew this and would face those consequences when he returned to Rygone. Hopefully, much of the circumstances surrounding his new family would be set aside until the war was over, but Chancellor Strom was unpredictable. "What would you have done if it was Tomas, Ed, or Victoria?" he asked.

"That's not fair, Troy. I was married to King Ben, and we raised our children together."

Troy's lenses were set to their usual brown, but Dia could see the anger flash across his face that darkened his eyes almost to black. "Do you not think I would've raised him just as carefully if I knew he existed?" he growled.

"Not my problem, Troy." Dia saw the others returning to the ship as their discussion was about to take a more heated tone. She flashed Troy a heated glance and said, "We need to shelve this."

Troy lowered the ramp, and Tristen, Renee, and Veronica stepped onto the ship. She looked at them all, but her eyes fixed on Dia in horror.

Dia slowly walked up to her. "Welcome aboard, Maria. Have a seat."

Renee laughed. "I knew she would be nice! You owe me a dollar, kid."

CHAPTER 43
INFORMATION

The team was only gone for a few hours before they returned to the mansion with Veronica, or as they all knew her, Maria Granby. Dominic was waiting for them in the curved room when they came out of the ship and walked toward the house. Dia and Renee walked on either side of Maria, proud even as she cast her eyes down, defeated. Troy and Tristen walked behind the three women, interested in how the rest of the team would react to their valuable prisoner.

Dominic said to Renee as they walked in, "I dig the dress. You need more."

She shot him a dirty look, then asked Dia, "What now?"

"We need to go into the lab and get as much information about the Coronians as possible to plan what comes next."

Maria said quietly, "I don't—"

"You know enough. Let's go." Renee grabbed her arm and led her to Brody's lab.

Penny and Brody happened to be with James and the two Dailings in the lab. James didn't react, but the humans gasped, and

Brody said, "The last time I saw you, you were heading toward the sportsbook."

Maria sneered at him, and Renee said, "That's enough. We need information before anything else, and I don't want bad attitudes." She pointed to a stool at the head of the lighted table. "Sit."

Maria sat down and stared blankly at the wall ahead of her. The rest of the team gathered around the table. Dia stood on Maria's right with Tristen on the left. Dia said, "Okay, Maria, we'll jump right into this. I know we're closer and closer to an attack by your friends. I need to know everything about their ship and weapons capabilities. How did they get here the other night?"

Maria took a deep breath, weighing her odds. The Coronians' torture would be much worse than spending a lifetime in the Ice Lake, and perhaps she could negotiate for a lesser sentence if she helped them. She glanced at her son and saw the desperation on his face. He no longer showed the desire to please her by helping the enemy. She glanced at Troy at the other end of the table and could tell he knew who Tristen was. Her dream of them being a happy family was over. She wondered if Dia Harlow would make a good stepmother. Of course she would. She raised three Kalowian royals, including one of their greatest kings.

"The ship from the other night was a Grigo destroyer outfitted with a second-generation Jump Drive. It was stolen off a Rygonian destroyer several years ago. They only recently got it to work on one of their ships."

Dia didn't react to the knowledge that the Coronians had somehow made a Jump Drive work on their ship, even though she was deeply concerned. "How many more Jump-enabled ships do they have?"

"None that I know of. Major Baryly was very proud of his ship, and it seemed obvious that his was the only one."

"What about the next generation? I know they have many ships, and their technology has advanced greatly since taking over other civilizations' systems. How many do they have that can make it here or to Rygone? How long would it take them to travel?" Dia demanded.

Maria had to think about that. She wasn't sure how long the days were on this planet compared to the other targets. She said, "I would guess they have about a hundred large destroyers capable of getting to this planet in ten or eleven days. That gives you six or seven before they're here."

"How many planets are they targeting?" Renee asked. "Will they target them all at once?"

That was something Maria didn't know. "Honestly, I'm not sure how many planets they want to attack. I know it has to be several, but I don't think they have the resources to attack all at once and be successful. I assume it would be Rygone—including Nexxus—the Kalow system, and Earth." She glanced at the Dailings. "And I'm sure Zole will be next."

Troy narrowed his eyes at Maria, making her feel intimidated. This was her first time in his company without being in control of the situation. His features seemed darker, and he had an air of anger about him. She couldn't help but think he looked taller. She quickly turned away and tried not to look so scared.

Dia snapped her fingers in front of Maria's face and asked, "Are we boring you?"

She brought her attention from Troy back to the conversation. "I'm sorry."

"We know they work from several planets in the Keplen system. Will they launch attacks from anywhere other than Darsayn?" Dia asked.

Maria shook her head. "No, the bases on other planets are mostly for diversion. All offensive military activity comes from Darsayn at the direct order of Premier Baxelhoff."

"How well do you know him? What do you expect he will do?" Dominic asked.

I know him better than I should, Maria thought. "I'm sure when Major Baryly's ship went down, he started getting more forces ready to attack Earth. He'll assume you're still here. The largest force will come here."

Dia sighed and studied the maps Brody brought up of Earth and the possible places the Coronians could attack. She was sure they would return to at least the western United States but wasn't sure if they had a way to track where she might be. She said to James, "Take Miss Granby back to the gunner and put her in the holding cell. Dominic and Renee, I need to discuss a few things with you. That's all for the rest of you for now."

Brody and Penny couldn't believe how different Dia was from Heather. They used to dictate every aspect of her life, and she just dismissed them from a military briefing. Dia realized this almost immediately and approached her human friends. "I'm sorry, now that I'm back to my usual self, I'm acting like my usual self."

"Do you remember when you felt like everyone was just using you for your powers and that you were just a commodity?" Penny asked.

"Yes. Why?"

"It might take Brody and me a little while to get used to, but you have power *and* powers. I'm glad you're back, General."

Brody nodded. "Yeah, I guess." He pretended to punch Dia on the shoulder and said, "Kidding—I like Dia too. Just don't lose all of Heather."

She smiled. "I won't. Actually, Heather is craving McDonald's right now."

"We're on it! Come on, Pen, let's introduce our new friends to horribly delicious fast food."

"Fine, I guess it can be a cheat day." Penny giggled.

They turned to leave, and Dia stopped them. "Brody, get enough for Maria too."

Penny said, "Aw, that's kind of you to think of her."

"Oh, not nice. *Petty.*"

***

After Dia, Renee, and Dominic finished the rest of their briefing, they walked into the kitchen to the aroma of chicken nuggets, cheeseburgers, French fries, and deep-fried apple pies. Dia knew Troy would probably only eat the pie if she let him, so he got chicken nuggets first, which he enjoyed, but he preferred the pie.

Brody and Penny reveled in the fact that two advanced alien races were in their kitchen, enjoying fast food. Score one for Earth.

Penny got quiet and asked, "So, when are you leaving?"

Dia answered her dear friend, "Tomorrow morning."

Penny just nodded, and James asked, "You're coming with us, right?"

Penny and Brody both turned to Dia. "Are we allowed?" Brody asked.

"Why wouldn't you be? And besides, we still need you, remember? There'll be a team coming back here. We're just going to Rygone to stage our defense," Dia said.

Penny beamed and exclaimed, "Oh my God! I need to go pack!" She skipped off toward the stairs, and James looked at Dia longingly. She waved her hand. "Go. She probably needs help anyway."

"So, I get to see more of your tech, right?" Brody asked.

Dominic nodded. "And meet Oscar. He'll love you."

Troy nodded in agreement with a mouthful of apple pie and mumbled, "Yup, he will."

Renee asked Troy, "How many of those have you eaten?"

"This is my fourth, I think."

Renee made eye contact with Dia at the end of the counter. She nodded at the general and kept the men engaged in conversation as Dia slipped into the curved room. She grabbed two glasses and a bottle of high-end whiskey from the liquor cabinet and walked out into the night toward the gunner.

CHAPTER 44
THE CONVERSATION

Maria was sitting on the small pull-out cot in the holding cell, finishing the food James had brought her. It was too greasy, but she ate anyway because she was starving.

She took notice of the super-advanced ship. She had never seen anything like it, even when living on Rygone. Oscar Strom pulled out all the stops. *I wonder what Baxelhoff would be capable of with a ship like this.*

She heard the bay door open and the reactor whine as a few other systems came online. She knew someone was coming in, and it scared her to not know who it was. *Please be Tristen!*

Unfortunately, it wasn't her son. Dia came around the corner and walked into the small space in front of the door. She didn't look at Maria or say a word at first. Maria watched as Dia opened a bottle of brown liquid, which she assumed was alcohol, and poured two drinks. Dia opened the small hole by the tray and placed one in her cell. She then turned, sat in a chair outside the door, and glared at her. After a few minutes, Dia said, "Go ahead, take the drink. It isn't going to hurt you. As a matter of fact, this is a thousand-dollar bottle of whiskey from Ireland. It's very smooth and delicious."

Maria didn't move at first and watched Dia take small sips of her drink. She eventually said, "You know, I would much rather be upstairs in bed with Troy, but we have all night. Get your drink so we can *talk*!"

Maria realized the drink wasn't a peace offering but a tongue loosener. She stood and picked up the glass, smelling the liquid. She cringed at the strong odor but took a sip anyway.

"Sorry, we're all out of White Claw."

Maria cleared her throat and said, "What is it you want to know, General?"

"Why do you hate your kind so much?"

Maria smirked and said, "I don't exactly hate my kind. I hate you and your family—and all of the old blood who control everything on Rygone."

Dia glared at the traitor menacingly, making sure to intimidate her. "So you partnered with our greatest enemy and are giving them information on how to take over Rygone, therefore hurting *all* of your kind. *All* of the refugees and Hanners."

"Once they took control, I would be the one to rule Rygone. Those individuals who took to the new way of power would be spared and given a great life."

Dia snickered, then laughed obnoxiously. "Are you serious? You sound like a dictator propaganda film. I read about this treacherous leader here on Earth named Adolf Hitler. He would have adored you and Baxelhoff."

Maria rolled her eyes. "You would know, wouldn't you, General Collateral Damage?"

"That was Colonel Collateral Damage. Get your insults right. I'm not perfect by a long shot, but at least my actions protect my people, not hurt them," She swallowed what was left in her glass and poured more. "Speaking of your people, you're a great mother. I mean, damn, keeping Tristen's identity from his father, making him a traitor to his people, *and* putting him as a spy right under Troy's nose? Incredible; I'm fucking impressed."

Dia was beginning to feel her whiskey. She looked at Maria's glass and said, "Drink."

"You can't make me."

Dia had the urge to pull a feeler from the reactor and show her what she could do but decided against it, at least for now. Instead, she stood up and went to open the door, prompting fear in Maria, so she drank the whiskey all at once. Dia lifted the bottle, and the other woman reluctantly put her glass on the tray to be refilled. Dia filled the rocks glass almost to the top and said, "Drink it."

Maria was now genuinely concerned but took the drink anyway. Dia glared at her as Maria chugged the strong spirit, cringing as she placed the empty glass on the tray. Both women stumbled back to their seats, and Maria said, "Why the alcohol? You don't want to speak as two respectable adversaries?"

Dia pretended to think. "Uh, no. Because we aren't. Too much female jealousy, am I right?"

The two women studied each other closely. Maria took note of Dia's uniform, seeing only the one star on her shoulder. Her usually immaculate braid was messy, a few curls pulled loose, and her makeup slightly smudged. But she was still powerful, still capable, still on top.

Dia observed Maria's haggard appearance. Her clothes were still the same from the night of the attack. She was dirty, and her hair was a mess. But beautiful, so lovely, and charming. Dia was always confident that no matter what, Troy would never stray. Yet this intelligent, tall, blonde beauty swept him off his feet.

Maria observed Dia's face and thought about exploiting her raw feelings, but Dia said instead, "I guess I'm happy for you both. I always liked Tristen. He was a good assistant for Troy and my brother. Let me tell you—he was popular with the girls. Would it be disgusting to say I once thought he was attractive?" She shivered and continued, "So creepy now."

"You thought Tristen was attractive?"

Dia nodded. "Yes, I did." She swallowed hard and became very serious. "You condemned your son, you know. What did you expect him to do if you won your insurrection?"

Maria didn't answer. She had been confident Tristen would be by her side and convince his father to do the same. However, the longer Maria was away from the Coronians, the more delusional she realized her aspirations were.

Dia swirled the last bit of whiskey in her glass and said, "Well, it's bedtime, I guess."

She stood up, took a pair of handcuffs out of the security cabinet, and locked one side on her wrist. She opened the door to the holding cell, approached a nervous Maria, and latched the other side onto her wrist. "Let's go. You can stay in one of the rooms. There's a bathroom with a shower, clean clothes, and a warm bed."

Maria was shocked and just stood there. Impatient, Dia said, "Don't make me regret this."

Maria hung her head and followed her rival out of the ship. Dia turned and powered down the gunner as they walked toward the house. In the distance, a storm was starting to form, and Maria heard Dia groan. Curious, she asked, "You don't like storms?"

"No, I like them too much sometimes."

Maria didn't press the issue as they walked into the house and through the curved room. Several team members were still in the kitchen, including Troy and Tristen, and they all fell silent, shocked. Brody started to say something, and Dia said softly but firmly, "Not now."

Maria was almost impressed at Dia's instant ability to exude power and still have the respect of those around her. Dia took her upstairs, and they went into the room right outside hers. Maria marveled at her accommodations. Dia showed her the bathroom, the dresser with clothes, and even how to turn on the TV. She unlocked the handcuffs and said, "Okay, don't even try to get out of here. Brody has a safety lock on the door, and there'll be a guard in the hall all night. Do yourself a favor and take this time to relax, get clean, and think about what you'll tell my father tomorrow when we get home."

Maria swallowed hard and asked, "Uh, will we see him tomorrow?"

"Yes, tomorrow. I didn't say to defend yourself. Tell the Chancellor how to beat the enemies you brought to our doorstep. You might even keep yourself out of the Lake."

With that, Dia turned and left the room, locking the bolt behind her.

Dia, still half-drunk, stumbled back downstairs to a group of stunned people and said, "We need to make a roster of two-hour guard shifts for Maria's door. She's locked in, but I don't want to take any chances."

Troy asked, almost whispering, "Why did you bring her in?"

Suddenly, there was a deafening clap of thunder, and the lights flickered. They all received a warning from the gunner about the cloaking program, and Dia said, "That's why."

She took a notebook out of a kitchen drawer and had volunteers take two-hour guard shifts. "Nobody, and I mean nobody, is to open her door unless there's an emergency." Dia paused to glare at Tristen. "She's rather convincing, so don't listen to her if she tries to pull anything. I don't think she will, but we can't be too careful. Now, everyone needs to go to their rooms and rest. Tomorrow's a big day. Good night."

The team, even the Dailings, all went their respective ways. Renee took the first watch. Then, as she, Troy, and Dia walked down the hall, she said, "You surprised me, General. I thought you would have left her out there."

"She needed a shower."

"Uh huh. Good night," Renee said.

Dia walked into her room, and Renee and Troy exchanged a bewildered glance before he followed his wife. There was only one light on, so the room was mostly dark. A streak of lightning lit up the chamber, and Troy saw Dia in the middle of the room, taking off her jacket and staring at the skylight.

He went and stood behind her for a moment. "That was a surprise."

"Believe it or not, I'm not the monster everyone thinks I am. Get this, she even called me General Collateral Damage. Of course, I corrected her with colonel, but you get it."

Troy put his hands on her hips, leaned down, and kissed the back of her neck. She moaned softly and asked, "You didn't want me to talk to her?"

"I'm just surprised you did and that you were cordial."

Dia pulled away. "Again, not a monster."

He followed her and said, "You know what I mean. This is an unprecedented situation."

She threw herself onto the bed. "Yes, it is. Let's not talk about it anymore. I'm tired, and I want you."

Troy was hesitant, knowing Maria was in the next room. "Did you put her there on purpose?"

"What do you mean? It's the best place to keep an eye on her." She knew. She just wanted to hear him say it.

Troy stretched out on the bed next to her and said, "Never mind." He pulled her over so they were lying on their sides, facing each other.

"Does it bother you that she's so close, Troy?" she whispered.

He nodded.

"Why?" Dia leaned in and kissed his neck. "If it makes you too uncomfortable, we can move. Her room is stripped down too much to move her."

Troy just shook his head and kissed her; he could taste the whiskey on her lips. He slid his hand inside her shirt and pulled it over her head. Dia moaned and pulled his jacket open. A lightning bolt hit very close to the house, rattling the skylight. Dia looked up and said, "This is a powerful storm."

Troy murmured as he kissed her neck, chest, and lips. Soon, Dia lost interest in the lightning and immersed herself in her husband. They made love, forgetting about Maria, forgetting about the storm, and thinking only about each other.

CHAPTER 45
LEAVING AND LEARNING

Troy woke to the sound of close thunder. He opened his eyes and saw that it was early morning, and the sun was just rising, but another storm was coming in from the west. *Is the weather ever quiet here, or are these storms attracted to her?*

Dia was lying next to him, pushed up against his side. He rolled, pulled her into his arms, and listened to her snore quietly. Troy smiled, thinking about how annoying it could be at times. He would take nothing about her for granted ever again.

A closer rumble of thunder woke Dia, and she stretched. She sighed, opened her eyes, then turned to Troy, gazing out the skylight. She cuddled closer to him and said, "We're going home today, Troy."

He pressed his lips against her neck and whispered, "I know. It's both wonderful and scary."

She nodded. "A lot is about to happen. I hope we can stop this war before it starts."

Troy nodded and held Dia close. He was afraid of what would happen when they arrived back on Rygone. Maria and Tristen would have to answer for their traitorous actions, and he was a conspirator. He asked, "What will you tell your father, Dia? About Tristen and me."

"I don't know yet. Part of me wants to hide Tristen, but I don't think Maria will allow that. I think she's going to throw your son under the bus."

Hearing Dia say "your son" was painful. "Which means me hiding him will be addressed as well," he said.

She was quiet for a moment, then said, "Not right away. My father is hard on you and will probably bust your ass personally, but I doubt he'll convict you of anything. Technically, you brought Tristen here for his protection, and you were looking for me. So I'll find a way to make it right." She sighed and added, "That being said, I can't guarantee how lenient he and the advocate general will be on him."

Troy whispered, "I know. I…" He trailed off.

"What, baby?"

"She ruined his life."

Dia took his face in her hands. "Which means going forward, whatever happens, you need to help him put it back together. If you make that kid even a fraction as good of a person as you are, he's set."

He pressed his forehead to hers. The only thing Dia ever asked for from him was to one day have a child. Now she was telling him how great a father he could be to his son with another woman. Surreal.

Lightning flashed in the skylight. Dia kissed Troy gently and said, "We need to get up and get this day moving. There's a lot to do."

They got up and took a shower together, trying—and failing—not to have sex. As Dia finished getting dressed, Troy went into the hall and saw Dominic sitting in the chair outside Maria's room. Dominic asked, "Good morning, brother-in-law. How's Dia?"

"Good. She's finishing up getting ready. How's the prisoner?"

"I checked on her when I took over about an hour and a half ago. She was out cold."

"Do you want some coffee?"

Troy tried hiding his nervousness from Dominic but knew he couldn't. The giant Florian asked, "You want to talk to her, don't you?"

Troy said, irritated, "I do, but I'm not going to." He repeated, "Do you want coffee?"

"Yeah, that'd be great."

Troy gracefully hurried down the stairs on his long legs. Dominic watched as he disappeared. A moment later, Dia came out of her room. She was perfectly put together and had the confidence to face the trying day ahead. "Good morning, Dom. Where'd Troy go?"

"He's getting me coffee."

She nodded and pointed her head toward the door. "That one?"

Just then, a knock came from the other side of the door. Dominic and Dia heard Maria ask, "Question, can I get some food?"

Dominic glanced at Dia, who nodded slightly in approval.

"Move back from the door," he said.

Dominic unlocked the bolt, and Dia opened the door. She had the handcuffs but asked, "Will you be good, or will I have to sic a twelve-foot Dailing warrior on you?"

Maria looked between Dia and Dominic and said meekly, "I'll be good. I promise."

Dia waved her out of the room, and they walked down the stairs together. Maria had found a pair of gray slacks and a pink blouse. She had her hair pulled up in a messy bun. As always, she looked flawless.

As they entered the kitchen, everyone else took notice. Troy and Maria's eyes met, and she looked away immediately, feeling his anger. Tristen sat at the island and said, "Good morning, Mother."

She smiled and nodded at him, then glanced around nervously. Dia said, "Tristen, take your mother into the curved room. We'll all be in there shortly for breakfast and a briefing."

Maria gave Dia a grateful glance and followed her son. Renee and Frank went in with them for added measure. Dia walked around the island and stood next to Troy, who was struggling with a coffee filter to make another pot of coffee. As she began to help him, he said quietly, "She makes me nervous. Why are you being so nice?"

"Sugar gets better results than salt, Troy. You know that personally when dealing with her, right?"

He nodded warily. "I'm worried about her being too close to Tristen. I just don't…"

"You don't want her to corrupt him again. Do you really think this crowd is going to allow that to happen? The moment we get to Rygone, I promise she'll be away from him for a very long time."

He glanced down, ashamed for being so anxious. "Okay."

Dia kissed him on the cheek and said, "Let me finish this. You've never even made coffee. When we get home, you can make tea."

He laughed, repeated, "Okay," and walked into the curved room.

Dia finished readying the coffee and helped Penny and James set out danishes, donuts, fruit, yogurt, and juice. They all made plates and sat down.

Dia sat down next to Maria, who said, "This house is lovely. How did you get it?"

Dia took a bite of a donut and said, "It belongs to the Dailings. Roger, who was killed in the raid to rescue me, owned it. Now it moves on to Frank and Peter. Penny and Brody also live and work here."

Maria looked at Brody across the table, talking to Dominic. "He's the one you were with in the casino."

Dia nodded. "Yes."

"These humans, they mean a lot to you?"

"Why all the questions?" Dia asked, getting angry.

"I'm sorry, I don't mean anything by it. I'm just curious, I guess."

Dia ignored her, picked up her tablet, and began working. When she was finished, Maria watched as she locked the screen. The background was a picture of Carl feeding the fish on the porch. Dia quickly turned it over. Maria remembered the video from the hotel. She wanted to say something so badly but knew the rest of her life depended on not pissing the general off.

Dia cleared her throat, and everyone turned their attention to her. "After breakfast, we need to get anything we're taking with us and load the gunner. I want to Jump in two hours, which will bring us to Baltica City right after sunrise." She turned to Frank and Peter and asked, "You'll be staying, correct?"

Peter said, "Yes, General. We've already contacted our leadership on Zole and told them of the events in Las Vegas and our leader's death. We're waiting to confirm what course of action we'll take from here." He looked at Brody and Penny. "When you return, this house will always be yours, even if we're no longer here. It will forever be paid for and maintained by our kind, and you're welcome to stay as long as you like." He turned back to Dia and added, "That goes for the Rygonians as well."

Dia was genuinely thankful for what the Dailings had done for her and the team. She said, "In the future, I'll urge Chancellor Strom to open communications between our worlds to develop a closer relationship."

They both nodded and bowed.

She turned to Troy. "Troy, when we arrive, please take Penny under your wing and show her our way of treating patients on Rygone. There's likely to be a need to treat many different species, and she can help you."

Penny's eyes went wide, as she was still intimidated by Troy but was honored that Dia wanted her to work with him. Troy nodded, then turned to Penny and gently patted her hand. "It's okay. I'm not the scary one, remember that."

Everyone chuckled, and the bubbly physician's assistant said, "I'm excited and honored, General!"

Dia turned to Brody and said, "You, High Colonel Conner, and Captain Ramsay will meet Dr. Oscar Strom, our brother, upon landing. I'm sure he'll have a tremendous amount of work to do to get the fleet ready to deploy."

Brody clapped his hands, threw them in the air, and yelled, "Yes!"

"Dominic, you and I will meet with the Chancellor upon arrival." She addressed everyone else and said, "I've notified Chancellor Strom that we'll be arriving there shortly. He and I both agree that we're keeping our entrance under wraps to the public for now. Crews are clearing the deck, and we'll land directly in the

Chancellor's bay." Dia stood up. "Let's get everything together and load the gunner. We'll be leaving soon."

The general nodded at Dominic, and he stood up and walked behind Tristen. She glanced at Troy, then looked at Maria and said, "Both of you, come with us."

Tristen started to panic but figured this was happening for a reason. He had no idea how many team members knew he was Troy's son, but they all knew he was Maria's. Mother and son were led out of the curved room toward the gunner.

Troy wanted to scream at Dia for not telling him she was taking Tristen into custody, which would cause too much suspicion. As the four of them walked out the door into the last of the rain, Penny asked Troy, "So, Maria is Tristen's mom?"

Troy nodded.

"Wow, that's crazy. Why's he in trouble?"

Troy cleared his throat and said, "It's very complicated. The general is taking him into custody for his protection."

Penny nodded. Changing the subject, she asked, "So, how many species of, uh, aliens, do you have on Rygone?"

He chuckled and said, "Seventy-two. There are three different classes. Like all of us except Tristen, Florians are the original inhabitants of Rygone and are immortal. Then there are the Hanner-Florians, which are any Florian-mortal species hybrid, like Tristen. Hanners aren't immortal but live between two hundred and one hundred thousand Earth years, depending on the mortal species and the Florian parent's age. Then there's everyone else. All species that can be injured, become sick, or die. Every condition requires a different treatment method, as does each species. Medicine on our planet is very complicated."

"Sounds like it. It means a lot that Dia thinks I can be of help," Penny said proudly.

Curious, Troy asked, "You spent an entire year with her as Heather. How different is she now?"

"Honestly, almost completely different," Penny said with a touch of sadness in her sweet voice. "Heather surprised us with how fast she learned at first and how cunning she was; it was amazing. But we controlled every aspect of her life. She would sometimes rebel by not coming to dinner or sitting in the garden and drawing those designs, but she always eventually did what she was told. The first time we took her in public, a restaurant, she was so scared. Carl had to take her out early because a loud noise scared her senseless. She was a little bit better in Las Vegas, but not by much. She relied on us for almost everything. But when I saw her in the kitchen yesterday, I knew Heather was gone. I want to think Dia is holding on to her alter ego, but I can't see it."

Troy felt sad about that. He saw a little of Heather when they rescued her. He saw her wonderment at the ship and how excited and relieved she was to see Brody. But the moment he returned her memories, that wonderment was gone. The general, his wife, had returned. He said, "Thank you for taking such good care of her. When we were separated, I had no idea if she would ever even be found, let alone make it to a place like this. I know that you had your reasons for training her to use the EIP, but there's no place I know of in the galaxy that would have a facility like this."

A tear ran down Penny's cheek. "We always knew someone had to be looking for her, especially Carl. She was too special, and it's nice to know that she came from such an incredible place."

Troy couldn't help himself. He asked, "Her and Carl, they were close?"

Penny was quiet, not knowing how to answer, and Troy said, "It's okay. She and I have already talked about the two of them. But I'm curious what you think."

"Honestly, I was rooting for them. I'm sorry. But there were just too many differences between them, and Carl was legitimately scared of her. It wasn't meant to be. And now? I'm glad it wasn't. But my heart hurts that he died."

"Truly, I am sorry for his loss," Troy said genuinely.

Penny leaned over and wrapped her arms around Troy, taking the Florian doctor by surprise. She said, "I'm so glad you're here! Please take care of our Heather."

Troy smiled and hugged her back. "I will. Now, we need to get ready to go. Is there anything here that you think might be useful to take medical-wise?"

Penny said, "Well, I have an area in the lab with stuff I used to work on with Heather. Maybe we can look at that."

As they walked together toward the lab, Penny asked, "So, when it comes to having Hanner-Florians, can you guys, like, be with anyone?"

Troy put his hands behind his back and laughed. "So far, we haven't come across anyone incompatible."

She smiled slyly and said, "Wonderful!"

***

Dia and the other three walked up the ramp onto the ship. She turned to Maria and said, "You'll be back in the holding cell. Tristen, please go with Dominic."

Maria watched Dominic walk away with her son and asked desperately, "Can't we be together? The Jump is quick, right?"

Dia opened the door to the cell, led her in, then closed it. As the door sealed, she looked Maria in the eye and said, "It is quick. And no, you can't have him with you."

Dia walked around the corner and into the small office by the bridge. Tristen was sitting at the desk, and Dominic was behind him. She sat on the desk and said, "Look, you've already admitted you're the traitor who conspired with her. I can't walk you up to my father and say that you're in the clear because you came clean to me. So much of the information you fed to our enemies killed thousands of Rygonians and our allies. I can't look past that, Tristen, no matter who your parents are."

Tristen became terrified, as he was afraid of Dominic knowing. Dominic saw his reaction and said, "I figured it out on my own, kid."

Tristen swallowed back his fear. "I'm ready to face my punishment, but I have a question."

Dia nodded.

"What about my father? The night I told him, I showed him the envelope first. He knew immediately I was the traitor and tried to call the authorities. But I told him who I was, and he made me breakfast and brought me here. He protected me. What'll happen to him?"

Dia shook her head, then glanced away, her intense gaze on the wall. She turned to Tristen and said, "I don't know yet. It isn't up to me. The Chancellor and advocate general will make that decision."

Dia was surprised to see anger cross his face and tears fill his eyes. "He's your husband! Aren't you going to protect *him*? I've watched you come into his lab for years, and you both worship the ground each other walks on! And now you're going to let him go down for protecting his *son*?!"

Dominic pressed his hands down hard on Tristen's shoulders and quietly said, "You're treading on some thin ice, kid. My advice to you is to shut your fucking mouth. Now."

Dia stood up and nodded at Dominic. "Lock the door. He'll be fine in here. When we get to Rygone, they'll remain in their cells until the guards meeting the ship remove them to the brig." With that, she left.

Dominic patted Tristen's shoulder and said, "Don't speak again about your father's involvement. Just don't."

Dominic closed the door, locking Troy's son in the office. Dia was standing against the bulkhead with her arms across her chest. She had tears running down her cheeks, and she looked at her brother and said, "When this war is over…"

He put an arm around her shoulders and kissed her on the head. "I'm here for ya, sis. I always will be."

***

The rest of the team began loading the gunner with the gear they were bringing. Most of it was Brody's equipment and the schematics for the suits and shells. In addition, Penny brought a few medical instruments she thought might help Troy.

As they were getting ready to leave, Troy noticed Dia wasn't on the ship. He went back into the house, searching for her. He went into her room and saw the glass door was open. He stepped out onto the porch and slowly walked around to where he knew she would be. She was standing in front of the fountain with the little fish, sprinkling the food around the bowl and watching them chase it. Troy asked, "Who will feed them after we leave?"

"Peter said they would ensure there's a caretaker at the house when nobody is living here. We had a cleaning service that we paid very well to keep quiet, so I assume that's who it will be."

"We're almost ready to go," Troy said quietly.

She placed the cap back on the food container. "I did it for his protection. I know you might not like it, but he could face a much harsher reality if I don't dictate the chain of custody he's processed through when he gets home. I'm sorry I didn't tell you; I couldn't risk you talking me out of it."

Troy just stared at her. He knew she had a lot on her shoulders with not just the Coronians but dealing with his family. She continued, "He's mad at me. He doesn't think I'll protect you because all you were doing was protecting him." She shook her head. "I've only been myself for a few days, and I already miss Heather. Let's go."

She placed the food can on the shelf and walked past Troy back into the bedroom. She picked up a bag on the bed and waited for him to join her. They walked out to the ship in silence. Dia didn't want to leave the mansion just yet. As they walked out of the curved room, she kept her eyes down all the way to the gunner. Reminiscing wasn't going to do her any good.

She and Troy were the last two on board, and she took the pilot's seat. Renee was in the captain's chair, and James was the co-pilot. They ran through pre-flight checks, and Dia checked the monitors to make sure Tristen and Maria were safe. Renee said, "Pre-flight complete. General, Jump when ready."

Dia took a deep breath and closed her eyes. Then, she slid her fingers up the controls and whispered, "Jump."

CHAPTER 46
WELCOME HOME

S ome of them had never been there. Some hadn't been in a long time. Some were only gone for a short while. But one had been missed the most.

Per General Harlow's policy, all DREX ships coming out of Jump into Rygonian airspace, especially over Baltica City, had to uncloak immediately after entering the atmosphere.

Penny and Brody watched the monitors on the deck as they came through a bank of clouds high above an extensive range of snow-capped mountains. Penny marveled at how similar the land looked to Earth. They watched as the gunner slowly glided toward what looked like the top of a massive building. As they approached, a voice in Rygonian came over the speakers and said, "DREX gunner 1, please authenticate."

Renee sent a passcode to the tower, and the voice said, "DREX gunner 1, you are authorized to land in hangar bay one. Welcome home, General."

Dia looked at James and said, "I'll let you land. I don't want to crash a brand-new ship in my dad's parking space."

"But what if I do?" he asked jokingly.

"Then he'll yell at you, not me."

James expertly maneuvered the gunner into the tight hangar, eased the ship into bay one, and completed docking. Dia could see the small group of people waiting for them. Her father, brother, mother, Jeannie Harlow, and General Smith. And four of Dominic's best guards. Her throat started to get tight, and anxiety seized her. She took a deep breath and pushed her feelings down. *This isn't the time to freeze, Dia.*

Renee opened the bay door, and as the ramp lowered, Dia saw how terrified Brody and Penny were. She smiled at her beloved human friends and said, "Walk out with me."

Once the door was fully open, Renee, James, Dominic, and Troy stepped off first. Dia, Brody, and Penny followed them. She looked around at the hangar she had spent tens of thousands of years working in and felt completely out of place. Rygone had never felt so different.

Dia's mother, Lady Pamela, was the first to embrace her. With tears in her eyes, she said, "I can't believe you're finally home. I can't wait to hear everything!"

"It'll have to wait, my Lady. There's a lot to achieve in a minimal amount of time."

Pamela peeked past Dia at Penny and Brody. "Who're these two lovely individuals?"

Dia turned and said, "Lady Pamela, this is Brody Patterson and Penny Singleton. They helped and protected me while I was on Earth. Brody and Penny, this is my mother, Pamela Strom, the Lady of Rygone."

Penny's jaw dropped. "Lady? That's so cool! Um, oh, I'm so sorry, it's a pleasure, my Lady."

Before arriving, Dia had made sure all of the Rygonians greeting the ship had translators to make the meeting of the humans seamless. She said to Penny, "Oh my, aren't you a dear. It's Pam. Dia is formal because of her own rules."

Shaking, Brody took her hand and kissed it.

"Brody, not necessary," Dia said, laughing.

But he was entirely taken by Pamela Strom with her long black hair, large brown eyes, perfect tan skin, and voluptuous curves. He said, "You're so lovely, my Lady. You look nothing like your daughter."

Penny smacked Brody on the shoulder. "Brody!"

He snapped out of it, and Pam was laughing hard. He said, "I'm so sorry."

"That's okay, dear. It's a Florian thing," Pam told him. "None of us look like our children. Wait until you meet Troy's parents."

Dia nodded and confirmed, "Oh yeah, nothing like him."

A short, dark-skinned man with black hair, brown eyes, and a huge smile joined them, and he and Dia embraced. He said, "Damn it, sis, don't scare us like that!"

"Trust me, I will again someday," she said with a smile.

He turned to Brody. "You must be Brody. Dia sent me a message about you. So you're interested in our technology?"

Brody almost went off the rails but caught Dia's eye. "Very interested. I think we can collaborate. Especially with the EIP," he said calmly.

Dia nodded to her brother, then said, "I have some other pressing matters to attend to. I'll catch up to you all later."

Renee put her arm around Brody and said, "You're with us now, kiddo. We'll all meet back in the Command Center for dinner. Right, General?"

"Yes, Colonel. See you then." She watched as James, Renee, and Oscar walked off with her human tech genius. She was a little jealous.

Dia looked around and asked, "Mom, where are Dad and Toni?"

"I'm not sure—oh, there they are, coming out of the ship."

Dia watched as her father and General Smith walked out of the ship with the four guards, Tristen, and Maria. She growled and said to Penny, "Stay here."

She approached Chancellor Strom and said calmly, "It's nice to see you, Father."

Knowing the contentious relationship between Dia and her father, Smith turned and quickly walked away with Maria and two guards in tow. Troy slowly stepped up to Dominic and Tristen, and she could tell something horrible was about to occur. The Chancellor stared at Dia and said, "You know I missed you, and I'm incredibly grateful you're home, but you brought two traitors here for trial, and I plan to do that quickly."

"You can't! She has valuable information we can use to end this war with the Coronians!"

"And him, Dia? What value is her son but a spy and a traitor who took innocent Rygonian lives?"

The situation was about to become very delicate, and now was neither the time nor place for that. Jeannie Harlow couldn't find out that Tristen was Troy's son yet. She would stop at nothing to keep both of them from being charged with anything and interrupt the urgent planning of the Coronian assault. Dia stepped closer to her father and, with a pleading tone, said softly, "Take them into custody now, but please, you and I need to talk before you go forward with charges. Please."

Warren Strom was not used to seeing Dia react so desperately, especially in front of subordinates. He also knew she had just been through more than he could possibly imagine, and she deserved his ear. He nodded and said to Dominic, "Place them both in the Command Center, holding cells apart from each other." He turned to his daughter and said, "Meet me in my office in an hour. I'm sure you're more than aware of the time-sensitive nature of our current situation."

She nodded. "Thank you, Chancellor."

He walked away quickly, barely expressing his delight and fear that she was back home.

The tension in the hangar reduced significantly, but Troy watched anxiously as Tristen was taken under armed guard. Dia walked up to her husband. "I'm trying."

"I know," Troy said with a nod.

Jeannie ran up to Dia and gave her a big hug. "I'm so happy you're here, honey! You need to come to the courtyard and see the murals!"

"Murals?"

Troy laughed. "Oh yeah, I forgot about that. You're gonna get as much of a kick out of that as I did. Maybe more."

Lady Pamela had arranged for a guest suite for Brody and Penny to stay in during their time on Rygone. She said to Penny,

"Let's get you and your friend's things, dear. I'll show you where you'll be staying while with us."

Penny nodded excitedly but was apprehensive about being alone with Dia's and Troy's mothers. Dia smiled and reassured her, "You're in the best hands around, trust me."

Penny walked off with the two matriarchs, and they chatted up the sweet human as if she were a visiting queen. Dia knew Penny was in heaven.

She and Troy stood alone, quiet. Finally, she said, "I want to go home for a few minutes before seeing my father. Can we?"

He put his arm around her and said, "Of course, my love. You can see the murals from the deck."

She was home but felt like she fit in less here than back on Earth.

***

Dia didn't know why, but she was nervous about returning to their apartment. As they approached, she saw the shrine outside their door with letters, cards, candy, and even panties. She cringed and laughed. "Man, there's going to be some pissed-off ladies around here."

"Not just ladies."

"Ah, really? Hm, interesting!" she said with a snicker.

Troy opened the door, and Dia reluctantly followed him into their home of almost eight hundred thousand years. Baltica City was ancient, but the incredible engineers kept the city running like new. Every year, a particular area of the city was remodeled from infrastructure, living quarters, government offices, and labs down to the restaurants and entertainment facilities.

Their apartment had been updated about three years ago, and it was very modern for their section of the city. Dia sighed as she looked around at all of the familiar fixtures. She whispered, "It looks the same. Why did I think it would be different?"

"I thought the same thing when I got home," he said. "My mother came in and cleaned while we were gone, so it looked good as new. It's strange how something so familiar can feel so foreign."

She walked over to him, resting her head on his chest. Troy was considerably taller than Dia, and her head fit perfectly under his chin. He hugged her tight and sighed. "I'm glad you're here, my love."

She whispered, "So am I. I'm not glad about our task. I just want to hide here, bake cakes, and read romance novels."

"What are romance novels?"

She giggled and said, "Books from Earth with a bunch of sex."

Troy huffed. "Huh, interesting. No wonder you like them."

"I need to get ready to go talk to my father. And then see what Oscar and our mothers are putting Brody and Penny through."

"I think they're both perfectly fine."

"Yes, you're probably right." Dia walked out onto the deck and said, "Where is the— holy shit! Are you kidding me?!"

Troy laughed hard. "That's what I said! Renee told me the citizens commissioned them only six weeks after we disappeared. I guess we were all but considered gone."

Dia studied the large painted mural of her dress uniform, complete with warrior ribbon and dagger. She said, "I like yours. You look very sexy. They even got your eyes right."

"Yes, my mother's doing. I've had nothing but curiosity seekers wondering about my dark eyes. I go one day without my lenses, and people get weirded out. It's rather irritating."

She put her arm around his waist and asked, "Do you think they'll paint over them now that we're home?"

"Boy, I hope so."

They both walked through the apartment into their bedroom, and Dia checked her communicator, seeing that she had twenty minutes before her meeting with the Chancellor. It took about five minutes to get to the Command Center, so she threw herself on the bed and tried to take a quick nap.

Troy asked, "What're you doing?"

"Trying to take a power nap, as I used to when I was in the Academy."

He laid next to her and asked, "Did it ever work?"

"Yes, when someone wasn't asking me questions."

"You're a jerk."

"Hmm, shut up." Troy started to poke Dia in the ribs to annoy her. She laughed. "Stop it!"

"I'm just trying to keep you awake so you aren't late to see your dad."

Dia rolled onto her side, opening her eyes to see Troy looking at her with a huge grin on his lips. She touched his face and said, "I'm scared, Troy."

His grin faded, and he kissed her on the bridge of her nose. "Me too, General, but we're who everyone is turning to, especially you, my love. I mean, look at those horrid murals."

"I know it." She stared deep into his dark eyes and said, "I'm serious. I'm leaving the army after this. I don't know what I plan on doing, but I'm done fighting."

He studied her face and saw the exhaustion of years of being Rygone's "Fighter." He was ready for her to be done too.

She asked quietly, "Do you want me to tell him?"

"Do I want you to tell him? No. Do I need you to tell him? Yes. Hopefully, he'll see reason if it comes from you."

"Warren Strom, listening to reason from his daughter. You have a lot of faith in me, Troy."

"Dia, be serious. You know I'm right."

She rolled off the bed and went into the closet. She got her long raincoat and a hat. "I'm still not ready to be seen by the public."

Troy stayed on the bed, watching her. "I'll see you soon. I love you."

Dia kissed him on the forehead and said, "I love you, too."

CHAPTER 47
CALM BEFORE THE WAR

Dia made it to her father's office right on time. The door was open, so she didn't bother to knock or announce herself before walking in and closing it behind her. She leaned back against the wall.

Warren watched the confidence drain from her face, and the little girl the kids in school teased because she was so small appeared. She said, "Dad, I can't do this anymore."

He stood up, walked around his desk, and stood in front of her. "Dia, please look at me." He waited until she glanced up sheepishly to ask, "What happened?"

She struggled not to cry in front of him, which was another thing she had done as a child. "When I didn't know who I was on Earth, I felt out of place. Now that I'm home, I want the freedom of not remembering my past back."

Warren pulled her into a hug, and she buried her face in his chest. He smelled of the shaving soap he had used since she was a kid. It had been a long time since they had connected personally, and it felt good. After a long, quiet moment, Warren said, "I was expecting you to come here ready to fight. I'm glad you aren't."

"I'm saving the last of my fight for the enemy. Contrary to popular belief, you aren't my enemy, Dad."

He kissed her on top of her head and said, "Sit down, Dia. I know we have a lot to discuss."

They sat down, and Warren said, "Now, the traitors."

"Yes, well, Maria Granby will be a decent, if not good, source of information, I believe. While still on Earth, the information we got from her gave us a reasonable timeline of when the Coronians might make it to different potential targets and what firepower they might use. I sent all that data to General Smith when we determined the time differences. Earth is closer to the orbit Darsayn moves in than Rygone." She sighed, exasperated. "Why didn't we know about such a close, significant intelligent species?"

Warren shrugged his shoulders. "I don't know, Dia. Now, the kid—that's her son, and he admits to being a traitor? Why did Troy take him to look for you?"

Dia closed her eyes and took a deep breath. "Because Tristen came to Troy the night before they tracked the signal from the EIP to Earth. He told him…" She paused, trying to find the strength to continue.

"Told him what, Dia?"

"Tristen is Maria *and* Troy's son," she blurted out quickly. "She became pregnant with him during Breger Dunes, and after she found out, she fled to Darsayn, where she hid Tristen from us and raised him to be a conspirator. She then planted him as a spy in Oscar and Troy's employ for twelve years, during which he fed her information about their work, especially the EIP."

Warren watched as a tear ran down the cheek of her stoic face, and he said, "Wow. This hole just keeps getting deeper and deeper. When does it stop?"

Dia began to truly cry, and she whispered, "Please don't take Troy away from me, Dad. I need him so much right now. I know he should've turned his son in and not taken him to Earth, but please…"

Warren could see the effects of Dia's deep-seated trauma syndrome coming to the surface. She was close to a breakdown, and he needed her to run this operation. He said, "Dia, I'm not going to arrest Troy. Even if you weren't asking me not to, his crime wasn't enough to lock up the best doctor on this planet on the eve of a huge fight." He glanced down at his hands for a long moment, then continued, "If it were one of you three, I would probably do the same."

"It's so strange to call Tristen his son. I don't think it's quite sunk in for me yet."

"Damn it, kid, you can't catch a break, can you? What're you going to do?"

She replaced the anguish on her face with determination. "I was an incredible mother to my children; therefore, I'll be a great stepmother. If he doesn't go to the Ice Lake for eternity."

Warren said, "I promise we'll deal with that after this Coronian invasion."

"About that—does it have to be an invasion?"

***

Dia and Warren spoke productively about the coming war for over an hour. It was close to lunchtime by then, and he said, "Your mother is making a very nice dinner tonight. I'm sure she'll want you and your new Earth friends to be there."

"Well, Mom and Jeannie took off with Penny earlier, so I probably need to go rescue her. She's a doctor on Earth, and I have her working with Troy."

"And the other one? Brokey?" he asked.

She laughed and said, "Brody! He's working with Oscar right now. I'll spend the rest of the afternoon with them testing the suit to make sure everything works here on Rygone."

"I want to see what you can do. I watched a few videos of the tests you and Troy did, and although impressive, I'm sure you've improved."

She gave him a sly smile. "Yeah, you could say that." She stood up. "This has been an excellent conversation, Chancellor. Thank you for listening."

"You as well, General. I'll be out in the hangar soon; I need to take care of a few things per our other discussion."

Dia put her coat and hat back on, then left her father's office. She had a transport take her to the hangar. When she arrived, Brody and Oscar were both carefully working on some sort of drive system. She approached them and asked, "I take it things are going well?"

When Brody saw her, he got excited and said, "Oh! Dia! This place is amazing! Thank you, thank you, thank you for bringing me! By the way, where's Penny?"

Dia swore. "I was supposed to check on her; Mom and Jeannie took her to your guest suite, and I lost track of time."

"Oh, guest suite, huh? Sounds fancy."

"Fancy by Rygone's standards, meh by the mansion's standards," she said.

Dia called her mother and discovered that Penny was working with Troy and his father in the hospital. Dia told Oscar that she wanted to test the suit and that the Chancellor wanted to observe. Oscar said, "Well, that might let the citizens know you're home."

Dia smiled. "Let it."

***

For the next few hours, Brody and Dia adjusted the new suit to ensure it was fine-tuned. Dia had not worn this suit yet as Mallory took the one she had in Vegas. She liked that it was lighter and didn't itch as much as the others. Oscar watched the human and his sister work, anxious to see just how far she had come.

Chancellor Strom called the top-ranking generals, the Harlows, Lady Pam, and the rest of Dia's team to the city's top deck. Everyone stood together, including Penny and Renee, watching Oscar, Brody, and Dia get ready to demonstrate how powerful a tool the EIP had become.

Oscar and Dia explained how important it was for everyone to steer clear of her for safety reasons. Then, using the translator disks, Brody explained what the suit did and how it made the EIP much more effective.

Dia went to the end of the south runway that looked out over the Odogen Plain. Even in the bright sunlight, the crowd watched her appearance change as she pulled the power from a tiny Wel Reactor fuel pod. They were amazed as they watched her body be engulfed in green flame. Her hair turned bright blonde, her fingertips were brilliantly white, and her eyes flashed like iridescent emeralds. Then, everything went away except for her emerald eyes as she pushed the power into the shell and suit.

Next, Dia turned her attention out to the plain. She reached her arms in front of herself and released a gentle flow of green flame from her fingertips. It stretched for a few tols down onto the prairie floor. The crowd watched, waiting to see what she would do. Dia reared back and brought her hands together in a colossal thunderclap. The deck shook as a massive eruption of flame and wind released from her hands and carved a perfect crevice in the plain for dozens of tols, stopping when she closed her hands into tight fists. Dia was still holding the flame out when she threw her arms wide, and the crevice widened by thousands of feet. Finally, with all the material hanging in the air above, she raised her arms high and dropped them to the floor, kneeling as all the displaced dirt, soil, and grass fell back into place, filling the crevice perfectly.

Brody tried not to beam too brightly as the crowd was stunned into silence. He said to Dia, "Oscar said you could destroy that ship." He pointed to a damaged DREX fighter on the edge of the flight deck. She immediately recognized it as her DREX that she and Troy fled in. She asked her brother, "Damn, you kept it?"

Oscar said, "Yes, I guess for just such an occasion. It still has the fake documents you forged in there as well. Those aren't needed, are they?"

She glanced at Troy, and he looked down in shame. Dia shook her head and said, "Stand clear."

Everyone stood away from her, and Dia walked close to the craft and examined the damage. She assessed the right side of the fuselage, where the cave wall scraped away her Commanding General seal. *That's in the past, Dia. It's time to show them the future.*

She stepped back a few feet and made a ball of green flame the size of a basketball in her hands. She threw it at the craft, and as it hit, the flare expanded around and enclosed the entire DREX. Then, she pushed out a big flash of heat, and everything within the ball incinerated instantly. Once the flame dissipated, all that remained of the DREX was a small pile of ashes.

With that, Dia ended the demonstration. There was no need to keep playing when they had so much work to do. She was aware that the Coronians might have developed the same technology that Oscar used to track the EIP to Earth. She wanted them to think she was still there, not here on Rygone.

***

The crowd dispersed, discussing amongst themselves the incredible events they had just witnessed. General Smith walked up to Dia and said, "Very impressive and terrifying, General Harlow. But that is what you worked for with the EIP, yes?"

"Yes. This weapon was intended to keep the peace, not start a war. Beginning with this Coronian insurrection, I hope for it to be just that."

He nodded and said, "Me too. See you in the morning."

Toni turned and walked away, seeming unsure of himself, which was not like him. Dia was concerned because he was the commanding general, and she knew the Chancellor had already discussed their plans with him. From what she could see, he didn't seem convinced.

Her attention was pulled back to the rest of her inner group. The one in particular who caught her eye was her mother. Pamela Strom was staring at her daughter with an unusual look on her face. It was almost as if she was terrified. She walked up to Lady Pam and asked, "Are you all right, Mom?"

Pam nodded and said quietly, "I've been watching you fight the battles of the galaxy for over one million years. This weapon could have stopped them all in one blow. What will you do to the Coronians, Dia?"

Dia was surprised she asked her that. "I plan to do what needs to be done to end this. To bring peace to everyone the Coronians have hurt, including us. Especially us."

Pam remembered the day she saw Dia in the hospital after being pulled from the swamp. Her daughter should have been dead, and knowing that the Breger Dunes attack, amongst others, were assisted by Maria Granby made Pam furious. She moved close to Dia and whispered in her ear, "Make them pay, Dia. And make sure those traitors do as well."

Pam placed her hand on Dia's shoulder and squeezed. Dia wondered if her mother's feelings for Tristen would change if she discovered he was Troy's son. Probably not.

Pamela Strom's demeanor completely changed. She smiled and said to the group, "I've prepared a wonderful dinner for a moment of respite and to celebrate our new friends from Earth. Everything is being set up in our apartment in thirty minutes. See you all there soon."

She flashed her brilliant smile, and she, the Chancellor, and Dr. and Mrs. Harlow all left together. Oscar said, "I need to go collect my wife, Michelle. We'll see you soon."

Penny grabbed Brody's hand and said, "Come on, I'll show you our pad. It's cool!"

Dia watched them start to walk off, and Renee and Dominic followed, ensuring the two excited humans didn't get lost in the vast corridors of Baltica City.

Troy and Dia were left alone again. She said, "I need to take this off before dinner. Let's go home for a minute."

"What about the crowds? People were able to see your demonstrations."

"I know. That was the point. My parents and upper-level officials keep telling me the people are on the verge of civil discourse because they think only you and I can save them. We're home. Let's show them we're going to try."

Troy smiled. "Wanna go to the mezzanine and get a close-up of those awful murals?"

She laughed and said, "Sure, let's show off a little."

***

Troy and Dia took the Flash Lift down to the courtyard. She was still in the suit but had released all of her energy, so her eyes were no longer green. Crowds of Florians, Hanner-Florians, Gorman, Bayron, and many others flocked to the courtyard to see the doctor and general. The Healer and the Fighter had returned to save them. Troy and Dia hugged, took photos with, and talked to the citizens of Rygone. Just over a year ago, they fled their home in hopes of saving them from the power of the EIP. Now they were immersed in them, hoping the EIP was the answer to their wishes.

Troy received a message from Oscar saying the rest of the group was waiting on them. Dia and Troy waved as they got onto the Lift. For the first time since before Breger Dunes, there was hope in the hearts of the people of Rygone.

They made it to her parents' apartment, and she took the suit off, leaving just the shell. Her mother and the executive kitchen staff had made too much food, but it was a great representation of what Rygone could offer the humans. Penny and Brody were the guests of honor and sat amongst some of the galaxy's most powerful inhabitants. Dia made sure James was at the table as he and Penny had become quite close over the past few days. Brody and Oscar were going on and on about their work. She hadn't seen her brother talk that much in years. *This is the way things should be. Tomorrow will make it so they can stay this way*, Dia thought.

After the main meal, the kitchen staff brought out Troy's favorite dessert, malson fruit cake. The recipe was the one Dia created while recovering after her crash. He nearly grabbed the whole cake before Pam stopped him, laughing. "Fiend! Get away!"

Troy was able to grab a small chunk off the side and uncharacteristically shoved it in his mouth like a child. Everyone laughed, and Dia placed her hand on his leg and said, "Nice one, honey."

Chancellor Strom watched the lighthearted activities going on around the table. The humans fit in nicely. Dominic and Renee were in their own world together. Oscar and Michelle were talking to the Harlows about trying to have a fourth child. Pam was sitting next to him, happy rather than depressed. But mostly, he observed Troy and Dia. He had utterly given up on seeing his daughter again, yet there she was, eating cake and joking with Troy. Warren narrowed his eyes and thought about what would happen tomorrow. *Tomorrow it ends, so this can begin anew.*

Everyone had their part to play on the following day. Dia said, "I know this has been a lovely meal, and I don't want the joy to end, but we need to rest if we want to continue having moments like these. Tomorrow will be a big day for us all. Everyone has their assignments, correct?"

Troy, Dominic, General Smith, and Oscar had listed certain individuals in certain specialties who would report to specific command post locations in the morning at 0500 Rygonian time. Dia and Oscar had estimated to within an hour when the cruisers, which were confirmed to have left Darsayn the day after the Las Vegas attack, would arrive on Earth.

A comprehensive Rygonian offensive had been laid out within a short time to protect their planet and several allies they knew the Coronians planned to invade. However, with careful planning, correct deployments, and the existence of Dia, they knew they could defend their own.

But would they have to?

CHAPTER 48
DEPLOY

After dinner, each family went to their own respective home or quarters. Dia said to Troy, "I'll be home soon. I want to walk Brody and Penny to their suite."

Brody and Penny were only a few doors down from Dia and Troy, so he said, "Okay. I'm going to shower."

She kissed him on the cheek and walked with her dear friends to their guest suite. Penny said, "This place is so interesting. Beautiful, advanced, but more sterile than I expected. Not that that's a bad thing!"

Dia laughed and said, "Yes, Baltica City is rather sterile. This is the parliament's home, government headquarters, and the location of our Health and Science and Research and Development departments. This is more of an office and research facility than a living space. Baltica North is the New York City, and South is the Beverly Hills of Rygone."

Penny said, "Maybe one day we can go to one?"

"Of course! South is the youngest and fanciest. It's where our entertainers and famous individuals live and work. One day, I'll have to introduce you to Perry Contreau. *He's* a Florian you'll never forget."

"If it's the youngest, how old is Baltica City?" asked Brody.

Dia thought for a moment. "Well, it had just been finished a few years before I was born, so it's about 1,250,000 Earth years old."

Brody choked on his glacier water and asked, "A few years before you were born? Like a million years, right? How old are you?"

Dia laughed. "We're immortal, remember? The passage of time is different in our eyes. I'm 1,248,153 years old. Troy is a year older than me."

Penny sat down hard and said, "If these cities and your civilizations are that old, how are they still here? That's insane!"

"Well, as I said, time passes differently for us. When a human is born, your life expectancy is about eighty years, so in a human's mind, their personal world needs to last for eighty years. We don't die, so we needed to create our world to last with us. Plus, Florians are very slow to reproduce. It can take a Florian couple dozen, if not hundreds, of years to have a child. There are only 798,684 of us." *Well, 798,683 without Daniel,* she thought solemnly.

"Is that why you and Troy—" Penny asked.

Dia stopped her and said, "That's a very long story, one that we don't have time for tonight, but I would love to tell you later." *No, I wouldn't.*

Dia walked toward the door and asked, "Did they show you the datapad to control the suite?"

Brody nodded. "Yes. I'm stealing it."

"I'll get you a nicer one later," she said with a laugh. "Good night, both of you." She turned to leave but stopped as the memories of everything that had happened over the past year hit her. She knew she wouldn't be home if it weren't for these two humans. She turned around, walked back to Penny, and gave her friend a huge hug. Dia waved Brody over to join them, and the three held on to each other for a few moments. Then, Dia whispered, "I wish Carl were here."

Brody kissed her on the forehead and said, "We all do. So let's end this tomorrow for him."

Penny wiped a tear from her eye. "Yeah, for Carl."

Dia smiled and nodded. "For Carl. And Roger."

She reluctantly let go and walked out the door. *Yes, this will be for Carl.*

***

Dia stepped into their apartment and could smell Troy's body soap, and she couldn't help but get a rush from it. She found him in his office, like usual. He looked up and asked, "Is everything all set with them?"

She nodded and walked into their bedroom. She lay the suit and a clean shell out on top of her dresser, ready for what was to come. She went into the bathroom and turned on the water. Dia examined herself in the mirror and saw determination but also apprehension. This move was hastily put together, and the lives of millions of the galaxy's citizens relied on it. She sighed and noticed Troy had come into the bathroom. He stood behind her, kissed the top of her head, and met her eyes in the mirror. He said, "Don't second guess yourself, General. This is going to work. It's time to defend ourselves the right way."

She smiled lazily and said, "Yes, I know. I've just never put together such a huge operation essentially overnight. I guess I'm nervous about the small details."

"I know. I'm feeling that from my end too. I have a whole field hospital in my mind and don't know how extensive it needs to be."

Dia whispered, "If it goes how I want, you won't need it." She turned and kissed him. "Now, go to bed. I'll be there in a few minutes."

He kissed her gently and left the bathroom. In the light of the open door, she could see him climb into bed. Dia took a short but scorching shower. Afterward, she pulled her shoulder-length hair into a tight, elaborate updo woven with her silver ribbon. Next, she silently went into their bedroom and confirmed that Troy was in a deep sleep. She dressed in the shell, suit, and boots.

Dia leaned over her sleeping husband and very gently kissed the top of his head. *The next time I see you, this will all be over. Then we can take that trip to the foothills of the Raltains.*

***

Dia left their apartment and silently went up to the hangar deck. The doors to the hangar were closed, hiding the massive effort taking place inside.

Dia walked into the hangar and saw dozens of flight crews making last-minute preparations for their DREX fighters and destroyers. All were fully crewed with the most experienced pilots Dia had. This was going to be an all-out air assault, so she needed the best in the galaxy. At the far end of the bay, High Colonel Conner, High Colonel Strom, and Captain Ramsay stood next to the gunner. They would lead the Earth team with one destroyer and four DREX fighters stationed strategically around Earth, cloaked. When the Coronian ships made themselves known, the Rygonians would meet them head-on. This situation would play out on five of Rygone's most prominent allies, including Zole. Baxelhoff knew by now that Zole had operatives on Earth who had helped Dia.

Next, she found her father waiting patiently next to a brand new DREX fighter that Dia had never seen before. She walked around the craft slowly and said, "Oscar has been busy."

Warren nodded and said, "He's needed to be. After you and Troy disappeared, I realized it was time to eliminate the tyrant. Help our people feel safe. They didn't have faith in me anymore. I needed to show them I still cared about their well-being. It didn't help much." He sighed. "They wanted you."

"When this is over, can we paint over those murals?"

Warren chuckled and said, "No, the citizens wanted them. They like them. They stay."

Dia rolled her eyes. "Are the other assets inside?"

"Yes. It's time to get this started."

The soldiers, pilots, engineers, and support personnel watched as the father and daughter who had shaped most of the civilization of Rygone moved to the middle of the hangar.

Warren cleared his throat, prompting the entire hanger to fall silent. "Thank you all for being here. For sneaking away and protecting your families from knowing what's about to take place. For so long, our great planet has strived to take care of its citizens and those of our allies. For too long, the bureaucracy has held us back from truly challenging the Coronians, and they have walked all over us. I've been a part of that bureaucracy! But no more."

Dia took over. "This operation, Operation Flashpoint, will take the fight to them." She pulled in a small amount of energy and bathed herself in green flame. "A year ago, my husband and I fled Rygone because we feared what this power could do. We feared that it could be turned against our own kind. Circumstances being what they were, I found my way to Earth, and with the help of some incredible humans, I learned to harness and perfect the use of this power. And now, I hope to use it to end this war before it even starts."

Huge cheers rose from the crowd, but Dia and Warren quieted them quickly, as the city still slept, and they needed it to stay that way. Warren said, "You all have your orders. You know which planet you are to protect and where to go on those planets to subdue the Coronian invaders. If they fire upon you first, you're authorized to return fire. Maintain constant contact with the operation commander, High Colonel Renee Conner, at all costs. If she gives the order, you will offensively open fire on your assigned targets. There's very little chance that will happen; not one shot will be fired if all goes to plan. Now, return to your ships; let's take this fight to them."

The crews and operational personnel ran to their posts, and flight crews began powering up their ships and getting ready to leave. Dia and Warren walked up to Dominic and Renee. The operation commander said, "We're as ready as we'll ever be."

Dia hugged her best friend and said, "This will work. It has to."

Renee nodded, and Dominic shook his father's hand. "Good luck, Chancellor."

Warren patted his son on the shoulder. "You too, son."

Renee and Dominic turned and retreated into the gunner. Renee had chosen a Florian co-pilot, Lieutenant Hanna Sefid.

Dia and her father returned to the brand new DREX fighter Oscar had commissioned for her. She boarded the craft and was immediately intimidated as the flight controls were completely different from what she was used to. Oscar sat in the pilot's seat and said, "I'm flying today, General. You're just my co-pilot."

Dia scoffed at her brother in shock and said, "But—"

"Sit down and deal with it, Dia. You have the shiny toy today," Warren said.

She looked over at the Asset in the seat next to her father. Dia said, "Well then, let's get this show on the road."

Dia strapped into the co-pilot's seat. Renee ordered all the ships to Jump out of the atmosphere to their respective planets. Those staying on Rygone Jumped to their assigned post and stayed under cloak in case of attack. The Flader Requiem Fusion Cannon on Nexxus was armed and ready to deploy if needed. Rygone was ready.

Oscar looked at his sister, and she took a deep breath.

It was time.

"Jump."

CHAPTER 49
NO MORE BUREAUCRACY

Troy's alarm went off, and he groaned, reaching for his communicator to turn it off. He stretched and rolled over to see if Dia was still in bed. She wasn't, but he noticed her blankets had not been disturbed. *Maybe she slept in the living room.*

Troy got up and shuffled out to see if she was on the couch; she wasn't. He checked the office, but Dia wasn't there either. He grabbed his communicator and was about to call her when he saw she had sent him a video message. Troy's throat tightened as he opened it. She sat in her father's office and said, "Good morning, Troy. I'm sure by now you're searching for me. I'm not on Rygone, just as many pilots and soldiers aren't either. My father and I implemented Operation Flashpoint early this morning. I've attached a file that details what's happening. When you get this, please get Penny and Brody and go to the operations center inside the hospital. There will be a live feed from many ships participating in this mission. I'm sorry I didn't tell you about this; nobody part of this operation informed their loved ones until after we left. We couldn't afford the Coronians getting advanced knowledge of our plans." She swallowed hard. "I love you, Troy. You know how I feel about war, but for me to be finished fighting, I have to end this one my way. I hope to see you soon."

The video ended, and Troy just stood in his living room, breathing hard, wondering where his wife and half of the Florian Army Air Corps had gone. He rushed to get dressed and ran down the hall to the guest suite. He rang the bell, and Brody answered, eating a pastry. He looked at Troy, confused, and said, "What's up, bro?"

Troy never understood the "bro" thing but said, "Dia and her father initiated a secret operation right under our noses. They and half the Florian Army Air Corps have been deployed. I need you and Penny to come with me to the hospital."

Penny was just walking out of her room and said sleepily, "Mornin', Troy. Where's Dia?"

"Probably Earth."

Her eyes shot open. "Huh? Why?"

Brody said, "She flew the coop with half her army, sounds like."

"Yes, now we need to get to the hospital so I can find out what's going on," Troy stressed.

Brody and Penny quickly got dressed, bringing their translator disks. Troy called for a transport to take them to the hospital, where they were immediately escorted into the operations center. He found his father there with his arms crossed across his chest. Troy asked, "What's going on, Dad?"

"It looks like Dia finally convinced her dad to take the fight to the Coronians. Look."

Troy, Brody, and Penny looked at a bank of ten monitors with views ranging from an orangish planet's outer atmosphere to a strange purple city to an aerial view of the Hoover Dam. Some screens were flipping to other cameras from worlds with more than one DREX, like Earth. The planet, location, and DREX number were listed in the corner of each screen. Troy scanned through them, looking for DREX 1. He asked his father, "Is she DREX 1?"

He nodded, "Turns out Oscar built her a nice new ship, but it hasn't shown up on any screen."

Dia doesn't want us to know where she is. Not good, Troy thought with growing panic in his heart.

John noticed Penny and Brody and smiled warmly. He pointed to a small door at the end of the bank of monitors and said, "They set up a nice spread for breakfast in that room. The sweet bread is very good this morning."

Penny was hungry, so she pulled Brody into the room with her. They were both shocked to see that John Harlow was right; the spread was huge. There were hot foods that looked like some sort of eggs, little tender steaks of some kind, and sweet bread with flavored cream. Danishes like the one Brody had were filled with fruit and strange nuts. A bunch of different odd fruits and vegetables were laid out. There were also carafes filled with at least ten different kinds of tea.

"Honey!" Penny exclaimed.

"Could you be any louder?" Brody complained.

She picked up a tiny glass pitcher filled with honey and saw dozens of them, some in different colors. She didn't know what to do or think when a kind female voice said, "You place the entire pitcher in the bottom of your cup, pour the hot tea over the pitcher, and the *balma* dissolves." She extended her hand to Penny and said, "Hello, I'm Raquel. Chancellor Strom's assistant."

Raquel was tall and had pastel pink hair that fell to her waist. Her light yellow eyes were large like Dia's but nothing like a human's. Her skin was most impressive, though. It was dark brown but had faint swirls of lighter and darker hues.

"I'm Penny, from Earth. Heather—uh, Dia brought us."

Raquel laughed and said, "I know. I've been anxious to meet you, but the Chancellor had me busy. But now, it looks like *they're* busy."

Brody couldn't stop staring at the beautiful woman. He had always taken a liking to redheads, but her pink hair was stunning against her incredible skin. He was utterly transfixed by her eyes, though. Finally, he squeaked out, "I'm Brody too."

Raquel laughed again. "It's nice to meet you, Brody Too." She pointed to the spread. "This is not everyday fare. Today is *Glacierli*. It's a holiday to celebrate the power of Rygone's many glaciers."

"Glaciers seem to be a large part of the culture here," Penny said with curiosity.

Raquel nodded. "Yes, the glaciers on our planet are unique to any others found throughout the galaxy. They don't melt, no matter the temperature, although many are partially hollow and filled with water with a healing quality seen nowhere else."

Penny poured a tea that smelled like roses over her balma, and she watched it dissolve. She took a sip, and it was delightful and fragrant. "I could get used to this."

There was a commotion in the main operations room, and they rushed back in. On one of the screens in the bank's center, an image appeared that had everyone either alarmed or cheering. Penny ran to Troy's side. He was staring at the screen, horrified. She asked, "What is it? Where is that?"

He said, almost whispering, "That's the view from DREX 1, Dia's ship."

Brody asked, "But where is it? What planet? It definitely isn't Earth!"

They watched Chancellor Warren Strom, his son Dr. Oscar Strom, and his daughter General Dia "Flashpoint" Harlow appear in front of the DREX and begin walking down a beautiful, manicured path toward a palace that looked much like the Taj Mahal. Hundreds of soldiers rushed toward them, and several began firing at the three Florians. Oscar and Warren were only slightly bothered, but Dia absorbed the energy, and she let it show. The soldiers closest to them watched as the Florian general became surrounded by green flame with her blonde flowing hair and fingertips as bright as the sun. She raised her hands in front of her, and they fled in fear, knowing what she was capable of.

Brody asked, "That's Darsayn, isn't it? The Coronian home planet?"

John nodded and said, "But why there? This is not a defensive but a very offensive move. What're they doing?"

Troy breathed, "She's done fighting. She's ending it her way."

CHAPTER 50
IT'S YOUR DECISION

The hospital control room on Rygone watched with bated breath, wondering what their leaders would do.

Most of the Coronian guard that was outside the palace gates had already fled, leaving the Stroms a clear path to the entrance. The tops of the palace walls were now lined with guards who had their weapons trained on the Florians, even though using them would be their own folly.

Chancellor Strom yelled, "Premier Baxelhoff! On behalf of the citizens of Rygone, I demand a meeting with you posthaste! We come here to bring peace to our planet and allies, but we are fully prepared to end this war with force!"

Several guards who felt safe on top of the wall began laughing at the three Florians. Dia let out a thin line of flame that spun into a rope. She threw it up to the top of the wall and wrapped it around a decorative pillar; she pulled her arms back hard, and the entire pillar came crashing down. She said menacingly in Coronian, "Next time will be the whole wall. Nothing in your arsenal can stop me from destroying your entire planet. Or the whole Keplan System, for that matter."

The laughing quickly turned to concerned murmurs. The guards on the wall and close to the gates began to move about quickly. Again, Chancellor Strom said, "We're here to negotiate peace. I know the Premier can hear and see me. We'll stay here as long as is needed until he's ready to talk."

***

Deep in the rabble of fearful Coronian soldiers, a small, unseen voice said, "Damn her, this isn't going as planned. Again."

***

Premier Baxelhoff stood in his chambers, staring at the monitor with the Stroms of Rygone standing outside the gates to his palace.

He screamed at his advisors, "How did a Florian Army DREX make it past our nets? I was told we could detect them when cloaked!"

"Your Excellency, this is a new ship. They must have changed the cloaking program again!" a female Coronian answered warily.

Baxelhoff knew the engineers on Rygone always responded to their technological breakthroughs swiftly. This was no different.

He fixed on Dia, glowing and mighty, standing next to her father. *I almost had that. I almost had her.*

He pressed his fingers to his temples to ease his growing headache. He turned around and scanned the chamber, looking for the one thing that could help him clear his mind. "Where's my wife? She was just here!" he yelled.

In the chaos that the advisors and military officers created, Premieress Lydia had vanished from the chamber. Much to Baxelhoff's dismay, the situation he was facing was about to get much worse.

Chancellor Strom received confirmation in his earpiece that the next part of their plan was in motion. He yelled, "You're about to receive a transmission from our DREX. I'm sure it will be an incentive for you to negotiate."

After dropping off the Stroms, the Asset in the DREX Jumped to a small courtyard deep within the palace walls. They expertly infiltrated the Premier's personal quarters and quickly and efficiently took Lydia and their daughters prisoner. The process took all of five minutes, and the Asset didn't have to fire one shot. The Premier's family went willingly, out of fear.

Baxelhoff glared at a screen open to a live feed inside the DREX. It showed his wife and daughters cowering together and handcuffed to the passenger seats of the craft. In the pilot seat, looking directly into the camera, was a figure dressed in all black, including a full-head mask that only showed their eyes. They had color-changing lenses that made their eyes a bright, unnatural purple.

Their electronically disguised voice said with anger and determination, "Premier Baxelhoff, as you can see, not only are we holding your city captive, but we have your family. It's not the way of Rygone to actively seek out war, especially if it can impact innocent citizens on *both* sides. But your constant warmongering and assaults on our sovereignty have made this necessary. Negotiate with our Chancellor, or we will unleash the damnation outside your gate. If you choose wisely, we'll return your wife and daughters unharmed. It's your decision how this proceeds."

***

Back in the hospital, John Harlow was in even more shock. He said, "If the Asset is with them, they aren't taking this lightly. Unbelievable."

The Asset. They usually worked in the shadows, rarely coming out, but they were the most effective secret corps agent in Rygonian history. Most of the covert training programs on Rygone were started by this one individual until they "retired" and began training a team of several agents to mimic their abilities. However, they would come forth and do what they did best on exceptional occasions. Since Breger Dunes, they were doing everything possible to fix what the Coronians broke within their society.

Troy couldn't take his eyes off the banks of monitors. Every once in a while, he would look at a different screen showing that word had gotten out to the Coronian bases on other planets, and they tried to mobilize. But the Florian Army was already there, waiting to strike. In minutes, Rygone had brought the entire Coronian force to its knees, all because they feared what Dia could do. He smiled to himself. *This is precisely what I meant for the EIP to do. Bring peace without firing a shot.* However, deep down, Troy felt a twinge of guilt about the source of his incredible weapon.

Troy fixated on the center screen showing the Stroms. A small door in the palace's large gate slowly opened, and two guards and an envoy came out. The envoy stood in front of the Florians and said nervously, "On behalf of Premier Baxelhoff of the Coronian Empire of the planet Darsayn, we extend an invitation to attend an armistice meeting. With our beloved Premier."

"Peace, not an armistice. That is non-negotiable," said Dia sternly.

The envoy stared at her warily. "It can only be the Chancellor and Dr. Strom. You're not to enter the city, General."

Dia shrugged nonchalantly and said, "No problem. I'll just hang out with his family in the DREX."

"General Harlow will stay out here. Right out here," said Warren.

The envoy nodded nervously. "Please follow me."

Warren glanced at his daughter, who had a sinister smirk on her face. She watched her father and brother go through the gate, knowing that Baxelhoff was only strong when he was winning the battle. She turned and sat down on the path mostly made of course sand and proceeded to draw the glass designs of Florian family birthmarks with her finger.

***

Warren and Oscar were taken into the elaborate palace. For the most part, Coronians, especially the men, were considered unruly and unclean, but their capital city proved otherwise. The city was filled with beautiful gardens and markets. The male beasts and female beauties of the species were some of the happiest citizens of the galaxy. Mainly because of Baxelhoff's system of rule that provided such a lavish lifestyle for his inhabitants. Seeing the two Florians walk by on their way to the Premier's chambers was cause for great concern.

For the next several hours, a tiny group of individuals shaped the future of a large part of the galaxy. Setting forth peace initiatives, negotiating families' returns, and restricting power to one of the largest militaries ever known. Dia willingly sat outside the gate as the proceedings took place. She was glad not to be in on the negotiations and just be the tool that kept the peace. Troy watched her sit on the ground doing nothing in front of the Coronian seat of power. Typically, he expected her to want to be part of the action, but she seemed at peace with her role. *This is the beginning of her change to a serene life. Thank the wishes.*

***

In his cell, Tristen could feel something big was happening. The guards outside his door were frequently changing, and he could hear them speaking excitedly, even though he couldn't make out what they were saying through the thick door. *Are we being attacked? Have Dia or the Coronians finally started the war? Why haven't they asked me anything else?*

He sat on his bed, waiting for a guard, officer, or his father to take him for questioning or to a tribunal.

None would ever come.

***

Baxelhoff and Chancellor Strom came to a quick and peaceful resolution. The Coronians would immediately stop their insurgency on all planetary systems in exchange for his family's safe return. Their condition was that General Harlow would leave Darsayn at once, without incident, and Flashpoint would steer clear only if a group of citizens from each occupied world assembled on Darsayn. They would remain on Darsayn as government emissaries until all

Coronian assets were removed. Once all parties were satisfied that the aggressors were gone, all governments would participate in a summit on Emerotl, a neutral entity, to determine a formal peace and trade treaty that would include the Coronians.

All would be null if Baxelhoff made one move to publicly or secretly go against the agreement. General Harlow would have free rein to stop the insurrection by force, however she deemed fit.

It took less than a day to stop hundreds of years of pain and blood. All it took was the successful creation of an all-powerful weapon bonded with the most significant military mind in the galaxy.

Peace was at hand.

However, would that have been different if Troy and Dia had never fled?

***

Suddenly, the entire galaxy froze in place. Every planet, ocean, life form, speck of dust, and molecule in Galaxy 148 came to a halt.

Dr. Helen Grace appeared on Darsayn and pulled General Dia Harlow to her feet, where the general froze once more. Dr. Grace got in her face and said, "If it were possible, your free fucking will would be the death of me!"

Helen disappeared for only a few moments before reappearing with a very bewildered Troy.

Unlike the rest of the galaxy, Troy's body was frozen, but he was awake and focused. His face filled with horror and confusion. "Wha—who are—"

She shushed him and said, "Troy. My dear, it's time for you to listen. It's time for you to stop hiding and become who you really are."

CHAPTER 51
148

Helen placed her hands on Troy's cheeks and said in a sweet voice, "Oh, Troy, you turned out so handsome! I've not seen you up close since the day you were born to Jeannie and John. They did a lovely job raising you!"

"Who the hell are—"

Helen seized his vocal cords. She said, "Now, only questions, and you must listen to each answer. Do you understand?"

He didn't know what to do or say. His mind couldn't process what was happening. She said, "Good. I can imagine you're curious to know what's going on. I'll start from the beginning, literally. My name is not Dr. Helen Grace, and I'm not a human from Earth. I'm the creator, manipulator, and guardian of Galaxy 148. This galaxy."

Troy stuttered, "Guardian and creator… how?"

"Oh, sweetie, you know how. Deep down, you've always known. I just haven't come and confirmed it until now. I am, indeed, a Beginner. My true name is Tealas. I'm one of the Original Beginners."

She took his face in her hands again. "And you'll not believe it at first, but I'm your true mother."

Troy's eyes went wide. He choked out, "That can't be. My parents aren't First Generation... I—"

"You're brilliant but have difficulty accepting things you don't understand, don't you?" She turned and walked up to Dia, still standing motionless, unaware of what was happening. She continued, "Troy, my sweet, you're not one of these rejects. You're a true Beginner, and I hid you amongst these outcasts to keep you safe until need be."

Troy had surprisingly calmed and comprehended her words, even though he didn't believe her. "I don't believe you. You're lying. *Prove it!*"

"Ohhh, temper, temper. You get that from your father, your real father." She sighed. "Okay, I'll prove it."

Tealas turned to the front of the palace. The front façade changed from stone to orange steel, and all of the guards on top turned to glass. Next, the steel façade fell away, and the glass guards toppled over, shattering on the ground. She turned to Troy and said, "That's the simplest of manipulation. I didn't create anything but changed the reality of those physical objects. All things, emotions, memories, and events, great and small, can be changed easily by the Beginner who created the galaxy they rule. As for me, my galaxy is special because of Rygone." She walked back up to Dia again and brushed her cheek gently with the back of her hand. She continued, almost in a dream, "Except this one. I can manipulate anything around her. I can change her path or circumstances, but I cannot change her actions and how she reacts to anything, even you. I've never figured out why."

Troy examined the piles of glass and began to understand, even if he didn't know why. She said, "Troy, you've known that you were very different from those around you since you were a child. You knew that even compared to the great Florians, you could easily far outpace anything they did. You remember everything from the most complicated medical procedures to what you had for breakfast three hundred years ago. You were ostracized as a child because of the darkness of your eyes. There's nothing special about them, but even the Florians couldn't accept something so different, and you had to change to ease their fears."

Troy couldn't believe that she knew all of that about him. He looked closely at her face for the first time and saw that he had her eyes, dark and strange. *Did she have those on Earth?*

"Deep down, you knew you had extraordinary abilities that you successfully kept hidden for over a million years. Hidden until you wanted to help your people, your wife, fight your biggest enemy yet."

"How much of my life have you manipulated?"

"About half. You've always been smart enough to make the right choices—until Breger Dunes. But of course, I manipulated some of that as well." She turned away from him, waiting for his response.

"What do you mean you manipulated Breger Dunes? That was one of the worst times of our lives!" he growled.

She looked back at him. "But was it? Sure, I made Dia's life a living hell. Every defeat she suffered, every challenge she faced was my doing, and even she couldn't make things better, which worked perfectly for making your life a living hell as well. But not all of it."

Troy was getting angry with the runaround. "What do you mean?!"

"Tristen. Dia tried for so long to get you to agree to a child, which *I* would've gladly given you immediately, but you feared who you were deep down. You were afraid that having a baby with her would be dangerous. Right?"

He took deep breaths and stared at her. She was absolutely right; that was precisely what he thought. He longed to have children with Dia, but the fear of what could've been scared him. Although heartbreaking, her love and devotion to him kept her from using her ability to choose to have a baby. She stayed faithful to him no matter what, and what made that even more evident was that this woman who claimed to be his mother couldn't change that.

He said, choking up, "You put Maria in my path? You orchestrated my affair?"

She nodded happily. "Yup, I sure did! I needed a grandson. And *he* wouldn't allow Dia to be his mother. Plus, well, it was probably a good thing. Her being such a variance probably wouldn't have been a good thing."

Now Troy became angry. "You sadistic bitch! Dia forgave me, but you couldn't have changed that if she had left! So why did you do that? And who the hell is *he*? "

"As I said, I needed a grandson. I needed to know if you could have children with a Florian, and Maria was a good choice. And *he* is your true father, Kherln."

"Even though she was a fucking traitor? A traitor who kept Tristen from me and made him in—"

Tealas smiled and said, "Yes, all my plan. If Dia's crash hadn't happened, if you hadn't felt crippling guilt for your affair, you wouldn't have worked so hard on—what do you call it, the EIP? Another thing that you denied about yourself, Troy. You were the perfect catalyst for that power because you *are* that power, but your 'healer' mentality held you back. I could've changed that, but I knew who was even better suited for it." She looked back at Dia. "How long did you try to bond that power to others? Pretending with Oscar Strom that the instruments you both built created strength? You told the Coronians that you couldn't replicate the results because it was a one-time thing with Dia, but that wasn't true. I was so excited when the thingy bonded with her."

Troy said nothing. He knew she was absolutely right about him. Right about the EIP being a part of him, not a synthetic entity. He swallowed and held back tears, struggling to break free of the frozen state she had him in. Finally, Tealas let go, and Troy relaxed. She said, "Don't try anything stupid, kid. You'll not like the consequences."

Troy walked up to his wife. Her face was relaxed, and she looked at peace and full of wonder. He touched her cheek and asked, "What're you going to do?"

Tealas said, "Make this interesting! This perfect ending to a horrible, drawn-out conflict that has destroyed hundreds of thousands of lives is too easy! I need you to destroy them! Or yourselves. The reason is complicated."

Troy whipped his head around and yelled, "*What?*"

"Oh, yes, my dear son, your ability to get her right here, putting the fear of annihilation into your enemy's mind, is exactly what a peace-keeping weapon does. It's too fucking easy! So it's time to make you all work a little harder for what we really need you to achieve. Because all of our lives depend on it, even mine!"

Troy went to lunge at her, but she froze him again and said, "It's good to see you have a bit of anger in you, boy. You're gonna need it."

Troy watched futilely as Tealas lifted her hand and went to snap her fingers.

She paused, though, dropped her hand, and wrinkled her nose. "That snapping of the fingers is overplayed." She turned and licked Dia's cheek.

The galaxy faded to black.

CHAPTER 52
REALITY

Tristen was still in his cell, reading a book, when everything went dark. His mind began to spin, and he couldn't control his thoughts for a few moments.

When he came around, he was no longer in his cell but on the fortieth-floor flight deck of Baltica City. He looked around frantically, and he couldn't believe his eyes. He had to be in the worst nightmare ever.

In front of him, Dr. Oscar Strom was standing on a platform. His hands were tied behind his back, and it was clear he had been severely beaten. On either side of him were two guards: one was a Florian Army sergeant, and the other was a Coronian beast!

What the fuck is happening?!

Off to the side of the platform, across from him, stood Premier Baxelhoff. He was looking on with smug anticipation. His mother was standing next to Baxelhoff, garbed in the ceremonial dress of the High Council of Darsayn.

Tristan's head was spinning, and he felt like he would pass out. A hand came down on his shoulder, and he looked to the right of him and saw Captain James Ramsay. He asked, "Are you okay, Colonel?"

Colonel? What the hell?

Tristen looked closer at James's uniform and realized it wasn't that of a captain. It was utterly black, and he had a cape draped over his right shoulder that went down to his waist. The insignia on his shoulders was a long gold bar with a black stripe down the middle. The symbol on his collar was two black swords piercing a red heart. James asked again, "Colonel, are you all right?"

Tristen feigned that he was feeling fine and just nodded. He turned his eyes to the ground, trying to figure out what was happening, and knew he had to be in a terrible nightmare.

He heard footsteps coming up behind them, familiar footsteps—his father's gait. As he passed, Tristen saw Troy Harlow step onto the platform next to Oscar Strom, who turned away in disgust. His father was dressed in a black uniform, much like James, but his was trimmed with bright blue. He also had a black cape, but the liner was also blue. The insignia on his shoulders was of three black stars trimmed with gold. Troy glanced at Tristen but quickly looked away and addressed Oscar.

"Dr. Oscar Strom, you are hereby charged with treason, heresy, and conspiring with the enemy. How do you plead?"

Proudly, Oscar said, "Not guilty because my actions are not crimes on Rygone."

The Coronian guard went to hit Oscar with the butt of his weapon, but Troy put up his hand and stopped him. Troy turned to James and asked, "Chancellor General, based on these crimes, what is the prisoner's sentence?"

Chancellor General? That isn't even a rank! What. Is. Happening? Where is everybody else?

James said in his usual quiet voice, "General Harlow, the sentence for this prisoner is death. To be carried out immediately."

Troy nodded at James and turned to Oscar, indifferent. Tristen had watched these two men as best friends for twelve years and couldn't believe what he saw next.

Death? He's a Florian! Shouldn't he go to the Ice Lake?

Tristen watched in horror as his father, one of the most honorable and kind Florians in the galaxy, pressed his hand against his best friend's chest. Oscar began to cough and sway. Tristen saw his father start to glow with a bright blue flame. His eyes changed from dark to blue, like iridescent sapphires. His hair went from dark brown to pitch black, flowing with the fire. A pure white mist trailed from the side of his eyes across his face, and his fingertips were a fiery red.

In less than a minute, Oscar Strom fell to the platform, lifeless. His life's energy and soul were now flowing through Troy Harlow's veins. Troy gently placed his hand on a strange device, releasing Oscar's life force into it. He turned and walked away quickly. Tristen was utterly bewildered.

As Troy strode past, he motioned for Tristen to follow him, but he didn't want to. After a few more steps, Troy yelled, "Tristen! Now!"

He quickly turned and ran up to his father, whose fast, long strides were almost too quick for him to keep up.

Tristen wanted to burst into tears; his entire world had been unmade. He glanced at his father's left hand. He was still wearing his rings.

Are they still Dia's? Where is Dia? Did he kill her too?

***

She opened her eyes and saw the morning sun pouring into the room from the skylight above. She took a deep breath, slowly let it out, and smiled. She pushed back the covers and felt the cool breeze coming in from the porch.

She clumsily stepped into her slippers and put on a warm robe. She shuffled onto the porch and walked around, knowing exactly where she would find him.

Heather came around the corner and watched him feed her lovely fish.

He looked up and smiled. "Good mornin', love."

"Good morning, Carl. What shall we do today?"

EPILOGUE

"I'm not thrilled by your recklessness, Tealas."

"When are you ever thrilled about anything I do, Kherln?" She stepped from the shadows in his bed chambers. He stood by the vast window, looking out over a bright cloud of undulating gas. They were deep in the center of the Universe where Beginner Kherln himself first came to be. It was a small nebula that remained unchanged since the beginning of time as he had begun it. *Bassamar* was the home of the Original Beginners, and their leader was not happy.

She couldn't help but notice how incredibly similar he looked to Troy and Tristen. There was no mistaking father, son, and grandson. Kherln wanted the cosmos to know who his heirs were going to be. Tealas said, "We're running out of time. It's time to throw Troy away and bring forth Genesis."

"He isn't ready," Kherln said. His voice was calm and smooth.

"After what I just did, he will become ready or..."

"Or?"

"Or we're *all* dead."